Hussy

C. L. Ellis

iUniverse, Inc.
Bloomington

Hussy

iUniverse books may be ordered through booksellers or by contacting:

iUniverse
1663 Liberty Drive
Bloomington, IN 47403
www.iuniverse.com
1-800-Authors (1-800-288-4677)

ISBN: 978-1-4759-5537-8 (sc)
ISBN: 978-1-4759-5538-5 (hc)
ISBN: 978-1-4759-5539-2 (e)

Library of Congress Control Number: 2012918914

Printed in the United States of America

iUniverse rev. date: 10/25/2012

I would like to thank my mother, Gerri Ellis for all of her support and love. Each step I have taken on my journey to here, she has supported. Her love, confidence and assistance continually encouraged me to complete this book and give others the chance to meet Ms. Lula Mae Carson, Puddin and other members of Friendly, La. Loving the art of reading herself she was the first eyes to read this book. After she completed it she told me it would be published if she had to do it herself. I would also like to thank Dr. Doreen Miller my acknowledge mother from previous spiritiual existence, her encouragement in getting me to go back to school made the difference in my life and I want to openly thank her for that. She actually came by and picked me up one day; and would not leave until I was registered in school. These two matriochs of love, strength and encouragement have helped me to stand in the mist of my most vunerable moments in life. My mother Gerri Ellis nurtured me and tended to my wounds and Doreen Miller never allowed me to look back. These two women would not let me give up. I also would like to thank my English 101 instructor from BRCC whose name is Dora Woodside. After she read one of my papers, she not only encouraged me to enter it in a constest but she told me to continue to write. . Oh and let me not forget my brother Hal Ellis for suggesting the title after I gave him a little taste of what the book was about. Thanks Hal. Oh and let me not forget my brother David and Q.T. Ellis, Jr. my dad for offering supportive input. As well as Ebony Lathan for having a listening ear and Van Lathan for constantly telling me to go for it.

I always, liked telling stories. I remember as a little girl sitting at the feet of my Great Grand Mother Ida Dixon; telling her stories about Bro Rabbit and Bro Bear and any other Bro animal I could think of. Brother Coon, Brother Mouse, Old man corn stalk you name it, I told a story about it. It was all worth it, because my Great Grand Ma, was either baking tea cakes, baking biscuits or frying the best damn chicken you will ever ate and don't mention her okra, shrimp, smoke sausage and tomato dish with a big slug of corn bread, lawd have mercy. Nothing made me feel more alive and loved than to see her face as it light up when I told her my little stories. She was one of the most beautiful creatures God ever created; not discounting that she had a heart bigger than the Grand Canyon and spoke the wisdom of God every chance she would have to impart knowledge to you. Not a day goes by when I do not think of Mama Ida.

After she passed, I did not tell stories anymore, nobody had time to listen. I grew up got married had a family and was living my life as I had expected. Then tragedy struck my twenty-six year marriage began to deteriorate around me. My life was changing, my world was being destroyed and my heart well it was literally cut in half. I hated each time it made a beat. Life as I knew it was gone. Lost in a maze of confusion and anguish, thrown into an existence I did not want to face having no other choice than to face my destiny. I withdrew onto my own planet and there is where creation found me, there is where I began to heal, there is where I found the other Chrystal. When you only have your faith or your belief to hold on to nothing else is relevant. That is also where the struggle is as well, because the Faith you held on to and the belief you have are part of the reason you were used. But nevertheless, you hold on, you allow yourself to be excluded from regular human activity. You change your location mentally, emotionally, and spiritually and there is where you find yourself alive again, on a planet that is a new frontier for the rest of your life. Or at least this is what happened to me. This place does not allow you to consider what others are saying or doing, it is a safe haven for you to die gracefully from one life to another. Yes, here is where you can be worked on; here is where your imagination and creativity are allowed to soar. Here is where you are bare naked to the Universe, bowed at your lowest and consumed with your grief; here is where you are skinned alive from your former existence. Here is where all your shame, pain, regrets and mistakes are taken apart weighted and removed. With each removal comes a sore, with each sore comes a scab, and under each scab is your healing. Here is where you crawl into the womb of existence for help. In order to have survived my death to my former life I had to exhist in another mental form sane or insane all I knew was my help was not available within the hands of humankind. Here is where I had to be resurrected into a new existence.

My life took a turn from one existence to another as if I was meant to live in this dual existence, one in chaos and one in spiritual limbo both confusing as hell. Creating while being destroyed, feeling pain as I release into my bliss and then being resurrected to a different perspective from what I thought I was. Most of my writings tend to channel back to time when people of my color were not well treated in this Country. Their image, their life styles and their religious affiliations all were determined and judged by those who used them as cheap labor and bed warmers. There is no doubt that much of what was being channeled to me was from the spirit of ancestors who wanted to have their story told, their way. I don't dismiss that there are energies as guardians and guides that are helping me along the way. Do not think this came easy for me; I did not know what to do about all this. Do I share? Do I keep it to myself? What should I do with it and why does it matter. All these questions went through my mind constantly at the same time, but that little voice you know the one we are not suppose to talk about, kept screaming share. I would wake up mornings and turn on the TV and someone would be saying "Put it out there, be your own miracle, put it out there, let them judge you if they may. I got you. If you have believed me for everything else, why do you not believe me now? Go ahead risk being considered strange by acknowledging signs, messages, and miracles why not be obedient and share your writings. I knew the answer to that; it was simple, because I had to suffer to get here and I did'nt want the feeling of rejection again. I didn't want to suffer again. And yes sometimes I question whether it is divine lessons or human egos that deliberately create pain in the lives of unwilling suspects. But realizing that all you have is that little voice your writings and saying you grab your pen or pencil and you write down what you are experiencing right then. Then run to your mother and share with her first, then you begin to share with others, but never do you fool yourself about human egos the critics need someone to criticize. The scholars need someone to ostracize and human ego needs someone to feel small. You even look at what you wrote or drew and you might not understand it or why you did it but you know you were driven to do it, so you share it. Here is where you evolve from a psychological perspective of being to the spiritual perspective of knowing. (All I am really trying to say here is when you have thoughts and ideas that pop up in your head work to manifest them. Everybody has a story that someone wants to hear.)

As the archetypes of my ancestorial memory bank come alive a world of colorful and intriguing people come forth. One day this wonderful woman appeared and started to talk to me. I had no idea how much she could talk. I soon realized she was a storyteller much like myself. I could actually see her living back around the late 1800s' headed to the 1900's making the best of what she had. Aware that she was blessed, to be where she was, but still not fulfilled, because she knew that things were not fair. In meeting this matriarch of past wisdom, I was introduced to how she saw the world during her time. Every word she expressed about her life was full of truth, daring a lie to be told.

She introduced herself like this "My name is Ms. Lula Mae Carson, best damn biscuit maker this side of the world and the keeper of oral records, just ask anybody white or black. I don't come from a long line of storytellers, so when you hear what I am about to say, don't think someone taught me, because no one did. I listen to what people say in everyday life, sometimes I write it down but mostly I remember it. I trys to keep most things in my head, cuase I know that folk can change writing to whatever they want; but as long as I got breath I am go tell it straight. Sometimes you need to be reminded of things exactly how deh was, and I am the one to do it. I am from a little town called Friendly, La., best damn town in the South and I mean best damn town in the South. We got our problems but our white folk aint as trashey as some, and is a whole lot better than others even some of black folk. Oh and let me tell yall something. Don't get offended about me saying "white folk" or "nigger " so much back doing our time that is how we talked when we by our selves and that is how we thought when we in mixed company. You know how most people do. Most people try to lie and make you think they don't talk different when in mixed company. Dem is the ones who want you to believe they different and tries to fool like they think we all really equal. Ain't a white man that started anything made anybody equal with him. Hell that goes for anybody else too. Na some of the words might make your hair stand up, but all I am doin is telling the story like I know it. So if you aint grown you bet not be reading this. If you is school teacher or one of them fancy speakers you might have a little problem understanding this common talk. Na don't get your hair all twisted and tangled and please don't get all flustered when you is readin what I am sayin. The writings and words in this story is about everyday people from my time, we aint' talk a lot of proper English and stuff. Hell for the most part we could not let white folk know we have use for to many words other than yes sir and yes maam. Even if we had read some of Fredrick Douglas's fine words we could not go around talking like it. Hell most folk, white or black would not be able to understand you anyway. Plus most of them was a readin Mark Twain, cause he made you laugh. Plus he wrote like we talked. We just plain old common folk and we talks like that so put up your red markin pens up; cuase if you don't' all you go be doing is marking in red. Na I must admit I am a little more well-spoken than most folk cause I keeps the fancy words I learn in my mind. But I is tellin yall stories about what people thank deh is hidin. And yall is nosey and want to know what deh is hidin too as long as you don't see your self somewhere in it."

After I listened to her introduction, I just sat back and wrote down every word she said. There she was this coco brown skinned creole with long wavey hair and these big dark brown eyes, wearing this pretty blue and white calico dress with a Spanish lace collar. Not to mention that she smelled like fresh magnolia and had her hands perfectly polished. Of course, all the people's names, places, and the incidents are strictly used in a fictional manner in her story, because she would never use real people to tell her stories. Anyway there I was caught up in the world of Ms. Lula Carson, best damn storyteller and bisquit maker pretty much in the whole got damn country. "Excuse me I hate to interrupt, but even though you sees me as a black creole I have a distinct Southern accent. Oh by the way some of the situations I discussed did happen. Some of the real evils done could not be hid, everybody knew about it."

CHAPTER 1

Meeting Miss Lula Mae

YOU KNOW WHEN YOU go have a summer as hot as hell piss in Louisiana because you only have one day of spring that you can remember. I cannot remember it being this hot though, this morning I woke up and I could see the steam coming up from the grass, I mean it was really steam. I was going to go and dig me some worms so is I could go catch me some of those big gagalies down at the bayou. But child when I stepped on the grass, it seemed like I was stepin in a tub of hot water. I own one of the prettiest pieces of property around these parts. And one of the my biggest attractions is my tress, most of the trees on my place reach to the sky so I always have good shade. Yes, sir when you pull up to Lula Maes place you go see, hundred year old oaks lined from north to south and east to west. In the middle of my yard is the oldest muscadine vines in the South. You know I have eight flower beds full of roses, gardenias and people come here to try and buy my st Augustine grass. Ain't to many places out here where you can walk on st. Augustine grass all the way to your favorite fishing spot. The bayou aint no more than a half of acrea from my house. Gives me a good little walk to get there, sometimes I ride my horse when I think I am go be catching a lot of fish though.

1

Everybody say my place is like heaven and normally I would agree. But not this morning I could not even feel cool under them big old trees in my yard. My bait bed was pretty full though got me some nice fat red worms to fish with anyway. I slowly walked to my favorite spot under my big old willow tree, you know, creepin like a cat, so I would not scare any fish away. I have willow trees planted all around my bayou keeps shade and fish love to lay under willow trees, they catch every bug and worm that fall off them into the water. Those fish must have been waitin for me this morning. Soon as my line hit the water one of them big old stomp knockers hit so hard he knocked my cork off and kept on going, but that sucker had a fight on his hand cuz he just met Ms. Lula Mae Carson, best damn baker, and best cook in all of Friendly, La., not to mention being one hell of a fisherman.

I had to stand up and lean back to bring him in though. It was a good fight he was one of those black humped back gagalies ooooooh child he gave me a thrill, and he go taste some good in my corn meal and flour mixture when I drop him in some hot hog lard. Yes indeed, Ms Lula Mae go treat this big black hump back gagalie right. No soon as I got him off the line and dropped me another line in the water another big sucker hit it, ooooooooo weeeeeeeeeee, na cher. I was fightin and tuggin with it, then my skills kicked in and I snatched that hook to the corner of his mouth brought him in. Baby it was one of the prettiest slabs you ever wanted to see. One of those black speckled sacalays look like he had muscles in his back; this must be my morning, my blood is rushing. I reached down and tied my dress up around my waist then, cause I knew it was go be one of those morning. The honey hole was sweet and plentiful, ready to bless my soul yielding her goods right onto my hook. Nay I usually catches me two or three big fish and some of them little brim bout three finger wide and that be enough for me. But Lula Mae was feelin right good so good I had forgot about the heat and the time of day, cause I took me a big swig of my homemade tonic I use to keep me from getting the rumortisim and I settled in. Then I remembers what my grandma use to say, she say "Gull if you start off catchin them big fish and they is a hittin back to back that means some big money is comin. Keep on fishing." Well this was just wishful thinking for me cause I aint seen no big money and I don't know where or how any thing called big money go come to me. Unless some old white person die round here and leave Ms. Lula Mae rich (ha na that is funny a white leaving money to a colored). When my line hit the water this time I saw the back of this big old cypress trout, but what that big fish did not know is Ms. Lula always fixed her line up to be able to handle one like him or one of them big old gar fish. But this fish wanted to fight and I wanted to make me some mighty fine fish croquettes so we was going at it. Hope yall don't think it was an esay fight, this big bastard was fightin like a gar. This son of a bitch was tryin to get off. When I looked up I was in that bayou but I got my hands on him and fought with him right to the bank. Yall know I had to straddle that big bastard, did I say big bastard aint fittin for a Christian woman like myself to cuss but this big bastard made me get my dress wet, and I am gonna be thankin about that when I scale him and gut him to, cause you know when you catch these you got to filay em right then and drop em in some lemon or vingar water. Oh some of yall might not be from the South or know about fishing, these trout is delicate and you have to use the vinegar or lemon to tuffin it so it will not fall apart when you fry it. I love fried shoe pic. Well let me get to fixin him up, thank God for my fishin shed, I got everything in it I need to stay here all day, cludin some more tonic. Yall know what catching this big old cypress trout remind me of? (He must be at least a 20 lb trout too.)

I got a cousin, he one of them black pretty creol men. Call me what you want he was different from some of them other black ones. This boy got keen features curly hair, his skin smooth like black puddin, he got big dreamy brown eyes, hell he is a tall straplin buck. The girls around here loved him even after he got married. He would come through hear once a year mostly during sacalait fishing time. His name was Jerell, that man knew the woods like an Indian and he must have fished every where in the south cause he knew where all the honey holes was. See when he came he bought his boat it was a fine boat too, it had a little motor on it so you could get to those honey holes where the fish was so big you thank you hung when they hit your line. You ever seen a brim so big you can not get but one in a skillet. Anit nothing like sitting on top of a honey hole where every time you catch a fish your heart stops. Child me and him would always fall out before a fishing trip was over. Sometimes I would land a cypress trout so big and pretty you know that he was go taste like heaven melting in your mouth when you ate him. I don't know what it is about these fishing and hunting men they have all kinds of superstitions and rules when you on they boats. I am go get me a boat just like this one, with a motor on it and show his ass. Now who am I fooling, I know I am not be coming back in the middle of the cucabug flats fishing. For one thang it is to far and another thang is the only women you ever see doing that is the ones who live back there. And let me tell you might want to deal with the men back here rather than the women, cause deh always thanking one of deh, men go want you. And another thang they can fight they ass off so you go have to shoot em. But any Jerrell would not let me put that joker on his boat. He would piss me off to high hell, cause I love me some cypress trout; all anybody want to give away I would take. Anyway catching this big shoepic made me think of him. He stopped coming around about two years ago after he got married and purchased his own place, here tell it is over 300 acres of good land. That man loves fishing so much he got 100 acres with nothing but ponds on it. They say he is making a good living from just letting people pay to fish in them. He must have stocked them ponds with some of the fish he caught, cause the words is every time your line hit the water you better lean back and get ready. Cazzie went up there around Old River to get some turtles, bull frogs and gar fish for the Major and them and stopped by his place. Figures he would move out round there that is where he spent most his time when he came here anyway. Aww Lord yall about to make me miss these fish doing all this talking. They usually slow down after a fight like the one we just had, but when you stop to fix em up it gives the water time to settle down some. No soon as I put my line back in the water another one of those big black gagalies hit it again. Then one them big old humped back bull brim hit, then another bull brim hit, oooooh weee Ms. Lula Mae Carson tearing them up. After this morning, I just might be the best damn fisherwoman in the whole of Friendly, La. By the time I finished using up my bait I had caught 14 bull brim, 14 of them big hump back gagalies, 14 of the big slab sacalays and about a 20lb cypress trout and nine of them little brim bout three finger size, I love to fry them whole and hard and eat em like cracklings. Yall like cracklins, I do I love the way them Cajuns make em. Ain't saying black folk can't make em good but them damn Cajuns well that is a different cracklin.

Huh, child if what my Grandmother said was true Ms. Lula Mae Carson was about to be some kind of rich woman. (This was a nice dream to have so I just keep it goin, better than what my real life was). Sun about to come up strong and it is already hot so the water is boiling. I had better get back to the house with my fish. I was leavin just in time too, cause them old stomp tail water moccasins can smell your fish. What I told ya? As soon as I looked up, I saw two of em just eyein me. What they did not know is I had my little 22 sitting right side of me. I keeps one in my shed, they lucky I did not feel like target practice. I hate killin God's creatures but I will. I went on and left cause if you know anything about them old black stomp tail cotton mouths you know they will fight with ya. I had to much treasure this morning to be running from a gang of water moccasins. Sometimes you can be out numbered on this bayou. I have seen so many moccasins going down this bayou a sane person would probably never fish here again. But I aint sane, aint no such a thang as a sane black person in the South anyway. We gots to be insane to make it here. Ain't to many sane white folk either. I am go have me one of them ice boxes delivered to my house soon, I just hope it don't blow me up. Can't trust to many new contraptions.

I sure wished the ice man be coming by right na cause I am tired and do not feel like cleanin all them fish, but since it aint nobody but me to do it let me get to scalin , guttin and filayin these fish. I got to get them to town cause Cassie, she is the head cook in the white folks eatin place and they had one of them ice box thangs that keep your food for ya. It was as big as a room and it keep thangs right good. Like I said I will be getting me one soon. Plus, she was going to fry some of them fish up for her and them girls. If I would have had some of them big old catfish she would take and fry that for them white folks, cause they love them some catfish and I love it too. Don't know why those catfish did not bite? I cleaned my fish and washed up and went on into town straight to Cassies' and of course them girls was talkin about all the mis- behavenin them white mens do when aint nobody around. Today they was talkin about the Sheriff Watson and how he likes to come in rub that hog lard all over Anna Mae, she his personal supply of colored girl women self. See we all figure that Anna Mae aint go never have another colored man all her life and that she just as soon keep that old low down red neck happy. Oh don't accuse me of mis naming one of God's children, that old Sherrif loved calling his self a red neck. We loved callin him one too, except we would always add sons of a bitch to the end of ours.

Was about 5 years ago Anna Mae and her husband seemed to be

doing okay, then Anna Mae gave birth to their first born child, old Willie Buck took one look at that little boy and say 'Dat aint none of mine.' Anna Mae swore that nobody else had been there but him, she say "Dis here boy just like his great great grand pappy dat's why he so light lookin and dat's why his face so narrow and his hair so red, cause he just like his grand pappy; Old Slave Master Johson from up there round Ville Platte." Old Willie Buck went on and took what she said, but he plowed her and plowed her and plowed her until she has him a baby girl. She was the sweetest lookin little chocolate thang you ever wanted to see. Anna Mae smart she told everybody how she had gave birth to her great, great , grand mammy, cause her little girl was just like her. She say " Lord, look at this child she just like her great great grand mammy black as Africa and sweet as sugar cane." Willie Buck went on bout his way workin, and tryin to take care of his famil; ignoring that his son was white as snow, with hair red as fire and a face full of freckles.

It was early one Sunday morning nobody in the fields, nobody fishin and nobody standin around givin that good old Friendly, La. gossip. For some reason this Sunday we went to the square said our how do ya dos and went back home, it happen that way sometimes. Willie Buck had been workin out of town in Sherriff Watson's brothers' field in Welcome, La. bout 20 miles up the road from Friendly. And he was not expected home till that next weekend. Nothing but the devil in hell made that man decide to come home for Sunday breakfast. He hitched him a ride on a hay wagon and headed straight home. When he got there, what he said he saw was his Anna Mae tuggin and lickin all over that old low down Sherriff Watson, (na that explains a lot, see Willie Buck had been caught about a year ago stealin old Major Whites hogs and instead of being dead they just let him work it off. But seems like Anna Mae was the one workin it off if you know what I mean). Willie Buck stood there in shock, said he heard the Sheriff talkin about sending his son off to a better school. Said he wanted his boy to live up North where people did not know who or what he was. Can you believe that red-neck trying to send his son away some where else so people won't know he black. Willie say Sheriff Watson said " Na look Ana Mae this here boy is special he look just like his grand pappy. He won't fit in niggerville, anyway his white blood done killed all traces of any nigger blood he might have and he don't need to be around a bunch of ignorant red-necks either." Willie

Buck say he heard Anna Mae agree with him then she commencin to take off all her clothes and the Sherriff started lickin, and smellin all up and down her thighs and her back like a dog in heat. Po Willie Buck, standin their scared, hurt and in shock as he watched the Sheriff ride his wife like a buckin horse but what hurt him the most was how much she was enjoying it. When he could not take anymore he screamed. And as the Sheriff jumped up he spewed his liquids all over that poor man. (You know our windows were not to high up so poor Willie Buck got a face full.) The Sheriff told Willie Buck no harm was done and he should just forget about what he had seen cause Ana Mae could only do what he told her to do. And then he told him "Nigger if you tell anybody about this or put your hands on Anna Mae I'll hunt you down and kill your got damn ghost. Na go fetch me some of that homemade outta my truck."

Poor Willie Buck went around for days like a spell was on him then one day that man just snapped and started talkin all over town to everybody he saw, till the word got back to Sheriff Watson's wife. Aww Honey that crazy white woman came in the general store and took a fit on the Sheriff. Na I usually could give a damn about that old sons of a bitch, but this time he was just out right shamed. And he looked right stupid when Ms. Watson said in a front of everybody that, "When God made sunshine he put it between my got damn legs you stupid bastard, but you to got damn blind to see it." And child no sooner as she said that Mr. Ellis said "Yes lawd he did" in such a manner everybody just got quite real quiet. Nobody moved cause they did not know what was about to happen, cuz it could have been a killing in there; but instead they all just left without saying another word.

Hum that's white folk for ya, too many nigga's heard that and understood it, dat made em shame for all white folks. You know the good God fearing whip slashing kind. Of course we had to stand there with this blank look on our face like we did not understand what was said. Even though every damn body knew we did. See that is what I am talking about, a thang is done or said and because of the color of your skin you have to pretend you are too dumb to understand; just so the people doin it to you feels like they have all the power. That is why I be questioning things so much. Aint tryin to be hard headed, just tryin to understand. Aint trying to buck nose with the good Lord just want to know how he so fair and we be treated so unfair. I been asking these questions for a long time and aint got no answer. Well the truth is I don't just want an answer I want a change. Well anyway I was telling yall about poor Willie Buck. That man went home that same day that happened in the store and took a brandin iron and beat that little boy to death (cause he was mad at his daddy) let me tell ya when Anna Mae saw all he had done she went screamin all through town. We was all standing around the Medicain Man wagon by then, cause everybody needed some of his healing tonic after all this commotion. He always came through once a month, bring in some of the best brew, I mean tonic you ever had. A couple of teaspoons and you felt just fine. So we standing around the wagon and here come Anna Mae riding like the wind screaming and crying like the devil had beat her tale. That girl almost killed that poor horse he was formin at the moth and all soaped up. She ran and feel down at Sheriff Watson's feet telling all Wille Buck had done. I aint never seen Sherriff Watson move so damn fast, he got on his horse so fast he knocked Anna Mae down in the dirt where all the black men thought she should be anyway. None of them even tried to help her up. If his truck would have been running he would have run over her and killed her as fast as he was movin. You know Sheriff Jones was high tailin it behind him on his horse, they ain't got him no car yet. When he got to her house and saw his boy lying there like that here tell that white man cried and cried and cried and cried' aint that nothing. Huh, who would have thought he would have given a damn about his little darkie boy. Child that man drank and drank and drank and drank for days. Must have been something special about this boy. I have to admit it seemed like he loved that boy. Truth is none of us aint' never seen anything like it cause that boy looked just like that old low down man. I bet if he lived he would have been a low down dog just like his daddy. These was very unsafe times in Friendly, La. and the surrounding areas especially for a black man or a boy. Sheriff Watson said he did not want to see a nigger walking the street of Friendly. Yall know he was wrong, cause he just wanted blood now anybody's blood. It is a good thang Jesus had already died cause if he had come along doing these times the good sheriff would have killed him for letting it happen. Tell me he hung a boy that favored Willie Buck, burned his family out, and beat his mother almost to death. That is why I always be asking you these questions good Lord. Wasn't none of this right, we had to put together money to get them folks to New Orleans to keep him from going back and killin them all.

Willie Buck was on the run. Cause the Sheriff put out all kinds of posters saying he wanted him caught and brought back to Friendly, so he could face his punishment. Na here tell, some white men caught him in North Louisiana stealin, and lynched him. When Sherriff Watson found out what they had done, he got in his truck and road up there and killed them men cause he said they cheated him by killin that black devil Willie Buck. From that day to now, no black man had better not even look at Anna Mae and her children. It is hard not to look at her though cause that girl is black as ten thousand mid-nights and she pretty. Long straight hair, green eyes, and nice keen features, yes she is a pretty child. She had them big old thick thighs and hips, an ass just like mine and that is a fine ass. I don't understand these white men, to say they make they women stay so small they love evey inch of us. That is why it hurt us so much that old bastard got her. And no man bet not even look at her to long lessin old Sherriff Watson kill em dead. And no white man had better even think about trying to share her or treat her like they do the other "nigger wenches" as they call us. The Sheriff has made it plain he'd kill a white man just like he kill a nigger, if he caught anybody trying to *fuck* with her and he meant that both ways. Poor Anna Mae, she was a marked woman for the rest of her life. The strangest thing I don't think Ana Mae minded bein his at all.

Anyway, I is just wanting to get my fish in that ice box so they won't spoil. I seasoned me some right quick so I can get Ms. Cassie to start some to fryin. I went on and started makin the biscuits and she started frying that fish and it smelled so good. When everything was done, oooooooooo ooo lawd we ate and ate and ate, until we could not eat no more. Cause nay all know that I was the talk of the town that day everybody wanted to know "What you caught em on?, Where was you fishin? What time of the day it was ? I told em I caught em on crickets, down by the bridge early in the morning. Na yall know what happened don't you, next morning everybody down at bridge white and black using crickets. Strange thang though the good Lawd was looking out for me and my lie, cause them people had some kind of fishing day. They all caught good fish, bull brim, sacalay, big old chinkapins, gagalie, shoepick, catfish, mullets, and Jessie Lee and her crew caught enough blue crab to sell em. They also had caught buckets and buckets of grass shrimp, for bait and they made a good piece of change off of them too. Looks like someone should have felt obligin and give me a little donation. Hummh all I know is one lie saved me from having to run people off my land. Cause yall know if they had not caught nothing, deh was go figure it out and was gonna be all on my property trying to find my honey hole. And for damn show, it was go be a problem, cause Miss Lula Mae don't give up her honey to easy.

CHAPTER 2

A Hot Summer

ONE THANG PEOPLE CAN depend on here in Friendly, La. hot summers and straight gossip from Ms. Lula Mae Carson. They can have faith that every Sunday, we go be praisin the Lawd. Of couse na that is after we done sanged and danced our feet sore in the juke joint on Friday and Saturday night. You can best believe we knew how to have a good time here and we knew how to praise the Lawd too. Aint nothing wrong with dancing till ya fart on a Saturday night. As long as you go to church on Sunday morning and stomp that Devil out. One thang here we all knows how to praise the Lawd, most folk don't do what he say, but deh praise him anyway. Ain't figured out why He ain't done struck down most of these here churches. I see a lot of things done in His good name that don't seem to fit what he taught. Now yall don't need to get mad this is how I see it; you can't expect a black women in the late 1800's to be to much different. I done praised mostly all my life, seems like something suppose to change in my condition. But I is still black, still a women, still in the South, still believing and still holdin on, na that ain't no reflection on me Lawd, that is a refelction on you. Since you see everythang then you see me tryin to do what is suppose to be right and you see how I fights the demons even when they seem like they winnin. For as I am concerned it is your move na.

It was the middle of July and it was hotter than a hussy in a pepper patch, or like them men would say "hot as a mare in heat", and child that is a hot mess. No body but a man want to be around a mare in heat cause she smelling so ripe. Bet yall mens like that don't you; but us women don't like that thought too much. Cause we don't want to go around smelling each other; exceptin for this girl we calls Sho Thang. We all calls her Sho Thang not cuz she was easy like some of these trolips. But because ifin a man tried to hook up with her it was a sho thang that he was wastin his time. But if in a woman came her way it was a sho thang she was gonna turn to lovin her real hard. I ain't lyin yall I had knowed about the power of this woman cuz many a women din left her husband and man and took up with her and stayed with her as long as she wanted them. Nobody wanna believe me but she is possessed with something that the preachers and saints can't do a damn thang about it; that is right I said damn. I wouldn't even look straight in her eyes, she could charm ya. You ever seen a cat charm a bird, that is what Sho would do to you. I know that for show and that is why I never would look her straingt in her eyes. See, yall I was to scared that the Jesus in me would leave and the devil in me would come out. Oh yeah, Ms. Lula Mae gots a little devil in her, that is why I am always askin for forgiveness, I need it. Don't nobody start to judge me, else I am go say look in your own mirror, we all do things that are wrong when nobody knows about it but us. So what if Ms. Lula Mae goes a little higher on her prices for her preserves accordin to who is buyin em, that is the American way. Plus when sugar goes to 5 cent a lb. white folk can pay a little more for preserves than black folk. And once or twice I told people some of my family living off in them big cities needs me to help em and church gave a nice size collection for that. My entire back forty had growed up and I had used my extra money to order me three of those store made dresses from New York City. I know I should have told the church I needed that money to get my back forty cleared and as good a member as I am it should not even been a problem, but there is always some nigga lookin to start something bout nothing. So I told em my family off was almost out doors and needed some cash fast and it worked. Somebody just judged me, but I don't care cause I aint really hurt nobody. Cause nobody know I was lying but me and God and so far God aint did me nothing yet. Oh! wasn't I telling yall about Sho Thang, Ms. Lula Mae gots to keep her thoughts, her real name is Beulah Mae Dixon and she was a looker and her family lived about 10miles on the other side of Friendly, La. They lived in the part of town we all talked about cause most of them people over there had children by they sisters, brothers and first cousins, so we figured since she was born over there she had to have something wrong with her. Anyway this is the only excuse we had for her being that way. The mens was all mad at her cause she usually got the women they wanted and they all wanted her. Not just cause she was pretty, but because the man that said he had her would be king of the town, hell he might be the king of the South. They all tried but they soon gave up cause they realized they would never ever have her. Wonder how that girl came up with some of the things I hear she do, hmmmm. I bet she nasty to but anyway I am go keep my way from her. Tell me she got secret thangs she know that mens don't know. I tries not to look at her to hard me. You know what the white men must have thought she was cursed too, cause they did not bother with her either.

Well we all pretty much got along here in Friendly, La. We knew the unspoken rules. Oh, yall people do not know what the rules is. Rule one blacks tend to business in Blackville only, and whites tend to business in Whiteville, and Blackville and blacks never ever show no disrespect to whites no matter how evil they is being to them, and blacks must never ever consider themselves as equal to whites cause that is not of God. Blacks can shop in white stores, cook in white kitchens, but cannot eat in white restaurants, whites can take what they want form black shops and eat in their restaurants usually free of charge. The black sheriff can only arrest blacks that the white sheriff give him permission to, and oh he can never arrest a white man. And child that might have been a good rule cause I doubt if it be one white man free. Black women can have white men, but black men cannot look at a white women longer than a second, or he gits his black ass tarred and feathered. And you better damn well know a black man bet not visit a black woman on the same day a white man is expected to come by. Truth is if a white man was seeing a black women black men had better leave her alone and that included the mullatos too. Na that is rule number one, Rule Number 2 is that if you do not follow rule number one you can and will be hung; Amen. Let me not forget this, always confess the evil in your heart and ask Jesus to forgive you. Pray for the people God put in charge, and keep in your mind that you are blessed because you have been civilized, better than the indian. Na these here is some of the rules of how to get along in Friendly, La. There are more but you would have to live here to understand. We had separate parts of town, separate lives, separate thoughts and for the most part we all pretty much hated white folks in our hearts and we knew it and they hated us too. You can't really love something you fear and that is the truth. Don't matter if we had moments of happiness or even pleasure we still had a kinda sorrowful hate for em, even if we liked em. Its like this, when somebody got the power to take your life and they treat you like they know they do. You go always be scared of em. And when you scared of anything all you want to do is get rid of it. But something happens on Sundays' we all started gatherin on Sunday's after church and it just worked so we kept it up. Our lives was totally separate exceptin for Sundays , Sundays was a little different. That is how this thing about the Lord confuse me. If He can soften hearts on Sunday why not everyday. We still had a place though but it just seemed different on Sundays. Could have been cause some of us was thinkin about forgiveness, some of us was thankin about love and some of us was thinkin about hope. But nevertheless you still had a place so not all of us was thinkin about the same thangs.

On Sunday in our little town of Friendly, La. we all would gather at the big gazebo in the center of town after about 2 or 3 hours of shoutin and praisin Jesus. Na that is one thang white folk loved to hear us do, praise Jesus, cause they knowed they done taught us Jesus is white like them. I bet if they knowed some of us thought Jesus was black they would stop us from praisin so damn hard. But on Sunday black or white we was all praisin Jesus. I hear it use to be a rule that we had to have our church after the whites sos God could go and bless them first and if he had any left over blessins he would give them to us, startin with the mulattos. That is why we ain't got shit na. Tell me Old Captain Buck Masters owner of half the South over heard one of his field hands talking to some workers. Tell me he said "Maybe they God aint so great since he cannot be in more than one place at a time." Say Old Captain say "Boy what is that you said about the Good Lord. I know you ain't tryin to figure like a man over there, nigger I'll take your tongue out. You son of a bitch. What was that I heard you say about the Good Lord?" You know he changed what he said, but Old Captain Buck gave him 10 lashes and made him stand in the swamp for three days. He was a lowdown bastard here tell. Huh, child them white folk hurry up and changed that Sunday service thang around. Aint that nothing. Cause, old captain overheard one of his field hands say that. We all start having praise service at the same time. One thang I am glad of is that we do not go to the same churches. I could not imagine sittin in church with them white folk, cause it would not be right. Hopin I could catch the spirit while sittin next to one of them sos I could knock the hell out of em in the name of the Lawd. Plus I figure, one day the death angel go ride and he go ride to straight over to the church of the people who say the Lord gave them the right to rule. And that is just fine with me cause I know when he come all the white folk go be in the same place so he won't be confused who to take. I sure am glad we don't go to church together, cause that would be a sin.

We aint never had a whole lot of mess and stuff like that cause we is all kinda po, in compares to the money other towns might have. We share just about everything and us colored folks remember the rule. Na. even though we all meet up in the center of town on Sunday, the difference twixts us still shows. You know we called the whites Mr. and Mrs. no matter how old or young deh is and they all called us by our first name or boy or gal. Our children even played games together as long as the black children let the white children win all the games. And no matter how smart they were, they had to play dumb. Maybe that is the reason our children stopped wanting to come to the center of town on Sundays. They did not care about the rock candy or peppermint sticks, they would rather stay home and eat tea cakes and pecan candy. Well anyway usually one of us would stay back on our side of town and keep them. We aint to much like our children playing with them anyway. Cause most of them was some spoiled little bastards with no manners. Hell our babies got tired of playing servants or cattle when they played with them little white kids. Plus, when they played by themselves, they was doctors, nurses, train captains, great speakers like W.E.B. Dubois, Fredrick Douglas and leaders like Harriet Tubman and Little Ida Runnin Tree; you know they played like they was well respected people. And our little girls never wanted to be maids, cooks and wives them girls wanted to have jobs like men, they wanted to be doctors, lawyers and professors. That is cause none of us ever told them that being a maid was a choice.

I told yall bout how we had a black Sherriff and deh had a white Sheriff, but we all know that every women wanted our Sheriff to be around whether there be trouble or not. Our Sheriff name John fine thang Jones. You know we gave him that middle name. Lord have mercy a woman must have made him cause he is everything a women wants to look at. You know the kind of man that have them big old broad shoulders, a slender waist line, graced with a natural manly muscle tone. He had that charcoal black skin that looked like black silk material, his hair was sorta course and wavey. He had them snow white teeth, and a man ass that made every women and some men in town just want to grab it. He smelled like fresh pine not to strong and he was as sweet as he could be, never asking for nothing and always lending a helping hand. How many times did I have to pray about every thought and stroke that I made when I would think about him in my private time? If you a woman and aint got no regular man you knows what I am talking about. Them times when you almost aching, feels like you go catch a fever or loose your mind if you don't release. This is the time you forget about all that shit the preachers be saying about you touching yourself. Hell I believe they put that in the Bible anyway to be sure women did not know what it felt like to be pleased. Since when God go give you some hands and fingers and then curse you for using them. Ain't nothing easier to get as a women aint been serviced going to a preacher man for spiritual help. Hell I bet all the men agreed to put that in the Bible sos they could keep the women from touching herself. If God did not want me to use my fingers He would not have given them to me; or He would have saw to it I had somebody to ease my tensions. If you think a tooth ache is something it can not beat the pain of throbbing lady self or pussy or whatever you might want to call it. Truth is I had a few men in my life that have missed the mark when it came to takin me on home, but lovely little fingers never miss, nope not one time. So take your judging hats off and grease your fingers.

Thinkin about Jones and my fingers reminds me of the time I decided to slip down to the creek and take me a swim in the middle of the day. Aint nothing feel better than a naked swim in a clear, cool creek. Well guess who I saw there? If yall don't tell I might just let you know that; I saw Jones and old Reverand Goodman's wife sister Lizzie laying on the sandy banks of the Comite River. Mr. Sheriff had took off his pants and all he had on was his under clothes, and they was wet. I forgot all about who he was with once my eyes focused on his body, all I could see was all of him. I mean his man- self was swole to the size of his arm, I could see it from where I was. Damn if that thang did not almost meet up to the size of bull's dick. I almost passed out at first, my women was throbbing child, my knees went weak and I was sweating, my stomach was tighting up, and felt like cramps was taking me over. I ought to be ashamed to say this but I my panties was so full of cream I could have opened a small dairy farm. Whether yall know it or not that is a sign of a good woman. Don't get all flustered and selfrighteous, this is what most women do when they see something they like. Exceptin for a few scared Christian women I know; cause deh is taught deh suppose to be ashamed for having normal feelings bout sex.

The Christian men must have been excluded when God sent out that rule, cause most of them I know is hoes and if deh ain't hoin deh is thanking about it. After about 5 minutes into watching him swim and play with her, I experienced one satisfying moment after another. I was enjoying every minute of this, I know what you thinking; but I really do not care. You probably wonder why I did not fall on my knees and start praying for the both of them since I caught them in the mist of sin and fornication. Well I was not thinking about Jesus right then. I did however wished I could be the one screaming his name like the good reverand's wife was go be doing in a few minutes. Then all of a sudden, Sheriff Jones stood over her and she pulled his under pants to the side and Ms. Lizzie started to lick and taste him like he was rock candy. Child she was sniffin his nut bridge, but most of us did that, we just ain't tell it. That is when I fell back right into a black berry bush, got damn, talk about being punished. I bet I came out of my day dream then. I could not even scream, cause I did not want either one of them to know that I saw them. Well, I did not get to many thorns in my behind cause the leaves was still kinda of green yet, but it still was not a good feeling. Then as I got up and looked back at them and saw how gentle he pulled her up, kissed her and held her; I forget about those briars and just started to melt again.

All this carrying on just made me think about this Cajun man I had feelings like that for. His name was Robeir, he was one of the finest rough men you ever wanted to see. Tall, sun burnt, thick man with eyes bluer than the sky, sho nuff Louisiana swamp livin Cajun. Yeap, a Cajun, he would speak sweet words of French to me and bring me filayed fish, shelled crawfish and shrimp, blue crab and honey by the tons. But most of all he bought me himself. We knew we could not tell anybody about our feelins for one another, neither one of us was prepared for what happened between us. We fell in Love, real heartbreaking, can breath love. I could hardly stand to call his name, without erupting, he moved me so . He was gentle, kind and he captured that part of a women that holds her most precious secrets, her heart. He had my mind because I thought of him every moment we were not together. Mr. Robeir Dabonshey treasured my body, he would never rush me because he took his time to touch every inch of me. I mean it yall he touched every inch of me as gentle as man could touch a woman. Robeir loved my bedroom, he said I must have had my bed made for a big man to sleep in cause it was so big. Well what he ain't know is this bed was made for a big man, it was made for Mr. Henry my mothers unlawful husband. He liked a lot of room so he had this bed special made out of 100 year old cypress. I had to spend most of my preserve money to make sheets sometimes cause I needed so much material. Robeir would love to stretch out in it and roll me on top til we fall off to sleep. He also liked the idea that my dresser mirror was right in front of it to sos he could catch a look at my hips wigglin. He was a good man and I think I loved him more than I ever loved anybody else or at least I tried too. I remember the morning I told him I was pregnant, he was full of excitement. I never saw him so happy he was like a school boy cuttin up his first frog. We must have made love all day.

He started telling me about his part he had back in the basin, and how once I got use to it I would fit right in. I did not know how to tell him I had went to see the root lady and she had already given me the tea. Right before he left that day I told him what I had done; I did not want to fool him. He looked at me for a long time as if he did not recognize me. And then he told me these words " Cher I have never been ashamed of you until now. I'll come back in a few days and if my baby is not here, I am no longer here." I said " How you go give me such a choice you know it is illegal for me and you to be married and even if it was not this can't work." Robeir say " I am man of the basin we make our own rules, we live by our honor, we keep our word and we take care of ours. You is mine and I am yours but if you done hurt my life inside of you I would not be able to see you no more cher." I knew when he left that day it was go be over cause I could feel the tea workin. He came back after three days and found me in bed weak and feverish, cause I had took to much of the tea. Then he looked at me with his eyes full of tears and he never said one word. He just kissed me on the forhead and I never saw him again, never. He ain't really love me no way if he could not understand why I did not want to have his baby.

Look at what happened to Annie Mae, just look at all the bad luck most folk have when they have them mixed badies on purpose. We was sinnin anyway something probably was go be wrong with that baby. My thoughts gets to me every once and a while about my baby. I wonder what my child would looked like. I wonder what kind of life I would have had with her daddy. I wonder what kind of punishment I was go receive for taking the life of my own child too. I know I am go get it one day. I think if I had to do it all over again , I would have my child, but it is too late for me to change what I did now. I will never give birth, not in this life. That is go be my punishment for killin his baby. You don't know how it feels to wake up hearing a baby cryin in the middle of the night and no one is really there; but I can't let it take over my mind. What I look like a black women with sense trying to have a white man's baby and believin that I could have a real life with him? What I look like causing more trouble for myself marrying a Cajun and movin in the basin. This ain't no life for either one of us, we can't have real love just something that seem like it is real. When I think of Robeir I think of how I really loved him, and I think of how I will never have that again. See God you just ain't fair sometimes, bring a man in my life who loves me but who I can't love completely. I don't know ifin I ever should really believe in you Lord, cause you allow some mean thangs to go on. I am go live the rest of my life in love with a man who I am dead to. But anyway I ain't mad at you shucks, I hate mosquitos and the basin is full of them. I would not want to live there anyway. I could smell sweet again.

It was a long walk back to my home. I took me a witch hazle bath, full of eucalyptus leaves, lavender and salt, it felt good to soak. My white hand woved cotton gown always made my body happy, plus Ms. Cresia had put a healing prayer on it. I laid in my soft bed and was satisfied over and over again as I thought about this day. Oh I guess you all thinking Miss Lula Mae aught to be ashamed of what she just said, well I am not. I am a full blooded woman with needs. I just aint lettin nobody meet them for me right na. Ms. Lule needs something to hold on to and dream about. I gets shames when I am talking to the Sheriff na cause I get moist, you know a little sweat on my woman self. I still remembers that day at the creek often. Sometimes, Ms. Lula Mae gits a little fast and winks at him, but I do not think he knows what I feel. He certainly does not know what I saw. He have not picked up on me yet. I like the idea that most people think, old Ms. Lula Mae plenty of woman alright but she won't bust a grape and they right I don't believe in busin grapes, but nuts is another thang. Unh … he one lucky man cause we takes care of him, we all feed him, we clean his house and we keep up his clothes. We just wants a chance to bend down in front of him and pick up something sos we could look back and see that fine smile on his face. I am just a twitchin right na . Lord let me stop talking about this man. Cuz John Jones is another story and I aint even sho I want to share that with the likes of yall. Seeing, that I am on a quest to keep my holiness. And believe me it is hard to stay holy down hear. Everything good is bad and every thang bad feels good. But, I thank God like sex, cause there is a lot of talk about it in the Bible. Looks like to me all people did was have sex and multiply in the Bible.

Well anyway this Sunday as with all Sundays, we all sittin around the gazebo drinking lemon aide and play arguing over who baked the best cakes . In our hearts us black women know full well these white women can not cook with us. We done had to take scraps and turn them into meals. We know how to take a hoe cake, fried fat back, and greens and make a meal. We know how to go to the woods and get spices these white girls don't know about. And don't yall thank we don't take home from they cubboards too, cause we do. You might call it stealin, we call it replacement for wages we earn but don't get paid for. But anyway when it comes to good cookin we wrote the books on that. But aint' nothin more arrogant than white woman who thank she can cook. She got to be the best damn cook and these white womens always trying to out do us everytime, when it comes to cookin. The only one of them ever won any contest was Sally White the Major's wife and the only reason she won was cuz Lu Bertha Williams baked her cakes for her. And in return she could get free groceries at her and the Majors' General Store. But you know what, we never let her know that we knowed that; after all she the Majors wife. Don't need her going home crying putting ideas in

20

his head, bout some smart nigger showing her up at Sunday gathering making her look bad. They will show do it too, if you make one of them shame or say something they can not understand deh goes home and rubs deh husbands heads, both of them and you are in trouble. In most cases us black womens have to work extra hard to keep them horney bastards relaxed. Instead of just coming in for a quick one they makes you rub em down and do extra thangs for them. Believe me when ever you had to spend extra time with one of them you really did not like it was like being put in jail. The only time them men really did anything real mean though is when one of them jealous wives keep on insisting. That is why I say Friendly's white folk is a little bit better than some in other towns. At worst you might get a slap across the face or a black eye so that evil bitch can see you been took care of. But what they did not know was most of them mens either be tryin to give you something extra for that or swearin they did not want to do it. Cause most of them go want to come back anyway and most of them do. You always have one or two of the bastards that try to make you think it was your fault, for not acting like a proper nigger though. Sometimes they would come by for months bringin jewelry, money, feed, meat, honey, material oh yeah, some of them would keep bring you gifts sos you can forget what they did. But that did not matter though, you can't pay a women anyting for raping and beatin her. These fools thought you could though, they really thought we aint have no feelins. Deh did not know Satan be shittin snow cones in hell before we be acceptin that shit. The only part I ever cared for is when they put they mouth on ya. I liked that cause seemed like you was in power then, you could bust em in they heads, or stab em, or even fart sometimes right in their nose and get away with it. You know some of them liked it when you farted too, these white mens is different. They some strange ones, well I can't say I mind all they bad habits, not all of em. One of em got hold to me one time and I swear I could feel his tongue in the back of my throat. That old boy there was gifted. He really thought he was doin me a favor. I thank some of them be tryin to practice on us before they get back to their wives. They be tryin to make love I thank. But like said when it ain't your choice it ain't your choice and child most times it ain't our choice. Plus we don't care, who say what we is all arrogant about our cooking and we know we the best. Cookin takes practice and since we deh maids and cooks we practice more than them. Hell our cooking is what keep us living or at least that is how we made a living. Child when we all get together without them white women we laughs and laughs until we cries about Sally's cakes. We beat them hands down most of the time, bakin and cookin. But just so you know, here in Louisiana we have the best cooks in the world, whether they be white or black. Some of them white gals knows how to make that fried cornbread, black eyed peas soup with them big old ham hocks, and lawd some of them can make the livin hell out of crawfish bisque. Aww hell just let me say, yes some of them white women can cook they ass off; mostly the ones call themselves Cajun. Kinda hard to tell the difference between their food and our Creole cooking sometimes. Of course, there has never been any competition when it comes to biscuits, cause I own that, hands down. Ain't a got damn soul in these here United States can touch my biscuits.

Anyway yall, while we all just sittin around debatin on our skills, separated from the mens and I means all the mens. Strange thang all the mens would get together on one side of the town square, laughin, talkin and drinking moonshine on Sundays. Look like deh all be having a good time over there, don't even seem like color matter. Deh just be laughin and yahain, like deh brothers or something. They have some kind of understanding them men do. Wish us women could have that, but we don't, cause we always competin with each other for dem men. I don't mind sayin I use to be right there in the race with em too. But your feets gits tired of runnin around in circles after the same town cock. So I just decided to be what deh call a virtuous woman. Just sos yall will know, I ain't had a man in a while either. Grace, mercy, being a good woman, and talkin to God ain't got me nothing but bein alone, with ten men who don't talk back. My heart kinda trembling, feet feeling sweaty, and my hands are burning, aww shit, there it is my eye jumpin. When this happens to me usually I am about to have some problems or some big trouble on the way. Last time it happened, this old gal from down in the flats named Tutt come round here talkin about she my sister and half my place was hers. I prayed about then I went to see Ms. Lacrecia, she prepared me a rooster foot. All I know is she ain't come around here no more, somebody told me she drowned back in the locks. Course Ms. Lacrecia ended up with the first fruit from my fig tress, but she was worth it. She was different from them others she always prayed to Jesus before she helped anybody.

Oh, Lawd, please, no trouble for me; not on a day so pretty only you could have painted it. Look like I could feel you smilin on us like we doin somethin right. Well is this the President comin into town? All of a sudden this fancy thang they calls a car pulls up, all long and shinny, with big sparkling lights like crystal balls, big white rims on the tires, with no top on it, sos you can see that snow white interior, look like this car was over one block long. Well the driver pulls up in front of our buggy station and a black man gits out with a fine suit on. Honey child it was black as tar with shinny gold buttons on it and he even had them same buttons on his shoes. He turned and tiped his hat at us, and we started giggling like school girls. The white women acted as if they was shocked that he had the nerve to speak, you could tell he was not from here. Thank God the men was too busy gabbing away to care. Then he steps around and opens the door. By na we is all looking to see who dis black women is got this man opening the door for her. We all looking cause we knows this got to be some rich women to have a car like this. After he open the door then he gives her his hand and this women stands up and you could have knocked us all over with a feather and put anything in our mouth you wanted to, cause all of them was open. First thang you noticed was her skin color, she looked like chocolate look like the damn sun was go melt her if she stood in it to long; I wish it would. She was wearin a red lace dress , low cut in the front and low cut in the back , that dress was fittin yall, it must have been custom made cause it fitted every curve on her body perfect. Then that heifer stretched out like a big old fluffy cat wakin up from a nap. Did I fail to mention that brazin heifer had just about all of her legs showing too, big old legs the kind them mens be hollering behind huh. She deliberately spread her ass and popped it as she stretched. If this ain't the low downiest two bit whore I done ever seen in my life. Shit maybe she is what I am feeling, maybe she is the trouble. All we need around here is another bushy pussy women needin her yard mowed. This ain't nothing but the devil, just watch how the white men go be fightin over her.

Well any way after she stretched, she turned and looked at all of us and smiled and what a beautiful smile it was too, she had all her teeth. It was warm and full of passion; it made you feel like she was an angel and you was lookin at a part of heaven. You know Ms. Lula Mae Carson was gettin every detail na, cause I know everybody go be comin to me for more information, you know the small thangs they missed. All us ladies smiled back while thinkin "Look at this Jezebel whore." I am sure most of the mens wonderin how much she go cost em. Look at em over there tippin their hats like gentlemen while they is fornicatin in their minds. I can tell yall and Jesus right na I am go hate this bitch. Oh we knowed what them mens was thinkin cause they was trying so hard not to look they was sweatin. Then all of a sudden Sally White the major's wife said " Girls, (and that meant all of us) looks like we got us a bit of trouble that just hit town." Then all of them white ladies nodded their heads in agreement. Well that was quite a statement I kinda liked to see them white ladies all flustered and some of them holy whores from my part of town was over there rollin deh eyes like marbles at her. Know what I just changed my mind about this woman. Here come some excitement and new blood in Friendly , La. I really found myself enjoyin seein them white ladies look worried and sweatin, cuz it was obvious that this women was not go be belonging to any black man; at least not any black man in these parts. Of course , some of the black womens was worrin anyway and that is because they did not understand the kind of women she was, you see. But Ms. Lula Mae had seen her kind before when I visited the Creole part of town in New Orleans. I had a cousin who worked in a good house and I had to stay there when I went to New Orleans. The only men that ever visited her was them white men and the women in the house keep themselves like this woman. You know the kind look so good you could drink milk out her ass. One thang for show we had to welcome this new trouble to town cause she was black and where else she gonna go but blacksville with us. Best I get in first and trouble the water, cause it is boilin right na. Look like everybody in Friendly done got scawled.

Well any way when the driver pulled her bags out of that car, her bags was just as fancy as she was. Then he reaches in his jacket and pulls out this long black wallet and gives her money. Kinda hard to miss a roll that big, cause it looked like it took both her hands to hold it. She looked like she was fussin at him as he carried all of her bags over and put them on the bench. She looked like a naggin wife chasin behind her husband and he looked like a man ignoring his wife, cause he just got back in that car and drove off, payin no attention to her. Na this is where the trouble started, that women turned and looked our way and Lord, then came the walk that shook the town apart. Backbone straight, a wiggle to set the fit of her dresss and a little stomach tuck. She moved like the wind was in her hips and that red dress made her look like a walkin ball of fire. This heifer had a small waist line in comparison to the rest of her fully developed devilsh body, some men don't like a women so full. When she walked everything was shakin and movin and rollin and bouncing all over the damn place. She walked like she was saying " I have some good pussy" and I know yall want to taste it. This ain't go be a regular problem she go be trouble. Huh that heifer moved like a cat, as she slid over towards us. (I says to myself the shit done hit the fan her in Friendly, La, cause this aint nothing but a bitch.). By now every man that had blood running through his veins was movin and stirrin about kinda nervously. Trying not to show interest, they can forget about that, cause they would have to be good and dead not to notice this wicked whore. Her skin like I said was like chocolate, her hair short though and real curly, you could tell she ain't never had no straighten comb in it though. Did not look like the men mind how short her hair was though, lookin all dazed and stupid like deh ain't never seen a whore before. You know mostly we all keep our hair long cuz it was more lady like. Honey we loved keepin our hair long too, cause you know white folk did not think we could have long hair. They thought most of us would have hair like this harlot but we broke the mold here in Friendly, cause most of us colored women had pony tails down our back, like a lady should. Most mens did not like no bald headed woman but, I guess that does not count for one that walks like she wigglin her hips through the eye of a needle. Shucks them men was forgettin about their wifes and their women, they was lookin like a pack of wild dog in heat. Na yall know this done pissed us all off, hell they actin like they ain't got no fine women here in town. (My mama always told me that the only creature more doggish than a dog is a man, and she ain't lie neither. I think I heard a growl or two.) Guess you could not blame them though cuz we was lookin too most hoes come out at night. Or maybe it was becuz we ain't never seen a women walk so free, even though hos is in the business of walkin they usually don't hold their head up as high as this one. Ummh Well if you thought lookin at her from a distance was something as she got closer she was something else. Breast like a pair of perfect grapefruit, (I hate her already) she had what yall mens call a perfect set and she knew it cause she brazin. She had us all kinda breathless like, we all sorta stunned a little, to us she was almost naked. Breast sticking out, ass stickin out, legs out back out all we really wanted her to do was get out. (God forgive me for what I am about to say but, "Look at this hoe".)

She said, "How yall ladies and gents doing on this fine Sunday evening." We all spoke back and looked in a wonder as if to say "What she go say next and how would we answer her?" Her next question was "Yall knows, where I could find a roomin house?" Na yall all knows that blacks always found roomin for blacks and mostly it was in our home. Course na we had a roomin house, but it only had three rooms. Most of the time it was full cause two of the tenants live there all the time. That house was belonging to Sarah Fay Brown and believe me this lady was not go be stayin there. Cause everybody know, Ms. Sarah Faye sleep with her Bible. Some even say she slept with the bible teacher too, but that is another story.

Well child here is where Ms. Lula Mae thought she was dreamin or drunk and I had not partook in the whiskey or my health tonic. The white man is something else, he feel he is owed to have the best of everything, even a whore. That Major White jumps right in and says "I think we may have as extra room in the town loggin house?" Ms Sally White turned three shades of red and blurted out " No way, we ain't got no damn room in our lodgin house for this nig ... Awwww women Louis" Huh, what? I could not believe I heard that a white man asking his wife to house a nig.. awwww colored woman in deh hotel. Well this is the first time I ever witnessed a man's dick speak for him. Haahaaa this go be good, I might writes me a book. I had started some pages a while ago and stopped but this go make it happen. Ms. Sally White said "Hell no, we ain't got no room, even if Jesus asked." Did she just blaspheme? "Louis, maybe she needs to talk to some of our fine colored folks to see what they can do for her. I am sure they can find her something. Then all the other white ladies says, "Amen". Well the Major must have had to much drink in him cause he turns around and says " Ifin we ain't got room in the lodgin house, maybe she can stay in our extra room Sally." (The Major was what you call smelling this woman and he done lost his got damn mind too. This is what happen when the dick in a mans mind gets hard.) The air was thick, so thick we was holding our breat. All of a sudden this devilsh heifer blurted out and said, " Oh I am sorry for not introducing myself proper, my name is Naomi Love, but most folk just call me Puddin , guess cuz I am so soft and smooth huh." Look at her sellin her evil ware already. Then that heifer winked and laughed so hard hell heard her. But it was how she laughed, a little out breath, lifting her breast with every chuckle and wiggling with every smile, in the meantime the sweat was droppin of her body like ice meltin and that dress was seemin to get tighter and tighter and wetter and wetter. I thank she was castin a spell. I have heard of women being able to cast a spell on a whole town before. Most of them go get themselves charmed by a powerful Obai. I think that is what she done did, this one ain't normal. I knew Friendly, La. would never be the same again the devil done sent his whore to town and she ain't playin fair. Then she said "Could some of you fine gents help me with my bags and show me the way to the loggin house". I hated em I hated every last one of em. You should have seem em, all them men, fummblin and sufflin over her bags like a bunch of fools. Like she was some decent God fearing woman that deserved some respect. I know one thang it was gonna be quite time in the bedrooms in Friendly, La. tonight. Cuz this Ms. Puddin din got all of the women pissed off at them stupid men. I know I won't be thinking about Sheriff stupid Jones ass; he walkin around stickin his chest out like a rooster on the yard. Dis nigga done lost his mind; I bet this woman here ain't gonna bake him one got damn bisquit or clean his damn house, he a simply minded bastard. I always had a feelin about him, he done just proved my doubts right; he is really stupid. I bet old Major White better have him somebody he can go to for something cause I am just about sho Ms. Sally won't be pleasuring him for a while. Sally White is a pretty woman with a decent figure too. But decent woman or not she ain't no match for this bushy pussy whore. (Lord please help my mouth.) Anyway, she got all her bags carried and she could have got herself carried if she wanted to. All I know is this Puddin as she calls herself may sound sweet but she is the devils'work . Ain't no God fearin Christian woman go have nothing to do with her and definitely not a God fearin woman with a man. Just goes to show all the thangs a man says he likes and wants you to be really don't mean shit when something different comes along. We all walking around here with hair down our backs, wearing modest dresses and keeping our self covered aint' what these fools tellin us they like. We all thinking we special some way. Huh, then comes along someone total opposite from what the good Lord say a women ought to be and these fools acts like she a Christmas present. So let me sum up this Ms. Puddin woman for ya. Short hair, full set of breast, wide hips, big legs and thighs; she did have a trim waist line though, but any ways you put it she still the big boned heifer that ruined our Sunday evening. Instead us all goin home full and satisfied, we just went home thinkin about who this woman go capture our tomorrow with her bag of devil tricks and lies. God help us Satan done unleashed his prize whore on our town. Why the got damn mosquitos not bittin? Maybe if this bitch get bite enough she will just leave. I have seen quite a few people say they have to leave here cause the mosquitos was too got damn bad.

CHAPTER 3

Monday Morning Sunrise

MONDAY MORNING SUN COMING up over the bayou, birds singing, frogs singing, rooster crowin , everything was movin about with exicitement. Look like everybody know something different done hit town. I knows from experience of course that all the talk today go be about this strange woman that came to town yesterday. Them white womens is talkin, the black womens is talkin; hell I believe the animals was even talkin, about them storm of rollin hips and poutin lips that came into our little town of Friendly, La. Na yall knows it is my duty to be the first one to really talk to this woman. So I goes and makes some of my special biscuits and pulls out my cumquat preserves my home made marmalade, and yall Ms. Lula even made a batch of tea cakes too. King, Queen, President or Govenor nobody in they right mind would turn down this basket. Na yall know I was really suppose to be goin fishin this morning. But anyway, I combed my hair back in pony tail, you know Ms. Lula had long flowing hair down my back like a lady should have. I put on my blue gunny sack dress, my fancy bonnet and sprayed my self with my homemade sweet water. You know the kind you make from fresh gardinas, honeysuckle, lemon and water. Hitched my buggy and to town I went straight to that loggin house. It sure felt strange goin to the loggin house to see a colored woman livin there. What was even stranger was when I walked in how quick Ms. Lucille greeted me, she was part owner with the Major and them. Child she hurried and told me exactly which room she was in upstairs. Oh yall should have heard that white women going on. She says" That harlot up there in room 69, has brought a curse on this loggin house. Her black soul being here is worst than the black plague. She ain't fittin to be here living amongst God's people he placed in charge of everything. She needs to be down there in nigg ... Aaah I means over with her own people. Na I am sorry for going off here Miss Lula Mae and you knows I always have been a fair and generous woman with all people but this has bought a curse on my business. The Major and Sally may be okay but I need money to keep coming in, cause this all I got to make my livin. And don't know God fearing Christian folk need to be treated like this. I am sorry I ever went into business with them. The Major is been bewitched. That women is of the DEVIL himself. Hard as we tryin to save yalls black souls from hell here come a black demon to waste all our time and make us sorry we introduced yall to the Lord. Not saying yall ain't God fearin people now after we done taught you all about the Lord, but yall still aint like us cause we chosen. My cousin said her prophet told her that yall is black cause your ancestors fought on the side of the Devil himself in heaven. And yall is black cause the Lord smote yall with lightening and burned your skin to mark ya. You know it is ashame to pay somebody back like this who saved yall from a certain hell. We been good to yall considering what yall tried to do to God, most places in the Bible where people tried to fight God, he had them all killed. I know some of yall is learned to be good Lula cause you is, and you knows your place too, you know what I mean Ms. Lula. She just don't belong here, you need to talk her into leaving. She should not have her black soul in this loggin house exceptin for to cook and that is all. It is wrong to make her think she is any different. I know I won't have any of my white girls clean her room or serve her. No way I disrespect the power the good Lord gave me by servin her kind. What you got in that basket Ms. Lula? Sure does smell good mind if I take a peek?" I looks straight at her and said, what's in this basket aint' fittin for one of the Lords people to have. It is just good enough to suit an old black soul like hers, plus we fixed it special for her. She looks me straight in the eyes and say, "Lula you might be mad about what I said but you know I is right. Look around you, we run this world and center of this world is the South. God made us over everything , don't matter how we got it, we over everything. So you keep what you takin to her because you and I both know if I tell ya, you will have to cook everything in that basked over for me. See what I mean Lula Mae. So I aint got no worries bout what is in it." I am thinking to myself yes, miss white lady, but you don't want Ms. Lula Mae mad while she cooking for you either or while any of her friend is cooking for you. You kin tell people who got good sense; the struck us with lightening that is why we is black. I just don't understand why these peoples is over us. "Take her what you got for her, yall probably what to posin her too. I hope it is posioned. Lord have mercy on my business. I aint go ever get any one to rent room 69 again. Miserable black witch. "

Well I goes up them long stairs and as I am walkin towards room 69, I started to sweat. Don't know whether it was because of climbing the stairs or because of what Lucille had just said; either way that was the longest walk I think I ever took. Knock, knock, lightly at first , then harder, when that door opened I was knocked for a blow. There she was Ms. Puddin, standin there in a snow white fancy robe child made of Spanish lace!, Spanish lace yall!, One thang I know she ain't have no shame cuz you could see straight through this robe and she was buck naked under it no gown, on under clothes just buck naked bushy pussy, you know it is something to be looking at a women and her nipples starin you right back in the face. Awww Lord she need to get her some scissors to her private patch cause the hair was stickin out like strugglin sapplins tryin to stand up.

I looks right into her eyes and says I brought you a welcome basket since you new to our town. She says" girl come on in here and let Ms. Puddin see what you done brought." As I walked into this room I was prayin that the good lord bless my efforts. No matter what my reason ain't no boby else came to welcome this poor soul. As soon as I entered the room, I was shocked out of my mind. As I looked up who did I see but Sho thang sittin on the table with a cat like smile of her face. She too had bought Ms. Puddin a basket, she had made a hoe cake(fittin for Puddin), she had black berry jelly, strawberry jams, fig preserves, pear preserves, slices of thick fried salt meat, and fresh milk, uuuuuuuhmmmmm you name it she had it. (By the way them fig preserves was mine cause everybody bought my fig preserves.) Sho thang really made me feel less of a person cuz awwww her reason for being there was true and genuine my reason for being there was just being nosey. I introduced myself again to Ms. Pudding " My name is Ms. Lula Mae Carson and I just wanted to bring you a welcome basket since you new to our town and all." Then Sho Thang say " Ms. Lula Mae I know you got some biscuits in there, throw me one. Oh, and be sure to get it right when you goes back and report to the ladies this morning. You can kinda put all their minds to rest , especially when you tell em I beat you here. " I thank that brazin huzzy be pokin fun at me. What she did not know is that her being there just made it all the better. Of course the devils children know each other and everybody knows Sho thang possessed. I turns around and bid the ladies goodbye, and lets Ms. Puddin know that if she needs anything she can just send word or come see me and I would be glad to help her with anything she might me in need of. Now I did my part, I went and took a welcome basket, got a chance to speak to this whirl wind that blew into town and I offered her my help. Even Jesus can not dispute that. Not only was the walk in long but the walk out seemed longer. I was glad to get out that room with all that carryin on goning on in there. Although I did not see on thing, can't nothing good or righteous be going on in a room with that Puddin and Sho thang in it. I feel kinda of dirty. I might even have to go over to the next Parish and see one of them Catholic Preist to get me some holy water , candles and ask him to get them demons off of me. I know it was demons in that room, cause one had possessed Ms. Lucille that is why she acting so damn foolish. That woman ain't never talked to me like that before. This women Puddin is the Devil. Now I am just to take up for Lucille for a minute. She was a good Christian woman most of the time. She always treated her girls real good, I mean real good. She paid the best wages, gave them all the sheets and pillow cases when she was switchin out. And for Christmas child she had a tree for the black children that nobody could out do. She was always braggin bout how many people she done brought to the Lord. Tell ya the truth I never heard her say nigger not ever. See how evil Puddin is she made this women lose all her love of God and tell me what she been hidin under all that holiness. I hope one of her little red head girls have a black baby.

CHAPTER 4

The Whole Town Is Waiting

WELL NA YALL THE whole town must have been waitin on me to come out of that room; or should I say, all of the ladies. Cause when I walked out of the loggin house the ladies started gathering around me like hungry chicks looking to get their morning feedin. Then my mouth started runnin the report, tellin em exactly what I had seen. So many question, so many assumptions, so much going on all at once, both white and black women questionin and commentin at the same time. Wanting to know where she from, how long she go stay, who she kin to on and on and on and on. I was trying to answer as quickly as I could. Then I looked up and sees Ms. Puddin lookin out of her window at all of us. That is when I felt shame, cause I knew gosipping was against the bible. But before I could finish beating myself up Ms. Puddin yells out of her window and says , "That is right ladies yall is got a hell whore in town, hot as tabasco sauce,sweet as marmalade and willing to spread her spices around." Then she turn and raised her gown up and showed us all of her beautiful black ass. It was a sight, looked like two full moon fillin up the window. Child ladies got to runnin and screamin just like they had seen the devil himself. I said to my self right then, we in a hell of a lot of trouble na here in Friendly, La. One thang for sho that women was smart, cause nobody complained to the men sos not to make them more curious about this whore the devil had sent to town.

Here tell the Catholic Preist was overflowin with women coming by his church gettin Holy water to bless their house and their husbands. And they all suppose to be good God fearin Southern Baptist. Po man they kept him on his knees prayin and blessing that water so much he had to call in another Priest from another Parish to help him so he could get some sleep. And lets not talk about Ms. Creashia, she was getting rich selling her keep your man mojo bags, but I gots to tell yall the truth mojo don't beat hojo. Ms. Puddin became the most talked about woman in the town. Hum I'd say even the state cause them white mens loved her see she use to sit by her window late in the evenin and sing. She had a sweet high pitched voice that just rang through the whole town. You know white people love money so ofcourse they gave her a job singin at the loggin house. That was the best thing they ever did, the loggin house was full every night. People would come by all day and make reservations for dinner. Old Lucille, even said that God heard her prayers so he made Puddin her foot stool by making her sing in her place. (I hate her.) I am tellin yall it was something about this women. (Yall all knows that the devil was the head of the choir in heaven). Strange thang about white people they love to be entertained so Ms. Puddin was in high demand singing at private parties for em . She was bringing more business to our little town than we had seen in years. Hell all kinds of big fancy cars be comin here every week end. Fancy white ladies in long flowing gowns and little dogs, men all dressed up in proper suits made of silk. We was becoming one of the most popular little towns in the South.

Child Ms. Lula Mae , was makin some sales too, cause for sho once all these new visitors taste my preserves they buyin em. As a matter of a fact all of us was makin money. Mens buying gifts for they wives, children and women. None of us was complaining though because one thing we knew and that was Ms. Puddin could not have all of em and anyway she might just prefer women for all we know. Well honey, them mens got together and voted to open up a good house here in the saved and sanctified town of Friendly, Louisiana. Na, they did not call it a good house but we all know that , that is exactly what it was. Cause honey child, no self respecting woman would set foot in a place called the Pleasure

Palace. We all knowed Major White was behind the whole thing too. We all felt sorry for Sally cause she was ashamed and embrassed how her husband was so took with the idea of openin a whore house. That might have been eaiser to swallow, for Sally, if she did not realize her husband was opening a singing house for his woman. We all know the men been having other women all the time, but this is too much. We might have our problems here amongst us but we don't appreciate nobody comin in makin it worst. Sally walking around teary eyed all the time, drinkin and throwing away babies. Good thing she had Tassay to take care of her. This is too much na, Sally going down. Yall knows what is about to go down na, them white women was gittin together to get rid of Ms. Puddin. I guess yall trying to figure how Ms. Lula Mae knows this. Well cuz them white women , talk everything over us just like we was not there. See they no we programmed not to mention anyting we heard. We did not tell what we heard about the husbands or the mens. Some of these women had regulars just like they husbands had. Oh, yes these women had history and they made themselves happy. I know not all their lives so easy. White men is a son of a bitch. What gets me is that the biggest ho was usually the biggest hell raisers and hard as hell on coloreds. Always something going on. Now we go have to side with Ms. Puddin to save her ass. (Did Ms. Lula Mae say that? I don't judge none of these women for what they do. Sometimes I want to cheer em on and wish em well. Then some bitch, say girl come here and get me some lemonade. Then I say fuck em. But these white men around here do some evil shit and I thank they all hate women really. But that is another story. Like I was saying in they minds they know we not go tell , cause we all knew our place. But in our minds we gaining information that just might come in handy one day. We disadvantaged and the only way we surviving is because of our wit. Let them tell it that is something we can not have. Every now and then I look to heaven and just wonder what in the hell is God doing? I know I am not a bad person, I know my mother was not a bad person. So why, why am I here in this place living this life. What make me have to be here, at this time a black woman living in the heart of the south. If this is some kind of test to see if I am go make it back to heaven it is not fair. Damn God it is hard to see you as being just. You know we having hard times down here. White man hate us cause we a constant reminder of what bein lazy get ya, a country full of niggers you can't get rid of . We hate ourselves cause we confussed, beat down and we have people tellin us how ugly we is. Plus all the love been scared out of us. We is sufferin down here and all we getting for all this trouble is the chance to call on you for help. We ain't gettin no answers, but what can I expect from an unseen God , who belongs to the white man. You know Lawd I think the only reason I talk to you is because I aint got nobody else to tell all these troubles too. Naw, back to these socializing Christian women talkin all of this trash in front of us. I know yall go think what I am about to say next is just wrong and down right insulting, but it is the way it is. See to these ladies we had no place, no value and no say,ceptin some of us girls ranked high with their men. Meaning we din learned how to get our point across to make thangs happen. If you rub any mans belly the right way you can make him purr like a kitten. Especially since most of their women down right could not stand em. You can't blame em either, babies all over the flats, parties with plenty of women but no wives allowed, beatings and big old empty houses full of nothing but thangs. Na, from the sounds of it, Ms. Puddin was in a lot of trouble. Mostly cause the men have lost it. See Puddin weren't no problem for us colored women, she was not in our part of town and most colored men could not afford her. Them that could was mostly married with good God fearing wives that would hit them in the head with the holy cast iron skillet of God if they found out he was messin with her. Na yall know she still a colored woman so we had to do our Christian duty and warn her of what was going on. So I listend as close as possible so I could get it right.

Na yall did not here this from me, it was the strangest thing to see how peoples especially women will come together when they all think they being threatened by another woman. Ms June Pickens the towns most reliable white gossipin woman and Bobby Joe Fields got together and started a petition against Ms. Puddin. Na why this is so funny to all of us is because Ms. Pickens's husband was this little weazle of a man never raised his voice at anybody and everybody knows how she bossed him around. But all us black women knew that Bobby Joe was seein Mr. Pickens yall know what I mean. So to see these two women workin together was a big laugh. Anyway that is white folk business. This tramp Bobby Joe became the talk between us colored woman when she joined the same church Mr. and Mr.Pickens went to and would sit on the same bench they sat on every Sunday. And here tell when the holy ghost would hit her and she fall out and Mr. Pickens would be the one to help carry her out the church. Lawd, we all use to just kill ourself laughing and whispering about that one. So anyways can you imagine how strange to see these two together getting papers signed to get rid of Puddin. (They need to be getting rid of that devil riding they backs, if you ask me. But who is asking me?) I went and told Ms. Puddin about the plan and I gave her a little weapon to use as well. Told her as much dirt on the do good white citizens of Friendly as I could, never knew she would put 100.00 gold pieces in my hand for it. Did you hear what I said, she gave me a 100.00 gold piece. Oh, and yes, I took it, blessed it, gave the church 10.00 of it and saved the rest. Don't care how dirty money is when it is blessed in the right hands it can do the Lawds work, Amen.

CHAPTER 5

Puddin Goes to meet the Major's Wife

TUESDAY MORNINGS, USUALLY AIN'T nothing special in Friendly, unless a brazin hussy is walking the street in a hot pink dress, clinging to every curve, with a low neck line and a high hem line. Huh!, somebody go have to tell that woman that we have small children in this town and they use to seeing decent women walk the street fully clothed. This girl is a mess. Next thang I see Ms. Puddin go shashaying over to Major Whites house. Sally White answeres her door in a loud voice she says, "Gal what in the hell you want with me?" Sally had problem when she answered the door cause Puddin say she looked like she was drunk. I guess she was full of her special coffee, full of all that Irish whiskey or some of that Tenessee special. Puddin goes into her house, we all waitin to see what happen next. For some reason the whole town got quite as a mouse. We just waiting to see Puddin come running out their with a shot gun in her face or better yet seeing her get a good cursin out. Ms. Puddin stayed in that house with that woman for over three hours; I know cause we was counting the time. When she comes out Ms. White smilin and wavin her good day. I was in shock , and yes I took me a swig of moonshine cus I was not belivin what had just happened. Of course I was the brave one to go over to Ms. Puddin and ask her what happened in there. Huh child she looks at me, Ms. Lula Mae Carson and says "Non of yo business girl you would not understand anyway ifin I told you. Anyway what yall care bout Sally, yall all say Ms. Sally is a sour old bitty. I says she is sweet as a ripe juicy plum from heaven's garden." (Puddin probably took over Ms. Sally white with her evilness. Ain't no telling what she did to that poor woman. I knows in my heart, she did something evil to that woman, cuz Puddin is the Devils' Whore and Ms. White is a Christian woman and she ain't no match for that kind of evilness). Well whatever her and Sally discussed it did not stop them women from signin that paper and givin it to the Sheriff who gave it to the Major who showed it to Puddin. Seem liken to me Ms. Puddin was more upset that Sally had signed that piece of paper than anything. When she saw her name on it she said "What a waste of a Tuesday morning. And you know what Ms. Lula Mae, I really don't give a flyin sideways fuck about what these people do or say to me. Cause it ain't go do me or dem no got damn good." Anyway things got quite for all while, no more big parties, no more business mens coming through, no nothing, them women shol had messed up some good business. But as all yall know nothing comes between a man and his money especially a naggin woman. So I am sure they was go come up with another plan. But they had to make it look like they were working on keeping the devil in his place. As much as they hated to piss off Puddin, they still had to keep up the images that they gave a damn about what they wives thought. So I guess that is why deh started goin to the good houses. One way or another a man go get to his hoe.

Well you know them white men had to do something. The women signin this paper was members of the Sisters of Heaven lead by Ms. Betty Righteous. You did not want her after you cause her husband knew the dirt on every white man from here to Washington. And Ms. Betty Righteous was his faithful and true treasure. The most holy Reverand Righteous Phillmore did anything for that women he could. One reason was cause she was born with a veil over her face, so she could see thangs and she knew the secrets of healin. But for some reason she had a bad feelin about Puddin, I mean it seemed like she was scared of her. She would not look her in the face, no sir and no maam, she never looked her in the eyes. Everybody know Reverand Righteous always had blessed oil, water and those sanctified handkerchiefs. But lately you could not get any cause sister Betty usin it all on herself every since Puddin showed up. That woman trying to keep her husband. She done even stop going by checking on the sick and shut in. Honey child she not giving a damn about no church business. As a matter of fact none of the ladies committies been doing any of the church business cause they so worried about the devil's whore in town. We really hated that cause one thing them white folk did do good was give you some good stuff for the charities. Yall it got rough seem like all the white women got together and stopped doing everything. So them white men got together and shut down operations for a while, just to keep their wifes quite. You know what I mean, the early morning and mid-day visists to our part of town got kinda scarce. Oh, most the time when they visited us it was early in the morning or mid-day cuase evening time was for their families. (Hyporcitial Bastards). We ain't care about that over on our side of town, we was glad deh had to slack up comin. Puddin gave us a break, for some reason them women thought we all was go end up really wantin deh men. Huh, they just aint know. What got me is how scared they was bout losin men that ignored dem most of the time. And for sure we did not want dem bunch of thimble dick low down bastards.

Next thing we know Puddin was not singing at the Loggin House, no more private parties, hell you could not eve hear her singing when you passed by her window anymore. The siren of Friendly, was turned off by a pettion of jealous women. Thangs got quite again, and life got kinda of boring, no more singing house, no more good time club in town and all the good houses was shut down tight as a tics ass. Mostly everything was normal except Puddin still stayin in the loggin house. Anyway we all just sittin around missin Ms. Puddin, or should I say missin the money that demon was bringing in. Child she was bringing in some money too. Everybody was longing for her to start back up exceptin for Major White, here tell he had started makin early morning stops at Ms. Puddin's room before he went to church on Sunday. I had been tellin myself all week long that I was not being a good Christian woman cauz I had not gone by to invite Ms. Puddin to Church. So, I grabbed some of my best got damn bisquits and homemade blackberry jam and headed to the Loggin House to invite her. Na yall I was not trying to see or catch nothing. I just wanted to do my duty as a Christian woman tryin to convert a complete heathen to the lord. See it is my belief that even though some people in the church do some bad things they know the lord and the lord know them so the Lord probably go give them a favor or two. But I just know Ms. Puddin was straight from hell cause she is a hot ball of fire and she steams up everywhere she gos and the Lord lets her live to test our Christian journey. Well any way here I goes to the Loggin room and knocks on the door, and it just opens up. Anyway child, I was not prepared for what I saw next. The Major was standin in the middle of the room; child that man was the first white man I ever seent turn black before my eyes look like he had been dug up from the grave. He did not even see me or he acted like he did not see me . I looked over to the corner of the room sos I could get a good description of it and rightfully so cause the last time Ms. Lula Mae was in it, I did not get a chance to really get a good look for myself. Remember na us colored women only cooked at the Lodgin House. You know Lucille only used white maids so blacks did not get to see the private bed rooms much and I did not get a good look on my first visit to her room. Ms. Puddin room has these fancy lamps all over it and she had them lace curtains too, the ones I always wanted to have, she even had one of them fancy white folk rugs. I calles it a fancy white folk rug cuz none of us blacks had one of them persaia rugs. Child she had one of them oversized velveteen counches a red one. (Ofcourse it would be red most hoes loved red). I got me a good look cauz I wanted my report to be right. I found it funny that Ms. Puddin had a dinin room set just like the one Sally White had in her house. We all knew about that snow white dinin room set Sally White had cause it was shipped in and it came in the middle of the day. I bet she planned it that way, so we could all see it. Well na her husband's whore got one just like it. Men ain't shit. I guess Sister Betty had a right to have some of her opinions about Puddin. I doubt if anyone eles had moved in a room and had it filled up with they own furniture and luxuries and such; paid for by another woman's husband and a white one too. My eyes keep movin around that room until I gets to the lounge bed in front of the window. Ooooooooh! Jesus sweet lord, what I had to keep lookin for, there was Sho Thang buck naked with all of her of her nasty fluffy showin , just, just , just laying there all calm smiling like a big old lazy cat. Oh Lord, Ms. Puddin was standin there with a little old short sleepin gown or whatever kind of gown that was showing all of her big old thick thighs(That woman had to have the most beautiful chocolate brown skin

God ever gave somebody). Oh Jesus , Major White must have come out of his shock cuz that man color came back then he went and pulled off his belt, swingin it and walkin towards them women like a mad man. Have mercy on my soul, have mercy on my soul, what was about to happen to me. I was trying to get the hell out of the way. He was cussin, swearin to the good Lord, sweatin, and swingin that belt like a whip. Oh Jesus he go kill em , he go kill em both and then he go kill me just for being there. All I could thank about was why it had to be me the one everybody always depending on to tell the story. Well, I just started cryin and prayin, then it all went wrong so wrong. Them two women started pickin up things throwin and swingin on a white man, hittin him, jumpin on his back and scratchin him. they was really whippin his ass. I knew we was go die. All us was go be found dead and buried under a tree.

Na call me what you want , I was tryin to get it all right cause I was go have to save my life. Yes, I was go tell on both of them and whatever the Major said happened is what I was go say happened as long as he let me live. Oh, I know some of yall thinking what a bitch. Well you do not have to survive in a place where your life is determined by some white mans' good mood either. So yes, I was go tell it. God knows I love the lord but Ms. Lula Mae was not planning to go visit him so soon. They womped on the Major until he came to his senses and just sat there in the middle of the floor cryin like a new born baby needin his mammies milk. That's when I picked up the jar of white lightin of the table to my left and took a big swig. I knew it was to my left cause that was nearest the door I was go run out of. Did not care who saw me drink it either cause I knew it was my last drink on earth. Ms. Puddin, went over to him and started rubbin his head and holdin and whisperin to him then she asked me and Sho Thang to leave. Na Sho Thang did not want to leave, but my feet was movin so fast my legs had to catch up. I can't say what happened when Puddin shut that door, but I can tell you I had a very interesting talk with Sho on our way home. I asked her why was she in Puddin's room showing her her nakedness. She sorta looked at me a little surprised and started laughing then she started to tell me what they was doing. Sho was laughin at me cause she could see how flustered I was, and I am sho my hard breathin gave it away too. Then all of a sudden out of know where she stops and turns to me and says Ms. Lula Mae, "I know you is a Christian woman and a good woman for the most part. But you probably aint' never been really made love to", then she licked her tounge around her lips and wiggled it at me. I wanted to run but then I wanted to stay. I was curious about this devil. I even think I wanted to awww ... anyway, Ms. Lula Mae ain't go tell yall all that . Yall don't need to know everything. I felt so ashamed I could not even go to church. Child I had to go home and take me a nice cool bath and pray for repentence. While I was taking my bath all I could think about was how that shameless demoness from hell licked her tounge out at me . I kept on prayin to Jesus to forgive me for being a gossip, and to forgive me for having hot flusters when I thought about her tounge. The whole time I was praying I was thinking about how that must feel, and since I had never had such a thing done to me before by a women my thoughts was intense, so intense my water eventually turned a milky white. If it is true what they say, about your thoughts in the Bible, I am on my way to hell for sure. My body temperature is hot and I can not cool it off. I am ashamed. I have to tell that truth, this whole experience lets me know that with all my saving and praisin I can truly be tempted and fall. Or just maybe Ms. Lula just had not had any kind of gratification other than her own fingers in such a long while ... she just wanted to experience a human touch any kind of human touch. It has been a long time for me and I burn sometimes, I burns sometimes real hot. Ohhhh don't yall judge me na, good Christians might not say it but they gets hot toooo. Well anyways I did not share what I had seen with the rest of the ladies cuz it was involving the Major. Since nobody came to see me in the middle of the night, or throw no bricks threw my windows, or burn down my sheds, I figure that the Major knew that I was not talking his business. And that was just fine with me.

Next day everybody looking for a wild cat that jumped the Major. Lawd have mercy some poor wild cat about to die. The Mayor told people he was out coon huntin and spooked a big boe wild cat and everybody knows it is bad to spook him. Really yall everybody in these parts knows you do not want to spook a wild cat and especially a boe. They can be dangerous, but in this case some innocent wild cat about to die because the Major got a whole of some real wild cats. Hear tell, about six wild cats died, did not matter cuz them Cajun's ate em. You heard me they ate em. Just like we eat bear, coon, rabbit, squirrel, nutra rat and raven hen, we can make anything taste good here in these parts. Like I said we the best damn cooks in he world. Later on that day here comes Ms. Puddin lookin for a place to stay here in blacksville. Of course none of the good Christian women offered her a place to stay. So me being a true Saint of God, offered my place. I have plenty of room and if I must say so myself one of the finest furnished homes in these parts. I could have more in my house but you never let these white people see you havin more than them. It just aint good for your health. But hell our men was making the furniture and things so we usually have the better made pieces than them anyway. It might have been made a little bit simpliar but it was made well. I ain't have no place to put all of her fancy furniture so Sho moved most of it in her place. She lived alone in a house big enough to suite two or three families. We been trying to get her to open up to roomers. Puddin looked like she just wanted to get a good nights rest. I guess it was a little worrisome living in a place where everybody hated you and now your main support was pissed off at you. I just stared at Ms. Puddin for a long time. What was so special about this woman. Did she have a powerful mojo or was she just nasty and loose. What was it that made you just want to take her in? She do have that beautiful skin, but she ain't no little women she full yall. What we call a big boned woman , full hips, everything about her full, not some little frail woman like we thank most men like. She had that short hair not long like most of us. It did have a little natural wave in it though and her behind always turned a corner after her. Don't know about this woman, exceptin the Devil must be helpin her. She could not have made the Circle C Club and I doubt if she had a blood line she could follow. Well any way that woman still had every man around town sniffin up behind her. Huh, after she got settled in to my house it became a regular who is who coming to visit. One night here come Roy Stamply he that New Orleans writer. The next night her come Mr. Mac Jober' first colored boy we know ever made it to a college. He was studying to be a big time doctor. Lawd we cherished our black doctors cause without them and our herb ladies we all would mostly be dead. You know white doctors would not help us. Yeah, child them white doctors would let us die everytime. Yall remember when that rash was breaking out all over the children and they was passing it from one to other. Well them doctors would not give our children any medicine. They said they did not have enough to go around. We had to send to New Orleans and get some help along with the swamp herbs.

We lost four of our babies though but that did not matter to them. The white doctors said they had to save the medicine for Gods chosen. No need to raise your brow or get pissed, that is just the way it was. But we learned, we learned to save our medicine when got it and we learned to have our own supply handy to. Sometimes we would have medicine they did not have and we watched em suffer too.

But yall know what is really pissin me off right now is Sheriff Jones. Na Puddin ain't never clean or cook for that man and here he comes bringing her flowers, fancy chocolates and sweet magnolia water, ain't that a bitch. I guess that is what you can get when you can wiggle your ass through the head of a needle. He looked so sad and simple, with his broke ass. Every night here comes some sticky dick man and on Friday and Saturday here comes them rich white mens with they little sticky dicks. Hell, Puddin givin my house a ill name. People is callin it the honey comb hide out. But yall I gots to say it was the most excitement I have had in a while. Some of them nights was so hot on my front porch all the moss on my oaks burned up. Child I ain't lyin. I would just be lookin and tryin to get me some tips. One day Ms. Lula Mae was go need some of this devil woman tricks. Shit you gots to fight fire with fire. thank I am lyin huh. I would watch her get ready for her dates. It was fun. First she would take one of them perfumed baths, then she would stand right in the middle of the doorway and dry her naked ass off. Then she would lotion down all of her skin, rubbin every crack on her body. I had to stop watchin her do that cause I think she would rub herself a certain way just because I was lookin. I started to wonder what the hell was wrong with me any way. But anyway she would put that gardina flower in her hair, then she would go to her closet and pick a dress. Yall know all of her dresses was fine and they all fit her like a fine pair of custom made leather gloves fit your hands. (Oh yall wonder how Ms. Lula Mae know bout them gloves, I have seen and known a few things mmmmmmm in my life, but we ain't talking about me na. Anyway I always wanted a pair of them kind of gloves, but mostly fast women wore them.) Every dress she owned fit her like that, like someone had custom made it for her. Well this night she was getting ready for this white man who I believed meant something to her. This was one I ain't never seen but heard her talk a lot about, umumhhhumm. She pulls out this hot pink dress low cut and a split all the way up to her pleasure patch. She slipped on a pair of stockins, with no panties (brasin hussy). So about an hour later here comes Mr. I am so damn lucky just a smiling. As soon as he sees Puddin the first thing he do is go inside his coat pocket and pull out this black box. Child I was strechin my neck to see what was comin out of it. All I saw was some sparkling jewelry, all kinds, earrings, neckelace,and I thank there was a bracelet and a diamond ring big enough to choke a small hog. Oh I could see good especially since she was standing there putting it all on at once. Then he pulls out his wallet and gives her a bundle of money. Then he gets on one knee like he is proposing to her. Hunh I almost fainted, I mean it, my knees gave out and I fell back on my little whatnot table and broke it to pieces. I hit the floor like a sack of potatoes. They both came runnin in to see what was wrong, the man he helped me up and asked me was I alright. I said " Yes , I am just fine". But yall I was shocked and a little mad to. I am a good woman clean, good cook, can fish, hunt and ride a horse with the best of them, shoot a gun like a marksmans, sew dresses fit for queens, and I know I got a gooda piece of pussy as ever told a slop jar good morning. So why I am not being proposed to. Why I can't seem to find a good man; and this whore(na don't be thinkin bad of me, everybody know she is a whore) got a man on his knees proposing to her. Huh. Anyway I went back to my bed room and they stayed in my parlor room. After about an hour or so I gets up to get me a drink of water and what did I do that for. Shit my life full of surprises. There she was standin in the middle of the room swayin her hips like a tree bendin in a hurricane. Then she started shakin herself, like jelly, everything on her body was movin. Then that brazin huzzie got down on the floor and crawled like a stalkin cat over to that man ... that is when I started to step back into my room slowly. I ain't never, ever mentioned what I saw her doin and I ain't never did nothing quite like that before either. She pullin his zipper on his pants down with her snow white teeth, then she look like she scentin him like them dogs be doing when they is in heat. Oh Jesus I could see it, it was his concern all big and swole standing straight up; that is when I closed my door. Na yall I did not see all what she was doin, but I did hear him screamin and moaning like somebody was killin him . I was needin a got damn ice bath na, but child I was scared to come out of my room. Na see that what she was doin that white man or mens never made us do that to dem. Probably cause deh knew deh was go have to do it back. I knew the devil himself was in my parlor room and he had got into Ms. Puddin and that man. I sure as hell did not want him to get into me. But yall them demons of lust was already workin on Ms Lula Mae. Huh I know cause my little man fell out the got damn boat and lost his got damn paddle. Bad thing about that is he did not have anyone to come along and throw him a rope. He just floatin straight up in the water bobbin like a cork , thobbin like he had a bad tooth in his mouth. Looks like I am go have to call on my hand husband for some help. Hehe ... I am human you know. This was it I had decided to have me a talk with Jesus first and then Puddin. I ain't go be going to no white mans' hell cause of some harlot. I says his hell cause if he owns the world and he lets us worship his God, then he gots to have his own heaven and hell. Ain't none of us go make it to his heaven unless we cleanin up, but we all will see his hell. Based on what life is here right na, I am sure I want to be a good servant in his heaven if I got to be somethin. Cause I sure as hell do want to see what his hell is like, especially for my kind. Cause if you ask me we livin in his hell right na. Good night yall. And good Lord I hope you wake up in a better mood tomorrow and really set us free.

CHAPTER 6

Puddin Makin Biscuts in my house

NA ANY OTHER MORNING that old cock of mine would be makin so much noise he would wake up half the Parish, but not this morning. I can not believe it, I did not wake up until 6:30, but to my surprise Puddin was stirring around in my kitchen. She had made some biscuits, fried some of my prize ham, made coffee and pulled down some of my fig preserves. She had some fresh milk and even had curned some fresh butter huh. Did not matter though, I still had made up my mind that Ms. Puddin had to go. I go miss all that extra money and them other fringe benefits. You can bet she paid me well for her room, well actually it was her mens paying me . I was getting high as 75.00 a week from each of em. Child the Lawd blessing me to be rich. Yes, I was gettin rich cuz I was savin every penny. See I knew there was no tellin when all this was going to end. When Ms. Puddin set my plate in front of me, it made me feel real nice, everybody likes to be served every now and then. I just wished she would wear more clothes. Most women had a certain amount of shameness about their body; but Puddin had no problem showing a her nakedness at all. I keep wanting to give her credit for being more than a hell whore, but sometimes you just got to face the truth. She charms you and she knows she is charming you too. There was something about this woman that made me feel real strange though. When I turned to speak to her, I could not get my words out. It was like a lump of bread was caught in my throat and I could hardly breath. Then all of a sudden, something snapped and I got from under her spell. That is when I blurted out "Ms.Puddin, we have to talk." She said "What about baby?" The way she said baby and the way she was looking at me made me fell like I was sitting in the hot sun. Let me see if I can make yall understand why I am saying she is of the devil. She spell bounds people with evil. I know I am an entire woman and I have needs and wants; but it never included wantin a woman. Sometimes when I am around Puddin I got to fight that devil. She be tryin to persuade me. "Did old bad Puddin scare you last night with all her shakin and going ons. Oh Lawdy, lawd, Ms. Lula Mae you did not see Ms. Puddin bobbin for apples between that white mans legsssss.. did you?" Then she did that evil devil laugh. On my Jesus I thought Puddin had lost her mind I aint seen no apples in that white mans' lap. I started to worry about her then.

I sorta looked at her with amazement and said "Puddin would you please put some drawers on? Why you don't wear no draws? You leaves the door open when you is washin and you stands up buck naked in the doorway dryin off your ass. I ain't never seen it take somebody so long to dry deh ass crack. And you do it so nasty, I thank you is doin it on purpose." "Well I is sorry my naked ass is offendin you so, we both women did not thank it bothered you so. And I don't wear draws cause I sells pussy Ms. Lula, why I might have to go to work at the drop of a dime. Who gots time to be pullin down draws. Once I see deh ain't got no sores on em, I gets to business. Plus Ms. Lula deh can't smell it as good if you gots on draws. A little cat funk turn mens on and believe me deh can smell it. Don't look at me like that girl. I ain't talkin about no rancied stank, I am talkin about a womans natural smell with a little hair funk to give it flavor." "Well do you have to sit in the middle of my floor and fan it Puddin, it is really getting to be a bit much." Let me git to my point, "Na Puddin all these different men coming in and out of my house is startin to worry me. People on both sides of town have been talkin about my house and the church ladies is just about to kick me out of the fold. And would you please stop layin in the middle of my bed with your legs gapped wide open, please. I done seen your garden more than my own."

While I am telling Puddin all this mess, I am already thinking about how I am gonna miss them stories she would tell me. They were full of devilment, all kinds of goings on. Some of them are from what people had told her and some of them were thing she had really done. One time we had just took our baths and powered down our bodies with some vanilla scented talcum and stretched out on the front porche to relax for the night. It was a good evening too, you could smell that confederate and night blooming jasmine filling the air with their beautiful scent. I had pulled out my best whiskey and made a fresh picture of mint lemon aide, set up the table and there we was sipping and swinging, me and Ms. Puddin. We was actin like two fine ladies would. After sipping on her third drink Ms. Puddin say "Ms. Lula you remind me of this lady I once meet named Ms. Bessie Bea Trim. She had a pair of balls big as black angus bull. You got balls like that Ms. Lula cause you let me stay here."

Puddin seemed to think she smart, I ain't show what she is. Ms Puddin told me this here women has her a man and a husband. She say "Ms. Lula Mae the day she got married, she had just got out of bed with her lover man and went and walked down the isle with her husband to be. When Link got drunk at the after party, Bessie went and got back in bed with her lover man. Na Link Trim was a big strong man, he was a logger and a trapper. Not so much to look at cause he wasn't all that pretty but a lot to hold on too if you know what I mean. He was one of those men did what it took to provide for his family though. So he did a lot of traveling where ever the work was. He was home 3 months and he was gone for 9 months. Her lover man was the traveling blacksmith named, Lawrence Kindle known by both white and black for being a damn good sharp shooter and one of the best damn fisherman in the southeast. Tell me he would go to the lake on a day when all the fish was sleep and come back with a string of fish. Nobody could ever prove it but it was said they all suspected he was having relations with Bessie. In other words he was shoen more that her horses. Ms. Bessie Bea was the head of the childrens choir, chair-women to the church social events and she was a mid-wife too. I believed people knew she was a undercover whore too, but they overlooked what she did. See she delivered most of the babies in her town both black and white." I bet she had some stories of her own. I would have loved to talk to her. Puddin say, "See Ms. Lula when you is a straight out chargin whore, peoples hate ya and talks about you. When you is a holy whore people over looks your deeds and lets you judge others. That is one reason I don't give a got damn about what any church folk thank of me. Come on let me finish tellin about Bessie Bea. Na she was a common lookin woman nothing special to look at; she just had a good mind. Bessie Bea had 12 children, three for boss, four she was sure was her husband's and the rest was a toss up between her man and her husband." All you could say to that was nothing. I am sitting her wondering how did this women even get to know Puddin. Cause even though she was havin some troubles did not seem like she would be friends with the likes of Puddin. So I asked her and she told me. "One day I went to see Ms. Cherice a Obay woman down round in LuChay to get me some tea; and this women Bessie Bee was getting some too. So we started talking." Puddin say she was just tryin to help Ms. Bessie be at ease for what she was about to do. Cause Puddin say she was go be there for a while. Because she had drank so much tea it took her two or three doses to get anything to move out of her. So she always had to sit for about three or four house. It must have worked cause that woman told Puddin all the details of her life.

Puddin say Bessie Bea told her and her two sisters were left alone to fin for themselves when she was about seven years old. First deh daddy left em , then he came back and they mama left em. Then she came back with a new husband took em back and gave a home for a little. Something was real wong with this woman because she took off again and left them little girls with deh step daddy. She must really did not care about dem girls, cause step daddys is known for rapin the girls and some of the boys too. Story goes their step daddy left them with the neighbors under the pretense he was going down the road to get deh mama, from dis old two headed doctor that spelled her. Tell me that man left and after about six months everybody realized he was not coming back. Bessie told Puddin from that moment on her and her little sisters had to fight to survive everywhere they went. People knew deh had no one to look out for them. So deh was tryin to use them as much as deh could. It aint safe for girls alone no wheres on the face of this earth. Them little girls picked up the habit of collecting double of everythin so when they lost one deh had a replacement. Poor babies from what Puddin say deh was always loosing everythang but each other; guess that is how they survived. It breaks my heart to think of dem babies in this world all alone findin for deh self. I ain't cryin for myself right na, I am cryin for dem babies. Puddin say that is why Bessie had so many children, she never wanted them to ever be all alone. She wanted dem to always have somebody to rely on.

But this 13th child she said was bad luck so she had to drink the tea. Bessie told Puddin her husband was a good man; as far as men go, but she could never trust he did not have another family somewhere too. So she always keep a spare man around. Puddin say she asked her "Girl that is dangerous game what if Trim start to question the looks of his children? You know mens do ask questions." Bessie Bea told her it did not matter about her children both her men looked alike anyway. Plus the day he question one of hers, she was ready to leave him. Anyway yall, this is a long story I just wanted to give you a little taste of the stories Puddin would tell me. Like the time she told me about how one of her lover men would always buy sets of jewelry, and he would give her the earings and the necklace to his wife. See Puddin had holes in her ears and she wore a lot of earings cause her hair was so short. I done come to the conclusion that men ain't shit, most of the time. Lawd I sure am go miss them stories Ms. Puddin would tell me. You know I thank her whole family is cursed, cause the evils of fornication is marked on them.

You know Puddin say her brother Cass was a hoe all his young life too then he married the woman of his dreams, Sandree Shoulay. One of them yolie girls down around Latnache Bayou. But here tell she took more of a liken to his brother. Oh yes, and that is not the worst part though, you know I don't think anyone in her family ever took to them. First child Sandree and Cass had was for his brother Mark. The only reason people know that is because, her time came due early and we all know she had been hip bumpin with Mark . You tend to know who fuckin the man you gots your eyes on. But that aint' the kicker; Mark's wife has been sleepin with her father-in-law and had him a baby girl. And child she look just like him. Deh is all some nasty folk, but what can you expect from people with bad blood in em. Puddin brother is cursed cause of who he was born to. Just like most of us, it is all accordin to who you was born to. So he just livin in hell, next child deh had died and Sandree got her self fixed and started drankin like a man. Puddin say she done turned from a beautiful angel to a ugly drunk. But maybe that is what Cass git, from what Puddin told me about him, he has been a cruel man.

Yeah child, Ms. Puddin told me some good stories. Sometimes when I have more time I am gonna share all of them with yall. If God spare me and say the same and I am still here, cause look like the towns women preparin a burnin wagon for me. Oh by the way when a baby is meant to come here it gets here not matter what. Puddin say even though Ms. Bessie Bea drank double that tea she still gave birth to twin boys 10lbs each, people say they had wide hands like a blacksmith. (Wink)! Let me get out of this day dream before I forget what I need to tell this woman about leavin my house. Then Puddin say "Ms. Lula remember when me and you was thinkin bout skinny dippin in the creek." "Na Puddin don't try and get off the issue here, my house is bein ill talked about and you the reason. Na I did not mind helpin you cause I am helping me too, but I am go be here when you gone." "Well, Ms. Lula why don't you just sit there and eat your food in peace so you won't have the gas. Let me think. Old Puddin may not seem like it but I got a lot of thoughts runnin through my head. Ifin this was just about a good fuckin I could get it all cleared up right away. I never haves a problem with that, most mens can't turn down a good fuckin. I ain't tryin to brag but if there is anythang I know all about it is that. I wish it was as simple as that." I am gettin pretty tired of Puddin thinkin she is God's gift to men cause she is gettin paid for it. She ain't the only one that can snife a man's under-nuts. Hell if deh kept right ain't nothing no better. Well anyway yall, I ain't have no problem with her servin me a plate of food cuase I is always doin the servin. It smelled good. So I went on and ate, but ate as slow as I could. Cause I knew when this meal was over Puddin was gone.

Well after Puddin studied me for a long while she said, "Don't you worry none Ms. Lula I will fix it." I looked at her and laughed cause she must not know she is the problem and these women did not want to see her comin or goin. Then Ms. Puddin said "Lets go stop all this talkin." She went to her room and started to get dressed. Huh, this dress, was not the usual dress. It was not low cut, nor was it hugging her hips. It was a satin pink dress with a high fitted lace colar, with them little covered buttons all the way up to the neck. It had that real expensive lace around the sleves accented with little embrodried red roses. Yall then she put on and silk white hat, child I almost died when I looked at her. I be got damn Ms. Puddin was standing there right in front of me looking like the preacher's wife. Then she said "Lets go." I said "Lets go where?" She said,

"To see the ladies doing all this mean spirited talkin about such a good Christian lady like yourself Ms. Lula Mae." I did not know whether or not this was go work, but I hurried up and hitched the buggy. The Lord usin Puddin like he used that donkey in the Bible, she go be the reason my house go keep on being well blessed. If yall could see my savins you would know what I mean. Oh bye the way , if you notice I did not say I had to change clothes. That is because I always dress as a presentable lady. But right na I just want to see if any good go come from this visit. First house we visted of course was the good Reverand Goodman's house since Sister Lizzie was the foundation of all the gossip. Yall remember what I told ya about sister Lizzie and the Sherrif, right. When we pulled up to the holdin post, we could see Rev and the Mrs. peepin out the window. I guess these find folks trying to figure out what the hell we wanted. Mrs Goodman came to the door and greeted us with sweetest lyinest voice you ever wanted to hear. "How are you wonderful children of God doing this morning?" My mouth open cause I was expectin deh dogs to come and run us off. Puddin jumped out the buggy and rushed to the steps and handed Mrs. Goodman a basket of goodies she had put together out of my pantry. No matter what Mrs. Goodman was thinking was'nt nobody go turn down my preserves. Lizzie was staring at us like she had seen the devil himself come walkin up on her front porch or even worse, one of them blind blues singers going around making all the church money. Yeah, they takes the church money when deh come to town, cause we all go to see em, even the Preachers go. We always know when to get our money right too. See they goes to the white folk first, then they come to us. So we have time to pull together all our spare money so we can juke with em. Plus we don't care bout them goin to see the white folks first cause we always get a cut price. Oh yeah, white folk love the blues. I don't know what the hell for, since I can't see why deh would have the blues. Maybe deh been havin the same dream I have been havin about deh judgment day. See Jesus comes back ceptin he is colored. Din he tells all the white folk "I been watching you people for a while now and I done seen your deeds. So here is your judgment. Tomorrow mornin yall go take the place of all the black folks and they go take yours." I bet that would be enough to make shit out the side of deh ass. That is just my dream though Lord. But however you come back if you comin back to judge what is fair, white folk is go be in a world of trouble. Ain't that some shit deh done wrote deh own punishment. Well anyway we ain't never mind dem comin to us last, cause they gots to come over here and stay. Works out just fine for us, we be going to bed late when them blues singers comes to town. Even the white folk know not to expect to be at work on time.

We all gits tied of hearin and sangin songs about God delivering Daniel cause he shol aint' deliverin us. No matter how much we sing them songs we still be in the same shape. See them blues sangers be tellin the truth about how we feel. We just want to hear songs that talk about how we really feel about life, and can't nobody tell it like a blues man. And seems like dem blind ones can scream the loudest and howl the longest. Lawd, child we loves to hear our blues men. Aww, lawd look at me off the track again. Anyway, we went in and sat at the kitchen table. Hmmmmm! well, I see old sista Goodman have been spending the church money real well. Seein as though we been putting money in a building fund for a new church and not one thing has been built yet. (laugh laugh) Maybe some of that money right here in this house. Looks like the curtains brand new, nice big kitchen, with a build in water and a built in stove. Plus, she got a brand new lazy susan table too and they not cheap. While I am noticing all these fancys, she puts the tea cakes in the center of the table so she could spend it around to us , just to show off. Yall know she did not have to spin the table to serve us no tea cake but she did. She nevermind be tryin to show off to me but she might have to do some explainin to the church, when I reports all this heavenly finess. I can not wait to tell this to the Ladies of the New Beaulah Jeruselem Baptist Church. She was not impressing me though, cause I could buy me one of them for each room of my house if I wanted to. Anyway we was just all talking and chitter chatter and all of a sudden Puddin said "We would like for you to go and get the Reverend for us now please, Sister Goodman." Huh, look at Puddin tryin to sound like she belong, callin Lizzie sister Goodman. Mrs. Goodman got straight up and went and got him like she was obeying orders. When the good man of God entered in the room I stood up in respect like a Christian woman should. Puddin just sat there like the no mannered harlot she was not showin this man no respect. Then Puddin starts to talk, listen at what she told the Reverand. "Reverand Goodman I have been a heathen all my life and I done been around some mean spirited people. But sir nothing beats the evil tongues of the Christian women here in Friendly. And not only that good Reverand some of the names deh done called me; hell I did not know Christian women used them words." She told about all the gossip and name slashing and such the women had been doing. Child she was a mess to watch, flingin her hands, waving the fan, and seem like she had mustared up some tears in her eyes. Puddin was puttin on some show. "Na Reverand Goodman the only people I know for sure have not used the language of the devil or his wicked way against me is your lovely wife and Ms. Lula Mae. No sir neither one of these ladies is spreading evil gossip about me livin with Ms Lula Mae. Everybody here in dis here town knows that Ms. Lula Mae is a God fearin woman, so deh know that if I was doin some carryin on she would not have it. They all around here makin up niggar stories. You know what niggar stories is Reverand the ones what we make up in our mind, then we sware to God deh is real." See we all could understand that cause we know if you thank somethin in your head long enough or if the right person say something is true, den it is true. Most people do that sometimes it helps them handle deh real life. I don't know everythang seem so messed up na. But look like this harlot with the devils tounge bout to make it alright. Then she said " Now look here Man of God "I know I am not a member of your fine church but I have a gift to go towards the building fund. A man with a heart of God such as yourself will need to add on more room for all of those new converts you are go have comin your way. See when people hears the story of how Reverand Goodman forgave the harlot like Christ did; people go come from far and near to hear such a man." I almost felt sorry for him but that went away when I thought aoubt how much money I am go lose if Puddin have to go. Then that hefier pulls out an envelop stuffed with money, it was over one thousand dollars in it I just knew it. After the good reverend counted it he started clearing his throat, and shaking his head, weaving and bobbin from side to side. He went into a sermon. Lawd have mercy the Holy Spirit hit the good reverend and he shook, I could feel him. I could feel that man, the money might have made him happy but the holy spirit caught a hold to him and made him shout, cause I could feel it. Then he said "The Lawd says all is welcome in his house and in his heart. Since I am Preacher here in these parts I will speak to my flock about the evils of gossip. I will put my wife over a committee of women to start a prayer group against this great evil."

He should have a committee over the whereabouts of his wife and how much Sherrif dick she done took up the ass. (Forgive me yall, please) Na yall I gots to say something right here we know Mrs. Goodman is the main gossiper, she started most of the ill talk, but it was not her husband she thought this harlot from hell was go get. Na she gots to pray against herself huh, serve that heifer right, too she ought be the last person to judge. I was just sitting there looking thangs over and all I can say is if money is evil then people is evil too; cause people love money. I wonder what the good reverend ever saw in his wife though, cause she is not just plain, she is just plain ugly. I really thought the Sheriff felt sorry for her that day. Na she is a black woman ain't never been spoiled by a white man. That could have something to do with her being so god awful ugly and she is ugly too; got damn. I means the kind of ugly that make you wonder what in the hell God was thinking about when he made her. She is some big old red bone ugly woman, with them gap teeth across the front of her mouth makin it look like a gate and her face pushed in like a possium, wide nose and that thang had nappy hair, that set up in the top of her head like a pineapple. When you ever seen a red girl with nappy hair. I ain't trying to say nothing but most red bone girls can get by even if they not so pretty cause they red bone, but not her, no Lawd, not her. She just got damn ugly. And we know she is a whore cause she threw herself on the Sheriff. Child Ms. Lula Mae sorry she got off track again. But I don't' understand Jones wantin her and I don't understand Reb wantin her. All I can say is her pussy must be so good she lick it herself. Well child any way Revernd Goodman started preachin and keep on preachin until Sunday and after he finished with the members on Sunday morning we ain't hear no gossip about Puddin livin in my house no more. That man preached like God done put a fire to him, lawd he talked about gossip, he talked about adultery and all kinds of fornications and when he finished there was not a dry eye left in the church. I think he picked up the largest collection we ever had that Sunday.

CHAPTER 7

Mashoe

WELL YALL, IT IS one of them lazy afternoons, you know the kind where the mosqitos don't even want to bite, the zombies don't want to get up, and the frogs to lazy to leap. My situation has changed in the community na. Instead of being a whore harborer, I am now the perfect example of a Christian woman doing her duty to please the Lord. I was just piddelin around tryin to cool off, sittin around my house in my fancy all white cotton night gown. It was a decent gown not them see through contraptions Puddin was always wearing. I was just sittin here relaxin in my swing watchin the sun slowly fade beyond the horizon and enjoyin the smell of honeysuckle and night bloomin jasmine as they filled my nose. My flower gardens, the sounds of crickets and other night sounds made my mind drift to the many things I had to be thankful for. It is kinda hard to just thank about all the bad thangs done happen to you on an evening like this. Seems like God is touchin you, tryin to let you know that even in the mist of heartarche and pain you can find peace and joy. That is a strange way to be; knowin that your life is not what you want it to be, exceptin for moments of grace and thankin God for that. Seem like every chance I get to thank God for something good I do; so much bad be going on. Well na thank you Lord for this right here. There is nothing more beautiful than my property at the close of the day. I swear the sun comes down to set right over my place on purpose, so he can kiss it good night.

Puddin was gone off with that rich white feller, you know the one bought her all them gifts and thangs the last time. The one looke like he was proposing to her. I wonder is deh done got married? Most of em just have pleasure with you and go on about their business, they never really want to marry much. He probably one of them criminals from up North. That could be the reason for his strange ways, plus Northerners don't like us down here no way, whether you is black or white. You know they calls us all ignorant and backwards down here. Tell ya the truth we is got some ignorant crackers and niggas down here but deh got em too. I hear tell they have criminals robbing banks in broad open day light; showin they face too. Lawd have mercy either you gots the Klans hangin down South or the white folk bank robbers up North stealin all you got. Blacks must be cursed is all I can say. We just work and die, and work and die and we ain't guaranteed heaven. But right na in my world all is well and all I want to do was sit here and rest my self on my porch praying for another cool breeze. Looks like the good Lawd was ignorin me about the breeze cause was no wind blowing no where. But there is some good thangs happening. I got my good graces back in the church, the new President a man named Hardy, den spoke out against lynchins down here and I am coming in my season. You know it take a white man with a pair prize bull balls to take on the South and deh lynchins. I know yall want to know what Ms. Lula Mae's seaon is don't you. Well every woman and man gots a season; it is the time when you are feeling your needs. For a woman such as myself that means I have to keep a lot of sweet oil handy. For people with somebody, babies go be made. I don't mind the sweet oil but I would much rather a hard warm body lyin next to me. I needs to roll my hips. Ain't nothing worse than havin a pair of hard lips and nothin to kiss. A lot of these woman around here grabs dem a young boy or two, but I have always been partial to a full man with a pair of ripe balls. I ain't sayin it is nothing wrong with getting one of them young studs, just letting yall know I prefer a full grown man . The good Lord go send somebody along soon and I gots plenty of sweet oil left . So I will be just fine.

I am just gald I am where I am right na. Wouldn't want to be in Tulsa, Oklahoma right na either them white folks done gone crazy and killed a whole bunch of black folks in broad open day light. Say they got the army to help em too. Yes sir and yes maam, they killed the entire town; all over a lie. Dis shol is a sad time for the poor black folk over there in Greenwood. My friend John Stanford told me the whole story. He had left there to go to New Orleans to get a house and set up for moving his family when he heard the news. Mr. Standord had got him a job on one of them ships, in the kitchen; making good money, child. I Know his wife was go be happy cause 8 months out the year he was go be on the water. Well anyway, when he got the news what had happened he rushed back home. Poor John say all his family was dead even his 2 month old baby. It is a terrible thang what happened over there, but hell so many of us been killed, we hear about thangs like that and just hope our white folk don't go crazy. Yall know down here in Friendly, we all gots us our good share of guns hid around. We go be some fighin muther fuckers if these white folk gos crazy. (Excuse my language but situations like this calls for cussin). Well anyway Mr. Standord came here to stay the night before he left to go on and take his job. He was sad man but he is smart cause he ain't nothing stop him from takin that job. See right now I can thank God I am no where near that place. So much saddnes in the Earth over there and them white folk still wakin around with the devil in cause deh know what deh did was wrong. I ain't worried bout what they did though cause aww one day it is go burn like Sodom and Gomorrah over there and the angels bringing the fire go be black. We done had a couple of homesteads burned down and all the peoples killed by Gods good soldiers.

We gots all these people suppose to be fixers and it don't seem like they really gots no power cause they aint fixed us yet. I be sittin here wonderin about all them tales people be tellin about old lady Mashoe. She one of the local fixers. Yall knows what fixers is right? They the people that get it done for ya, what regular people can't. Ain't never saying I aint ever went to one but it was for medical reasons and that is all it was for. Aint like some of them women puttin mens' suits in deh closet so they can draw him and keep him. What the hell go happen when the suit rot. Or gettin a pair of bull nuts cuttin open and writin the man name you want on a piece of paper and dippin it in your monthly, then ya put it in the bull nuts. Once you bury dem bull nuts in a cemtary for three days the man willy ain't go get hard for nobody but you. (Na don't yall go runnin out there spoilin no bull nuts, cook em and eat em, that is the best thang you can do for a good pair of nuts, eat em.) We have two here in Friendly, that do some serious thangs or atleast people say they do. One everybody talk about going to cause she calls herself a prophetiss instead of an obay woman, but it is all the same. Then you got Lady Mashoe, nobody wanna tell when they go to her; no sir nobody tell that. But you knows lots of people going cause she gots one of the biggest spreads around and all she does is what she does. I am always thinking about these people, they got the power to fix, so I been wondering why ain't none of em ever fix our low down situation. Like I said ifin you can fix some thangs you ought to be able to fix all thangs. So, here is what I really thank; some people know how to talk and listen to nature. But nature only concered with healin, then some people only know how to talk to other spirits, but deh only concerned with thangs that concern them. See them people who listen to nature, she tell them healin secrets. And everythin eles people do is just by chance, I don't know if all works I figures is it just by chance. But I don't take no chance with it.

I read dis book by dis here fellow named Henry Bruce . He say exactly what I thank, all peoples both black and white have deh supersititions and conjurs, one to keep em back and the other one to keep em comin back to them for help. Seee I believe that if Mashoe' give you a shoe string and tell you to tie it around your waist with the man name you want one it and you git him. You probably was go git him anyway. I believe if you hope long enough somethins is got to happen. But I do remember this time when Mashoe took 5 black eyed peas threw in the air and said some words and the people who house she did that in front of moved out the next day child. She did it for this old white man who wanted their land and he got it. He paid em for it but them people did not want to move. Then I remember this time Jeb Walker was doin a lot of evil talk against the Major. Well Sally had one of her girls take her to Mashoe, say Mashoe had her get nine red onions, cut a hole em and write old Jebs name on a piece of paper, cross it out and stuff it in that onion. Jeb Walker ain't spoke in five years, he got four more to go before he will be able to speak again. We know how many years he got left cause after the first three years Sally went back to Mashoe and asked her to change thangs around. White folks always forgive each other. Mashoe told her he had nine years not to speak, if her or the Major wanted to take his other four years no problem with her. But she told her for show somebody had to do the rest of the time left, cause something she called a "fayo spirit" would take vengeance. That is why I don't mess around like that you all ways gots somebody to pay. Let me tell yall this, Mashoe ain't nobody you want mad at you, for one thang too many white folk owe her favors and the other thang is she talk to all kinds of spirits. She ain't talkin to the right ones to help us colored folk, cause we is all messed up.

Mashoe' had one of the finest mens god ever blew breath into his name was Thaddeus Jones, one of the finest catches around. The problem with him was that he was married to old lady Mashoe' and nobody understood why. Na we believing they married cause they say so, none of us ever went to a wedding as such and we don't know when it happened. He bout 20 years younger than her too. We all thought about him. Every woman around wanted to just look at that man. See he had this cold black hair, and this smooth black chocolate brown skin and he had them gray eyes that just would look right through you. Lawd he even walked like he was gliding and he was gifted too cuz when a man built like that you sees his person, even if he not trying to show it to you. Oh lawd, he was nice, well any way he waited on Mashoe' hand and foot and he loved her more than anything; you could tell that. We never understood that, Mashoe' not a bad looking woman, but she shows her age. One day we here dis young girl named Carol Jean comes to live with Mashoe' she bees about 12 years of age. None of use had ever seen this child before and we did know who her people was. She was a little mulatto girl, we thinkin maybe she one of them children who got away when all that killing was going on some years ago. Oh, yall don't know about the time all them Mulattos was being killed from here to Texas. Oh yeah, child somebody was killing em up around here. The white folk had gone crazy. Choppin em up with axes, I believe. Na we don't know who, cause ain't nobody telling that. High as 200 regular black women was killed in Georgia and about 400 Mulattos just because. They was killing so fast they even killed a few white folks, the found out later. A black man still had to pay for that though, cause they hung Willie Chamberlin because they say he give them the name of a white family instead of a mulatto family and they kilt em. Every body know that was a lie, or maybe not, but for show one white family got their just due. That is a shame for me to say, but yall ain't living down here in this shit, and this is some shit.

We don't fool with the Mulattoos much cause they is strange as the white folk. You know they marry each other to keep the color huh! But that is the same as rich folk marryin they family to keep the money. They had they own way and did very little business with us regular black folk, deh good builders, though. You want some cabinets built you call one of them, if they come you go have something else to show, that is if they come. Every now and then one of them would marry a dark girl and his family disown him. Not all of em bad, but that is the same with almost everybody exceptin most white folk. The only reason we cared about what happened to them anyway was because Mulatto or not they is still black and that was some kind of low down thang to have happened to our people. Here tell quite a few other black families was kilt too. It is always the same if one black was thought to have done something or was being punished for something, we all had to pay for it. We was all figuring on why these killing going on and all we could come up with was that; the white folk trying to get rid of anything black that is white enough to fool them. Then when they gits tried of killin em they go start killing us regular blacks to make it look like we at war with each other. Aww yea honey we know the game by na. We all wondering who them white folk think they foolin. They even tried to make it look like we was doing it. They had a lie goin around say a voodoo lady was doing all the killin cause she was owed a debt. Who them white folk thank they lying on, everybody know that Sister Queen Hanna Marie was a kind and loving women, taking care of peoples needs, healing people and loving her Catholic Jesus. I am just saying anything black that might have done any kind of good is always being attached. Yall, know Sister Queen Marie passed on the year I was born in 1881. God rest her soul. I always take me a patch of green grass, moss, pine needles and fig preserves when I go to her grave. It is always good to leave a gift. Anyway none of us believe that some voodoo sacrifice had anything to do with them killings.

White people is crazy when they gets together and if they the wrong kind of white folk somebody go get hurt. When they gets on killing sprees one of em sooner or later will say "Lets kill all them niggars and there they go burning down our houses, raping us, hanging us, tar and feathering us, you name it they do it to us. I thank they gets possessed cause mostly they would come at night but lately they be comin in large groups in the broad open day light. No shame, no shame. They go on for days, killin and picnickin (pickin a nigger to kill) and ravashinging, until either they gits tired or some bleeding heart loose one of their prize niggers and feel he done suffered to much a loss. Yeah, there are still are some prize niggers left. You know the ones, seem like they living a bit better, gits aways with a little more and always looking at you like you bet not cross an eye at them. They ain't got no other skill except for being a good nigger and deh is the best nigger you ever wanted to meet. They will get you ass lynched too. Some of em try to act white, lookin all down on ya. But we know deh just playin the good niggar game. Of course yall know we use to loosing our men, women and children to lynchings, but this axe murdering well it was just down right evil, catching people in they sleep and cutting em up. From here to Texas, they killing Mulattos, seeking to find what they created cause they foolin em right and left, marryin em and lovin em to death. Yes, indeed these white folk really do thank they God. They the ones created the mulatoos and now they tryin to kill em out. Sorta like you did us Lawd. Lawd what is these times coming too. We just been put here on this earth to be beast of burdens, barin the masters babies, burdens, and all his frustrations on our backs. Yall better stop me cause I gets all off the subject, but you gots to understand there is so much happening now a days, somebody got to tell it. Na back to this little old gal and Mashoe.

Well the story goes that Thaddeus took a spell and ravished that girl. That nigger ain't take no spell he just got drunk and raped her. Everybody knows it too, that girl was eighteen firm and fully packed. Mashoe aint have not business leaving her there with her man any way. Most men that is a man was go at least try to say something to that girl. But I guess ifin a child come to you at 12 and is livin in the house most men would have seen her as they own child. Let me stop lyin most of em would wait till they think she old enough and try. That is how men is dogs, plain and simple. They say Mashoe' had gone down to New Orleans to do some work for dem drunes tryin to start their own church. See yall it don't matter how close to white ya is you aint. So when you trys to do white folk thangs like startin churches without them you go need some extra help. One thang bout Mashoe the only color matter to her is green. I ain't show bout all these hear witches potions she make, can't say deh is real or not. Just know a lot of people use her even them dagos. Hell Mashoe is a rich woman and she go always be rich, one man come have her put it on somebody and the other come to have her take it off. How we know this is because of Mr. and Mrs. Jack. Well here tell Mrs. Jack found out her husband was seein Martha Louise so she goes to Mashoe for help. Well Mashoe told her to fill a jar full of water and put Martha Louise and her husbands name in it. Then take that jar and put it in the river during a rain storm. Supposily puttin their names in the water and throwin it in the rough waters would cause so much confusion between them Mr. Jack would leave Martha Louise alone. Well it worked cause Mr. Jack came to hate that woman. Well Martha Louise knowin something was wrong and went to see Mashoe to take off the fixin. Mashoe told her to write Mr. Jack's name on a piece of cow hide and bath with it for three full moons. Well honey after the third full moon passed here comes Mr. Jack back with Martha Louise, here tell Mashoe made as high as five hundred dollars between the three of them. Anyway Mashoe had to go to New Orleans to do the work so she left her cousin Irene Tedford at the house to watch over it and make sure everything else was being kept in order too. Guess she was not watching enough, because everybody around here knew what Thaddeus did to that girl. Know why yall , cause she cried everyday all day and half the night. She cried no matter what anybody said to her. You could not make her stop, that child eyes had closed up so much she looked like a chinaman. Ain't no body do Thaddeus nothing cause they knew Mashoe would and the white folk did not care. Being raped was just common for black women. If it was'nt the white men it was the black men; did not matter they all raped us. I bet he wish he had killed her though; that child let the world know what he had done to her.

Irene says when Mashoe came home she looked at Thaddeus called him in her bed room and closed the door. Irene said them doors was thick and hard to hear through but as loud as Mashoe was talkin she understood every word Mashoe was sayin. Say she asked "Why Nolean crying everyday? Why is she scrubbing all the time? What is wrong with her Thaddeus? The child seem like she done caught a spell." Irene say he started screaming like someone was brandin him with masters initials. "Mashoe you is a evil woman after all these years you mean to tell me you don't trust me? Why you want to accuse me of takin some girl I am with you cause I wants me a real woman not some girl. All the thangs I done done for you. How you go believe some lyin child and a bunch of gossipin women?" But Irene say Mashoe tolt him she knew what he had done; say she told him everybody in town knew what he had done and they was not all a bunch of gossipin women. Tell me that man went to tearing up the house and everything. Kickin over the furniture, breakin the windows, and stompin like he was on fire. Say Mashoe' told him he had till the risin of the sun to leave her house cause their was not nothing else they had to talk about. "Then Irene say she told him, "Everyday you thank you is a free man Thaddeus you just steppin closer to death cause he just waitin for you to catch up with him. He got your name from a faithful servant Thaddeus." She put one hell of a hex on him. Irene say then she heard some whispering and after that Thaddeus ran out the back door, screaming like somebody had just tarred and feathered his low down ass. The next morning Thaddeus be found in the swamp done hung hisself. Some people say the Lugarou got him. I can believe that cause we all know the Lugarou is a Cajun demon and he probably would rather hang a nigger than eat him. I leaves them Cajuns and they demons alone, the only one I ever want to see or know is that Fifalit, he the one leads ya to treasure. Oh and sometimes I sees deh Traiteurs casue deh got all the healin herbs you ever want to have. I don't mess with them Cajuns and they stuff much, cause child something goin on with them people. I know one thang my use be love you know my Cajun man I told you bout early, well he told me to keep a mirror on my porch by the door sos to keep somebody named M'su Diable out and I do. Anyway before Thaddeus left dis here world he left Mashoe this here note on the wall in her parlor it say " I am on my way to hell Mashoe and I go save a place for you gal, the Lugarou comin for ya". We ain't never found out what she did with that little ole gal, cause she disappeared just like she appeared. We aint never found out what she said to him, cause she whispered it so low so you could not hear that part. Some people say she used hex words on him she learned from the old conjur women; others say she told him the girl was his and that is what drove him mad and made him kilt hisself. Whatever the case that Thaddeus Jones took his life and is naw waitin in hell for Mashoe' to take her place besides him. Never understood somebody chosing to go to hell cause if I had a choice I would not be living in this one. He go be waiting long damn time cause

Mashoe done found her another man who seem to be lovin her just as much as he did. I doubt if she go leave this here earth anytime soon. I shol do feel sorry for that new fixed man she got. He bet not cross her, hell we bet not cross her.

Yall, know I am just thinking. I can say what I want on these pages and to the Lawd. That's why I like talking to me. Sitting here tryin to figuring this thang out. See one thang I know, them white folk always looking at us smiling is cause they happy that they got somebody to rule over and they thank the smiles on our face is because we happy deh is our rulers. You know cause deh is good Christians, but they don't really know what is on our minds. Deh can't even thank like us our lives is too different. Most of the time we smiling just to keep from cryin. We smilin cause sometimes we too scared to frown, we smilin cause we hopin that God go look down on us and have mercy, we smiling cause we ain't got no choice. We ain't on the auction blocks no more and they don't sell us like they use too all open in the open for every one to see, we just livin on colored blocks, workin for less than we worth, fightin for Masters scraps with no place to go. Sometimes we up and most of the time we down, but on Friday and Saturday we be carryin on like heathens across the track in coon town. We all live across the track in these nice little blocks full of shot gun houses for the most part. Ofcourse that is if you live in the town. I don't. They took us from the plantation and moved us cross the track, how bout if bet ya if deh find out the land across the track worth some money deh go take it all back. Then they go move us in some shit in a brand new shit din to keep us quite. Somethin not quite right about this whole situation, between black folk and white folk. Seem like the God they telling us about is all in deh favor. I ain't really seen a damn thing he done did for us yet. Even though we have our own little section of town deh give us, white folk still come and do what de want to do over here. I feel one day that's all go change, but I may not be here to see it but it is all go change oneday.

I come to remember when Sally White and LuBertha Dumonqi was sitting out in the gazebo having their mint juleps at 9:00am in the morning, good Christian women taking deh tonic .Well deh juice must have got to em cause they decided to make fun of how we talk. Sally say "Lula what is dis here empty bottle doin on the floor?" I says, "I don't know Ms.Sally. Is you wanting me to move it." She says "Is you, is you", what kind of nigger talk is that?" I am thinking in my head. White folk always talking about how somebody can't talk, cause we don't sound exactly like them. Well hell what they need to sit and figure out is we talk just like dem. Deh taught us to talk, so if we talk ignorant, we talk like them. Na we talk like em but we don't sound like em, we gots rhythm when we speak, probably cause all we did was sing in dem fields. But, we deliberately tryin to use different ways of saying thangs so we can sound schooled. Na we don't sound to schooled in front of them but we knows how to sound schooled. Our teachers we have teaching us how to use correct English. Don't know what makes these southern crackers think they talk so right, plus a lot of dem can't read either and we know it. Na, ifin you ever get to met a fine northern gentleman, you will here some real educated talkin, all proper and stuff. He go sound different from one of the Southern gents, cause he go sound smarter. Na the southern gent he go sound prettier, but that northern man go sound smarter. Lawd forbid if you meet up on one of them old Englishman; you go here some real strange talking then. You aint' go ever understand a damn thing he saying. Cause deh invented English which is a foreign language and ain't real American talkin no way. I wish I could tell them both that ifin a man from England heard both them talk he would think deh was both ignorant; but I like living. See that is how deh got us, deh have the power to take our life. Anytime somebody got the power to put you back in chains and take your life deh got the power. We aint' running a fair race in this life, and if by some chance we start to beat em , they shoot us with the gun that started the damn race. That is why I don't run.

We always sangin to the God deh taught us about and He tellin us in His word to pray for them and obey them like deh is Him. Well, damnit they ain't Him. How you go beat somebody with cat of nine tales, stab em in deh side, nail holes in em, skin em and a whole lot of other evils of the Devil and expect them to love you? How you go kill someone husband right in front of them and expect them to trust you. I got a whole lot of these how you gonnas. This is for you Lord, I always have had my doubts about you. I am scared to have these doubts, lest your wrath come down on me. But, you got to answer me something. Why you let us be slaves, then declare us animals, then you let us be sorely mistreated in your name. Either you just the God of the white folk or you hate colored folk too. Which is it? We still singing songs about coming to meet you around the throne. We still praizing and jumpin up getting full of the Holy Ghost or something that is makin us forget for a minute. And we still going back to a shack, facing the same demon you put in charge of us. You might have delivered Daniel, which makes me think he had to be a white man. But for sure you ain't did one thang to deliver us. No sir, you ain't did one thang. If you free a mans' body from slavery and his mind still in slavery he worst off than he ever was huh. Plus, what is the use in freein a man who to scared to speak up for himself and the ones that do speak up always end up dead. I know that is how they do it in this time. Remember that man named, David Walker; he died before I was born in 1881. Well anyway he told them white folk somethin in writing about how he felt about all the evils deh was doin. Here tell some good old faithful nigger poisoned him. Na I don't know for sure that an old faithful Tom did it, cause you know how white folks lie even about history, but I figure ifin you speakin out against white folk you ought not eat out in places. Deh can always get you in your stomach. But it stand to reason some old nigger killed him casue he was poisoned or so deh say. Plus we could not eat in the same places deh could anyway, so who else do you get to do your dirt, but someone just like him, well lets just say someone his color. That is right git his own people to kill him then you really can not blame the white man. That is what I thank they did to him. Ms. Tora Lee Goodman, Reverand Goodman's sister who lived in Charleston, North Carolina an educated woman told us about this man. She also swore she was never go come back down here again. She said the ignorance here just made her too sad. But she sure believed that somebody good nigger kilt him for deh master's right to be right. Na Lord, I am about to give you a situation and I want you to fairly answer it; if you feel you need to be fair to somebody black this morning. What if I snatched you from heaven, chained up your hands and feet, kill your children, starve and beat your wife half to death, and fix it where you can't speak your language would you keep comin to me for help? Well would you? I am only talkin like this to you cause I don't know who else to talk to. Plus, just by chance you woke up on the good side of bed you might talk back if too many white folk aint' callin on you and you might want to show somebody black some mercy. We all around here singin when we get to heavbun to see ya, we go all be free. For what I am seeing heavbun got a back door, we gonna use that door to get in and we go be cleaning white folk mansions. Ifin what I am saying is blaspheming, you gave me this mind and you gave me this mouth, and you gave me a brian to figure, so it is all your fault. Cause see Lawd, I gots a mind like a child and you my daddy. I figure we must all have a mind like a child cause grown people just don't let folk keep doin them the same thing over and over again. But us do. Yes, sir we keep a singin, workin, and toilin for these good Christians and they keep on lyin, killin and mistreating us. Oh! Is that you Lawd just put the thought in my head about the Quakers who helped us in slavery. Well, I says this, ain't nothing special about doing the right thang especially when you have the power to do it. When you have the power you have the power.

CHAPTER 8

What Beulah Want?

NAW WHO IS DIS coming interrupting my time alone with you Lawd? I had plans for myself later on. Me and my bottle of sweet oil. Child dis here is Sho comin down my walk way. I got my thinking cap on na. What is she doing comin my way? Well anyway she comes up to the porch and ask me where Puddin at. I tells her Puddin gone with her soon to be husband. Sho turns and looks at me and says " Puddin ain't got no soon to be husband. " Honey child I rared my shoudders back with pride and looked her squre in the eyes and tells her Puddin gots her a rich white man that is crazy about her. I saw him on his knees beggin her to marry him. Ifin she is smart she will marry him and go off and start her life over. A woman like her ain't go git to many chances for a marriage proposal." Sho says "Puddin ain't go ever marry no man. She just as confused as she can be. She really ain't made her mind up about a lot of things in life yet." Aww , looks like Sho might be taken with Ms. Puddin. Poor child she about to be as hurt as a squirrel in a dog yard. I told yall there is something about this woman. Now she got Sho in love with her too. She round here pining over someone she say don't even know herself. Plus her devil ways ain't go take over Puddin that is why the Lawd done

71

sent her a rich man to keep her in line as a woman. Sho can give it up with her evil persuasions.

Anyway I says "What do you want Sho?" I know all I wanted was for her to get the hell off my got damn porch. I just got them damn Christian hyporcrits to leave me the hell alone about Ms. Puddin so I don't need Sho comin by here all the time. I don't think they will let me off if I start hanging with her. Plus, I was at peace and telling a story to myself and talking to you Lawd. Not my fault she running around like a bitch in heat after Ms. Puddin. She done really put a bee up my ass, cause she messed up my moments with you. See I believe moments to yourself is valuable. You know them times when you do not want anybody around you, not anybody. You just want to sit be your natural self. You sweat a little, fart out loud, yeah I said fart out loud, belch, and just stretch out like a big old lazy cat sunnin. Then every na and then take a sip of a muskadine tonic, rub your thighs together and touch yourself for a minute or two. You know what I am talking about a natural moment. You can't have a natural moment with folk around. It is impolite to fart and belch in front of people let alone rub your little pleasure patch. These type of things can only be done in a natural moment. But now here comes this confused hell bound thang bothering your peace. She says " When Puddin gets back here you tell her I came by. I want her to come see me quick, we have a situation to discuss." Then she turns and walks off but she had a different walk not like a man, she strutted off like she was a hot woman. I mean she was movin her hips back and forth like ripples on the pond. This was kind of confusing to me cause she usually tried to walk like a man. It really did not work for her either because she was so curvey. We use to calling her the man girl and a few other words, but we knew she had the same thangs we had between her legs or at least we thought so.

You know there has been stories about her having a lady dick or something like that. Here tell here woman part is extra large, but I always figured that was just cause she was rubbin all the time. She could have been as much woman as we is, corse I would have loved to see ifin she did have a man's concern. Child, that would be the highlight of my reportin. I have a large woman piece myself but I rubs a lot too with my hands. That is probably all they lookin at for real, but you just don't know about people they is strange and she is different she just might have a man's concern. Ain't our fault she let them devils possess her though and set her apart from us. I rarely thought of her as being a real woman, because of her habits, real women just do not like having women all the time. Unless you a whore like Ms. Puddin then you do what the money say; I wonder if Sho payin Ms. Puddin. Hmmmm, today she must have fixed her self up for Puddin. Her hair was beautiful. I mean beautiful, I never noticed how long and silky it was. That gul hair past her behind and smell like she cleaned it with magnolia water. Then I notices too, that she was a right fine lookin woman, a real find looker; the kind that could have any man she wanted. Child I had to stop my self. I was paying too much attention to her. That is what happen when you is not prayed up and demon come on your porch. So anyway as Sho walked away her hips still gigglin like ripples on water with her head down as if she has lost her best friend, Sho made me feel bad. I don't know what got into me but I called her back to me and as she turned I saw the most beautiful sight I had ever seen. Just as she turned around the light from the sun highlighted her entire body and she looked like an angel of some sort, dark or light she looked like an angel. As she walked towards me, I was shocked at how much of a woman she really was. We never paid attention to her female qualities because we all knew she liked women and not men. Plus some thangs you want in your circle and some thangs you don't and she was one you did not want to be seen with. Any of yall saying anything different is a liar or you like my cousin Christina who says heaven big enough for all kinds of folk. But that is another subject all together, cause Christiana son fixed our hair, made our dresses walk with a twitch and her daughter got a full got damn mustache and a deep voice too. God sho was confused when he made them. Like said that is another subject. Plus they always on the moaning bench praying for deliverance. As a matter of fact we ain't seem them lately here tell they both moved to California.

Sho came and sat down in the swing next to me. I got up and fixed her some cool lemonade. As we sat down in the swing drinking lemonade, I asked her why she did not like men? She turned to me and looked at me with the hurt look a little child had after a bad ass whippin and said, "Why you don't want to know why I never went to see my mama and papa Ms. Lula ? I looked at her puzzled like cuz, I ain't no where she was comin from. Then she said "I don't like men cuz men don't really know how to love you". I stood up and looked down on her and said " What do you mean girl the good Lord made men for women. I Know you thank your way is the way to go, but God made men for women. You just got to give them a chance." "No, Ms. Lula Mae not me. My papa would beat my mama because he loved her. We had a strange house Ms. Lula I was like my daddy's other wife most of my life, nobody ever knew what was really going on in our house. They really did not, we looked like we more normal than most folks over where we lived, but I think we was worst than them all. I use to drink wormwood tea to ease my pain cause as soon as my daddy finished beating my mama he headed to me. I remember drowing in his sweat and smell of his arm pits. Lord I hated him. Between the tea and the white lightening I almost did not feel a thang. I would pass out and wake up and my mama would be there cleaning me and telling me that if I did not tell anybody what he had done and just keep prayin to the good Lord he would make him stop. She'd say " You just watch child, God go send Gabriel himself and he go take care Mr. Hanable Dison you just watch." So I got tired of waiting on God to send in Gabriel Ms. Lula. I went to town to see the Sherriff. Huh, I knew she had made a mistake then; you can't go to man who is known for rapin and ask him to help, cause ya daddy is rapin ya, poor child. Yes, Ms. Lula I broke the code; I went to the white law to tell on a black man. I heard people say that if you needed help and somebody hurt you, the law would help ya and I believe that and I believed that a white man would jump at the chance to put a nigger in jail, so that is why I went to the white Sheriff. But no Ms. Lula, that is not what the law man did. He looked at me and told me to go into the back room he was going to get a lady to come in and talk to me and look at me to see the damage. I went in that room ready to put daddy in jail. But instead of getting some help he looked at me and said "You must be runt down there by now if your daddy been breaking you in. I don't want none of that." So he locked the door and pulled his gun out on the table where I could see if. He said "Na I am go have to teach you a lesson about telling a man's business in his house. And if you bite me I go hite you in the head with this pistol." All I could thank of is when did white men see black men as men. Then he put his privates in my mouth and he gagged me over and over and over until I started throwing up. I am glad I did to cause it went all over his shoes and pants and it sure did stank. When I begin to shake and cry he punched me in the nose and blood just went everywhere look like he had broke in a new lamb. We all knowed about how some of them men liked lambs cause they just like a woman. Din he kicked me in the back of my head, Ms. Lula onto the dirt street and told me if I told anybody he would kill us all. Don't know who I was go tell it to, but I almost told anyway, especially if it meant I could get daddy killed. I stayed quite a long time Ms. Lula. I stopped talking cause talking only made things worst for me. I use to sit alone a lot under the house or find me a hollow tree. People could not hear me cryin down there. See I had a lot reasons to cry Ms. Lula. Most people thank I don't care about what I am or who deh say I am but I do, I do. I don't have rest at night cause I am usually waitin for the Devil to come and get me. Cause all yall say I am a demon. I don't know if I am a demon but I do know I will never be a women who wants a man. If that is what makes me a demon then I am. One time I was down by river and I found this cave right near the bank. It was all sandy like a beach or something, so I went into it just exploring it. It went a long ways under the ground. I was happy I thought I had found my way out of this hellafide life God choose to give me. Then I realized I was headed straight to hell, I expected to see the Devil himself pretty soon so I was tensin up for a fight. He one ass I wanted to kick and since I could not get to heaven to fight God, the Devil would do. Hell both seem to be one in the same to me; did not matter which one I served I got hurt. Was not no Devil down there; instead I ended up staring an alligator right in the face. Shit you know what that meant? I was bout to be his dinner. That was scarry enough but when my eyes could see parts of human bodies, I peed on myself. I held my breath Ms. Lula, I held my breath and I eased all the way back out of that cave. That is the only time I recollect that God was looking out for me and that is the only time I recall ever saying thank you God. Cause I don't owe God thanks for nothing eles in my life. If heaven ain't so, hell is on Earth. From what I see heaven on earth for white folk and hell is on earth for black folk. Girls white or black aint safe, so dis here God gots to be a white man who hates women. I looked at her and said "Girl don't you blaspheme on my porche, been enough of that done here dis morning." Corse she ain't know what I was talkin about, but me and the Lawd did. See I know that the Lawd go forgive me cause I am in his mind I talks to him. But I ain't show if he go forgive me ifin I let a heathen curse him on my porch. She had to quite that she done already decided which way she gonna go. The Lawd can change anything ifin he want to, right God. I am thankin if I gits to come back here on Earth, I wants to be a white woman with long red curly hair. I always loved that red hair. Go have me a bunch of servants I hope deh is every white person I ever met in life and I hope deh is black as the tar I am go feather deh ass with. Amen.

Two years passed after my problem with the Sheriff and one day my mother came in screaming like the devil himself had attached her. Old Mr. Dison had fell with a condition, it made his body sick on one side so he could not move he could not talk. That nigger had had a stroke. I said right then maybe God is real and maybe God did answer my prayers. I looked at him laying there eyes looking at the ceiling not wanting to look at me cause that bastard know I am smiling at his old ass. I am thinkin to myself dis go be one man I go enjoy fuckin. My mother would have to leave me with him to watch and care for him while she did her day work. See, sometimes the people who you treat the worst be the ones have to clean your shit. First day she left me I just stared at him, walked around him and slapped his face over and over, thinking about how the sheriff put his self in my mouth. I slapped the shit out of him. His eyes all wide and teary, looking like he dun seen the devil himself. Well he was seeing the devil, it was the devil he created. It was me, I am his devil. A devil is one or two things something you scared off or something you did dirt to first. See we all is devils Ms. Lula we just thank we not. I took a tree limb, a little one and I forced it in his backside, Yes, Ms. Lula I did that, like he forced his self in me. I shoved it and shoved it until I saw blood. Then I looked in his face and I said to him " God did not kill you cause he was leaving you for me.I am go kill you Daddy Dison." that is what I would say to him. I go kill ya Daddy. It was the look, the look in his eyes that almost made me stop. So I stopped looking in his got damn eyes. I went snake hunting one day and turned over a log full of baby snakes, gathered em up and put em in his mouth one by one. I don't thank he could feel em goin down his throat, though. I don't know if deh did him anything or not, but I liked putting then snakes in his mouth, liked seeing him tryin to keep his mouth shut. I hated my mother and I hated my father and I hated God all three of them did nothing but hurt me over and over again. God still was hurting me cause he letting me hurt him. Well anyway one day my mother came home early and she caught me doing some low down dirty shit. I was using his old ass as target practice with my sling shot, yes I was , he could not move so he was a good target. My mother beat me and beat me and beat until I had a bowel movement on myself. The only reason I took it was because I did not want to hit her back and I deserved it some kind of way. Then that bitch had uncle Buck hang me from the ceiling over that shit until my nose bleed like a river. One day she go be next. I don't want her to die yet. I want her to age then I am go come back when she can't help herself and fuck her up. If there is a God he go give me that pleasure. She so lowdown, hell would rather her go to heaven.

That old bitch sent me to live with Uncle Willie and his family for a while. Every body was talking about her doing that casue they knew she needed help. So people was wondering why she sent me away. Did not have to worry about her telling what was going on cause she was to proud. Well anyway, I thought I had landed in heaven, when I first got to Uncle Willie's house . They went to church every Sunday, their family was well respected,in the community. Uncle Willie was the head deacon and Ms. Albertha his wife, was the church cook and as gentle a woman as you could ever want to know. They believed in populating the earth though cause they had 12 children. All of them worked hard and all was as well mannered as any child you could ever want to know. Lord, the cooking the cooking was incredible and they always had a big fat chocolate cake or some kind of sweet treat; not just on Sunday but on every day. Every day yall, Ms. Albertha had cake, or peach cobbler, black berry cobbler, or peaches and dumplings or black berries and dumplings you name the sweet she made it. Oh, and the coconut cake, nobody not even you can beat that Ms. Lula. Well she don't know a got damn thang about my coconut cake. I aint' never entered it in a contest but if I did I bet I would win it. Aint but one other person give me any competition bakin and that is Sally's whites girl Lu Bertha Williams. Believe me baby if I wanted to I could have the ribbon for best got damn coconut cake in these parts, maybe is the United States. I been blessed with a gift for cookin. Huh, you gots to go hard to beats me baby, and at your best you ain't go beat me but you can be proud if you tied up with me. (Ms. Lula Mae sucking her teeth na ready start some baking later on). Ms. Lula, Ms. Lula, what is wrong looked like you is taking a spell. Are you alright? "I am find girl what else was you sayin na."

OoooWeeee, I said, na there is a God, and he just might have started liking me, cause I have landed in heaven. I should have known this was too go to be true. Well Ms. Lula one day Uncle Willie was going fishing and I asked could I go. My cousins was shaking their heads something fierce, like no you do not want to go. Especially the older girl Anna Marie she was like come with me Buelah. I am going to a quilting circle, you will like that, we all pull out our patterns and colors and go to work. Well she ain't know me I hated anything to do with sewing. I use to help my mammy make my dresses and she would always make me a new dress when Daddy Dison had took me. Didn't yall ladies use to always talk about how I was the best dressed girl in town? And yall know what people come to think of it we sure did. Sho always wore some of the prettiest dresses you ever wanted to see, every since she was a litte bitty girl. I guess yall know I got three angels speaking to me and third one good, one bad and the third ones' name is shame. I am feelin pretty shame now just listenin to this child tell her story. So anyway Ms. Lula, I said no, "I love to fish so I am going to go fish." I loved fishing Ms. Lula, ain't nothing like catching one of those big old bull brim, that take the sanker right down to the botton of the water ifin he can. Nothing feels better than pullin and tuggin that big bastard to the bank. She right too, I love a good fish fight. That girl better stop my pole stay ready.

Everybody standing there looking but not saying nothing, then all of a sudden Ms. Albertha, say, "Willie, you best behave or I promise ya the Lawd go take vengeance." I started not to go, but I figure she must have been talking about something personal between them. I figure they was shaking their heads no, because most young folk did not want to go fishing in their spare time cuase most times you had to fish to eat. What they did not know is I loved to fish, more than I love to eat em. Well while I am walking to the pond with Uncle Willie, I just started talking rattling on about the dirt my daddy had done me. Then I told him what happened when I told the Sheriff. He stopped in his tracks and said "Girl, don't you know better than to tell a mans' business out of his house. Aint nobody ever told you that you not suppose to tell the law no matter what go on in your house. Seems to me you got some demons of lust following you around here gal." My heart dropped, here I am scared, mad, in another hopeless situation that I cannot do a thang about. I just realized I hate God, got damnit I hate him. I knew I was in trouble Ms. Lula Mae cause as he was talking to me his face changed. He looked like the devil, the same look I saw in my daddy and the sheriffs' eyes. I did not see that good God fearing man anymore. I saw that look of sickness, the look that meant everything he was about to do to me was right in his mind. Dis time I hope I die, I hope I die to hell. Fuck, heaven it might be some men there, so fuck heaven. Then he pulled me close to him and said "Na you go do to me what you did to that white man you little hot trollep." See, tears they don't mean nothing to a devil, the devil likes tears and they don't move God either, cause my eyes stay full of em. Yeah, I was cryin, crying cause I knew it was about to hurt. I knew no angels was go come for me, I knew no Jesus was go get off the cross and fight for me. I knew no law was go punish this man and I knew I was just a nobody who splipped threw the cracks in heaven and fell to an unforgiving Earth. I knew this time I was go die, cause I wanted too. I was thinking in my mind, "Dear God that hate my soul, please kill me now, curse my bones so that I will never grow old. Please, please kill me now, before the pain starts. Take back your breath of life, crush my heart and burn my soul so that I never come to Earth again. That was the end of the world as I knew it . That was the final death for me Ms. Lula. He was standing there about to put his self in my mouth. I swear, seems like all my guts came up at once and I threw up blood. When he jumped back something strange happened, the tree branch he was holding on to broke into. He tripped and hit his head on one of them bald cypress tree lungs. He hit it hard Ms. Lula, blood was everywhere and he was laying there kinda shanking and moaning. Trying to talk. I looked at him and says "What Uncle Willie you tryin to ask for forgiveness. God aint and I can't forgive nobody. Seem like he was tryin to get me to pitty him. Na this part here Ms. Lula is where yall church going Christians calls me a heathen. I tried Ms. Lula, God knows I tried not to do evil. I tried not to do what I did. With all of my strength I pulled the rest of that big branch down on top of that muthu fucker, until his head was all the way under water. I watched as his eyes bulged out then he just stared at me like I was the only person he could see. Then I left running back, like the devil and all his angels was on my heels. Aww, the feeling, the feeling, I had was so good and so right, yes all my insides was alive. No pain for me, no pain for me, no hurt, then I remembered that necklace the old obai woman gave me for raking up her yard. Shit it worked, she said I was not go be harmed no mo, it worked. It worked. I was sure that he was dead; yes I killed him. Well I did not really kill em the coonde raun killed him , the power of the obay. I was out of breath when I got back screaming and crying telling Ms. Albertha what had happened in part. Told her I could not get him to move, maybe she and the children should go and try to see if they could get him out. Ms. Albertha turned around looked a little sad but not like she was go die without him. She said honey child by the time we get back your uncle Willie be gone on over to see Jesus. I am sending the boys to get the undertaker. All of a sudden Ms. Albertha starts to sing this song sorta goes like this " Oh, sweet and powerful lawd, dis earth we come and do your will, one day you will call us back in your bossom. We toil and toil, silently moaning and cryin for freedom. Beggin you good lawd to come save us and our children. We pray and pray seeking your favor, to help us lawd as we sojourn in the place full of hard times unpaid labor. Singing sweet bye and bye till the morning come and one day you sends your angels our way. Mr. Willie done gone to meet Gabriel and Michael at the crossroads of life. A church going man doing the best he can din meet Gabriel and Micheal in the holy land. Now Mr. Willie will rest in peace in the Lawds righteous hands. Never to return to this blessed and cursed land." Like I said she did not seem like she was hurt at all. Ms. Lula, what I am really trying to say is that it seemed like she was relieved. Seem like this was something she wanted for a long time. Maybe, that necklace was not what worked, maybe prayers like the one she just sang is what worked. But, I don't care something worked. If God tryin to get in my good graces, He done let to many things happen to me na. It is go take a walk on the water miracle or raise the dead miracle to win me over. Scratch that raise the dead, he might raize up that bastard Mr. Willie.

Even though I knew Ms. Albertha seemed like she did not care I felt it be best for me to get the hell out of there. I left walking back home, but before I could get three miles down the road, here comes Ms. Albertha and her girls. They surprised the hell out of me cause, as far as I was concerned I was go be hitchin rides, walking and running right back to Friendly and they was go hate me cause they might figure I killed Mr. Willie. Ms. Albertha took me all the way back to my mother's house, and gave me a coin purse full of silver and gold. She smiled at me and said, "I guess the Lawd was just looking out for you child, like he was looking our for me and my children. Tell people round here we go be selling our spread. We moving to a place called Chicago; A big city with big city ideas. No lynchings I hear, good jobs, lots of eligible educated men, you might want to think about going with us we got plenty of room." Everything looked like it was turning out for my good. Except my mother would not have me back home. When she opened the door and saw me, she called me a dark cloud from hell. I figure that the ony reason my mother had me was becaue she could not get rid of me anyway. It was said she had got rid of several children cause she ain't want to be no mother. Here I am no home, no hope and no love. But I did have a good bit of money, fifty dollars exact. I put it in my shoes for safe keeping. I realized mens tear off your dress and your drawers but they never take off your shoes. Just in case I got in a bad situation again, did not want them to get my money. I went all over town trying to get work, nobody needed help. All I got was no or we don't need no empty wagons around here takin all our business. Hard enough for a black to find work and especially for a girl who goes around talking, about the low down thangs been done to her. I needed work, because I could not let anybody know I had money, cause they would take it, plus it is the inheritance for my children, if I ever have any. Here I was with money, I had no were to live and could not spend it even if I wanted to. Well I soon realized that even the devil had a heart. My mammy who could not offer me a place to stay, got me a job with Ms. Rose Deluche'. This is low downest woman that ever lived on earth, but she took me in. I was her slave, but it was better that what I was use to. She never beat me, she never raped me, she never paid much attention to me at all. She just referred to me as her pet like her cat or dog. She never paid me either. She said I could not afford to pay her rent to live in such a fine place, so she just charged me my wages to live there and take care of here ass. She had so much money she never missed how well I paid myself. Plus, she drank so much she was never sober enough to care. One thang she saw to is me reading and writing, she said "I don't won't no ignorant niggar doin my business, to easy for you to steal and say it was a mistake." So that woman taught me every night until she was sure I understood.

Every body know about her demons. I would drank to if I were her. After about a month or so proving my loyalty Ms. Rose, gave me town privelges. She started sending me to do all the shopping. She was starting to look real bad these days. I could have felt sorry for her, but she was damn evil sometimes. One time she looked at me and said "Beulah it must be hard being you, a pretty little nigger not fit to do nothing but clean white folks shit. Must be hard being born to serve. I doubt ifin anybody ever prayed to heaven and asked the good Lord to make them a Nigger." Then she said "Why am I trying to have an intelligent conversation with you, you probably do not understand civilized conversation." "Then she just laughed, I would laughed too, because she must have forgot she was teachin me the white folks way. But what this woman did not know was, I was living better with her than what I had ever lived in my life. Hard work never bothered me. So cleaning house, cooking, washing, working the garden was something I found pleasure in doing. Plus, nobody was beating me, or throwing me down ravaishing me or whispering about me being a demon. Ms. Rose aint know I was go do every thing I could to keep her living well. She ate the best, I used everything I saw Ms Albertha do. She put everything in her pots; sage, rosemary, basil, green onions, bellpeppers, garlics, thyme, lavender, lemon grass and a melody of other herbs in her food; that is what made her food different. You could throw a bull after eating one of her meals. Well anyway I was cooking for her like this cuase I did not want nothing to happen to her. I use to love giving her a bath though, she had a nice body. She stayed small, cuase she never ate a lot. She had a real nice body. I would bath her with rose soap and lavender water. Then I would dry her off gentle, brush her hair, oil her feet , get her tonic and make her a little sour salad. I calls it sour salad cause she liked them bitter dandelion greens, lemons, and vinegar water on it. I only tasted that once, see that was her doin not mine. I just fixed it like she wanted it. Sometimes that man would come around. He lived way off in a place called France. He would show up bought twice a year, come stay with her for about a week and leave. He was nice to me too. One time he gave me a real box of chocolate from France. I ate and ate and ate until I was plum sick. I still got the pretty box. I had a strange feeling for this woman, the more I took care of her the more I wanted to take care of her."

"I was in town at the general store and saw my mother on day Ms. Lula. She looked at me and for a moment my heart became soft. Then she gave me a look that only an enemy could truly give someone they really hate." She said "Poor Albertha is alone with all of those children now to raise." " A lump came in my throat. I begin to sweat and my heart was pumping so hard I thought I was going to die right then and there. Cause for some reason, I just knew what was next. But to my surprise, she said a group of KKK caught poor Willie down by the river and beat him to death and left him by the bayou dead. Say he had wondered off on the wrong side of the property line; over by them Rasues place. Yes lawd, they killed your Uncle Willie, a good Christian man and left the likes of you still here. God go take vengeance on the Rasues." "I looked at my piss po excuse of a mother and started laughing and I laughed and I laughed and I laughed until I could not stand it any more. Maybe that is the reason I got that 50.00 dollars. I never did understand that. But it was 50.00 dollars, that is my life saving now, my inheritance, my future, I ain't go never have nothing less than 50.00 Miss Lula. Anyway, that day was the only day I saw my mother show any concern for me. Cause I continued to laugh, with tears rolling down my eyes, I laughed." She looked at me and said "What in God's name has the devil done to you child?" I said, "Whether it be the devil or God at least one of yall is dead. Cause if I had my way you and daddy would be with Uncle Willie right now mama." "That was the last time I spoke to my mother. Next time I see her or daddy I want to be looking down on them in they last bed on earth. That's right I want to be looking down on em the next time I have to see one of em." "Child, that is not nice,watch yourself you might leave before them for saying thangs like that." "I do not care Ms. Lule I got my business fixed, I am go be burned like a piece of wood. Aint' a man or woman on this earth go git to look down on me when I die." Well, I don't know why it bothered me when she said she was go be burned like a piece of wood, cause I had figured she was go burn in hell anyway. I guess it bothered me cause most folk don't want to have anything to do with burning and death. That usually meant you was in hell. But come to thank of it that might not be such a bad idea. Who want a bunch nosey niggars and evil crackers lookin down on em. She ain't go have to worry about the white folk they just go be glad she gone sos they can get the land back.

"Like I said Ms. Lula men do not know how to love a woman, at least none of the men I ever meet did. Daddy loved mama so he beat her, he love me so he raped me, Uncle Willie, well Uncle Willie seemed like he loved me cause he was so kind. But the first chance he got, he tried to hurt me too. The law, well I will never trust the law again, the law is a lie. Plus, I should have known a law made by white people was not for colored people. You don't make laws to protect your animals Ms. Lula. Oh by the way, I did not give up on men Ms. Lule. I never felt nothing for a man, boys always did sniff up behind me, I aint never wanted none of them.

I would have been this way if a man had not took me and did harm to me. Ofcourse them taking me made me hate them all the more though. I never wanted a man Ms. Lula, never. So after all the things they did to me, I deciede men don't know how to love a woman and I know what a woman really needs. I ain't go ever give a man a chance to hurt me ever again. First of all I ain't go trust em. Second of all I carries this nice little darenger, it don't' miss. See Ms. Lula I will never put myself in a position to get hurt by a man again. And you know it is a known fact in these parts that if I get a bead on ya, you shot. Plus Ms. Lula I fines that women appreciate a gentle touch, a sweet word, a compliment and a listenin ear, so I ain't shame of what I am. I am mostly shame of people that look at me and think I am some sort of demon or devil. People who don't see my spotless house, my fine garden, my charity work with the children, or my help with the homeless people down the track. No, Ms. Lula the people here they don't see none of that. Just a devil filled demon, strange and different from them or revealing a part of them they think might exist. I got no regrets and ifin a man could come along that I could ever trust I'll be his friend; but my lovers will always be women. I tried not to be like I am, I tried, and sometimes I wonder why the good Lord made me like this. Then, I thank maybe He just like a lot of different kinds of folk, ifin he made me and I am in His image like the Preacher say, what does that mean Ms. Lula Ma? What does that mean? You thank He mean and hateful just making people different so other people can have someone to mistreat? What you thank on that Ms. Lula? I don't know Ms. Lula a lot of things I done heard about God aint' true. I hear people say God will hold your hand, my hand always been empty when I am in trouble. I hear people say God will heal your broken heart my heart aint never been fixed, plus I came here with a broken heart. I hear people say God will take care of your enemies. Exceptin for one that got kilt by accident all my enemies still livin and since God is suppose to be a man Ms. Lula I understand why I always got fucked most of the time. I aint trying to be hateful or disrespectfull Ms. Lula but I am as confused about all this as yall is about me. So Ms. Lula I am just gonna keep makin women feel good and wanted, like I want to be treated . Does that answer all your question about me. Get it right cause I know you will be tellin all your friends about this here piece of news first chance you git. Tell em this too, if God created me like I am to condemn me he is as evil as the Devil.

CHAPTER 9

Prayin for the redemption of Beulah

WELL I GUESS YALL know I just hung my head down, I could net even look up. I never heard nothing so sad in all my days. Beulah just like all the rest of us, trying to find her way in this here big old world, searchin for this thing we call love. Poor child just told me she searching for something she don't believe in. See I guess she think love exist like some Santa Claus or something she is waiting for a big gift that just drops at your door. Well I can tell you that aint true cause if God was go be droppin gifts of love at anybodies door it would be mine. What that girl needs to know is that you have to work to be loved and you have to work even harder to love somebody. I could have started my speech on how love is real, and how God loved us so much he gave his only Son and all, but none of that seemed like it would have made any difference. I did not say another word. She told me about myself rigth to my face, cause God knows I believed she had a demon in her and I still do. But now I realize she don't know it, so I am willin to try to help her out. See, I knew something good had to come out of this. She just don't know that if a good enough man came along she would never look at another woman. I smiled on the inside, cause this poor wounded girl was just like the rest of us. Scared of being raped, either our brothers, uncles, daddys, all step daddys, sheriff, mayor, store owner, drunk low red neck up the road, we just got fucked by everybody just like Beulah said. Oww Lord forgive me for using fucked, but there are no other words that would describe the burden you have given us women. I am starting to believe you just might be white and don't like women to much, cause I know them white ladies life anit all that pretty, yes sir, I know. Beulah sat there for a minute or so, then she just got up and left without saying a word. I sat there swingin on my porch trying to hold back the river of tears that was flowing down my face from the story I had just heard from a injured little girl in a women's body. See I believe she never had a chance to grow up so she just stayed like she was, a hurt little girl running around looking for some help and hopin for some love.

I know all of what happened to her was terrible but this girl still ain't countin her blessings. She was blessed in the mist of all that trouble. We all know that Ms. Rose Delauche left her money, no body know how much money cause Ms. Delauche took it all out the bank and kept it at home. This girl gets to live on prime white folk land all the days of her life; corse na when she die the city go take the property. Reason being is because Rose did not leave it to Beulah legal; but as long as she live she can live there. See not all the whites is terrible till the day they die some do some good thangs. I don't know why but they do sometimes. I remember the Jonsaques, some of the riches plantation owners in the south. You would have thought they was the low downiest too but they wasn't. Slaves did not get beat there, you got to stay with you family and you buy your freedom from em. Oh yes they was a strange group for down here. I don't remember the older ones cause I was not born yet but deh is a legend of goodness for blacks. The younger ones grew up and started farming and huntin and anybody who wanted to stay with them got paid fair wages and had they own real house. A house not a niggar shack. The story goes like this, the Lawd sent the yellow fever plague down here and it was killing people every where. Most places did not allow deh blacks to take the medicine but them Jonsaques, gave all they servants some and here tell they did not lose a lot of them either. That is not the half of it. All they servants had birth papers, married papers, baptisment papers and they tell me that deh let them have books to read. Na people don't talk much about them teaching negros to read, cause that was against the law. See not all of em do bad thangs. But so many of em is so low down til you forget about people like them Jonsaques. Dem some fine men too. I remember I was swimming at the creek on one of them hot summer days. Anybody down here know ain't nothing better than finding one of them little creeks with a sandy bank to take a dip in. Feels good wading in the water and finding a deep spot for swimming. I had took me a horse ride, on one of them early summer mornings, when sun woke up with the dew. Had me a little tonic in my canteen, some cold fried chicken, figs, ho cake and some fresh honey. Everything I needed to get me through the day. It was a sweet essence in the air, little flakes of white flowers fallin from the trees, grass still wet and the sun just bearly heated enough to warm your hands. It felt good to be alive. Old Sadie was thirsty so I took to her to the creek to get a cool drink. She drank, I drank, aint nothing like some sweet creek water. Sand was still kinda wet though, I like that so I can see where old low shoulders been slidin around. Old Sadie sorta laid out and wallowed and muddy up the water, when she was finished I tied her to tree stump on the bank. Then I put my blanket out and rolled up my pants legs and cooled off my feet some more. It felt so good I got down to my under clothes child found me a deep hole and jumped in. Surprise the water was warm like it had been heatin all night. Next thang I know I felt this hand on my back it was Frank Jonsaques. He turned me towards him and he had an evil look in his eyes. I knew right then that I was go be in trouble if I tried to swim off. He kissed me right off and I mean he kissed me, like he wanted to. He smelled like the creek and his arms was full of man strength I could not believe what happened next. I kissed him back, as if it was not a world of hate separating our kind as if we had the right to do what we was doing. I kissed him back for everytime I did not want to kiss back. I kissed that man until I was drunk. He took his hand and gently touched me, he touched me like he needed to touch me. He touched me like he had been wanting to touch me all my life and I felt alive in his arms. I burned, hotter than a heated brandin iron. I burned for this man. Every part of me was shakin, like I had just met the love of my life. When he laid me back on my blanket he looked at me with those deep green eyes and I lost my breath. I lost my got damn breath, because he kissed my stomach, and looked at me, then he kissed my breast and he looked at me, he kissed every part of my body and he looked at me. I never since had a man look at me so much. I never felt this way exceptin for, well lets forget about him. Some people might figure I should be ashamed, but I can't see how. I can't see how such a moment could be bad. I laid for hours with this man, creamin in his arms and drunk with his every touch. We lay, we eat, we drink and we roll into each others arms and hold on for dear life. When we let each go we felt as if we done pulled something out of each other. The second time in my life I ever tasted a man so sweet. The first time in my life I did not care what I was doing. The first time in my life I ever exploded so hard. Just thinking about him gives me good feelin in my bones. It was like we both knew we would never touch each other again so we held on to the moment we was having. He needed me and I needed him and that is all it was that day. We met each others needs. Well you know what; I gots to go. Memories are just that memories, you use em when you need something to make you feel good. You only use the bad ones when you need a good excuse to be mad.

Well goodnight yall, I think I am gonna turn in now. I think I have heard enough for this day. "Na good Lord it is me Lula Mae Carson, a gossip, sometimes a foul mouth woman, a fornicator to Lawd, cause you said we all sin but I am truly your child. Sometimes I lust Lawd, but for the most part I try Lawd I try. So I am coming now to ask you if you would touch Beulah and heal her heart, first, from all the evils been done to her. Keep her safe for the rest of her life and forgive me. Forgive me Lawd, no Lawd forgive all of us for how we have judged and talked about her behind her back. She need our prayers Lawd she don't know she have a problem , help me to pray for her relief. I would ask you to help me to keep my big mouth shut, but Lawd you know I have to get all the facts right and made for this purpose. It is my duty to set them gossiping hypocritical church ho's straight. I have to let them know the truth so they can stop all that low down talk about this poor child. Once I finish with them she won't have to worry. Ifin I hear anything from her after I talk to them, she go have some of their secrets to tell. I bet none of em would want her to know some of their business. Especially, the latest one with aww one of the church ladies giving pleasure to 13 year old boy. Yeah, child we got some problems in the holy land. Goodnight and tell Gabriel when your children call him he needs to get them six wings a flyin quick. Seem like he slow handling black folk business. No unless you got a angel special designed for us with one wing and prayer, we be expectin Gabriel to get to us just as fast as he got to them Hebrews. Oh by the way I meant to tell yall that the Jonsaques was suppose to be Jewish people, but they changed their names so they would be safe here in the South. Guess they did not want old Pharaoh and the Klan comin for them again.

Chapter 10

I found me some books to read

Ummmmmmm, umm um um m nothing like the smell of a early spring morning, seems like you can smell perfume from heaven. The sweet honey suckles, oh my, the aroma of my roses, sweet magnolias , and pine all mixed up at once, oh, lets not forget the lemon grass, oh yes , the lemongrass it was heavenly. See yall, all these nice smells go all through my house every morning when the spring givin birth. Plus, I always keeps me some lemongrass planted, it is good for ya. It keeps away snakes. The old folks say it is a good drawer of strength and spiritual powers, honest to God and some say it is pretty good for lust. I know one thing it is good for the stomach ace, and the flying gas, shoot you can even make a paste out of it and rub it anywhere you got an ache and it will work on it. Yes, Ms. Lula Mae love her some lemongrass. I got me some more plants, planted in my back garden, rosemary, sage, basil, lavender, thyme, nice sassfrace tree, good yucca, (old Indian lady told me bout the yucca plant. Deh call it the God plant. She say Little Bird it is good for washin your clothes and hair and it keeps the rumtism away. She calls me Little Bird cause she say I eats like one.) Keeps me some morning glories too, cause I harvest the roots. Lawd I can't keep em people be runnin over here paying high as 5.00 for one root, especially when they can't get them John The Conquer Roots. Ms. Lula, ain't sick to often yall cause I got all the medicine I need growin in my yard. I got some other plants growin too, but I ain't go tell yall all my business. Just every naw and then I might share some thangs, but you aint' go ever know all my business. See all my business ain't all the business you need to know.

Well I have started reading these books. Oh, ain't nobody wanting us to be reading still and they ain't making it easy for us to learn. When we was getting books for our school house, it took us two years to get them delivered. We had to teach our children out of one book for two years, so them white folk thought. We was stealing they books from they house and using them in our school. Shol was child. We was stealing any book we could and the teacher was teaching words from em. We even would get their newpaper too, sos our children would know the latest white folk news.. We always brought them books back. Most white folk don't pay any attention to us as long as deh can look up and see us smilin. See deh thank when we smiling we is thankin on the goodness of the Lawd, we actually be thinkin bout how good it would feel to stomp deh ass. We would have all died for stealing them books and we would certainly died ifin deh could read our minds. But that is another story.

Na these books I got ain't stole; how I got these books I am reading is because they was throwing them away. So I sneaked em out of the garbage. I am liking some of the stories, but who knows what is real in these here books. White folks is such big liars and all, and since they wrote most of this I am reading, it ain't probably nothing but some white folk lies. You know they put lies in books, shucks, like putting in the good book, a slave ought to love his master. Slaves should have been trying every chance to kill master. We all knows that is a lie anyway. It is all we can do to love the white folk right here in Friendly. The truth is we ain't lovin em. If in any of these sons of a bitches would have the power to have us on they farms right na, putting a whip on our ass they would . Truth is they do keep us in line, tell us where to live, have us clean their houses, and steal back most of the money they pay us. The more I think about this situation, the more unfavorable God is seeming to me. The one thang that save the Lawd is that I know white folk will change anything they want, casue they can. So, I pretty much know the Lawd did not tell them that.They made that up to justiy them having slaves and to keep them slaves in order. They also did it to keep us from taking vengeance for how bad they treated us, so deh put that in the good book of the Lawd to keep us from killing them. See, as hard as a a black person's life is here on dis here earth, them canivin white folk know we do not want to miss heaven's goodness and go to hell. Cause after this place we go need a heaven. And I really do hope there is two heavens one for them and one for us. We is tried of cookin and cleanin for them folks. Deh put that love your Master in the good book so they could sleep comfortable at night knowing we not go bust they heads in deh sleep, but if they get to treating us any worse, they ain't go be here no more. Deh just ain't go be no more, we is gettin pretty tired, pretty tired of all this mistreatin. Oh, they smart na, I done figured that. You got to be smart to have the power they have and they have the power. But, we done figured out a long time ago that some of these things they tell us is what God say, we knows it is what deh say, cause they think deh God anyway. See the white man he thank he God believe me he do you can't act like they do and do the thangs they do and not thank you is God. Enough about these white folks and their lies I am just wanting to thank God for this moment right now. I just wanted yall to know I got these books, cause they had throwed them away and nobody saw me get them either. Like I said they know we is educatin our selves and they know we can read, but deh sho ain't trying to help us learn more than them.

Yall, fancy dis, you live in a place where you just a person. You protected and every thing that is done to you is fair. Sounds like heaven don't it. This place is reserved for white people only, for you will find no black people there. With constant pleas and lowly hearts we begg and bicker and tear each other a part. What master did not do with whips and chains , he took our nature and changed our names. I cry in the morning and I cry at night. I cry cause we ain't got no heavenly weapons to help us win dis here fight. I cry cause I am helpless and small and not counted as human. I cry cause I don't know what we did to make God so mad as us till he let us be treated so bad. I cry cause my tears is the only thang that washes away the stains that are in my heart for a moment. I cry cause I am women and that makes me even less. I cry cause ifin I don't these white folk go hang me for sho. I am not one of them great speakers or anythang, but I have words that come to me like this. I kinda keep that do my self. If you tell people you hear words you either a witch or crazy and I aint' either one. But one thang I am is a human with feelins and hopes and dreams and one day I will be free. I will be free to speak my mind and live in peace. Nuff said about that. I am ready to live.

You know I woke up thinkin different than I thought last night. I woke up with a new understanding. Getting a new understanding about thangs you was wrong about feels good sometimes. I am woke up prayin for Beulah, I mean it, as soon as my eyes opened all I could do was say "Lord have mercy on that hurt little girl in a woman's body. Please sir Jesus look out for her and help her with her change." When the Lawd put it right in your face and make you have to swallow back your words and thoughts you done had about someone. You will wake up too with that person or thang on your mind too. Seems like I been doin worst than them holy whores at the church. But yall have to understand how strange a woman she seemed to me. I knowed about womens on womens but Beulah the first one I have been real close to. I did not know what to thank, plus somewhere in the Bible it teaches you to hate folk like her. That should have been the first thang should tipped me off that something was wrong though; cause the Bible also teaches that I ought to love people who hurt me. And just like I said to hell with that I should have said to hell with treatin this child like she got the poxs. I can admit when I am wrong; plus I guess what she doin aint so bad. I lady finger myself all the time and I am sure that is all she could be doin too. Sometimes if you just talk to a person you can save yourself a world of guilt. Well all of it can't be blamed on me cause she ain't never gave us no explanation until now why she is the way she is. Lord I love my kitchen. I love my house and I need you to help me to love the white folk here in Friendly more truly, rather than just smiling at dem demon son a bitches like I really care. Ifin you want us to be truthful and faithful you have to do the same for us you doin for dem white folks. I am tried of tryin to cross Jordan with out a life raft. You know my heart and you know that if they gave me any reason to love em true I would. I got to tell you the only ones of em I ever feel sorry for is the women. The mens got to damn much power for pity. But, I am trying Lord, I am tryin to Love em likes you love em. I am bein obedient to your will and askin you for help so if I don't change it must be our will. If you do not make it be so then it will not be so, but I am beggin like a good Christian is suppose to do, Amen.

Please help me Lord cause I is just a traveler in land not meant for me, so please see me through to the other side the right way. Amen.

One thing I can say is there aint a house in Friendly , have a kitchen as beautiful as mine. Even the white women have to admit it. See I hand painted my walls and so I had time to decorate them with crasanthromoms, roses, and magnolias on them, not another kitchen like it. Them flowers looks so real you want to smell them. Oh honey child my kitchen is so neat and organized everything in it is nice, and you know that it is because I keeps it that way. See I love how easy it is for me to go straight to everythin and get what I need to make me a fine breakfast. My jellies on the second shelf, my cane suryp on the counter, my flour in the ben next to my brand new ice box, (oh I did tell yall I had been so blessed to have bought me an ice box. Got three of us black women here in Friendly with one na; the Good Reverands wife, and ofcourse that old snooty French women Ms Louise Lebouf (with her stuck up half white ass). She even got them white folk confused, god knows you can not see no blackness in that woman. Her eyes blue as the sky, her hair blonde, her ass flat, her breast big, and her got damn nose turned up. Just like them stuck up mulattos. I put my table right in the middle of my kitchen so I can place everything on it just right. And my flower sack apron hanging over my washing counter, everything to my liken . A smart woman knows how to make nice aprons from flour sacks. All my life has been pretty much straight based on my color condition, can't remember when I ever really had any big situations not common to black women. See we have it broke down, we have our regular problems we know we go have at some times, like rape, beatins and bein kept in a low place. Then there are those problems that just come from no where; like Puddin. But mostly my problems comes with not saying the truth to these white folk. See I know God is judging me harsh, cause he hate a liar. But they want you to lie to them like it is the truth. They like hiding the truth right in front of your face. And I am one hell of a got damn liar when it comes to dem, gots to be. You can't tell a man holdin your life in his hand that you know he ain't worth a shit. While he telling you, you is free and you know it aint so, even the govberment is in on that lie. They be doin thangs right in front of your face na, and tellin you de whole time they is doin something else. Like gettin ya to work deh land and makin you thank deh go be payin you fair. Frank Henry worked old man Amos

McCoy's land for seven years and when he thought he had earned the right to have it in his hands. McCoy told him it was for his own good that he keep the land in his name for a while sos the Klan wouldn't take it. Well he made him work another seven for protectin him from the Klan which was him. One thang about these white folk they knows how to keep each other lies, meanin they tries not to let the real bad business go beyond deh own hears. I laughs at that; I ain't never seen a black woman with little ears. They all the right size for listnin to everythan pass deh way. And sometimes deh trys to make you not see what is right in front of your face, like Mr. Philmore Davis for instance.

Let me tell yall bout Mr. Philmore Davis. He was from a long line of plantation owners, like everybody else in the south who was not black. He keep every part of the land his daddy left him. He almost had built his own little town. Na look a here, he ain't have nothing on that place but mens. All kinds of mens, but not one women. Na us good towns people say he is doing the work of the Lawd, giving men a place to come and worship without the temptations of a woman, helping them get started over when they come home from prison and the army. Most colored people around here aint dumb as some people thank. If he was doing the work of the Lord so much, then why I done personally sold goods to women who looked like painted jezebels coming in and out of that place. Na, don't try to confuse me na, I said no women lived there, I did not say they did not come there. Child some of em had on so much pancake powder you could cut it with a knife. A few of them woman was so big I know deh had to get they dresses special made. Some of them heifers had hands like wood cutters too. Every summer Mr. Phil would go off to Paris and every fall he came home with a new so called friend. You know the food was not good, on that place, unless Mr. Phil had somebody come in and cook it. Doubt if it was too clean either, cause I ain't meet a man yet could out clean a woman. Na this is one place you don't get nothing about. They grow deh food, make deh clothes, and serve deh God right there on his spread. I tell you what I thank, I thank that Mr. Phil is a man like Sho. I thank all dem mens is his and I thank all these white folk around here know it. They just don't want no colored folk to know it for sure. I figure they shame. That puzzle me cause they ain't shame of nothing else. They don't seem shame when they is preachin the word of the lawd and sendin us up as scrafices to appease Him. No, sir I don't see no shame then. No one thinks we really capable of thinkin and that is lie. Reason they think that way is because of this, we sees clearly what is being done to us. But see we understand that because we don't have power, we don't have a say. But what they don't understand is we understand that. I remember one day I was aww at the general store, these two old Cajun men was talking, I think that was old man Labedo and Mr. Tugee'. They was talking about how to send a dog mad. Labedo say, " You beat dat dog head Tugee' and later on ya call him to ya and give him a pat and some food." He say " Din a hour later after he done forgot you call em and beat him again, hard. Din ya call back again and love him, give him something good, pat him on the head and send em off. If ya do that for about two weeks, he go stalk ravin mad. But if you do it to a nigga he go keep coming back, thinkin you go one day start to treat him better; so how can you say they is human when they ain't got the sense of a dog. A nigger is a fine machine God made for us to use. Only problem is God made him so dumb we have to spend most our time trainin and retrainin em." Hearin them old to red necks talkin made me wanna pee in some coffee. See that is what they been doing to us, so they thank we stalk ravin mad or like old man Labedo say we is less than an animal. But, that is a lie we just made up good, cause we strong and if it was all even and fair, we be just as powerful too. But nothing is fair here for us not even death. I figure we doin alright to say we in hell. That is why I know hell gots some beautiful places. I live in a beautiful place in mist of hell. Plus see both dem men talkin, neither one of em could read and they both had to make marks for their names. So see deh ain't got the sense of the animals God give them to oversee. And both of them needed to quite talkin about dogs cause they both smelled like wet dogs anyway. Since they being so low down let me tell yall why old man Tugee so mean and hateful. See him and his wife real religious and he one man believed that you is suppose to populate the earth. God did not like him though cause all he got was one girl out of that wife of his. Her name be Caroline Tugee' considered the most holy and up right woman in these here parts. Can't say she was ever too mean to us colored cause she just did not deal with us at all. It was like she did not want to see us cause she knew that what they was doing to us was against the good Lords will. See she knew damn well we was one hundred percent human cause she believed just what the Bible say about how all us was made. And unless Adam and Eve was part animal that meant we was all human. That woman could preach the Bible if she wanted to but she was too busy raising their daughter to be a holy woman. Well anyway that little Cassandra Tugee got to be about 13 and wanted herself a boyfriend. Here tell old Caroline caught her behind the house kissing him and child she tied that child down and scrubbed her private parts with a pot scratcher. They tell me all that child insides was scrapped raw and she scrapped off her special part, yall know the part I am talking about. Well the child got sick and started runnin a fever, Caroline knowed what she had done so she did not call the white doctor, she called one of them creole traiteurs, but it was too late and that child died. Well old Tugee' blamed the traiteur and went to her house and drowned her. I guess the Lord must have whipped up on Caroline something bad, cause she wrote him a letter and child that crazy woman killed herself. I guess she aint' believe God was go forgive her, after all she had killed two people. Tugee could not read her letter so he had they preacher man read it and after all this he been one of the low downest sons of bitches God ever put on the face of the earth. But I guess you can't blame him cause his whole family got killed by the Bible maybe that is why he blaspheme so much. But I guess you can not blame him.

See that Mr. Phil, I always knew he was too nice to colored folk to be regular white folks. He give to the childrens Christmas festival, he donate all his old clothes and furniture to the colored churches and he sends at least two colored childrens to schools out of state, called boarding school. He do it every year, he use to send both boys and girl, but na he only send the boys. See what I mean? He just too sweet to be regular. I ain't saying that there are not some good hearted white people, that will help colored folks, he just gave so much and such nice thangs, even the white folk had to mention it. Hell they wanted some of his throw away thangs too. Na this is how I speculate on him, I don't know for sho but I am almost 99% right about him and them mens. Everybody haves needs and you can't tell me that a place like that full of mens aint full of somebody that needed some attention. Ain't none of them ever come to town to much for nothing. They almost did everything out there, and by the way I am just being mean and jealous bout what I said about the cleaning and cooking, here tell you can eat off the ground and what you eat taste so good you don't care. Na that is what one or two people said, can't be all that good cause I aint never sold them none of my preserves or biscuits.

Na yall bet not repeat what I am about to tell you about Mr. Phil. Last Fall I was taking me a ride past his place and his back gate was open. I tied my buggy and just took me a walk over by his big gazebo and that is when I saw him. He was holding this other person with long, long blone hair so gentle and sweet, I had to watch. By the time my eyes really got straight I noticed it was another man. That scared the hell out of me for two reasons, if they saw me they would have kilt me and if mens treatin each other like that they aint go need us women; hell he was touchin him like he was fine bone china. I felt strange though not only did I feel warm watching them, I also felt jealous. Yall can repeat this if you want and I will say you're a lyin. Even if you readin it I will say what you readin is a lie. Don't want know evil white mens in love with each other following me to the grave. I eased my ass away and never told anyone this until this moment right here. I think I was jealous cause, I figure some woman somewhere needed to be treated like that and here it is two mens havin the nerve to be lovin on each other like that. They taken away from us and that just pisses me off. I guess everybody got deh likes and dislikes. Just like some people is more gifted than others. God gifted colored mens with some handsome sized concerns and he blessed the white man with tongues that kin touch the back of your throat. So I guess we all got some kind of gift, but looks like the gift of a man touching another one like that should just be kept aside for women. Thank God niggers gets killed for havin white women, cause if we have to compete with them and mens we might as well all be like Sho.

It is got to be something wrong over there, I figure they must all be doing what I saw him and his friend doing cause them men not like the black baseball players; I ain't never seen any of them down the tracks tryin to get satisfaction. Child them baseball players loves them some women when they come to town to play deh comes for comfort too. And every now and then one of the local gals gits lucky and lands her a husband if she ain't to pickey. Some of us is pickey as hell and usually them is the ones lonely as hell too. I remember when we was making suits for one of the traveling teams, me Sandra Faye, Marie, Theloa Johnson and Poonanny and ofcourse everybody was talking about this new player, who was welder too and he was lookin to move here. Well he was some pretty, blad headed though, but lord was he a fit man. Sandra faye comes up and says "Look a here girls this new player say he comin to town is mine . I dreams about his fine ass every night" I bet her sheets stank. Then she "I am trying to get to him fo yall holy harlots slide round to him and I just want to let yall know I done had him bout three times and I am late. God I hope I am pregnant." Na the truth is I thank she is tellin a got damn lie plus she ought to know that pregnant slickness don't mean nothing all them players had about three or four chillins aroud town. But anyway let me make yall laugh. All of sudden Theola Johnson said " Girl you can have them pretty boys I likes me an ugly man myself, cause he know how to give a pussy a black eye." Child that broke up the room. Now we understand why Henry Bulldonge' always hanging around doing everything she want. Look like he been given so called giving her pussy a black eye and bet he done swole her lips up too.

Na Sandra know that just about every woman in Friendly done had they share of them baseball palyer. If I tell yall the names of some of the good women of friendly, white and black that got they heads full of corn silk down in the corn fields with them boys when they came to town you would take a spell and not be able to speak. Huh! I could almost do what I want around here, cause I know so much. But I also know if you start to make people scared of you they will get rid of you and the easiest thing to do is get rid of colored folk. Strange thang this life you can have power but can't use it, and that somehow makes the power a burden. All of us pretending like we know what we doing, like we understand why we here, or how we got here and none of us no better than the other one. Can't nobody answer it; so I figure somebody just sat down and said this is how we go do it. Or something like that anyway, yall do not let me keep getting off of my point. I just don't know why colored folk had to be mistreated so bad. Maybe people just don't like thangs different from them. Maybe different is something to be afraid of. Maybe different means they might have to change something they don't want to. I can't answer for why being different means you go be mistreated, I just know it do. Thangs is being done right in front of your face that is wrong and because you don't have power you have to take it. It is the truth, try livin here being black like me. I bet you aint go like it. Huh, I thank God he made me a listening hear and a speaker of the truth. I have value in these people community, they need me to repeat the truth to them. That is why I don't believe what they say about talking and telling stories in the bible. Probably some rich person, say ,

"Put in the good book about too much talking, that way they won't be sharing our business with each other." That did not matter casue they spoke so freely over us like we was not there we got all their business and we talked about it.

Some of they mess worked though, cause they got us so separated and confused we tend to hate one another. We don't trust each other and some of use will sell out our mama for a few crumbs. But you got to understand that is just how we have had to survive. Not all of us but sometimes it is hard to tell what a person might not do. I remember one time I mentioned a little gossip that turned into to a big mistake and caused hurt to a bunch of people; It was a story about Betty Wronge'. Her girl said that every Tuesday, Mr. Warlee' would come over and she had to leave the house for three or four hours. She said he would always bring her cheese, and French bread from New Orleans and send her on her way. Oh her name was Ora Lee by the way. Na yall know that Mr. Warlee' was as married as Jesus is holy. So I repeated the story to Cazzie, no harm intended cause I knew she was not go say a word. Well I was wrong about that she was talkin in the kitchen and one of them white gals heard what she had said. And any way to make a long story short; it got back to Betty and it was a big mess. Betty did not believe that Ora had said a thing and she was blaming Cazzie's girl, cuase she would always go by and get the sheets and pillow cases for cleaning and ironing every Tuesday. She fired Cazzie's girl and as soon as I heard it I went to her and told her I would tell her where they heard that foolishness from if she give Cazzie's girl her job back. Well, I told her that Ora was the one who was telling her business. Anyway she fired Ora and to let you know how low down she was she did not hire back Cazzie's girl either.

Let me change something I don't want yall to believe that all of us colored folk hate one another cause that is not true, we have been known to prey on one another. Some of us us tend to hate our own but then again some of us hate everybody. We been separated from each other since they brought us here, old from young, dark from light, field niggers from house niggers, bed wenches from cooks, and piss po to po hell. Soon as us was suppose to be free we stopped coming together to fight; instead we started fightin each other for crumbs. White folks made us like that though, but we carried it on. Our biggest problems is with ourselves, them white folk done beat the pride out of us, we just ain't got none left. See ifin you too black you gots to much Africa in ya and ifin you too light , you gots to much master in you. That is why you got the circle C Club for them paper bag colored negros, the Frenchman, the browns, the high yellows and them jet black ones. See we see it like that and for some reason it is so normal for us we don't thank nothing wrong with it, we be sayin " Look at his black ass or look at that high yella bitch we adds color to everythang. We can't come together, dark mens don't want dark womens , less she Puddin. Light mens don't want light girls , unless they is dem Frechmans and you know the marrys each other to keep the color in. See them yellow boys na they go get them a real dark woman, cause they tryin to weed out all that white blood em. See them black ones they go git them a yellow girl cause done been made to believe they black skin is something to be ashamed of. See they hate that deh is so dark and the last thang they want to do is recreate their pain. Oh yea they be in pain, cause among they own people they be called ugly black names, that is why they hate themselves. I thank that is why we are still suffering, we have not come together. Hell, I don't want to be too dark myself; I really don't, I won't be able to wear no colors. The light skin negro hate hisself too cause he too close to white and the dark skinned negro hate hisself cause he too close to Africa, na ain't that just a bitch, excused me Lord. Oh na child don't thank we the only ones, them white folk have some problems too. All white womens trys to stay the size of little girls, see they mens is got a problem with wantin children, oh yes I believe that. Most little black girls on any body plantation was broke in about eight years old. Them white mens loves little girls and deep down them white womens knows it that is why they starve deh self to stay little. Most of em be so frail you can blow em away, I know it hard from the white mens to feel too manly ifin they can't reach deh woman honey pot and ifin she too big he sho nuff can't reach it. And then again yall something else is strange about them white men, sometimes you catch em visitin them big old gals that hold farts between deh thighs till deh bath. I is got a lot on my mind it is a wonder I got any room to keep up with all the happens round here. Lord it is hard to keep the faith and trust in you while you is letting people keep a lock on our minds. I keep hopin that you send an angel with the key to unlock our mind and help us to see that as soon as we start to love each other we will be truly free. I doubt that is go happen anytime soon. But anyway some rich man put that in the Bible bout gossiping bein bad to keep us from talkin bout them. I am telling you I bet that is why they say that; rich people is some sneaky bastards with money.

CHAPTER 11

Reverand Two Wings Johnson Coming to Town

FRIENDLY IS ALL ROUSED up today, Rev. Two Wings Johnson is coming to town, with his thunder guitar. Let me stop right now and tell yall about this man before I go any further. If you ever wanted to see a real prophet of God, well Rev. Two Wings Johnson is him. His real name is Sancified TW Johnson. He was named after the prophet that baptized him. The TW belonged to the reverend and the the sancified belonged to the Lord. I hear tell when he went down in the water and came back up seven doves from the lord flew over his head and sanctified him a preacher that day. Some people say looked like he was walkin on the water, but I know that is a lie; cause the white folk would have killed him. They say people got healed and some got good fortune that day, some even changed their life. This ain't no folk story, see he was baptized by a white traveling preacher from Listinigar, Alabama. Everybody know ain't no white man go tell no powerful stories for no black man. Tell me when Two Wings came up out the water he said the Lord told him for to let all the white folks come in the water so they could get blessed first and then he let the blacks come in after them, and they was blessed with whatever the Lord had left. It did not matter though I hear everybody there got what they needed that day. Na most of the time Friendly, is a little town that is ignored, we don't have any festivals of course we should, I have been proposin a biscut festival for years. These good town folks just won't take the effort to do it, probably because they know I am go be the center of the whole festival. But, Lord child when Reverand Two Wings come to town everyboby knows about us and is headin our way. We have one of the largest tents in the southeast put up when he come to town and we always have to put it up by the water. The good reverend believes the water has something to do with eternal life. I do not know about all of that but I do know every obay women, two headed doctor, and preacher as far away as Georgia will be here by the end of the week. Everybody working from sun up to sun down getting deh wears ready to sell. I don't have to because I stay stocked, see I have to stay stocked; somebody always buying from Ms. Lula Mae.

Child you aint' never seen nothing like Rev. Two Wings though, long black cape and a snow white suit with red shoes, help him stomp out the fires of hell, aww Jesus I am feeling the spirit right na just talking about this good man. Yall thank I am lyin but there is some thangs you just can't explain and Reverand Two Wings is one of them. Where in the hell he get them red shoes from I don't know and that smokin guitar ain't white for nothin cause it strike like lightening when he pluckin it and Lawd he can pluck that git fiddle. Child that guitar is a work of art, got his named carved in it, and when he play it you can hear him as far a five or six miles up the bayou. Ida Banks getting all her daughters ready like a bunch of cows in the pasture waiting to be picked for slaughter. She always linin them up in front of the traveling preachers trying to get them married. She got six of em and aint none of them is married or have any children. She is just cursed all the way round, nobody even want to get her girls pregnant. They are some nice looking girls too. Long cold black hair, nice keen features, strong and structured bodies like ballet dancers, yes they are some good looking girls; they just so got damn tall, hell they taller than all the mens in these parts. Poor Ida she is trying to get at least one of them married off. Them girls kinda of strange, always together they do everything together. They make each other's clothes, comb each other's hair, teach each other go to church with each other and they have one big room where they all sleep. Ida's husband Bill Banks left her over

5 years ago. Said he left to go out west to get a job on the railroad. But that is not what really happended. One night that man got drunk and told Ida he knew he could not have children and he was wondering how in the hell she had six girls for him. Johhny Faye, their neighbor at the time said you could here them screaming at each other miles down the road. Some how Sheriff Watson got wind of the fight and showed up over there says Johnny Faye. Tell me he took Bill off to jail to cool off. The next day Sheriff says he let Bill go and that was the last he saw of him. Sheriff said Bill had told him he was leaving Ida and going out west to get a job on the railroad. Now yall think what yall want, I have my own thoughts about this situation and what really happened to that man. All we know is Bill had been seeing Hattie Freeman for over 12 years and she never had one child for him. Yet his wife at home had six girls for him. We know Hattie was not a failing woman cause when Bill left she had three head for Wilber Right. That is all I am saying about that. She ain't never did me nothing so I ain't got to tell her business.

We all excited everybody gittin ready. All the sisters from every Parish around tryin to come out and do their spiritual duty so they can get blessed with seats in the front row or near to the front as they can get. I bet yall thank deh trying to sit so close, sos deh can get hit by the spirit first; hell no, deh tryin to get so close so deh kin get a good look at Reverand Two Wings under plunder. Cause you know he start off without that robe on, and he wears his pants sos you can see the fat meat of that thang. I truly believe that the spirit directs that man to put that robe on sos you can keep your mind on his message. Thank god I done got over that; hell I got tired of working my fingers to the bone for a front row seat to look at something that is going to leave me frustrated. I ordered me a dress from New York City yes I did. I am not go even tell you what it looks like. I am wearing it for the Lord so I can't tell you about it before I show him and every body else in town. Yes Ms. Lula got her a store bought fancy dress for this occasion to praise the Lord. Na to show yall how special this man is old low down Sherrif Watson done provided protection for him during the revival. The baskets be so full of money you would think you was at the First National Bank. My personal thought is that old Sheriff is watching how much money coming in so he and the Major be sure to get their right part. We always laugh at that because old reverend Two Wings, had a special made basket ,they had real deep bottoms. His faithful servants said the Lord made him as shrewed as the snake, cause he gave him white folk wisdom. See old Rev. had an extra bottom in them baskets where the collectors stuck most of the money that don't jingle in. Yes, he was a smart man, that what happens when the good Lord bless you with brains. He got protection and did not give away half of what that old Sherrif and Major thought. I don't know how people think they are suppose to get the money the Lord done gave people. Seem like I read somewhere that a man should not steal, or maybe I am wrong maybe the sayin was, black men should not steal and lie. If that is it that explains why the Lord let the white man get away with stealing and lying so damn much. Did I tell yall I gots me a Hattie Simmoms dress. She is a black lady that designs clothes in Paris, France. These days you can get them dresses for a good price.

The choir ordered new robes cause you don't want to be looking any kind of way when this man come to town. Of course I did not agree with that whore red they ordered, if it were not for those white colars they would look like a bunch of holy whores up there, corse some of them really are. Guess you wondering why we call him two wings, well that is because he always singing that song, I got two wings to vale my feet, two wings to vale my face and so on. He had two wings to vail everything except for his dick, huh. We all knew he had over 28 head of children, from here to Georgia, to Chicago and down in the delta of Mississippi. I guess he is doin what he suppose to, cause the Lord did tell us to multiply the earth. He pretty slick too, cause he got a way of making you do what he want without you getting mad. Like for instance if a white person come in the tent and all the seats is taken, he will say "Git up and let our good white folk sit down; you know they here cause the Lord sent them" and of course us well behaved blacks will git up everytime, showing our Christian obedience, aint that some bullshit. I am glad he ain't never pointed me out for that one, cuase I would have folded my arms with a big hell no and I probably would have said muther fucker too. Yes, I said it, hell no muther fucker would be my answer, don't try to judge me either cause I ain't saying that to the Lord I am saying it to his corrupt man. You know God uses all kinds in his work. I go along with a lot, but I have my own thoughts about things. Don't make since for me to get into a fight with all these good God fearing folks by myself, cause I am just go be out numbered. Some people say it is beneficial to let them seats go to the white folk. Dora Sims say when she gave up her seat, somebody slipped 5.00 in her hand, but it did not do her any good she put it right back in the collection basket, cause she stupid. I would gave back one dollar and kept the other four.

Come next week we all go have us a nice wind fall and a good shoutin time, I always say ain't nothing wrong with shoutin till ya stank. Most of these holy do rights full of shit anyway. Seems like that is the only time we all lets ourselves go, other than when them blues singers and baseball players come to town. (Oh Lord I am laughing to myself right now; thankin about all the sellin goin on.) Life is hard when you not in the right color skin, just ask any black man or woman you see. We stay tied up most of the time, either we bowing down to some ignorant cracker can't even spell his name or we cleaning some old stuffed up, scared ass white woman's house pissed off at us cuase her husband got a bunch of little half white pickaninnies looking just like him running round. We don't git to let our self go much. So whenever there is a time when we can just release we do it never mind if it is a holy man or a devil singin blues man, or some of them well endowed baseball players. Life ain't easy for people who got stole from there homeland and bought to a foreign land, lied to, beat, rapped, murdered, and deemed an animal. See Lord that is why sometimes I can't believe you, I just don't know what to say about you. Then again I could be callin on the wrong God, seems like the God of the white man really ain't the God of the black man. Na I ain't meanin you no disrespect, just in case you is both our God and is pissed off at us about something. But what I really thank is dem white folk done beat our God memory out of our minds so we ain't got no choice but to see if you gots any mercy for us dat ain't dressed like a Quaker. Cause your white man don't and his scared ass women ain't no better, mostly cause she is in slavery too, it is just a different kind. See na I think I might be on to something, see I want to know how the God of the White man can be a fair God to the Black man. Seems to me if I am a God for somebody and I am on their side, I ain't go do anything to make their life harder. I figure if you give us the same rights as and we all suppose to be from Adam and Eve then we ought not have to bow down to them no more. What Master you ever know wanted his servants to be equal with dem, that is why deh is a master. I figure if you telling me to pray for my master and ask you to bless them, you surely can not want me free. I figure ifin you let my children be made alligator bait and my babies be hung on trees for Christmas tree decorations you can not mean me any good; no disrespect meant from this old ignorant gal; none meant at all. You did let us git free from the auction block, it just ain't registered in our mines yet. Then again I don't know maybe you freed us cause you got tired of seeing your chosen people doin such evil thangs to deh sisters and brothres, cause if Adam and Eve is true we is all sisters and brothrs. I thanks that is the reason you start openin doors for us poor heathen colored folk. Only thang is you ain't opening them doors to fast and we still suffer plenty heart aches. We still on the plantation ceptin na they call em our neighborhoods. I still ain't figured out the white folk yet though, cause they calls us animals, yet in their society it is shameful to have sex with the animals. They have little half human and half animal babies walking around with their faces, but they call us heathens. I would like to know what you really is all about. I would like to know how you came up with some of your rules and how you give us over to such mean people. I guess it don't matter much we got so many black preachers spreading around the Masters message he ain't got to do it no more. I don't know the name of the God we use to call on cause nobody let us keep our God, but I do know that I ain't called the right one yet. Cause when I do He go show up for me like the Isrealites' God showed us for dem when deh was crossin the red sea. But until he show up I beg your mercy cause I know we be blashpheming your image. We all do it cause we gots a bunch of names for each other like niggers, crackers, dagos, rice patties and a bunch of other low down names us peoples come up with for each other. I figure like dis ifin we is all in your image, den you must look like a nigger, a cracker, a dago, and a big belly rice eater. Ifin I am wrong bout what I just said din your good book is wrong cause dat is what the preachers tells us even the white ones slips up and say we is all made in the image of God. See when dem white folks be callin me a nigger, I be sayin God is nigger too and one day he go kick your white ass for me, you sons of bitches . But it look likes to me since deh kilt your son in such a mean way, they done scared the hell out the heavenly host cause aint no more delivers din showed up here tryin to change nothin. Well anyway I is tryin to live a good life, but a good life ain't got to much excitement in it.

CHAPTER 12

A Good Man in a Bad Situation

SOMETIMES I WONDER IF I could just let my self go though and trap me a good man in a bad situation. Well, let me not say trap. Let me say find a good man with a bad woman. I would rather say that. They got some women around here who got a good man but he just ain't enough. In a small town like this everybody knows who they are. I just don't get it, some of the worst whores on earth ends with a good husband that forgives her and loves her no matter what she do. Like, Ms. Rosalee Fouche'she something, no shame, no cares it seemed like. Na look her husband last name Watson but she felt her family name had more worth so she uses her family name. See what I mean she so evil she ain't even take the last name of her good husband. Na this woman use to walk to her smoke shed, to the mail box and sometime up the road in her underwear. Let us not talk about how she would have a drink on Sunday with the mens and tell dirty stories. We always felt so sorry for her husband. She ordered him around just like a little child. That is ofcourse when he was not prentending like he could not hear her. Most people thought Mr. Henry her husband was pretty much deaf, but I know for sure he was only deaf to her voice. See I was on the fish bank with them one Saturday evening and Miss Rosalee was just a calling Mr. Watson asking him to catch her line, he never moved a muscle. She looked at him and said "You old deaf bastard don't know why I bring my ass out here with you. You just ain't worth a fuck Mr. Henry. I don't know how you heard that preacher when he asked you to say I do." Mr. Henry just sitting there with a smile on his face study pullin up fish. I am thinking to myself, I know he ought to be glad he cannot here her. Poor Mr. Henry, wife just cussing him out and embrassing him all over town. Bout a half hour passed and I ran out of bait, so I barely whispered to myself, "Shucks I am out of bait and the damn fish just starting to bite good for me. I wonder if Mr. Henry will let me have a few worms?" Yall know that Mr. Henry turned to me and passed me a half bucket of worms and winked at me. See old Mr. Henry was just deaf when it came to Rosalee. I figured he was tired of having to jump everytime she opened her mouth so he just played deaf. That probably was a good thing for him cause all she ever really did was cuss. That is how I know people can hear you and not hear you at all. I can't say I disliked Ms. Rosalee, because she would give us all something to think about other than our situations. I would just git so tickled when I would be coming down Fouche Rd. and look up ahead see this big tent on two legs walking towards you. It would be Ms. Forche in them big yellow draws, headed to where ever she decided to go. Child you could make a dress, a shawl, and head covering with a pair of them big drawers. That woman ain't have no shame not a bit, big old firm tits that stuck straight up to the sky, look like she could supply milk for half the parish and a big old yellow jungle ass big as one you have ever seen. And Lawd on hot days when sweat drippin off ya, you could see her actual ass crack, the crack , the actual crack. Poor Mr. Watson, he just a good man in a bad situation.

My mama use to say that Mr. Henry Watson, was good man in a bad situation just about everyday of my life. See Mr. Watson was married to Miss RosaLee Fouche, not cause he wanted to but because he had too. She was a loud woman like I told yall but she was full of laughter everytime you saw her. She was one of those big boned high yellow gals. Straignt hair, kinda green colored eyes and they tell me that when she was born and the midwife slapped her on ther ass her first words was "What the fuck was that for", then they say she pissed straight up in that woman eyes everybody know she cussed before she could walk. Ms. Lousa say when she was makin her confirmation, when she got to the alter for the Priest to bless her she asked him "Why Jesus made it so got damn hard to be a Catholic?" Good thang she was not mine cause I would have tore that ass up. Child this woman cussed in front of the preacher, white folk, childrens and everybody, with no shame. I always wondered why nobody did or said anything to her. I hear tell she performed special favors, for the white folk, nobody knows exactly what that was though. Na I got a rumor from listening to Becky Trimmyass one of the sweetest white women around these parts, that Rosalee would be setting them up with black mens. Before yall go spread this all over town and say it came from me, I was ease dropping so I may not have got it all right. But sounds like to me Becky was telling the ladies at their monthly meeting that if they wanted to do it safe just call Rosalee and she would know what to do. Na I don't know what they were referring to exactly but that is what she said. Ifin you tell anybody it came from me I am go swear to your God of heaven that you be lying on me. Some thangs you don't want to be responsible for spreading. See Ms. Becky was one of the few single white women in our Parish, sweet as pie. Ms. Trimmyass never had no children, no men friends and did not have much company either. But if you needed help, go to her, if you needed a loan, go to her and if you needed to talk to somebody , talk to God, but she was a good woman. She did not like nothing but the Frenchman though, that is all she allowed to come around her house to do anything. Her handy mens was William Roberashow, he hunted, Luke Forneyeah was the only man who tended to her fields and Jake Colliyea' built everything she had. You ain't never passed there and saw no darkies on her place, just the Frenchman. People have said some mean thangs about her but I ain't go repeat them. That woman has helped more colored folk than God.

Well anyway Roselee was married to poor Mr. Watson and my mother had been seeing Mr. Watson for over 20 years. Yes, my poor mother feel to the temptations of the devils ways. She let her lust make her fall in love with somebody's husband. I don't know what to say about that cause it was wrong and there is no way to make it holy except, it felt right to see them together. They loved each other and you could see it, but it came from the devil, so it was not good love. Everybody understood why Mr. Watson and Rosalee stayed married but that just made him look like he ain't have no back bone. You know we don't like men who ain't got no backbone. Most folk knew Rosalee had regular men friends that visited her and you know they was having relations. Let me explain this sos yall can understand it. Here tell it, Rosalee daddy said that Mr. Watson had better stay married to Rosalee the rest of his life since he spoiled her. Old man Tate Fouche told Henry if he left Rosalee he would have him killed. Told him even if he die he would leave enough money in his will to have him killed if he left her. Mr. Fouche hated Henry cause he messed up Rosalee's chance to marry that well to do old Frenchman Mr. Francis Lebouf. Who is now the husband of that Louise Lebouf. Well let me stop na cuse they is another story. Anyway that old man Tate did die and he did leave in a will that he would give 500.00 to the man that kill Henry Watson if he ever left his daughter. They says Rosalee just laughed and laughed at the reading of the Will especially when it seems her daddy left her pretty well off but under the conditions that she never put Henry's name on any of her accounts. Humn guess old man Tate meant to let Henry Watson know just how much he hated him. Na that was a real demon bastard. He hated that man til the day he died.

Yes, indeed I remember most Sunday mornings after church Mr. Watson come by and bring us hams, and half of cows and wagon loads of greens, and sweet potatoes and spend all day with us, just like we was one big happy family. Mama would always stand on the front porch and waive goodbye to him till he disappeared and say "Poor Henry he is a good man in a bad situation." I never knew what she meant until I got older. See mama and Mr. Henry was having relations and everybody knew it. Mama was the head stewardess of our little church you would think somebody would have said something, but they did not. Maybe it was because Mr. Watson's wife, Rosalee was a Catholic and she never came to our church, so people kind of ignored the fact he had a wife; to most men around town she did not even count as a wife. We all know she prayed to statues too, she had some around her house. So she was pretty much considered to be a heathen. Mostly we thought all Catholics was hell bent peoples anyway, praying to statues and all, the whole lot of them. Plus since they was not married in the Catholic church we was told the Catholic people did not even accept their marriage either. Talk about having a way out. Well one thang for show Jesus was not a Catholic.

But not all of the Catholics was all the way bad, cause that lady Ms. Coneair, one of the sweetest voodoo queens you ever wanted to meet was a Catholic too; but that woman ended up being a Saint I tell ya. She turned out to be a healer and a comforter doing the Lawds work. We knew God had sent her, cause she could tell you things that came true or was true. She healed one of my first cousins from the croup de salon (a evil hex). Yes sir, somebody had put some spirit snails in her food and threw a bottle filled with chicken guts and cats blood under her house with her name wrote on papers stuffed in the it. We cannot figure how them snails got into her food, she is a particular woman and do not eat out, she just don't eat out at all. I don't care who cooking she ain't go eat it. I remember a few times I felt my feelings hurt because she would not even taste one of my biscuits. Anyway that was her loss, but she ain't ate one yet. Well she got sick and my auntee took her to Ms. Coneair, she gave her a spoon of healing power and said the words. Well my cousin passed them snails for one month it was a mess too cause my auntee and them would have to burn up her movements everytime she had one. I am not exact about how long it took but one day them sails stopped coming out; she got well again and a new man showed up for her too. Yes, Ms. Coneair, was sent hear to bless us. Sometimes people can be on the other side and still do the Lawds' work. You know them Catholic people do some strange thangs, buring candles in the broad open daylight and all. Cleaning away the spirits with the smokes, they do, out in the open, the things we do in private; or when we go to see someone like Ms. Coneair or a two headed doctor and have them do it. You have to be a wise practicioner to be able to master this world and the spirit world. But if you living right you should not have to keep going to see Ms. Coneair, burn candles all day or pray to statues, you should just call on the good Lord and know He or whoever will hear you. So you know something is wrong since they burn them candles every day all day, maybe their God need a lot before he pays attention to them. I try not to know to much about them kind. It can all get a little confusing, because they preach about Jesus too, but they act like he need a lot of help, cause they have all of them Saints around him for backup. That could be the only thing that blacks and whites of Friendly agrees on . We don't talk to statues, or burn candles unless it is for ... never mind. What I am trying to say is everybody in Friendly, was mostly good Baptist, even if quite a few of the people around was doing that Catholic thing. That is right, even though a lot of folk was being made to be Catholic, we liked having good old fashion church here. Put on your Sunday best, bring you some slippers and get ready to settle in and hear the word. We all had to bring our slippers, cause after of hours of stompping out the devil your feets gits tired.

Not having a picture show here made church the second most popular thing to do. The juke joint hands down was the number one favorite, but we not suppose to admit that. Nothing better than seeing a good show on Sunday; sometimes I don't know whether it be the holy ghost has people jumping up and carrin on, the guilt from what they was doing or if they foots be done gone to sleep. My foot went to sleep in church one Sunday and I started to stompping to wake it up and before I knew it the holy ghost had sent about three fine brothers to my rescue. Sometimes it ain't nothing but the devil himself trying to test you to see if you really sincere about the Lord. I am sincere about the Lord, but the Lord knows about our conversations, the ones where I am asking for an explanation as to why I have to be in such a bad way on this planet called earth. Why have I been denied the right to just be myself, and why in the hell don't a damn good woman like myself at least have a study good man to spend some time with. Ain't like I don't deserve me a good handy man, somebody to rake my edges, mow my grass, service all these rusty pipes around here and do a little tree triming. Yall can judge me all you want, I ain't trying to be no saint, because saints don't have any needs. I am a woman full of temptations and yes, I want me a good strong man, but I can admit that. I am always amazed at how many righteous devils I been around. Seems like the people doing all the judement is doin all the doin. Child anyway my mother, Mr. Watson, and God go have a lot of talking to do. I wish I could hear them explain to the good Lord why they sinned so long. I also would like the good Lord to explain why he did not strike them down for disobeying his commandments. Cause they did them all, lying, commiting adultery, coveting, fornication etc …, so I would just like to here what the good Lord go say to the both of them. Just my luck he go say "Henry, for a good man in a bad situation you did good we go let you in. Then he go look at my mother and say Lubertha Needee, because you took on the sin of Jezebel go to hell." Yeap that is about what He will do, blame the women.   .

I was always amazed at how everybody in our church knew Mr. Watson was married and who he was married to; yet, they still welcomed

114

him like he was the good Lawd himself.(Hypocritical bastards). They all would say he was a good man in a bad situation. He and my mother stayed together until his death. That is how we have such a big spread. Since Mr. Watson could never get any of Rosalee's money or land he bought his own land and gave it to my mother. We could only buy land that them white folk allowed us to, but I figure one day they go be sorrow for selling us all the bottoms. I got a feeling in my black bones they go be real sorry. But I know that sorrow won't last long because deh go find a way to steal it back from us. Cause that is how God sets up his chosen people from what I see. Even if they give you of something by accident, they figure out a way to get it back on purpose. I bet we ain't go own half the land we own now in times to come.

That is how Ms. Lula Mae got over 2000 acres of land. Prime land, my soil is rich, my bayous is full, my pecan trees full, fruit trees bare the sweetest fruit you ever wanted to taste. Oh, yes cause of their sin I am living pretty damn good. Looks like 1 am being blessed by the sins of others. Mama never told me Mr. Watson was my daddy, but I could not guess who else it could have been. After Mr. Watson died, do you know Ms. Rosealee's old croaked ass attorney tried to take that land from my poor mother. Talking about it was right that Rosealee have that land, cause he bought it while deh was married, he was a no good old bastard. Said Mr. Watson was wrong for leaving it to my mother, casue she wasn't nothing but his hoe. I hope he died of the croups. Rosealee was the one made him stop, they say she told em to leave my mother alone, cause the only place Mr. Watson felt like a man was when he was with my mother. Rosealee told em her daddy made damn show he would never be much of a man being married to her, so Ms. Lubertha Needee' my mother was his true love. That old attorney of hers' keep on pushing until he made him some money. He made up some papers for Rosealee to sign giving my mother her part of something she did not have any parts of anyway. I thank he was trying to get it for himself; you know after my mother passed on he tried to come back and buy it from me. Or should I say he tried to steal it from me. That old devil offered me a dollar and a quarter an acre, everybody know it was goin for at least 15.00 an acrea if you white and 5.50 if you black if you selling. If you buying it is 20 dollars an acre if you black and 5.50 an acre if you white. I am not complaining we just glad we could own a piece of the soil we toiled in to build these people country. But if you find anything more croaked than a white man you let me know where that creature at cause I am go run to him and find out what he know so I can use it against them white folks. They something else, teaching you how to love somebody who got they foot on your neck. I ain't never said we was the smartest people, we just more resilant than others. That is why I be talking to God all the time, I am trying to get me some answers about this thang. But like I said the God of the white man, don't seem to give a damn bout colored folks, in most cases.

CHAPTER 13

Company Coming

LAWD I JUST KEEP going on back and forth tellin you what you already know. Let me get up here and make enough breakfast for me, Bealuh and anybody else that might just drop in. After all I makes the best biscuits that God ever tasted and that is something you want to share. Oh, today feels nice you can feel the warm sunshine smile on you through the window and the breeze, it feels like sweet honey taste and my pine trees making it smell fresh and clean all over my front yard. I think I am just gonna open the shutters all around the house. Maybe a good man in a bad situation just might be passin down the road and look this way and … anyway forgive me lord for being such a forward thinking woman. Just then I looked out the window and who I sees comin down the road in another fancy car with the top off. Lawdy mercy it is Ms. Puddin, smiling and throwing her hands up; I can see the life in that woman. I just laughed to myself and think what it must be like to be a woman so free. Child this heifer in a big long sapphire blue car, with shinny metal all around it, big white tires, and white leather seats, ummm ummmmm, (na Ms. Lula grinnin from ear to ear all excited like child seein Santa Claus for the first time, cause life din come back home.) that car pull up and out jump Puddin all dressed up and wearin pearls child. I mean strings of real pearls and diamond all on her fingers , she looked like a summertime Christmas tree. (All she was doing though was showing off, don't nobody need to wear that much jewelry. Well lest say most decent women don't). My head was swimming everything was happening so fast. Lawd, I had to take in so much then this man the got out. Oh Jesus, he was a beautiful man, I almost can't speak. He awwww had on all white clothes, everything he had on was white. He was brown with silky straight hair. You could tell he had some good blood in him. Puddin says "Ms. Lula Mae Carson meet Steve." I loved seeing men in all white, his hair shinned like fine polished silver and his skin was as brown as mine and he had a smile that made me blush. I was so caught up in lookin at him Puddin had to get my attention back. Lawd Ms. Lula Mae had went somewhere else. Anyway, I hurry up and invites them in to get relaxed and child I hit that kitchen. I pulled out my prized thick bacon strips, the finest ones in the South. Oh honey child, my pigs win prizes. This rustler was coming through and had some men on his trail and he needed some money for some pigs. I needed some pigs and he solded me four black Berkshire pigs. I ain't reckon the name did not mean anything to meuntil until I killed first one. That is when I realized I had something special, yall. When I slaughter a pig you ought to see the white folk comin to get my meat, poor black folk can't even get any meat lessen I give em some. The white folk pay to well for it and you know what else they buys the chitterlins too. Our white folk here knows how to eat, hell we trained em on what is good. Everybody know I have the finest pigs in the south don't feed em nothing but that sweet corn from my fields. I just put my oversized black cast iron skillet on my stove for some serious cooking. Pulled me out some salt meat too and put it on to boil, then I am go fry it. Ifin yall ain't from the South you probably don't know how to eat fried salt meat. Puddin like the bacon but she loved that fried salt meat and fig preserves together with the biscuits and melted butter. While I am whirling around in the kitchen cookin. Steve says " What you cookin?" I says, " I am cookin the best damn biscut you will ever taste in your life, bacon, fried ham shanks, fried salt meat, eggs, fresh ground grits with my homemade cheese in em, warmin up some of my fine fig preserves, and blackberry jams, already got the best chickoree coffee you'll drink and some fresh squeezed orange juice. See that big old Satsuma tree you passed comin in here makes the sweetest satsuma's in these parts and that is the juice you will be drinking. " Shit ain't a better cook in the world than a Southern woman, whether she black or white.

That man came and grabbed me and hugged me so tight he almost took my breath away and I almost forget he belonged to Puddin, I felt a tingle. I aint had a mans attentions in a while. Excuse me yall, as you can tell Ms. Lula needs a little tendin to mmmmmmmmmmmmm anyway. I aint no easy women to get next to, but believe me if in a piece of wood was on my lap a fire would start. Meanwhile Puddin in her room changing , getting ready to take a bath and singing up a storm, that what she do when she happy. Huh, this fine man named Steve is something else. I only says Steve cauz when I called him Mr. Steve he looked at me and said " I aint old enough to be your Mr. anything Ms. Lula Mae. I call you Ms cause that is what Puddin said to call ya grand dama." Lessin yall is ignorant of a different language, dama means a fine lady or at least that is what he had told me. Then he looked at me long and hard with them deep black eyes and said "There are a few names I have I mind for you Lula . Bella is one, Senorita; but for sure you are an extremely beautiful and curvaceous woman Ms. Lula Mae. You titillate my intentions. Maybe one day you might feel gracious enough to grant me a little punta . But for now, where is my dama pintada? I figures he is talkin about Puddin so I says "She probably in the tube by na." "Oh by the way Ms. Lula you can call me anything you want to." I din cut my biscuits out na and ready to put them in the oven, when I turned and looked out the window what I see, here comes Beulah. Uh Jesus Lord have mercy here come some confusion to this nice morning. That is what I get for tryin to walk down two roads, but Lord you know the temptation I am having, somethin trying to keep me out of heaven. Na that's a place to go Heaven; but the way I figure, it just go be a little bit better than here for us colored folk, cause the Lord go be right there. But the white mens still runnin it and soon as the Lord turn his back deh go kick our ass. Oh Jesus what is going happen here this morning? Beluah she was all dressed up all girly like again, she looked like an angel comin down that road. She too had on all white and her hair was swayin down her back with the movement of her hips, huh she even had one of them big old magnolia flowers in it. Awww Lord, I am thinkin na, that it is about to be some real trouble here cuz Puddin was in there with Steve and here come Beulah. I aint know what to do but pray and I don't think God is listening at me right naw. But I prays anyway, Lord please don't let no fires start here this morning in my blessed home that only you could have gave me; Amen. I hurry up and started settin the table since almost everything was ready exceptin my damn good biscuits.

Beulah walks up to the door and I could see her lookin in , like she was tryin to see somethin. I know she saw that big old fine car. I opened the door and she said "How you doing on this fine morning Ms Lula Mae? I sees you have some company." I says "Fine Beulah what can I do for you? I was'nt expectin to see you this morning." All of a sudden her face changed to that of a mad dog she said "Where Puddin at, that is what I am here for." I says she in the tube , why don't you come have some coffee with me. I'll set another place at the table for you. I was sorta hopin you would come by (na I am lying too shit I am losing more and more points to my trip to heaven)". Beulah looks at me and says "Okay coffee sounds good." Then I turned to take my fine biscuits out of the oven for just one second and when I turned back around that heifer Beulah was gone. You know I did not take to kind to that either cause she was disrespecting my privacy by just going all through my house without me telling her to. I knew she was going straight to Puddin's room so I is just waitin for the rukus to start, but there was no sounds of screamin or fightin. It was quite as a Catholic wake in there. I looks up and here comes Puddin, Steve and Beulah to sit down at the table and eat. I know what happened, they thought about this fine cookin I had done and decided to eat first and fight later. That is what good cookin can do for you. We all sat and ate fine, honey I mean we ate fine, until none of us could move. Then Steve says to Puddin , "Go put on something real cool Senorita, let that beautiful skin of yours free it self and breath for me." Child my heart beatin fast na cuz I knows about Beulah and Puddin, but I don't know if Steve knows. Puddin gets up and goes to her room and comes out in something that is to say she might as well have been naked in. It was a pale blue wrap around lace and satin robe thang with some white lace flowers to cover her private parts, but since it was lace and well yall know what was showin .Look like Ms. Puddin pussy has a full mustache. Huh that is strange she must have stopped takin the hair off. I, I , just don't deserve this. I started prayin again cuz of the look on Beulah's face. Then Steve goes to his car and brings in this contraption that makes the music from these little flat round things. I had heard about them and had seen them in the shoppers catalog, but I had never seen one in real life before. He called it a victrola. Aint nobody around here had no victrola cause aint nobody gots time to sit around and listen to one plus who got that kind of money to throw away on a toy. I likes the gramophone oh my I likes it a lot. I wish I could here myself on one of them talkin machines , cause I have a pretty voice too, high soprano. God gave it to me cause he like hearin me over other folks is all I can say, cause you can hear me over most other folks in the choir. Then Steve opens this little box he had and in it was full of the white man's devil, big old long cigars, and a bottle of hell brew smelled so strong when he opened it, you could not even smell my pines no more. Look like I could just smell the devil cause I knew hell was in my house. Anyway Steve gives us all a cigar and a drink. Speaking of that drankin, I only have me a taste on the holidays mostly of real hard liquor, cause I takes my tonic almost everyday. Tell ya one thang though I never do like dem white ladies mixing mint and lemon in they brew making hell punch. I guess cause I likes the way whiskey taste all by itself. Aww well let me not lie, I like a mint julep every now and then too. I knowed I shoulda said no, me being a Christian lady and all but I aint had no good time for awhile, sitting here trying to get to heaven, and missin heaven right here on earth. No, not this time for Ms. Lula Mae. I know that never havin any fun is not good for the soul so I am go do my soul some good right na and pray about it later. God go forgive me, he forgive dem preachers and seem like he forgive the low down ass white peoples too. I hope I ain't pushin my luck cause I am just show us colored folk done did something to God and he still is pissed off at us.

We all know everybody needs to have a good time sometimes. Child I drank and I smoked them cigars and before long I was singing like a bird. I was prancing like a proud mare , you know from the music coming from the gramophone. You know some of them cigars had a different kind of bacca in em, smelled like awww, well I can't say what it smelled like but it sho did make ya feel good. Make ya thank a lot too, but it sho did not stop ya from havin a good time. Huh, know what I don't believe, I know of anybody with one of them gramophones. You would have thought I would have seen one in them whore houses in New Orleans but I ain't see none there. So I was glad to dance and listen to it, sos I could really have something to tell em on Sunday in the Town Square. I likes having things other people don't' have, like common sense. Most black folk around her so tied up with what they don't have and worried about deh life deh never stop to think about a damn thang. If deh smoke some of these cigars deh go start thankin though. Anyway people round here likes to get drunk and fall out so deh can forget all about this shit hole of a world us black folk have to live in. Ain't nothing wrong with tryin to forget thangs that hurt ya, hell much shit been done to us we probably go have us a liquor store on every corner before long. I am go keep my hopes up cause I know if the devil put dem liquor stores on every corner to help us forget, the Lord go put a church right across the street to make us remember.

Na don't thank I am go report everythin cause I aint; you never let folk know all your business, some thangs just for you and God and some thangs just for you. Hell if these folk around here knew how I questioned God they would call me a evil heathen; both sides the black and the white ones. See me, I ain't never believe I could not question somebody that is suppose to take care of me, punish me and bless or curse me. Yes sir ree, I am go question him, ain' t saying I have got to many clear answers but I can tell ya I questions Him. Plus, I think that is some white folk shit anyway, cause deh thank deh God and they don't want you to question them even if you see them hangin your sons or rapin your daughters, sayin they came up with thangs you came up with to make your job easier or just takin what you done worked for and destroyin just for dirt.. Na ain't that some shit, somebody is beating the hell out of you, taking advantage of you and you not suppose to question them. I bet them folks get together and laugh until they cry about us. We got all the sayings and they got all the blessings, money, priviliges and deh got a personalized God who done gave them every got damn thang under the sun. That is why I don't understand us colored folk sometimes. Ifin a white man don't like somethin and say it is wrong, we don't even question it. Most times we agree it is wrong especially if deh aint beatin the hell out of us. I done seen it happen a white man write something down and make it seem right and colored folk thank it is, especially if they thank deh Master image go be proud of them. Even though deh would not talk about Mr. Philmore with us colored folks, deh would exchange looks with you when he or his men came to town. That was the only time a colored person was allowed to turn deh nose up at a white man. And that also was the only time you could look dem in the eyes for a long time too. See deh wanted to stare at you to see if you was agreein with what they as thinkin and naturally since colored folk wanted to be excepted by em they agreed. I just as well tell them to kiss my ass. I sure in the hell ain't go judge or treat nobody bad cause a white man feel somethin wrong with em. I tell you what I am getting pretty sick of this shit. I know there is a God, but I don't think he is nothin like what they been telling us. Plus it is some trickery about concernin this religion thang, oh don't you worry Ms. Lula Mae go figure it out.

Well anyway, I decides to take me a little walk outside barefooted, the grass was warm and tickled my feet and sun just laid gentle on my head, lawd I felt so good, oh my , I felt so good. I had forgot about Puddin, Steve and Beulah. I was feelin right pleasin. I was feelin like a women in need getting ready to be serviced. I wanted to see our own Sheriff come strutin by, with his gun holdster hanging low on his hip, with them bow legs and that fine man structure all swole up and aware that someone was staring at him with lust in their eyes. I did tell yall that he had a fine body didn't I; he just look like a man that was born naturally fine with all the muscles in the right place, every muscle on his body was in the right place. I have not seen a man yet look as good as he does with his shirt off, not too much muscle, but just enough to make you want to touch him. I would touch him alright, over and over again. I is feelin sorta drunk, drunk with passion, stomach quivering, arms sorta weak, breathin sallow, jittery, and my precious puffy little wonder is runnin a race with my heart. I am a mess, what I am feelin and wantin is suppose to be of the devil and evil, but it makes me feel good and alive, especially when I can complete the feelin. Oh Jesus, is I am ever go see your face, I gotta ask cause if it is true that you is sinnin even if you thank of something I am in a shit load of trouble. (By the way that is another truck load of shit used to keep you in line. See how master got your mind na you worried about what you thank. And people wonder why we drank so much across the tracks, huh.) I had to start walkin kind of fast because my knees felt like they was gonna give out at any time and I would find myself laid out on this warm bed of grass. I still can not figure what is wrong with me touchin me, that just does not make sense to me. I done told yall before, I figure mens put that in the bible sos we won't know that they don't really know what deh doin. So deh tryin to keep us controlled so deh can slip dem stinky guggie dicks in us at deh leisure and make us thank deh is doin us a favor. In other words deh tryin to keep all the pussy to themselves. Ain't that nothing men want so much control over us they don't want us to touch ourselves.

I walked to the end of my walk- way and started to break a sweat, child, mainly because my mind was more on pleasin myself than worried about what some sneaky peeper might thank if they walked up on me. Anyway if someone did they woud be trespassing if I did not want them there, hell I just might lay out here for a minute or two. Oh did Ms. Lula Mae tell ya I have one of these walk- ways that start from the road, goes over the bayou,and then it goes through a small garden. Where I grows some of the finest mustard greens, potatoes and herbs you ever wanted to see. My garden of fresh herbs is one reason why my food is so much better than most others. And why my legs some of the finest shaped ones in these here parts or so it been told. It takes a few minutes to walk to my front door from the road and it is just as long a walk when I have to go gather herbs. See all that walkin I do keeps my legs pretty. Most people coming to visit me use the gap on the west side of my spread, because it is easy for wagons and cars to come through. I likes it better when they come that way too cause I can see them, that is why I had all the trees cut down on that side of my property. I want to have a good look at who is coming up to my house. Well anyway I got myself together begged for forgiveness again and started back to my house. I am always beggin for forgiveness, cause it seems like everythang that makes you feel good is a got damn sin, or so that is what they tell us.

I could hear loud talkin and swearin comin from my house, sos I get a move on then, cause I am thinkin it done started. They waited until after deh done ate my good breakfast and na it has started. What kind of devilment is going on in Ms Lula Mae Carson's house. Aww Jesus is you done left and sent in the Devil, to show me the way to hell. Cause you know it is go be some shit if people cuttin up in my house. But when I gets closer to the house I could smell the welcoming aromas of cigars, fine whiskey, and lalic water all mixed up together comin through my windows. Ain sho I like my house smellin like a juke joint but any that is another story. I immediately started to feel shame, cause I had figured these people was fightin and gettin ready to tear up my house. But lawd have mercy that's not what had started. Steve and Beulah was dancing and I mean they was dancing close and nasty like and when Steve turns around to twrill Beulah, his concerns was poking out mmmmummmmummm, way out. And I was glad of that cause what they did not know was it was'nt go be no tearin up my house. I had my little pearl handle derringer with me . Usually when you hear people gettin all loud and carrin on trouble is right behind it and that is all I was thankin when I walked up. Cause you know it is go be some shit if people cuttin up in my house especially on a morning like this when I am feeling kind of drunk and satisfied too. And yall know that whiskey will make your true feelings show, help me lord. Then here comes Puddin strutin as fast as she could meetin me in the middle of the room and puts her hand on my neck and says "Come on old fineeeeeeeeeeeeeeeeeeee Ms. Lula Mae, come on and join us little party." I already told yall Puddin is the devil's number one whore so you knows a person cannot hardly resist her. "Girl go on with that foolishness I am yet holding on." Lord knows I tried to resist but everybody sayin come old fineeeeeeeeeeeeee Ms. Lula Mae come on, all of em includin Mr. Steve. I fought with every Christian fiber in my poor old sinful flesh, to resit the devil, but that fleeing thing did not work for me. It was to many of them demons for me to win. I was not prayed up and I did not have any prayer warriors with me either and the angels must have been at a meetin in heaven; cause was'nt none of them around. The demoms of lustful temptation came over and over took me, I was bein tested like Job. My flesh joined in that party they was havin, but my spirit was absent with the Lord. I aint go tell yall what kinds of temptations and brazin acts was forced on me, but Sodom and gomarrah would be ashamed of what we did. But I am go say that I ain't never socialized like that before or after that in my life. This is one of the moment in your life you know happened and you know you liked it, but every Christian and moral fiber in your mind and body is tellin you, you done went to far. But damn, it felt so good until I would rather think of it as a moment of blessed weakness. Don't judge me cause I know every body alive has had moments just like that, if not the same situation one that could come close to it. Ifin yall thank I am gonna let yall sit here and judge me, you done lied cause I ain't. One thang I know is that everybody got skeltons in their closet. And ifin you listen real close you can hear em rattlin.

Me and Beulah became very close friends, I understood her better after that day and she understood me a little bit better too. Puddin and Steve stayed a few more weeks. Making every moment worth having them around. But Puddin being so damn good at what she does was startin a rukus, her regulars got win that she was back and wanted to see her. We all knew that was not good for anybody. So Puddin and Steve moved some place they call Cuba, that place where Steve got them cigars from. I guess yall thinkin I should be sad or worried cause Puddin gone. Well child Puddin left me well off. She left me jewelry , she left me over 8,000.00 dollars plus the money that I made off her livin with me and the tips her visitors left for my fine meals made me a rich woman. Na don't yall get the notion that I just laid around and collected money like a landlord; I worked for some of it . See an idol hand is the devils whore house. So you knows while Puddin was entertainin I had to do somethin. So I cooked, and yall know it was good. Some nights I would make a pot of crawfish ettoffe, or Crab meat delon with rice, sweet peas , mustard greens, corn bread, fresh biscuits and pecan pie. I always had a pecan pie made, them mens loved pecan pie and hot coffee, Lord Jesus they did. So yes I made some money by workin and it was not on my back either. I also sold many of my fine jellies, jams, pecan candy, and fig preserves to these fine customers too. Say what you want to say all men love good cookin, whether they good men or bad men, white men, black men, china men, Indian men, all mens love good cooking and good clean food like mine is worth a gold mine in California. I had a few of them men make me offers too child. I didn't take em serious, though, cause I knew better, but it was the thought that counted anyway.

You ever watched how people mouth move when they are eating something they love. It is different, looks like their tongue and their teeth makin love to one another, really. That is how people look when they eat from my plates of food. Oh and by the way, Steve left me that fine music player too. I know I will be havin a lot of visitors na because no one else in town had one of these. Can't wait to see them white folk face when they sees a colored woman has somethin they did not have. (Bastards … oh lord forgive me here I am callin them no good white folks out of their names. When, instead, I should be thankin you for givin me something they ain't got. My worst problem is go be the colore folks, see casue deh go try to start some shit. Once deh fine out deh not go just be droppin by listen to my machine. Deh go git jealous and try to find a way to take me down. I feels sorry for them all, but fuck em, dis here is my blessin.) I know Puddin ain't no saint but she is been an angel to me, cuz I is rich, yes maam , and yes sir I is rich yall. I really don't have to take no shit no more because I am a pretty rich woman, but I would have to leave Friendly, in order to enjoy spendin my money. One thang for show I would not be able to spend it in peace here and even if I could what would I spend it on. Ain't a damn thang in this town worth buyin. Got all the land I need or want to handle, about to add on to my house ain't but one thing missing for me right this very moment and that is a good hard leg in my life. Oh and you can't order to much from the catalog, cause either you ain't go get it or you go have to answer some questions bout what you got. Don't you just hate nosey sons of bitches?

CHAPTER 14

Somebody Has Moved In on The Johnson's Place

THEY SAY THAT SOMETIMES you get blessed in the strangest ways and I guess I have to admit that. Puddin done blessed me more in my life than anybody else; then again she could'nt help herself. God is the God over everythan so if he want to he can make a hell hound like Puddin bless a godly woman like myself. Huh, I always was a little judgemental and a little stuck up especially when it comes to them harlots see cause they would cause a good man to get caught up in a bad situation. Na that is different yall from a good man being in a bad situation. I keeps hearin a little voice telling me I must show a change in myself sos to be a good example of a good Christian. That is one reason why the Lord sent Puddin in my life. Because of her I done pulled my nose out the air and I ain't to ready to judge people. One thang I know you can'nt just look at a person and tell ifin deh is bad. Whether deh is black of white, but you can be pretty sho ifin deh is white you ain't deh equal and deh probably go do you somethin low down. Na, Lord you knows I need your to help me stop being so noisey and gossipin. I am placing all these burdens I have on you, sos ifin I do not change it must be your will that I continue

128

to be just like I am , Amen. I am just go try to keep to myself in your presence , since I have some secret business of my own I would like to keep quite. One thang I know your good book says you have to forgive me, for whatever I do; that do count for black folk too huh. And it ain't none of yall business what it is either, I hate nosey readers.

Plus, there is a rukus in town na, all about this new fella that just moved in over at the old Johnson homestead. We don't know much about him but since he moved on old man Johnson's place we just all thinkin he must be some kin to them Johnsons. Deh was a strange group of people. About 20 years ago bout 15 of them moved in on a piece of land that all of us thought was fit for nothin but sloppin hogs. But them Johnsons built up that land up and made the best sweet potato farm you ever wanted to see. They worked the land and had babies and worked the land and then one day they all just moved away. Na I don't know, but some folk says that old man the daddy, had eight daughters and all eight of them was pregnant. Strange them girls all being pregnant cuase there never was no mens from town ever go over there . No one fooled around with those girls. Ms. Johnson was a little worm of a woman, here tell old man Johnson married her when she was seven and started her to having babies as soon as she could. He suppose to have had a boy or two but we never seened much of them . They would always go one town over to get their supplies and trade. They even had a nice shack, course none of us got a good look at it until they all had left cause it was somethin about them Johnson's . Not that you was scared of them but they just did not seem like the kind of people you wanted to get to know to well or piss off. Hell, they was down right unusual, stranger than white folks to us. Like I said they all left at once and nobody knows where they went to or why. Soon as they left the place a committee of us Christian ladies took it upon ourselves to do the Lords works. It was me , Sister Goodman the preachers wife, Lizze Ross the best singer in the choir, and Winney Degre' the leader of the fund rasing committee. With our Bibles in hand, some of them Catholic folks Holy Water and blessed oil from Reverand Two Wings we was ready to do battle with the devil.

Child yall should have seen all of us in our pure white baptizing gowns, full of Holy Ghost fire marchin over to the Johnson's house singin with sister Lizzie Ross leadin the meter. She say "Lawwwwd we goin down to do your will, seeking to runnnn the Devil off. Here us as we call him out Lord and runn him quickly back to hell." and as we got closer to the house the windows looked like black demon eyes was lookin out of it. Somebody had painted all of them black with white circles right in the middle. Owww wee Jesus feel like something is all over me right na just talkin about it. We made a circle right in front of it and started to shout out the 23 Psalms, while others was shoutin out the 119 Psalms and the other was readin a prayer from the Catholic church. Since we did not exactly know what was going on over their we wanted to blessed and rebuke the house first. Just in case the Johnson's had any evil spirits there, we was bout to send them following dem Johnsons's. A lot of people leave a place and leave their evil spirits with you or in your town. We was prayin yall, sweatin, turnin all around, singin with the voice of angels, stompin with the authority of warriors and rollin with the tides of righteousness. I could feel the spirit taking over my body, yes Lawd we was havin a time. And then all of sudden Sister Goodman says "Lets go in sisters, we need to walk through the house and bless the grounds." Everybody knows I am the gatekeeper so I told Sis Goodman, I would stay at the gate with Gabriel and the good book so when they ran the devil out, I would help Gabriel hold him down, by the reading the word. So they go in all of them. Singin, praisin the Lawd and beatin that tambourine loud enough for all of heaven to hear. Then all of a sudden Sister Ross and Sister Degree came runnin out that house cussin like two sailors in a bar. They went tarin down the road like deh was in a horse race. Neither one of em was lookin back givin a damn bout what was happenin to us. Then my heart stopped when sister Goodman came runnin out of that house throwin up her hands, eyes bucked out of her head, hair standing straight up and screamin the name of Jesus. At least she was callin on the Lord instead of cussin like a sailor. I just shook with fear, I knew the Devil himself had got hold of her. Lord Jesus here I am standin by this got damn gate with a got damn book in my hand and I don't see no got damn Gabriel no where. My heart stopped especially since dem other two so called prayer warriors took off tarin down the road like a bunch of unsaved heathens with no God on deh side. (I can't wait till the next general church meetin.) Child din all of a sudden sister Goodman fell on the ground, and I noticed the Devil had a fur coat and was wearing a mask. It was one of the biggest bo coons you ever laid eyes on. The kind of coon hunters stand around and talk about for a hour or two waiting for the taxidermist to come. I knew I had to be careful, when I saw that. I realized then I would have rather seen the devil. Cause if I did not hit that coon right, I had a problem. But I really was not worried about it to much, because I am more than just a damn good woman, I am a got damn good woman. Thank God sister Goodman wore them ugly thick haired wigs, cause if not that old coon would have been bitin and scratchin up her natural head child. As I turned and looked by the the gate, there was a hoe handle layin there. I took it and hit that coon right behing the neck. That was all she roll yall , all she roll. A hoe savin a woman of God. I got to tell ya, that turned out to be some good eatin. I took Sister Goodman back to my house, cause she had to be doctored on right away and she needed fresh herbs, tea, and some strong whiskey to help her out. Yall don't know the pain she was in, cut up, bite up and bleeding, attacked by a coon. Well, I had it all, whatever she needed to get better Ms. Lula Mae had it all. That is why I keeps me an herb patch, people always need somethin. The other two sisters had already went and told the Reverand so he came by and got his wife. I let him know what time the coon would be ready. I had to clean and musk him first, then let him soak in my seasonings, so I let the good Reverend know he would be ready to eat on tomorrow. Of course Rev. being as greedy as he is wanted to know what I was having with that coon. I told him the usual candied yams, mustard greens, cornbread, biscuits, blackberry cobbler and some spring punch. "Don't you worry Ms. Lula you won't have to eat that all by yourself. I am go bring decon Wilson and brother White." "Bring a donation when you bring them too okay Rev." That is what I said to that bold as man. I invite him to my house and he invite the church. As long as they leave me a nice donation they can eat it all. I don't care too much for havin to many left-overs anyway.

Anyway back to this man, I been settin my eyes on, his name is Big John. I been watchin him from a far off you know, like a descent woman would do. He seem to be kind of a brazin man to me wearin them overalls kinda snug pushin his concerns almost right in your face. He ain't makin nobody blush but them white women though. It has been about a year or two na since Puddin been gone so life seemed pretty borin na in Friendly; exceptin every single, women is tryin to get big John. Looks like Mr. fine thang Jones done got some competition. I am not as forward as some of dem juke joint harlots, so nobody knows that I have put my bonnet in the runnin for that man. You see yall I lives by myself, and I spend a lot of time talkin to myself and God, na God don't answer like regular people do. God listens to what I have to say and then God gives me the right to figure out the right way to do a thang. I found this secrete a long time ago. See you knows about God and God knows about you, but since God don't force nothin on us , we have to know ourselves the right way. Na the Preacher says, God picked him to tell us the right way. We believe it cause we want to. God never told me bout a Preacher he picked. But some of them men speaks with power when they is tellin you all the stories in the bible. I mostly thank it is the stories themselves got the power not the men. Like I, remember my Great Grandmother use to tell me stories and then I would tell her stories all about Bro Rabbit and Bro. Bear. Lawd, forgive me yall cause yall probably don't even know what that is. But anyway, I know God, is suppose to answer our prayers , the way you want them to be answered. Child it never hardly happen that way though, you have to do somethin. And a lot of times if you really listen to them Preachers they send you a secret message in their sermon, tellin you, you have to do something to move the spirit of God. Most of the time deh doin involves a large collection plate full of guilt from Friday and Saturday night sinnin. I ain't never figure out why God make me pay man so He can forgive my sins. Cuase if you look at it that is all we be doin, payin a sinner like ourselves sos we can git favor from a God who says we been set free from condemnation. Now that is another story don't get me started on that. Plus the only reason I keeps my thithes up is sos the church will come to my funeral. So maybe, I have been stayin to myself to long, maybe it is time for me to step out and do somethin about this situation. I am over here all alone, wastin these good grindin years on fingers and promises. Hell when a good women reaches my age she is seasoned to perfection and she knows what she wants. That Big John just might be the kind of fella I need to fill my pantries full of nuts. Hell these empty mounds of passion need more than fruit to be satisfied. Nuts is good for ya ask any doctor. Na don't say you heard this from me but some womens goes to the doctor and he gives them pleasure to make them better. Oh yeah, deh can't keep no secretes from us. Child some of them was goin to this doctor in Mississippi and he would use these different thangs on em to make their lady passion spit. But that is another story; can't tell yall everythang at once.

CHAPTER 15

4:30 in the Morning on my Way to Town

WELL ANYWAY I HITCHED old Lula Bell up last night and she ready for her trip to town, this morning. If you go trade in Friendly, you have to get to the Town Square early so you can get your place to set up your wagon. Course that was only for coloreds , you know the white folks could have any place they wanted. I thank the lord not many of them wanted to set up at all. The only ones ever really set up was Ms. Lucille Ledaey. Now that is a women, most times we always takin about how helpless the white women was but Ms. Ledaey was not in that group. She was a formed women solid a a rock, long black hair, big green eyes the color of grass almost, and an ass like a colored woman. Oh yes, she had some ass on her. You could not use the word niggar around her even if you was colored and she made the best muskadine wine in the entire South. Lucille won prizes for her wine, the President of the Country would order cases from her. She would call you her sister in front of white folks and you was to scared to say it back. Cause when deh catches you by yourself they tell ya, "Don't let that crazy white women get you hung. You ain't no sister to a white woman or man." I be thankin to myself you sho is ignant and you is a partial heathen too, cause you don't believe the shit you wrote in your own Bible. But then again I don't believe that Adam and Eve shit either. But ifin it was true I keeps puttin two and two together gettin a bunch of half crazed children that spread out a cross the world that became us. You know sister and brothers children go be simple minded. That is why we hate each other so much cause most of us is simple minded. Now I am not tryin to get off the subject of Lucille cause she is an important lady. But I just want to show yall how peoples with power do.

About three years ago, I went to deliver some of my goods to the Babasheys' house and Chris the college boy and one of his friends was havin one of them talks where you had to have been studied the book to really understand how deh was thankin. They keep on talkin like I was nothin to worry about. I remember the subject cause people don't go around talkin about the conscious and the subconscious. From what I figure, the conscious is what you is thinkin about all the time, you know the thangs that be on your mind. And the subconscious is the thangs that be put in the back of your mind. Follow me na, I believes that the Bible makes incest allowable, and that is why people is so crazy. See Adam would have had to have his daughter and Eve would have had to have her son and then the children was go be havin each other. Here me na ifin that is the truth then, it been put in our minds that incest is a divine order. Cause God made Adam and Eve and yalls Good Book say we is all sisters and brothers and if that is the truth I understand where the term muther fucker comes in. I use to thank that was the worst thang to call somebody till I realized God approves it. Na ain't that a muther fucker. And ain't them two boys some real dumb asses sittin in here talkin around a women who gots wit just like dem. Deh never thought about that casue first of all I am colored, second I am a woman, and third I am poor or so they thank. When people haves a lot deh really do thank deh is gods. But see ifin some of our college boys was in the room deh would put them to shame; well maybe not cause that could cause a killin. Ya bet not out do em, rich folk will hound your ass for the rest of your life if you out do em. I want yall to know you ain't dealin with no regular person here Ms. Lula Mae gots plenty of sense. You thank I am go ever talk like this around any other colored folks, hell naw. Deh be the one go run tell Master, or deh go sit around judgin you so much you go have to put your foot up one of deh ass. Dis really do help me though cause now I understand why we is so messed up we all comes from sisters and brothers children. What else would you expect? We is all a bunch of crazy muther fuckers and that is the reason we hates one another. It take a real fool to hate deh own kind.

Na back to Lucille, her husband went off to war and was killed right after he got there. She had sixteen head of children and they lived on the old Lestworth Plantation. She ain't have no men friends to help her and these white heifers around here was so jealous of her deh wanted her to fall down, yall know why. I guess when you is made of good stuff nothing kin stop ya. That women start growing beans, corn, sweet potatoes, rice and sugar cane instead of cotton. Din she leased out her pecan orchard, so she was makin all kinds of money from that, plus she got all the pecans she wanted to harvest. You could not beat out her pecans she has one of the oldest and largest orchards in these parts. Child she would hire people from all different places to work for her. Plus she got quite a few women who lost their husbands in the war livin with her too. Her house is full and seems like everythin she does ends up bring blessings to her and others. She is a sweet and kind woman, just as good as gold. Makes you wonder about the good Lord, people who seem to be good just have some bad times that hit them. Her children was not like the rest of the kids, they had manners and would say yes maam and no maam to colores as well as whites. I hate plantations and I don't usually go near em, but when she haves her annual harvest celebration, I takes whatever I have and head straight over their and enjoy myself. Plus you ain't never had a cochon de lait until you have had hers. Well anyway if you want some good cooking, finely made clothes, cakes and pies, you stop at her table. And by the way if you did not order one of them pretty apple pies you can't buy one. She also made sweet potato pawn, oh lord you ain't had none till you have had hers. She liked my biscuits and my fig preserves, so most of the time me and her would just trade. Ms. Ledaey was the only white women who had a regular spot she keep all the time at the market. A lot of the money she made from the market she used for the real poor people. You know she got Tandy Williams help when the night riders burned down her house and killed her husband. Ms. Ledaey rebuilt her house, gave her children clothes and gave them a years worth of saving from the market. That is where she made her mistake, when she gave Tandy all that cash money. That girl left Friendly and did not even say a thank you goodbye to that good women or none of us either. You can't help some heathens, cause some people just ain't shit.

Like I said the market was mostly run by us black folks cause, child people from all over loved buying our preserves, fresh picked black berries and our pickled melatons. But the black berries all ways went first. I don't blame em for buyin all the black berries ; cause deh so worrisome to pick. I grew a few patches of them, but after the red bugs ate me up a couple times, I started buyin them myself . Plus I hated taken those turpentine baths. Another thang I forgot to tell yall about Friendly, we are known for having some of the best dirt in Louisiana. Rich and black full of nutrients, that produce the best of anythin that is grown in it. We ain't the richest of people but we got just about the best of everythang in nature God could give you, except fairness.

Yall, know I was in town by 4:30 waitin for folks to come bring in their goods and buy my goods. I sorta likes to get my pickins first. It is one of them foggy mornins everythin still damp by the dew; I calls these my sho nuff sacalay mornings, cuase on mornings like this I always catches me a big mess of them pound and a half sacs. Sos I am standing next to my hitch and all of a sudden this big thang brushed up against me and almost knocked me down. But before I could fall he grabbed me with them big strong hands, it was that Big John. Well I started gigglin and straighten out my clothes and he looks me dead in the eyes and says " I am sorry maam did I hurt you?" I giggled for a few minutes and finally blurted out and said "No". Then he pulls me real close and says "Aint you that rich lady that lives at the end of colored town with all that pretty land?" It is like I heard him and like I did not hear him I was still feelin kind of silly na, cause just the feel of that mans strong hands on my back was movin me real strong. My head was swimin, and I even felt a little sweaty in my funk pocket. I sho hope he can't smell me. See I was in the arms of the one man that I was willin to have to pray for forgiveness about. Child I was breathin so hard I could feel the heat comin out of my nose. Finally I gave him an answer back. " I be Ms. Lula Mae Carson and I do live in our family homestead but I do not know about all that rich stuff." Every body knows it aint suppose to be no rich coloreds in Friendly. Then he says " You shol is pretty." I said "Thank you sir you might want to let me go." Then he says " I might not want to let you go." All of a sudden I jumped and pull away from that demon filth casue I

could feel his concern was on the prowl. I showed my disapproval of that
. Then he looks right at me and smiled as if to say it is okay if you liked it.
He was a brazin man and I don't think he was a church going man either
(He was'nt slick enough). Big John was indeed a big man, he was strong
lookin, solid, thick and he had coco brown skin, with course brown hair,
and light brown eyes, pretty but because he so solid you just notice the
solid built of this buldgin man. You can call me a whore if you like, that
man had some dick on him. And it was so hard I could feel the heat of
his grizzle on my on my lady self. He is a fresh man, I mean a fresh man,
but damn he smell good, like fresh pine.

Before we could say anything else , here come Sally White , you know
the Major's wife. She says, "Ain't you the carpenter my husband said was
coming to build up my sewing room?" I know I ain't no man but ifin I
was, I sure as hell would not want this this big old thunder dick nigga
around my wife or woman or nothin. As usual the white women go pass
him around from house to house first. Before long one of these white men
is go wake up and put words in against him. But that ain't go do em no
good cause when a white woman decide she wants somethin she can be
quite demandin. Ifin they don't let him do the work they won't be able
to sleep in their own beds. Then she turns and speaks to me . "How are
you doing this fine morning Lula? "Fine", I says. Did'nt feel like calin l
her Ms. White so I just answered fine. She standin there lookin at me
from over the top of her spectacles as if she wants me to leave so her and
John could talk. I am standin, she standin, then John answers her and
says, "I is Big John Patterson. I meet your husband over in Welcome. He
said he was lookin for a town carpenter and he even offered me a place
to stay if I wanted to fix it up. Well I guess I am your man maam." Sally
tells John to come by after lunch today sos he could get started right away.
As soon as she left my mouth just opened up and said. "A big man like
you probably be right hungry so early in the mornin, not unless you have
found someone to cook and clean for ya.." Hmm, his name is Big John
Patterson, not Johnson, so maybe he is not kin to them Johnson's after
all. I hope not. Seems like the Major must have given him permission to
use the Johnson's place. Hell he probably owned it, they always take our
land when the old folks die off. Plus most of the time we can not afford
to keep up more than one place at a time.

John says, "I don't need someone to cook and clean for me although that would be nice. I am in need of other thangs right now Ms. Lady. I am right hungry na but I will have to wait till everybody gits here with their goods. I am needin some more tools and some fresh wood sos I can make me a new table and some chairs." I says " You a furniture maker too?" He looks at me and hold up his big hands and says these hands have built houses and made baby beds, they strong but gentle. I am whatever you need Ms. Lula." When that man said that, "Have mercy on my soul" is all I could think of in my mind cause I knew I was going to hell for this one. He just made up my mind for me. Then, I says " I been needin some work done around my house. I wants me a new porch and I wants me a back porch to go all the way around back of my house, which means all the back bed rooms will need doors added to them too, so you can walk out from the bedrooms to the porch. I always did like that style of house, it is just like Annie Richards's place." We say reeee chard, she says Richards. She passin but that is another story. "If you come by after you get your supplies, maybe you could tell me how much you will charge me for the work to be done. I really need it bad." He looked at me right then and said "I can get that wood later and seems like I might have somethin sweet to eat this morning after all. You got some honey? Why don't we go and see ifin I can give you what you need na Ms. Lula, the market can wait. I am pretty hungry na." It was just like I could feel him inside of me and I know he could feel me, hell he could smell me, cause I could smell me.

I don't care what yall think of Ms. Lula Mae I have every bit the devilment in me to get to Big John before them white women pass him around. He might say he would not dare touch one of them and all that, but that ain't nothing but a negro man trying to pretend like he would not dare touch a white women. Them lying bastards know they want it and they want it bad. Men like danger and adventure, so when any man is faced with the chance to get somethin that somebody tell him he cannot have, he go get it, if he get the chance. I don't so much care about all that business between white woman and black men, to me if people brave enough to do it let them do it. I know enough to know that when people is attracted to each other it don't matter what anybody else thinks. I think the only reason the white man is tryin to scare off relationships between their women and black men is because they want their women to look to them for everythin. They want her to stay controlled by deh money and power cause those are their real dicks. And they know that when needy white women and that mistreated black man get together there is go be some serious "fucking going on' as Puddin would say. If you make people hold back their feelings and kill them if you find out that they have them; when they do get together they go catch up for all that time they was apart. See that black man's concern is goin to be angry and hurt and that white womans lady self is go be stroking it soft and long pettin it and tryin to calm it down. Everybody knows most white womens have pussy like a jersey cow that is why the black man like em deh ain't got to ever stop diggin in. And you know what you have when that happens is, well yall know … That black man go swell up with passion and that white women go receive every inch of him. See the black man's body is a machine full of passion. You want his sweat to drop down on your brow, you want his strong arms to grab your ass. You want him to plow as many rows as he can in your sweet garden, you want him to grind your wheat. Hell, I don't blame any woman that wants her one, that know what he doin as long as she leave me some. Even if they don't, I will still be okay, I gots a few gray boys I can call right now if I wanted too. And aww they not the average ones either deh hung like black angus bull. I always get the exceptions. Oh we calls our white men gray boys, cause most of them represent the confederacy whether deh tell ya or not. You ever had a southern gentleman call your name in the dark, listen … and then deh got big appetites too deh eats everythin livin or dead, deh eats it.

CHAPTER 16

Ms. Lula Mae's Treat

ALL THIS TALKIN GETTIN me fired up. I know one thing on this earth for sho this morning; unless one of them white girls done slipped in the barn with him already, I am going to introduce him to my pantry in a few minutes. That is why I say, I am in trouble of hell fire, cause I know what I am doin and I can not wait to do it. Hell anyway fornication is not a sin if nobody else don't know about it. I always did like a big broad neck man, buldging with passion. Plus everybody who would judge me if they found out about my great sin, I have piked for. So aint no reason for me to give them a second thought and if the good Lord don't strike me down then I consider this one of those times the Lord forgive and forget your deed. I been good most of the time can't see why the Lord would want to kill me for wantin somethin that he put in me. He did make me so He knew what feelings he put in me. Na , I am rushing home so fast I did not sell one thang. My heart was beatin so hard I felt like I was about to pass out. That Big John got on his horse right next to my wagon and I could see his concerns, yes, I looked and I looked good, because all that was doin was getting me ready. The ride was not helping me either because they had not graded the road and it was some bumpy ride . To much more of this an I ain't go need him.

Child when I got to my front gate I rushed right in my house and started makin biscuits and fryin bacon. While screaming over the noise of clatterin pots and skilets telling John what I needed to have done. Child I had that kitchen lite up with the smells of biscuits in the oven, coffee, bacon and fresh pussy. Althought I wanted to walk in my house and go straight to my bed room. But I hit that kitchen first; tryin to act like a lady. Big John says " Ummmmm ummmmm Ms. Lula I can hardly wait to taste it." I excused my self and went to the bathroom to freshen up. While I was rinsin the soap off my face John must have eased up behind me, cause when I stood up he was standing right next to my behind and lightly touchin it with his concern. Then he said in a deep sweet like voice "Thought I heard you call me Ms. Lula did you need me for somethin?" I choked as my eyes watered with passion and my knees felt as if they were goin weak and I said " No John I never called you out loud, maybe you heard me thinkin about you." Then he pressed his concerns up against me again a little harder and it felt like he had a smokin gun in his pants. That is when I helplessly fell back into his arms like a little baby. He turned me and kissed me and I lost my direction. Then he touched me gentle like a feather, and swayed me back and forth like the wind gently blowin a swing. I ... I could not think, I was moist and anxious. I was angry at myself, but my body well it just ignored me and went with his flow. John had thrown me away, I could taste honey on his lips and I was so warm my body was drenched in sweat. I mean I was so moist my thighs felt like I had just oiled them. I was trembling, and well ... I pulled away for a minute, just to catch my breath, see I was drunk. My lips were meltin and head was swimmin, and and and, I started touchin him and feelin the strength in his arms and broadness of his back muscles, and that smell oh my god that smell behind his ear, and then I smelled them damn biscut. I started to let them bastards burn. But I ran to the kitchen and got them out the oven just in time. I looked up and John was standing in the kitchen still smiling,he said " Them biscuits smell as good as you taste Ms. Lula. " I said what you know about how I taste, and then that brazin man fell to his knees and buried his noise right beneath my waist and that is when my knees went out. The next thing I knew he was guiding me backwards to my bed ... about a hour or so later, I was still shiverin. Yes, I was still shiverin, I needed that and apparently he did too. He reached over and grabbed my whole woman and gently tugged me towards him and gave me the pleasure of his strong gentle hand. Three minutes later I was so relaxed I could not feel my legs. I was thinkin to my self, "It is gonna be alright now Ms. Lula, it is gonna be alright girl. If they ain't got this in heaven, I do not want go." Aint' often you find a man you will use his hand on you after he done piped you good. All I know is right na I must be blessed. And if these feelins is from the devil I am go ask the good Lord to take it from his side and bring it to our side.

When I could get up I immediately went to the bathroom to wash up , I did not want him to wake up with a nose full of ass funk. But he must have got up first cause when I put that wet towel to my face all I got a wiff of his man self. That is the problem about livin with men you never know where they have been and Big John's ass and nuts all over this towel. I fixed him a plate fit for a king. That man ate and ate some more, and I felt good cause he ate all I cooked. He looked good to sittin at the table with the sun shinnin through window bouncin rays of glory off his body. Lord this was a blessed mornin here. Then it happened he told me it would take 550.00 to do my job. I almost fainted, all I wanted him to do was build me a porch around the back of my house, do me some of them French doors, add some windows, add an extension to my front porch, add me another room, build me one of them nice gazebos' , and get my house ready to start getting electric and plumbing. Hell I almost fainted again. I told John I had to pray about this , he said fine but while I was thankin he would have to start Sally Whites house first and then no telling who else might get him to obligate. I got my ass up and I went right in and got him 250.00. He left my house this mornin full, satisfied and 250.00 richer. Did I just pay for a man?

Chapter 17

John Started Working on My Job

The day seemed like it was passin by so fast; I guess cause I have really been busy. I aint had no more vistors all my work done and I just laid around thinking about what a blessing I had just had. Aint that something, I just called the best sinning I ever done a blessing. Next thing I know I had dosed off to sleep. I must have been real tired cause I never go to sleep this early. Na I must have been sleeping pretty hard cause I slept till the next mornin. How I woke up was cause I could hear some noise but I thought I was dreamin. You know that haze you are in when you do not know whether it is a dream or real life, cause in real life you are not expectin it and in a dream you can not see why you are doing it. All I could hear was the sound of hammerin and the clangin of stuff. First I turns over and over until I realized the noise was real. So child I jumped up and went to grab for my trusty make it right. That's my shot gun full of scatter shot, it is just a little sawed off present from one of Puddin's old suiters. I sure like it to cause if you aint suppose to be on my property and I aimes it in your direction, I really don't need to have a bead on you to hit you with it. That is why I call it my make it right. When I looks out the window it was Big John makin all that noise and stuff. I sees him , but he did not see me, I ran back to my bed room and grabs my comb and brush and gets in that bathroom and start fixin myself up. Yall know I put on my powder pink satin robe. I don't need to tell you who gave that to me. I walks to the kitchen and I yells out to Big John, I says "I wasn't expectin you so early this mornin, hell my rooster had not even crowed yet, how you can see in all that dark. He says "Ms. Lady it is a full moon plus I likes to do what people don't expect. I had to get to workin early sos I kin finish you early. I have to get to Ms. White today and start on her. Anyway I thank your rooster is a little tired it is kinda hard on a cock when he the only one the yard" First I am thinking how you go finish me early, you can not finish this job in one day or even one week. Then I says under my breath, I bet you do have to get to her. I ain't go lie on Sally White she is a looker, that is why I just don't get the Major. She is a pretty as a picture, she is one of those red heads, pale skin, big green eyes and a face full of freckles, but she is pretty. I am standing there just looking at him, thinking just how much of Puddin's harlot tricks I can use on him. Shit dem white gals like to suck the strength out of a man so I better be quick. Cause I don't intend to leave them anythang to suck. I ain't got a pair of poutin lips for nothin.

Now ifin I was a real wise woman I would see the signs that this ain't right, first of all I keeps thinkin about Puddin when it comes to John. I keep thinkin about some of the things she told me men really likes a lot. I bet she could take one look at John and tell me every thang he liked. I am thinking about a situation Puddin told me about. Not all the people she talked about was worldly peoples some was of Gods' chosen army. See some people thanks about evil and sin all the time and some people just bumps into it. Puddin told me that sometimes you just want to do things because they make you feel good. You know it is not good for you to experience them, but the experience go make you feel so good you do it. Puddin says, "Sometimes Ms. Lula Mae a man comes along that you want to have. You look at him and you just want to give yourself to him. Not for the money but because you want to. You give yourself to him totally, you hold him like he is yours, you love him strong like his is yours. His smell alone makes you come and his touch send stocks like lightenin through your body. You can just lay your nose next to his nuts Ms. Lula and inhale his scent. The whole time you with him you don't even think about money, you just want him." Well I am thinkin to myself when she is saying this "How a harlot go want to lay down with a man and not think about money?" Then she looked right at me and says " I know you don't believe me Ms. Lula cause you don't figure I have a soul, let long the ability to have feelins for a man." Hell I am scared now cause the devil done got in my mind and is able to tell Puddin what I am thinkin. "The truth is Ms. Lula you run across situations like that every now and then. It ain't good for you though, cause while you holdin that man and feelin like he is yours you forget what you really is. So you whisper sweet words of love in his ears and tell him he does not need to leave you a dime. He lay there and hold you, he rubs your feet, kisses you sweet, then yall takes a long nap. Then the truth hits you in the face when you go to wash up and come back out to see, not only did he leave you money but he left you huge tip. Then reality hits you Ms. Lula you are nothin more than a bought favor. These are the times when you look up and thank God that you are good at pretendin. See I pretends a lot Ms. Lula, I pretends a lot. Sad thing is when I am not pretendin most folk think I am anyway." I thought to myself "Lula you are really a self-righteous bitch sometimes." Yall know what it is too early in the morning to be so serious. But that Puddin left me a head full of stories, I am go share them with yall, don't worry. Cause if you readin this and din got this far you like Ms. Lula stories. And child I will tell you stories all day long as you helpin pay my bills. Ms. Lula Mae is tryin to get all the money she can, casue she needs to live good, so thank ya for readin this here story. Course yall is gettin way more than what you paid for, the dirt on peoples is worth more than money if you use it right.

" Plus Ms. Lula we usin green wood and sometimes it will swell so I need to get it seasoned and everythin. I hopes you don't mind me comin like dis, do ya?" Hell I had almost forgot about Big John, then I looks at that man and says " John have you had somethin to eat yet? He looks at me and smiles and says "Nothing but a little bit of beef jerky, but even if I had already ate Ms. Lula I still would want some of what you got." Then he looks at me and smiles a devlish smile. I looks off a little and trys not to let him see me blushin. Cause I hopes John don't have in his mind he go be comin over here sharpenin his tool when ever he likes. Child I started cookin like the Reverand was comin over. Yall already know I made them biscuits, went out to my smoke house and got some fresh salt pork and pulled out them figs and the honey, cause he seem to like figs and honey, to sweet for me together though. See I noticed that when he ate the other mornin he put both of them on his biscuits. He almost pissed me off coverin up the taste of my biscuits; most people eat em naked. I put on the water for my cheese and garlic grits and made some fresh coffee. Na a breakfast like this would not be right unless you have some fresh orange juice. Since it was still kinda dark I tried to ease out in my pink satin robe and knock down a few of them oranges. I calls them oranges but the white folk says they is a Satsumas. I don't care cause deh always namin somethin different tryin to make you feel more ignorant than them. Deh is got damn oranges, deh grow on a tree and the juice is sweet , good and orange. Na yall know I was not tryin to be forward, but I had to put them in my robe cause I forgot to bring out my bucket. I could feel Big John's eyes goin all the way up my thigh cause you know I had to raise my robe way up to my waist. He ain't come messin with me though, he playin with me like a cat playin with a toy. I goes in and start rollin the satsuma's to get them soft sos the juice would be eaiser to squeeze out. I was thinking about Big John's muscle while I was squeezing them oranges. (bad girl Lula Mae, bad girl) Johns all of a sudden stick his head through the window and said in a sort of breathless way, " Woman you is about to drive me crazy showin me them big brown thighs and the smell of all that good food. How long is I got to wait fo I can dig in?" Na I ain't sho but I thank that man was pullin on his concern when he was sayin that. Lawd that man show needs to watch what he say. Then I says, "The coffee is ready do you want some of that right na, before the rest is already." He says " I likes to enjoy somethin that good all together. I kin wait till everythang is ready for me." I starts to laugh to myself. See Big John just don't know, I got husband on my mind and he who I want for right now.

Well any way I calls John in to eat and he goes into the bathroom to clean up. Yall I am just thinkin how good it would be to have him everyday. I feels like he just might be the one I needs, owww Jesus I do need him. Then all of a sudden a hand comes up the small of my back and, and a moist tongue on my neck and the next thing you know I just gave in. Yes I gave in to his touch , yes I did. I am a good Christian woman and I aint been touched in while and we need to be touched or at least I do. But I feel like John is takin advantage of me in a way. Because everytime John comes to touch me I cannot resist him. He makes me fornicate and my religion tells me that is wrong. In a way I want to say no, but my evil flesh wants every inch of him. My spirit be saying no, no, no, but my body be sayin get all you can get. Lula Mae, blessins come in all kinds of disguises. Sometime lifes is just too damn hard. He is takin me against my Christian will, but he is givin my human nature what it needs. Then he lifts my robe and starts to feel my thighs Jesus this sinful body was feelin good my lady-self was thobbin. Daylight done broke and the sunrise was like watchin God paint, there is nothing that could ruin this moment, not one thing. As I was lookin out the window all of a sudden I sees this big old long yellow shinny car pullin up and comin straight cross my got damn walkway. Damn, who ever it is I hate em. I says "John stop looks like I got company comin." I know this, who ever it is, lost stranger or needey neighbor, I ain't go be to nice to em. I also know whoever it is they do not know me very well, cuz I tells people to park deh cars at the road and walk up to my house, if they not using my gap. I don't want no dirt road in the front of my property like some of dem colored folks back of the tracks and I don't want my fine bridge broke. You tell trashy people deh don't appreciate nothin and these must be some of them well off trashy people cause deh in a fine car.

A white man from Mississippi made that bridge for me. He likes me a lot; I had took care of his ailing wife until she got better. So he had decided to bring her here and leave her with me so I could take care of her all the time. I needed a new bridge cross the creek cause my old one was getting kind of weak in places. Well honey child, that good man saw my need and built me a bridge. No charge no, nothin, that man had men from his railroad crew, to come by and build that bridge for me. Now I am not much for people from other countrys but some of the chineese men was exceptionally good lookin. Most of the time all they did was smile and talk about you, right to your face. I say that because they was not like us they had their own tongue. They could talk to one another and you could not understand one damn thing they said. I did not pay too much attention towards them, cause they was hell bound folks. The white folks say if you don't know Jesus you can not see the kingdom. Since these people can't even talk Jesus tounge I know deh hell bent. Na if deh God is the real one when he come back and we can't speak His tougne and plead our case, guess we is goin to their hell. These poor heathens here go be talkin to deh statues like the Catholics. They was easy to take care of cause you could not feed them folk a thang, they did not eat your biscuits, your cake, your nothin, deh ate what deh bought to work and that was it. Made it easy for me to go on about my business, cause since I had done my Christian duty by askin, I was done. Na Mr. Paul did not seem to trust them much either he always told me to keep them out of my house. He always said he did not want anythin to happen to me. I took real good care of him and his wife. Na them is two fairly descent whites, never heard em once say nigger, or wench. Mr. Paul was known as a stingy man, but he had to spend money to get me. He did have some problems though, na here he was seein Anna Bell Carson, no kin to me she is a white woman. Na the only reason why I am sharin this is cause yall is payin good money for this story, sos I have to tell yall people's shameful business, cause that is what we likes to hear.

Anna Bell was a strange kind of woman to figure out. Everybody knew she did not like men mistreating women, casue she hit her son-in-law in the head with one of them cast iron skillets for beatin up one of dem bought girls. Nobody ever took up for them when they got deh ass whipped but she did. Plus she was never mean to us blacks. She always gave good money to the Christmas funds, she could cook a mean jambalaya and she had the sweetest smile you ever wanted to see. Oh let us not forget to mention that she never missed a church service or family day celebration. Mr. Paul's wife had went mostly blind so she never did know that the man she thought was comin in cleaning up and cookin for her was really Mr. Paul's hoe, Anna Bell Carson. Yeah child she would dress up in men clothes and put on a hat and be walkin all over that woman's house with her in it. She managed that womans house and her husband, she had over three children for him, everybody knew that but poor Ms. Karen Ann. We all knew it most colored folks be been knowin things about dem white folk personal business. Yall all knows white folks is strange in a lot of ways. Ain't nothing for a sister to marry her sisters ex husband, huh or even her husband. When they falls in love the falls in love and they go all the way in. Some of em leave home and some of them kill off each other. Deh is dangerous when deh is in love and ifin you ain't the one deh lovin, well all I can say is get the hell out of their way. See when a man or woman lose that certain feelin for you and have it for somebody else; ain't nothing you can do will right to them. You talk to loud. You don't talk enough. You need to work harder. Your cookin don't taste the same. All this means is that somebody else scent is in deh nose. Anyway the reason he had to get me was because Karen Ann was getting worse and worse and they know if she had died the whole world would have said they killed her. Cause when a woman can get in your house and go through your thangs your ass is in trouble. Cause dem hoes will try and fix ya when deh is that bold.

Like the time Vivian Johnsonee had just built a new house with her husband Larry. Well her mama got sick and she had to leave home for month or so. Child Mr. Johnsonee move his hoe right in her house. I can not tell you how many times both us black women and white women wanted to kick her ass. He tried to tell us she was his cousin, and even though we did not fool with them Frenchmans a lot we all knew better than that. Can you imagine leavin your home you done just built and your husband done moved in his hoe. Na that bitch is sleepin all in your bed and shitin out your toilet. And ifin that hoe believe in fixin you might just end up sick or havin to kill that bitch. Child a hoe that will stoop so low as to come into your house is low down enough to try and fix you. Honey we all wanted a piece of her. Well when Ms. Vivian got back home the white women had her come over to one of deh quiltin parties and it just so happen one of dem mentioned a rumor about this mulatto who had moved his woman in his wifes house. Vivian went home and got as many people as she could to come and help her clean her house and of course many of us came to help too. Child we found bottles with roots in em, onions with names stuffed em, and eggs in all her closets, one thang for sure if the hoodoo did not run em out of there the funk would have. Well anyway Ms. Vivian sat up all night waitin on his ass, child that coward did not come home for a week. Vivian had everybody come and get any furniture deh wanted. She gave it all away. Then she sold the property to dem low down Rankins (Nigger haters from deh soul. If deh put us all on a ship and needed somebody to jump on it to kills us; all dem damn Rankins would jump on. Doing their duty for the South.) They hated the idea that a nigger had a house like that, so deh paid her so much money nobody could afford to buy it back. Like deh would have sold it. Deh put a full rebel flag in the yard and painted it red and gray. Well child when Johnsonee come back to his home he was meet with shot guns and dogs. In other words he was fucked. So yall can see why no matter how much it looked like Anna Bell was helpin Mr. Paul, it was just low down of them to do that poor woman like that.

Anna Bell is a hoe I and so is Mr. Paul, but there is somethin descent about them both. I really believe she could have taken care of Ms. Karen Ann and not hurt her one bit. I am telling you the truth. I know that is hard to believe but I do believe it. Her children are kind kids, her house is almost as clean as mind and she keeps herself real good. Three children and still got a good shape for a white woman, mainly because she had a behind. Don't know where in the hell she got it from but she got one and a set of the devils dumplings like you ain't seen before sittin in the front of her chest. Yall know what I mean huh, she had big milky white tits made you want to bite into like dumplins. But I don't know about having my husbands woman take care of me on my death bed. Why would a man's woman want to take care of his ailing wife? Both of them are strange to me. Well anyway I started feeding Karen Ann some of my good old mustard greens and squash from my garden and she started to get better. Oh by the way I also was feeding her my chicken soup medicine, and my special teas, awwww huh, yall want to know what that is don't yall. Ain't telling ya.

Mr. Paul was some kind of fine white man, he had olive skin, broad shoulders, one green eye and one brown eye just looked like they pieced straight through you when he looked at ya. I ain't to much on white men but that one was worth the time to look at. I took good care of him and his wife. There was nothing he could ask me to do that I would not do with a big smile on my face. What is yall thinkin in them evil minds of yours just cause I said I took good care of him and his wife don't mean he got any special treats. I just made sure all his meals was cooked, every evenin he'd come and pick up his cookin and cleanin and I saw to it that everybody else did what they was paid to do. If you thinkin I got that bridge built for special favors, stop your evil lies. You bunch of wicked demons, Ms. Lula don't sell no favors. I keep waiting for Jesus to come and straighten yall out. He wanted to build me that bridge cause I deserved to have that bridge built. The folks tell me that my bridge go outlast the judgement day.

Anyway who in the hell is this? By na John started to behave hisself and I am mad as a cat fightin a hound dog. Ha, Ha, Ha. Child I put my hand on my hip ready to use words dat ain't nice when , I sees who gittin out the car, shit! I mean oh Jesus it is Puddin, got damn. She had lost a lot of weight, but she still look good even though she was a little frail. Everything bout her the same she just small. Her hips did not look like trees swayin in the wind and her thighs ain't clappin thunder when she walk hell her skirt ain't poppin like whip no more, but she still is good and damn pretty though. It never fails, as soon as a good woman gets her a man, here come some hoe. Anyway I had to catch myself and pretend like I was glad to see her and the truth is, any other time I would have been glad to see her, but Big John was here and I know Puddin was gonna mess with him. Puddin comes right on in like this is her house and says, "Heyyyyyyyyyyyyyy Ms. Lula Mae, I bet you been missin me?" Then she shimmies her shoulders and stretches out her arms and hugs me like a nasty man would. You know how they do it, grab you in the small of your back and bend they knees, and hump into you when they hugs ya. That is exactly how that heifer hugged me. "I know you is surprised to see me and I know you wants to hear all about what old bad Puddin been doing, huh Ms. Lula Mae?" Truth is all I wished right then, was for some angel to come from heaven and collect this demon from hell. I keep tellin you I am wonderin about what the hell God is really doin. Soon as I am about to get what I want, here come somebody I have to share it with.

"Child I din been through somethin. Girl what's that I smell? Is that some of your damn good biscuits? Huh seems like I am just in time." Right after she said that Big John comes out of the bathroom, oh Jesus, it is about to be some puttin on in a minute. Puddin kimbowed her legs and rared back on them. Child Puddin lite up like fire flies in the evening time. "Ha yall doin? Who is you Mr man?" "I am Big John and you?" "Why your mamma named you Big John instead of just John?" "Well miss she tells like this, she said I was exactly like my daddy in every way and his name was Big Leroy. So she named me John. As I grew people keep callin me Big John so that name just stuck around." " Well fella, what the big stand for?" John was lookin at Puddin very strange now with wonderment in his eyes. "Maam I never though about what the big stand for; maybe I should have asked somebody." " Maybe you need to ask your mama." "Can't do that lady, my mama passed on about 9 years ago." "You don't have you a conjurer, Mr. Big John, somebody to call her back here sos you can talk to her?" Puddin burst out and started laughin, that is when I broke in and called everybody to eat. There is some kind of feelin in this room. I do not know whether it is me or whether it is Puddin or whether it is John but there is a different feelin in here now. I can't eat much, because I got Puddin on my mind. Feels like somebody done put the evil eye on this house, let me go outside and spit three times in each direction sos I kin bind them demons till I gets to me a two headed doctor. I trys not to use the same ones all the time.

"I hope Ms. Lula Mae can not read my mind cause I like her a lot and she is real sweet; but that woman Puddin over there is one of them woman than can rub up against you and make you spill your seed. I can tell she got all kinds of thangs she knows how to do. I can tell, she soft, she pretty and she smell so fresh and nice. I can smell that women, and that deep dark skin look like somethin to eat. Got damn she got my balls liftin. If I get the chance I am go cock her like a shot gun. I got to try her out maybe once or twice. Most women like that cost to damn much, but once she get a look at stiff dick she go be like all the rest of them women, and break down for me. Damn I can not get that smell out of my nose. She go drive me crazy until I gets to bury my cock in her. Big John go show her why deh call me Big John. I likes a women like her when you calls her a whore and rub a little spit on her ass all she go do is take every bit of it.

"If Lula Mae think I am go pass up a man with a concern as big as that one on Big John, she can just start prayin for help right now. Cause old Puddin have every intention of fuckin Big John for nothin. I always have been able to tell a cocksman and he one. He go grab me by the ass and stuff his meat in me to the hub, then he go slow grind the fuck out of me sos to show me he in charge. Cause yall know when a man have a concern that big and he takes his time to please you he is a real dicksman. I is tellin ya that man right there, that Big John, he knows how to please a pussy. What he don't know though is he can dig to China ifin he want and he can whip that meat like a coach whip, I am go swallow up every inch of him and latch hold to his nuts like a snappin turtle. One thang about me I appreciates special thangs and when I get em, I don't play with em. See he is use to dick whippin women and I am use to pussy whippin men, so we gits together, we go be some fightin muther fuckers. Lula already think that I ain't nothin but a mis guided demon so anything I do she should expect it. I hope Lula Mae don't think I give a damn about what she thinks. The last encounter we had was so intense I almost fell in love with her. Plus if she ever tell me shit I am go remind her how I was pickin her hair out of my teeth for a week. I hope she done realized she needs to shave that hairy faced pussy of hers."

Lawd, look like I can see what everybody is thinkin; cause everybody kinda quite and uneasy. I am still bothered cause of how John was touchin me earlier. I just looked at John and thought to myself, maybe he just ought not be in my life. I know I want him and I know he want me, but I also know if he gets the chance, he go stove his dick as far as he can, in Puddin's funk pocket and she ain't go object to it one bit. The first chance them two get to be alone they go stick together like dogs fuckin. They might intend to just do it once but they go continue until the excitement is over. I can smell em both, huh. If Puddin wasn't holdin that one time we all spent together over my head; I would go and stir up some of my church sisters and we would handle her real good. All I have to do is make the right comment in front of the right people and Puddin's ass could be out of here. But that is what I get for being caught up with a whore from hell. "Oh, Puddin sweetie, would you like to freshin up now? I got me a new water pump. Child that water come in so fast it almost fill up the tub with one good pump. I had Mr. Holmes come put a burner in the bathroom sos to keep the water warm too. Come on baby lets, get you all confortable." "Lawd Ms. Lula Mae you always thinkin of ways to be comfortable, that is what I like so much about you. You ain't go let the modern times pass you by, as they invent it you get it. Oh, I really do like them new lace curtains, must have cost you a pretty penny or two. But you can afford it, can't you Ms. Lula Mae?" This is one time I can say I wish Puddin had somewhere else to go. She ain't nothin but trouble for me. Big John sittin over there all uneasy like cause he know what kind of woman she is. Men say they want a lady, but when they can smell a good whore around they gits an itch. I ain't no fool. I know that most men likes a good hoe; hell Puddin proof of that. Even if she was not around, I can tell you men likes a women to feel free when he with her. But if you deh women and gets to free you scare em and they want to start to doubt you; that is why they need whores. See she is made to do what he to scared to let his wife do. You know what I mean. See if you start in on him and go for yours the way he is goin for his you scare him. He lose his control cause he know you go get pleased, with or without him and that scares him, in a lot of ways. One thang I can say is that I don't have time to be worried about what a man is thinkin when we having relations. I am too busy gettin all the enjoyments I can, because I know it might be a while until it happens again. What I am sayin is I delights myself. I don't give anybody the power to satisfy me. Long as I can remember I have always had a good relationship with my little funk pocket cause I kept my hands in it. Not all men the same, not all women the same, but when it comes to enjoyin relations everybody ought to be thinkin the same. Know what that is, satisfy yourself. That way you never come up short. That's right baby first you have to know yourself, then you have to know what you like, then you have to make it happen for you. That's right baby, make it happen for you. I always figure that if I keep tellin God about all my faults and sins, he will just keep giving me extra time to work on them. I got a lot on my mind now. You can rest assure ifin a man ain't around, Ms. Lula Mae can always give herself on good fist fuckin.

Big John was standing outside smoking on his pipe in the heat of the sun na , with one strap of his overalls on his shoulder and the other dropped down and little sparkles of sweat was dropping off his brow. I know he is probably thinkin what in the hell am I doing with a woman friend like Puddin; because she is such a forward hoe. Hummm he looks so good standin in my yard next to my favorite cypress tree, whose limbs he was usin to hang some of his tools sacks on. We go have to talk about that I don't want him breakin down my limbs. He even looked good dirty to me, hell I just like that man. Puddin interrupts my thoughs with her forward way, "Well na looks like somebody done found someone who makes her special pleasures notice the goodness of life, huh Ms. Lula. It is kinda good to see you showin you have needs just like the rest of us worthless sinners of the devils seed. I bet you ain't did nothing since aawwwwwwwwwww … "Look Puddin we said we was never going to talk about that time again na." " Well since you are feelin so strong about it I guess I won't say nothin about it again." Then Puddin comes close over to me and as she stroked the back of my neck with her finger lookin at me like I was a piece of fresh ham or somethin, she said "You know I fell in love with you Ms Lula. You sweet and you warm and you good to the taste." I hate this bitch, she sure was makin me very nervous now. She found a weakness in me and now she is go use that on me for the rest of my life.

CHAPTER 18

What you Doing Back Here Puddin?

I SAY "WHAT YOU doing back here na girl?" "You know Ms. Lula sometimes even us devils finds passion. You know when it is real passion too, when you are with someone who absolutely thinks they are better than you; but in a moment of passion they give in to your every touch. Now that is some real power. I been around Ms. Lula, people pay me to know things that make them feel good. It is alright to experience different feelings, cause variety is the spice of life. But nothin is better than actually pulling out the deep needs and passion of people. See we been made to live in a box Ms. Lula, people tell us everythang to do. They tell us what is right to feel, to do, to live and to die; thank of it Ms. Lula everything you do somebody taught you to do. Anything you do outside of what the church tell ya is an original sin, and anything you do outside of the law is a crime. And in between them both is a bunch of boarded people waitin till someone tell them it is okay to have a good time. Well that is a bunch of bullshit, how somebody go tell you what is right for you to feel. Hell, everythang make you feel good is a sin. Drinking, smoking, lusting, loving, eating, wanting, cussing every got damn thang make you feel human is a got damn sin. Maybe being human is a sin, seems like it to me. People all boxed in fightin to get out, but they scared, they scared of what they go find out about themselves. Fools follow rules, made by other fools who aint got a clue, girl. Take sex for a minute, we all boxed in. Somebody done gave us rolls, we each suppose to have a roll. Women think they suppose to be so lovely and lady like while they is making love; when actually they suppose to do whatever it takes for them to be satisfied. Instead of apologizing for every little pussy fart, embrace em, some women ain't got enough cushion to make fart. Most women think they can't feel certain things unless a man gives it to them and that is not good for them. When you don't understand that you have the right to embrace your pussy you don't know when it ain't being embraced right. I tells all womens to embrace their pussys and let them know they are appreciated. Instead of layin there like a log waitin for somebody to cramp deh pussy, deh ought to be crampin some fine piece of man pleasure. Some of them looks at me like what a hoe know about a relationship so deh ignore what I say. And then deh man meets me, and I am somethin else aint I Miss Lula Mae. See it is the excitement and the surprise they get when they understand that I go after a nut just like a man do. But what deh don't understand is that it is my job to make them spit out that dick flam. See when I am rootin like hog, I am just tryin to hurry up and get to the next customer most of the time Ms. Lula Mae. I fucks like a man Ms. Lula and I know it is the truth cause I done had a few men who done had men tell me so. Hell I even had a few of dem as regular customes. Ain't nothing like being sent to heaven on bed of lust. You sent me to heaven Ms. Lula. I think about that day we spent together a lot. It was one of the hottest moments I have ever had in my life."

Don't you just hate it when a bitch know somethin on you that she can use against you, especially if she is an immoral hoe. She want to have somethin on a good woman. Sweat is just running down my face, cause I don't want to be reminded of all of that. I want to forget it. I want that it never happened and I am pissed off at God that he let it happen to me. What am I suppose to do now the devil have the upper hand on me? Where is Jesus when I need him? I will never hear the end of this. She got me, this is not a good feelin. Now I am startin to think evil. See that is why the Bible say come out from among them. What the hell is dick flam? You keep company with whores you end up getting fucked. I will pray for using this dirty language later but right now it is makin me feel good. Here I am a good woman all wrapped up in the devils mess. Plus I am tired of Puddin talkin like she the only woman know how to please a man. I ain't never left a tooth print on a concern I ever been with. And I ain't never heard no complaints bout nothing else either.

"Miss Lula, Miss Lula , what you got on your mind girl, you so far away. Don't worry I ain't go tell nobody, no maam, I am not go tell a soul. This little pink thang in my mouth done caused enough trouble". "Puddin I am just thinking about all the times I done messed up in my life and I wonder if there is any true holiness left in this world. Seems like I have failed the Lord." "What Lord you done failed Ms. Lula, the one up in the sky, lettin our people die and suffer, you better call on somebody else, cause that God you been callin on, ain't payin attention. Saw Carri Bea before I got here she told me that Louis was hung over by Sefaw River. Here tell he had been stripped of his skin. How many times you thank he called on the Lord? Ifin God is got blonde hair and blue eyes he ain't mine and if the devil got blonde hair and blue eyes, he ain't mine either. Don't remember a time I done called on the good Lord and He went against white folk to help me. Can you remember a time that done happen for you Ms. Lula." I started to tell her how many times the good Lord done helped me with white folk but why argue with Satan's whore, you not go win.

Puddin said "Just wait until I tell you why I am back here, and how got damn rich I am." My eyes set a fire now Puddin got damn rich, well that means more money for me cause I just started chargin her for her meals, and her lodgin. Don't yall think hard of me, business is business, if Puddin had not needed a place to stay and paid me so well, ain't no way I would have anythin to do with her kind. But like I said she was makin me rich. As we walked to the front porch to get Puddins bags, Big John leaped from the porch and almost ran to her car and started grabbin em. Studpid bastard, he bout to give up a treasure chest for a few rusty coins. You should have seen how Puddin eyeballed him, shameless strumpet . She looked at him like a cat eyeballin a bird. I almost had to grab her and pull her back so she would not touch his concerns. Puddin just smiled sort of devilishly like and says to me "I show hope you get that one girl cause he not just fine he real fine and biggggggggggggggggg too, yes lawd, na na na he is a big one child. Ms. Lula me and you go carry these two cases here, don't need no Big John's help with these." Lawd have mercy they were heavy as hell. Maybe because they was made out of something called crocodile skin and they had real gold and silver trim, listen yall real gold and silver. I figured that is why she did not want Big John to carry them. It was a hard walk back carryin them heavy bags. I hope she leave one of these suit cases with me. That heifer went right into my room and threw those bags right in the middle of my damn bed. Of course I had my snow white embroidered sheets on my bed with my crocheted pillow cases and my Spanish lace spread on it. I felt like really hurting her. Old bitch. I am sorry Lord but she made me call her that name (*Did I tell yall my family is known for having the whitest whites in these parts.*) I can't tell yall everything about how we keep them clothes so white, but here is some of it .When you are washin your clothes cut up some lemons and put in your water and let them sit for about a hour then you rinse them clothes real good and they be white, fresh smelling and clean, clean, clean. "Pudding you can just move them bags off my bed, you know I don't like anythang on my bed, so move them bags na." Puddin looks at me and laughs. "Girl what I got in these bags kin buy you the bed and the store it came out of." "I don't give a hoop in hell what dem bags kin buy get them off my bed." Puddin just laughs and move the bags to my cedar chest. I says "What you got in here girl?" "Open a bag Ms. Lula."

Lawd have mercy I almost fainted when I opened that bag and saw all of that money. I immediately turned to see if Big John, God, the devil or who ever was looking through the window 'cuz I did not want anyone to see what I was seein. Hundreds of hundred dollar bills, neatly tied in bundles, 20's, 10's, 5's , gold and silver pieces of all kinds. Then Puddin opened her bag and it had just as much in it. She says it was 350,000.00. Pussy pays Ms. Lula Mae and sometimes it pays real well." I was sweatin now, my mind heart and soul was disturbed. I did not know what I might have do to get my hands on some of this money. All I could think of was owning my own bed and breakfast, a fancy one for colored folk to come to. You know the kind of coloreds that would spend good money, for a nice place, not the ones figure you suppose to give them a deal just cause you colored and deh is colored. I always figured that was shit, see I don't believe I am suppose to give all I have away to somebody cause they colored like me. They don't ask the white folks for no deal and they pay full price and more for what deh buy from them. But whenever they come to buy from they own they wants a deal. Hell we done already paid double for what we got and then our own folks wants us to give the rest away to dem.

Already this money, Puddin and the Devil is causing problems. You don't know what you might not do to get your hands on all that money and disappear. I started feelin real scared and I know I had a blank look on my face cause I was in a real daze. I could see Puddin's mouth movin but I was not makin out the words she was sayin, not until she grabbed me and shook me. I ran to the window again but this time Big John was lookin our way. I hurried up and went outside to see if he needed anythang. "John you need something?" "No Ms. Lula , why you ask?" "Oh, I just thought I saw you lookin our way and I figured you might have needed somethin." John looks at me kind of strange like and says "No if I need somethin I can get it." Then he turned around and went back to work. Puddin sittin in the middle of my bed with her legs gapped open like a lazy cat, that girl ain't nothing but a gip. She says, "Na Ms. Lula what we go do with all of this money?" "Get off my damn bed Puddin, just because you have all this money don't mean I want you to ruin my spread and cases." "I can buy you a store full of sheets and cases Ms. Lula." "But you can't buy my time and my mothers time and my grandmothers time, it took years to make these. Na let me help you move them cases off my bed girl." "You got to be the damnest fool women in the world Ms. Lula. I gots all this money and you givin me a hard time about some damn sheets and cases. I will move it but you just lost youself some money for that. I was gone give you 100,000.00 but now you gets 90,000.00." I almost fainted, then Puddin grabbed me and held me in a strange manner. It was the devil's way, I knew there would be a cost for any parts of this money. But she is a lie old Lula is strickly dickly, unless some demon heifer has not cast evil spell on me. Like her and Beulah did some time ago, I swear before God they charmed me.

Evenin time done rolled around, and I can just smell my confederate jasmine, magnolia, and gardenias ridin on the breeze of glory comin through my windows. Then I looks at Puddin and says "Look Puddin I am not go lose my soul to hell for no amount of money. I do not want to be bothered with your foolishness." I sure would hate for her to take a fall down my steep steps in the mornin. Lawd please keep Puddin's evil hands from off your favored servant. "Where we go hide this money Ms. Lula? You know being a black women I can not take it to the bank.

Ain't no black nothin is suppose to have this kind of money. If I go to put this in the bank them white folks go find a way to take most of it from me if not all of it." Much as I hate to admit it Puddin was right we ain't really had no real big problems with our white folk here to much, just a hangin or rape every now and then, you know the usual. If Puddin took that money to the bank them white folk would be damn rich and if they let her keep any money she would be damn happy. More than likely deh just go kill her and take it. This kind of money can get you killed. In all of our excitement we had forgot about Big John. Then I hears this voice "Ms. Lula I need to have a little more money to get the kind of wood you want." Damn Big John standing at the damn side window. I wonder if he saw the money. I hurry up and gave him a hundred dollars. He looked at me and said "The wood will only cost 20 dollars Ms. Lula." "Just take the 100.00 you might need somethin else. Since you got to go to town, you can just come back tomorrow John. Me and Puddin needs to catch up, you can leave now if you want John." " Ms. Lula is that woman go be stayin here with you now?" "Yes she is John." "I don't like it and I don't like her. She ain't your friend if I wanted to I could get her right now." " I am sure you could John I bet yall could get each other right na. But you don't have anything to do with who stays in my house. I beg your pardon. I thank you need to know you workin for me at my house, my house. One person makes decisions here and that is me." Child you have to get men straight in a hurry, cause they will take over your possessions, if you let em. But I ain't about to give up one damn bite of ownership here, no maam and no sir, this is Ms. Lula Mae Carson's place. I am the shack bully here. Na this niggar got some nerve. I beg pardon for calling him a nigger. I hates that word but that is what he actin like a ignorant fool. Oh, yall I calls white folk niggars too, I sure do. Cause they some ignorant muther fuckers sometimes too, yes deh is. They make me sick preachin God while they hangin people. Got me so messed up I can not stand hyms about rivers, and you will never see me on a picnic, never. And you would not go on one either if you knew what it meant. "Good day John, take your time gettin here in the morning, Puddin likes to sleep late." Why in the hell is it takin him so long to get his tools together. I am go tell him not to hang all them belts on my Cypress tress right now before I forget, cause I don't want my limbs to break off. Guess that lets yall know how ignorant John really is. People with good wits don't do nothing to destroy mother nature, unless deh is ignorant.

" Puddin I have a place you can hide this money." Then I pointed over to my closet, I have a secrete door in there where I keep all my secret papers, jewelry and other things. Once Big John is gone we can hide all this treasure. No sooner than I said that, Big John comes in my bedroom, he did not even knock on the door, me and him go have to have us a talk. He goin to far now, he makin hisself to free in my house. " Ms. Lula I am about to go now." "See ya tomorrow John." Once I am sure John gone I started to look for other places to hide all of this money. "Puddin girl how did you get all this money?" "Remember that Cuban man I was with Steve, the one with those big cigars, then she looks at me all under eyed and stuff; she made me blush with shame. I told yall know matter what, she is still the devil's whore. "Yes, I remember him." "Well he took me to Cuba with him and we was doing okay; life was good. I liked deh food it was close to ours and I liked the weather too. Not eatin well was not why I started losing so much weight. I was the partyin, child they partied and partied and partied, dancing took most off these hips off; well that is part of the reason I lost them. The other part is because I been worried for my life and the life I might have in me." " Puddin is you pregnant girl?" Could be but I thank I am going to see Ms. Cherice soon as I rest up. That is why I am so sad these days Ms. Lula, no husband and got damn baby. Anyway we gits married and thangs seemed to be goin just fine. But, Mr. lover man Steve could not keep that dangerous snake of his in his pants. Steve went out on me and got some little rich girl named Liza, knocked up. Them Cuban people did not care that me and Steve was married or should I say the rich ones did not care. They told him our marriage did not count anyway because I was not a Catholic and I was a hoe. They were just being down right hateful and down right low-down Ms. Lula cause I had not done one thing while I was in Cuba. Well maybe one thing but I am sure that nobody knew about it. What I am tryin to say is any where you go in the world and stay if rich people there you go dance to deh music whether you like it or not."

"One Saturday evening we at home in the bed and this big old fat man just walks in our house after his son kicked our door in. Mr. Rameriz , his name, he is full of rage, cursing and swearing to high heaven. He tells Steve if he did not marry his daughter he was going to kill him, me

, anyone or anything that tried to stop the marriage. I said "Well we is married, and we was married right here by the justice of the peace. The next day Steve gets a visit from local constable the same man that married us. Mr. Jenevous informed me that because Steve's parents refused to come to our wedding and because Steve was Catholic and not married by a Priest, we was not really married according to their tradition. What he should have said is "I am scared to death and if I can not get this undone I am go be looking for another job," cowardly bastard. Got damn Ms. Lula , that was the first time I ever felt like a nigger in Cuba. Mr. Jenevous then said that he had received something from the government office about us having to leave the country because my papers did not seem to be in order. You know that was something they made up. You can tell little miss rich girl's pappy had greased somebody's palm. He said I had two weeks to get the hell out of Cuba. I started cryin and could not stop. Contania our maid told everybody she knew, what the Rameriz family was doing to us. The local people liked me more than I thought because some of them stood up for me. Maybe that was because I would sang and shimmy at they little gatherings. Ms. Sanchez and her family, Mr. Artist and his family and several other people who had been married by the constable said if my marriage was not acceptable then so was every citizen who could not afford to pay for the Padre and the church. It started to get real divided in our little town real quick. Apparently, a lot of the town people worked for Mr. Rameriz and honey child you know they protested for old Puddin. They were not going to work because he was being so low down to me. They know he was wrong plus I thank they all knew his little princess was the princess whore of the town. One thang about Cuba the regular people is just that, regular people. It was a good run but you can not beat money, no sirree, you can not beat money and power. Must feel good having enough power to play with people's lives and destroy em if you want to. Yes maam, must be good to have that kind of power. Somethin us colored folks in America don't know one thing about. When Jesus paid the price to set the captives free, there must have not been any colored folks around the cross that day Ms. Lula.

Everybody knew that Mr. Rameriz was just a fool when it came to his daughter. Some folk even thought he might have been so pissed off cause he wanted to be her first. From what I hear Steve really was not the first, his chauver was. It was a mess, but the people did not back down, they all agreed that Steve and Liza was wrong and the only way they could get married was that I gave him a divorce. And the only way that would be accepteable is if I had been unfaithful. Ain't that a bitch, somebody thinking I was faithful. But the truth is, I had been faithful, for the most part. This was the first time in my life I ever heard that word and my name in the same sentence. Most of my life I have been a fuck machine and that is what I was good at; screwin and bein a two timin hoe. If there is such a than as faithful, so me it. Who are those people bein faithful and how you know deh really is? "What you mean if there is such a thing Puddin, there is a lot of faithful people in this world girl." "Well they sure not faithful to God from what I see Ms. Lula. I done had so many of God's men He ought to give me a free pass to heaven. Cause I seem to be working for Him all the time. Ain't to much difference between me and a Preacher man, he sellin the ticket to heaven and I am sellin the ride."

" Ms. Lula Steve tried and tried to fight them off, but they were givin him trouble on the streets, tryin to stop him from workin, you know he is a music man. Deh was harassin his family and makin threats. He started coming home later and later, then he started to resist my touch. That is when I made up my mind that I was go have to look out for myself. I had a meeting with Mr. Rameriz and told him that I would publically announce that I was unfaithful to Steve so our divorce could be accepted by the church. He immediately asked me how much. He said "I know you have a price, women like you always do." I told him I wanted one million dollars, yes one million dollars. You should have seen how that old fat bastard choke. He said "I will give you 50,000.00 and you will take it." I told him I needed to start me a business and I might be with child so I needed one million dollars. He says "I will give you 250,000.00 or I will just see to it you and your little cloud of shit end up in heaven or hell, your choice." I thought to myself we will both go meet in hell, cause heaven meant for people who give a damn. Well anyway I caught him give me the look and I took it from their. See, I thanks like a man; soon as I saw he might be interested he was have to tell me no, but I knew that was not go happen. I says "Mr. Rameriz you wonderin why I can charge for my pleasures? Puddin you didn't." "Yes, I did Ms. Lula." He said "Yes". I says "Why do you think that my price so high? Could it be I am so damn good at pleasin the dragon?" Then I walked over to him real slow and he let me touch him and rub up against him. I took my time and touched every part of his old fat round body. I touched him until he shivered and shivered til his knees got weak. I was sniffin him and lickin my tongue behind his ears and he was standin there like he was in shock. He was easy too, cause he was one of them men who liked to be rubbed on and I rubbed him. I had him all messed up as long as I held on to his man piece; he was like a baby suckling for its mammys' tits. He liked to be tickled too, big bitch. Know when I really got to him Ms. Lula? When I laid out for him like a rug. Then he wanted to know if I would stay an extra week. I said "Fuck no you old bastard, just give me my money and I needs cash." But you know what Ms. Lula that old fat bastard had a certain smell about him though sorta like juicy sweet coconut milk and pineapples. Yes lawd he did smell good, guess if you that rich you can pay for someone to keep yo ass clean for you. He was not a bad salad to toss after at all. I enjoyed myself for a minute or two and I mean a minute or two he shot off all over his self girl and me too, had my damn eyes burnin. He better be glad I am leavin Cuba, cause if I was not I would take all his money and all his cabannas too. He was not a bad lookin man he just was fat and he was so fat cause he was so damn rich. It did not matter what he looked like anyway. When you is rich you can be as ugly as hell, fat as a bull, and low down as a honorie rattle snake, people still treat you like you the most wonderful thing there is. Most of the time regular people is laughin at them rich folk though. Cause they know if deh did not have any money people would not even see them. It is true a lot of dem rich folk would not be shit if deh did not have any money. Thank about some rich folk you know, na thank about them without deh money.

I know the people was thinkin he wanted his daughter for himself, but it was something about him made me feel like maybe the people was wrong. He was just freaky, and we all got a little freak in us don't we Ms. Lula. Hmm, he did not seem like the kind that liked babies, but then again you never know. Oh, see this big old as diamond ring, he just threw that in. Na I don't know much about the value of a diamond but that thing was as big as a pecan. Hoein looks like it is passin holiness. A good man up against a bad women ain't got a chance, and if he up against Puddin, he done for. I ain't seen a good black woman or a white woman with a ring like that. What is goin on Lawd? "You know Ms. Lula a man ain't nothin but a orange on the tree of life. You just roll em and roll em then you squeeze the juice out of them; like you would a ripe orange. Ha, yes maam a pair of soft hands and some sweet lips can beat the hell out of a stubborn ass hole, Ms. Lula.

Any way child, then I goes to Steve and tell him that I din talked to them rich folk and they says I must be gone before Sunday or they go kill us both. There he go pacing and cussin me, so I just stopped him and said "Look nigga I ain't tryin to stay here, you need to give me some money so I can get the hell out of here and save both our lives." You should have seen the relief on his face Ms. Lula, chicken shit ass nigga looked so relieved he could shit his pants. He sure as hell did not want to die for me. Then he tells me that he go give me 5,000.00 dollars as a going away present. I laughed at that shit and told him I needed at least 30,000.00 to get started. That son of a bitch started calling me all kinds of low down bitches, then told me he should have left me in the hoe house. I love the hoe house so you know he could have kissed my ass with that one. Then he swung at me while callin me a cheap ass, to bit dick suckin hoe Ms. Lula. That is when I cold cocked his ass with my elbow behind his neck who the hell he thought he was Master or something, I could fight his ass back. I learned that elbo move from a cheatin gambler. She use to gamble with them men and when deh get a little rough she act like she leavin the table, din she hit from behind with that elbow. A women like me gots to know a lot of thangs. I knocked him down and straddled him. I said " Steve if you say one more filty word like that I am not go divorce your sorry ass. Ms Lula don't' ever tell me nothing good about men, cause deh ain't shit. All of a sudden he started grabbing me and grinding wanting me to make him feel good, while he cursing me out. I pulls my dress up way over my head and let my breast tickle his nose, he was like a baby hungry for his milk, and as soon as I was sure he was real hot and bothered I got up. Then he said "What the matter with you? Why you stopped?" I said "Us cheap to bit hoes, likes to be paid first." I was not thinking about him anymore Ms. Lula because when I finished with him he was gonna to be broke. And I ain't got time for nothing broke, exceptin this heart of mine and it ain't go ever be fixed. See, Steve's family had some money too, so I know he could get whatever amount of money I wanted. Plus, he took me from my country , which I don't give a damn about, and brought me to his, he owe me. Now let me tell you this, in Cuba you are much freer being colored than what you are here. But you either poor or rich and that is it. I knew I was about to leave so I was go get all I could get before I go. I had to have something to remind me I was just as human as any body else, and enough money was just the trick.

Steve was go marry his little rich girl, pretend like he love her, have a new family. So he really won't need the money I took from him; he will have all of hers. I never will forget the day I left Cuba it was early on a Friday morning, nice and warm. I put on my white dress, my white hat, my white shoes, and my white lace gloves had my driver Miguel take me to them rich peoples house. I looked like a virgin getting ready to be sacrificed. You should have seen how they was all looking at me when I pulled up; like I was some kind of monster or something. You know those rich Cuban ladies was thinking how much better they were than me and feeling like they had won some kind of victory over me because little Liza was getting Steve. She wasn't gettin shit, cause Steve had this special thang he needed to have done before he could really start to have a good time and I bet she had no idea what that was. It is kinda hard to be a woman who know how to tickle a nut. The servants lead me into the smoking parlor, normally ladies were not allowed in the smoking parlors, but since they did not consider me a lady, that is where I sat until Mr. Rameriz bought his fat ass in the room. First thang that som of a bitch did was ask me if my hands were tired. Then he wanted to know if I would meet him on this other island for a few weeks before returning home. I just laughed and thought to myself, "Puddin old girl if you stay one more week you might be a millionare." Then another thought hit my mind and said "Or you might be dead." I decided to take them cases of money he had for me and leave. I figure a rich man like this could buy as many Puddins his bank account could afford. I did not feel like playing with my life. You know I ain't got no shame, but if I would have been here in the states, I would have spent the extra time and made me some more money. But something about this situation made me want to just take the money and get the hell out. On my way back to the house I had my driver take me to the church I had to see my Preist. Plus I needed some blessings over all that money so I gave the Padre a whole sack of it. See I still was in Cuba and I might need some favors accordin how everybody was go act. See girl I was not home free yet. I confessed to the Priest as much as I could before he started sweating and coughing, he took off to the back of the church and almost drowned his self with that so called Holy Water. As he stood looking at me as if he had seen el deablo himself. I reached in my bag and gave him another 1,000 dollars. When I counted out that money on the table he acted just like them Baptist preachers act when you give them a bunch of money. First he looked at me like he had just seen Jesus, then that man began blessing me, giving me all kinds of little cards, burning incense and casting down any and everything that would come against me. I actually felt pretty good then. See Ms. Lula no matter how much of a devil one might be, one always wants some kind of favor from a Holy Man. Now I am headed to Steve to go bid him goodbye. When I went in the house Steve was standing in the kitchen doorway looking like he wanted to cry, head held down and stinking of alcohol. I did not want to show him any kind of feelings but I just could not help myself. There was something about this man. He may have met me through whoring but he married me and he took care of me as best he could take care of anyone. When I caught his eyes piercing my very soul I started walking over to him like a snake crawling on the ground. Then I starts to unbuckle his shirt real slow like, then I unbuckles his pants, I looked at him for a long time. I knew it was gonna be my last time. He was sweating like he had been caught in the rain, part from drinking the other part was he knew he was about to let go of his precious Puddin. I knew I was not going to see him again for the rest of my life so I wanted to make good of this last time. See no matter what I say about him he was a good lover. He just stood there letting me kiss him,. I was kissing his thighs, he knees, his ankles until I worked my way back up to his silky chest and round the back of his neck. See he was a neck baby, that man loved to have his neck kissed. Oh god Ms. Lula he smelled so good a mixture of the alcohol and his man musk almost ran me crazy. I dried every bit of his sweat with my tounge. I started to move all around his body girl, he has a nice body. He was letting me have my way till he saw how much I was enjoying him. Then he started acting like he was trying to fight me off, but once I grabbed a peach off the table and rubbed it on his piece that was it. The next thing I knew that man, had started grabbin me and kissing my neck, rollin my hips, and grinding on me like the wheels of a mill. Then us fell back screaming with pleasure, relief and pain.

Then all of a sudden Ms. Lula that devil looked at me like he wanted to kill me. He says "Get away from me you evil bitch. You have el deablo in you and you will get what you deserve you hateful whore. I looked at that nigga dead in his eyes and said , "When did you think about that before or after this here whore drank all of your nut milk, you sorry bastard. You are just like Mr. Rameriz, want it , need it, but wants to be better than it." Lula he started moving towards me like he was going to kill me he ain't know I had me a darenger. Just when I was about to pull it out, old man Rameriz and his driver pulled up. The old man came in the house his self and asked me if I was ready to go. Huh, I looked him dead in his eyes and told him "I have to clean up first, because I had just had some useless seeds waste all over me and I wanted to be sure that I did not carry any filth back to my country. Course you know Mr. rich man did not mind especially since I had given him a little taste of Puddin. Child I ain't even trying to pretend like I am anything nice, because I am not. I just know how to survive. Now do you see how I am a rich woman na , Ms Lula? I am richer than any white woman or man here in Friendly, hell I might be richer than most whites in the state of Louisiana, maybe in the US. Well maybe not in the US, but I got these po crackers in Louisiana beat. You know this is all between us right Lula Mae, I don't want the whole church and heaven to know all my business. What I want you to do is take 50,000.00 of them dollars and put away for your self. I thought you said somethin about 90,000.00 at furst. "You is just playin right Ms. Lula. I was just talkin a little shit. But na if you don't want it?" Well if I am go send my soul to hell at leaset it will be the rich side of hell, cause I am taking this money like I took all the rest. "Hell yeah, Puddin I want this money. I ain't stupid." See yall this is a blessing from God. I remember the preacher preaching that God would take the money from the evil ones and give it to the righteous. I am the righteous and Puddin is pretty damn evil, shit anyway I did not wait one more minute. I took all my money and counted it and banded it in small amounts so I could spend it a little at a time. It would take me a life time to spend all this money. Child Ms. Lula thinking about movin on up out of here. I is tried of always being alone, tried of these old pecker wood's shit. Tired of trying to be so damn holy, tried of not having myself a nice time when I wants to. I am just tired of the same old place. I have heard about fine places across the bayou for sale, most of dem was old plantation houses. Of course, I would burn the house down and rebuild it to my liking, cause I hate them plantation houses. They remind me of so much pain

I hate to look at them. But that is just a dream, cause I would still have to explain where I got all the money from, shit we can't have nothing in peace. I know some of yall thinking why would she want to burn down such beautiful houses. Well I hates all plantations, can't see the beauty in em, cause they ain't got none. Everybody know they was evil places that killed babies, rapped women and men and worst of all they treated people like animals. Sorta like how people in the South still is. If you in the South and you is black you know about death knocking at your door, sometimes deh wear white hoods and sometimes they don't' but deh all praizin Jesus.

I started to think bout me having me some strong black buck wigglin inside of me, makin me like him so much I want to pay him. Ms.Lula just tired of the whole thing around here. What if it really ain't no heaven or hell and it is just some white folk lie to keep niggas wishing for a better place. But I know the truth see as long us is they black in America us go be black in America. I keep hoping and praying for justice for what is been done to us, but I got a deep feeling in my spirit that justice + black folk = hangings. White folk get justice, black gets injustice and is just the way it is. I am starting to think it is all a lie anyway, cause if a black man did not write nothing in the Bible. Then how the Bible go be for him. Cause I believe if a colored man had anythang to do with the Bible he would have put somethin in it against treatin colored folks so mean. Maybe it is just a book to keep us scared to go to hell and keep us hopin to get to heaven. Maybe it is just to keep us controlled. Wonder were all the black people was back in the Bible days, because they sure ain't telling me about no black people in that bible. All I hear this Bible preaching is loving your enemy while the enemy is hanging our men and raping our little girls huh. Oh Lawd, forgive Ms. Lula , I is just thankin bad. Most of us want to believe in heaven, cause life here on earth is hell for us, so we really don't want to go to a hell after we die too. If it gets any worse than this just write me out of extience all together. Oh, Lawd forgive Ms. Lula it is the money that is making me question you so much. When you gets money you gets some bad thoughts, you feel powerful and eternal. See the Preacher was right money is the root to all evil or maybe I been evil all the time, some of these thoughts I din had before I even had this money. Ifin you is kinda poor you worry bout your good name, but ifin you is rich or gits a lot of money from some where you don't give a damn about your good name. Hell you can buy you a good name, but you can not buy a thimble full of piss when you poor. I sure am gonna be doing a lot of repenting for my thoughts. I thank I agree with that Preacher man that said the lack of money is the root to all evil. Cause if you ain't got none you will steal, lie and murder to get, ceptin if you white. Hell deh gots all the money and deh is still killin, stealin and lyin. But deh is doin that sos deh kin keep it. Guess you can't blame em." Ms Lula", "Yes Puddin, " "Come on over here and give Puddin a back rub please. I is tired and I needs me some rest. Just a little nap before we head out to town." I moves over to her and gives her a long satisfying back rub; then I goes and make her somemore bath water that woman loves to soak in the tub. Probably cause she has a lot of filth to wash off. Hell I started to bath her, she done gave me 50,000.00 in cash.

I ain't den thought about Big John for a while, sos after I made Puddins bath water I goes to check and be sure he ain't no where sneakin around. You can't trust people these days. I looks and looks and no Big John glad he gone. Then my mind goes to thinking all about me living abroad and seeing places like Cuba and that place called New York, and that place them rich white women goes called Paris, France. I am thankin na about how free I am, not having no children or man to tie me down. I got me 50,000 plus 12,000, and a chest full of sapphires, rubies and perils. I is almost as rich as Puddin, but I ain't telling her cause she is the reason I have all this money. It all came from her gents, bows, and hoes'. Ummm huh I can smell my night blooming jasmine now coming through the windows, while the sound of Puddins sweet soprano voice is singing in the tub. So I goes an puts on that song machine and listens to the sounds of people making music, yes people singing on a machine. I do not know about heaven much, cause I ain't never been there and ain't no heavenly person brought me a damn thang. Hell the ambassors of heaven ain't doing nothing but taking money from me. Neverthessless, Puddin on the other hand is making the disciples of hell seem awfully good and gernerous. She is the one making me so happy these days. Lawd life is a wonder, here I is just a little old poor girl from Friendly, La. And now I is a rich lady and all I did was be kind and open my house and heart to a women that nobody else wanted to be in the company of. If they knew what I knew I bet each and every one of them would want Ms. Puddin in there life now; excepting for them white women, they would kill her and take her money. Well not all of them; don't get me wrong there are some good white folks around but it is hard to find em and even once you find em, you can not give all your trust to em. Cause deh white, deh not like niggas deh sticks together even if deh don't like each other.

Sun going down na the birds is singing, Puddin is singing and the people on that music machine is singing. I am feeling free in my heart and my soul is at rest not worried about a thang. I am not even thinking about heaven now, I don't want to go there na. I wanna stay here on earth and spend some of this money, and live like I am in heaven. Just when the sweet smell of my gardina bush hits my nose a hand touches on my shoulder and scares the living hell out of me. I means scares me so bad I sorta wet my panties, (huh that mean my fresh smell be gone na). Child it was Big John , standing over me a grinning and lookin like he wanted to eat me for supper. Oooooouuuooouooweeee, I sure did not need no man touching me right then, especially one so strong and half dressed. I had to catch myself quick, I says "Big John put on a shirt right na. I mean it na, stop all this carrying on na." But on the inside I was a ball of fire wanting to give in, but Puddin here and I do not want anymore of that sharing stuff going on. I am figiting and sweating, swallowing and scared to death, Lawd don't let me give in. I wish I did not give a damn about nothing. Uh, I really ain't so good, I am just controlled that's all. Then I says, "What you want any way John , I thought you was all tied up on another job?" That devil looked at me and says, "I guess you don't know what I want Ms. Lula you being a Christian lady and all." Even though he said that to me it was the way he was looking at me as if he was go charm me or something. Twas'int nothing but that old demon in him then trying to get me started up. Just then Puddin comes out the bathroom half dressed and looks at John and says "Man is you climbing up the wrong tree there baby. Ms. Lula ain't go do nothing but pray for you and herself. Ain't no squirreling go be going on around here, so if you looking for some nuts you better go pick you self up some pecans."

Well right then I did not know what to say, but na John turns and looks at Puddin like he could not stand her and as he walking off he says, "Ms. Lula I will see you in a few days I will be working over at Sally White's house. Puddin I hopes you is gone when I get back." I tells John good evening, and Puddin yells, "Why don't you wish in one hand and shit in the other field hand and see which one fills up first. See Ms. Lula see why I don't cater to, too many niggars. Deh ain't nothing but a bunch of fuck dogs. Hell most mens is nothin but fuck dogs whether deh black or white. Deh is just a bunch of hot and bothered fuck dogs Ms. Lula Mae." What Puddin did not know is me and John done smelled each others musk.

CHAPTER 19

Dinner in Town

"WHAT YOU WANT TO eat Puddin? I am ready to make you whatever you want." "Make me what ever I want, girl you not go cook for me tonight, we is going into town and get us some of then white folk to cook for us at the town kitchen." Huh, na first of all Puddin know ain't no white girls cookin anythang over there in that kitchen everybody know that be Jessie Mae Williams and her girls cookin everything over there at night and Cassie and dem cooks the day shift, so anytime you goes there the food is good, anytime. And furthermore ain't no way we can go over there and eat in them white folk eatin hall. "Puddin we not go be allowed to eat in deh eatin hall. I ain't never seen no body colored sittin at a table in there girl." " Child what you mean, you just watch and see. I eats where ever I want to . Girl Lula Mae you is to damn fretful and scary once I gets to goin I gets dem white women to like me just as much as dem white mens do. See I got persuasion and deh is all green. It is all how you handle yourself girl, get dressed." Child I was getting excited, so I started puttin on my nice pristen white cotton dress with them little blue embroidered roses on the collar and the lace pockets. It is one of my Sunday go to meetin dresses and I sprayed some of that fine sweet smelling perfume

Puddin had gave me along time ago. She had said it was from Paris sos, I did not wear it a lot, but this was a special evenin. I was go eat at the white folks eatin place and I wanted to smell good, and I wanted them to smell me smellin richer than them too. I could hardly wait to roll into town with Puddin and that fancy car of hers.

Let me straighten my living room up a little before I go; never know how you might come back home. Just when I was about to sit on my blue silk sittin chair, Puddin came in the room and what did I see? Well like I told yall she was a little frail to me but she be just right for them white folk, deh believe in bein thin. Our should I say the women has to be thin, cause the men lets they belly get as big as they want. Well we all knows why they like they women so little, short sticks can't stretch to far across a wide road. To tell ya the truth, half the time when deh be throwin down us grown women deh mostly gettin thigh pussy. Cause we is known for our big asses and fluffy thighs. That is another reason why our babies get raped at early ages deh be tryin to get em before deh gits to be grown women. Maybe that is why our mens is so big they have wide roads to cross. Yall know what I am tryin to say, so I ain't go spell it out. Well na I gots to say that the Lawd made most people to suit each other acceptin for most white men and his woman. Cause dem girls is made so wide and deep they can handle a couple of bow legged dicks. And most of their men gots lots of balls and short bats, from what I hear. Let us not get of the subject. Na Puddin still had that way about her, still full of life and passion. Puddin had on a yellow silk dress with little diamonds all over it, casue she likes to show off. It was low cut in the front and the back, it had a long tail on it like a wedding dress, and a split all the way up to her glory hole and of course it fitted her waist line. It had a chaffon like collar and the sleves were see through, she had on a wide white hat and silk covered gold shoes. I said, silk covered gold shoes and no stockings of course, cause she is a nasty woman. I never understood why that woman would not wear stockings, even a hoe ought want her legs to be pretty and of course her face was made up perfect. But you know deh all knows how to put that war paint on deh face. I just looked at her in shock; I looked at that woman cause no matter what she did she just looked damn good. Child them silk gold covered shoes with rhinestones on them ain't never been seen in Friendly, La. before. Ain't seen one white woman with a pair of them on.

Then she looks at me and say, "Lula where is you goin dressed like that!" I says "I am going to eat at that fancy white folk place with you." She says "Child let me see what I can git you to wear and please let me make up your face." I says, "Make my face up. I ain't fittin to let you put no harlot paint on my face." Awwwweee na lord here it go just when those words came out of my mouth, I seen somethin on Puddin's face I ain't never seen before, she looked embraced and hurt, she even dropped that proud head for a moment or two. I guess she could see that I felt sho nuff bad about what I said , everybody know I ain't one for trying to hurt anyones feelings and less lone Puddin's feelings, especially not Puddins'. I tried to throw it off but she just looked at me and says, "Okay Ms. Lula I ain't go paint you face like mine is." I turned my head in shame and started to cry, and then I say , "I am sorry Puddin, I am sorry for just being an ignorant woman sometimes." Puddin being who she is says, " You aint ignorant Ms. Lula you just speaking how you has been raised to believe. I is a loose women to most peoples. I know it is hard for a good Christian woman like yourself to have company with me. I is grateful to you to Ms. Lula, you is the only friend I have really ever had. So ifin my friend says she does not want to be made up like a harlot, then I ain't go make her up like a harlot. Come on girl lets go have dinner."

Just then all of a sudden something snapped in me and a fire took off all over me. I says "Damit to hell Puddin make me up and give me one of those hot dresses too we go burn up Friendly tonight." Huh, child Puddin could not have been happier, she pulls out some of her older dresses when she was thicker, and started to dress me, ha ha ha na baby. I had on a blood red Spanish lace dress, with black baby doll trim and a side split up to my knee, it was low cut and it was off the shoulders, (Na of course I have really nice shoulders from all my hard work) and that dress was huggin my hips like a starvin man holdin on to a loaf of bread (Na that is tight). Na here is the kicker, she gave me a pair of brown silk stockins, with the seam up the back, ifin it was not for that seam, it would have looked like my legs was naked. My legs was dressed like the President's wife. Then she puts my hair in an up do sos my face can show good and then she puts a red silk Camellia in my hair. I am not lying I never thought I could look so good and I was looking very good just as good as Puddin. But then again I always did look better than her cause I am a clean woman. Child we goes and git in that fine canary yellow car with those snow white seats and puts down the top and here we go me and Puddin headed into to town to be truned around at the door; I am sure of it. I sittin straight and tall to be sure every body in town and the country see me. I wonder who that horse belongs to about three miles up from my place. I have not noticed any body coming around lately, did not see a brandin mark and did not see a rider. I keep my head turned towards my house and that horse. That horse looked familiar, maybe it was someone from town scoutin early for dear tracks , you know Jake Toulea one of dem cajuns killed a 18 point buck back of my corn field last year that's probably him tryin to get lucky again or maybe some one tryin to sneak down to my favorite fishing hole. Well if deh is, deh can just have it, cause this one evening I looks to good to be running off someone body fishin or huntin. And ifin deh is tryin to get in my house I done made arrangements with Ougalla to watch my doors and windows, good luck to em with that one. Cost me one thousand for that obaya to bring him in. Ummmm Puddin was not saying much, look like she was in a deep thought or something. I was just enjoyin the ride. The air smelled sweet with the blossumin of the flowers, oh my god the magnolia trees were just showing off na. The smell of them made you think that if there were any gardens in heaven they would have to be full of magnolia trees, gardenia bushes, honeysuckle vines, confederate jasmins and night bloomin jasmins, that is what my roads was lined with. The sky, lord the sky was a wonder of colors, purple, deep green, beautiful blues, sun light yellows, deep pinks and reds with warm sheds of orange yellow streaking through it. This is a moment I will always remember and feel deep in my heart; I think I would call this a sense of peace. The wind blowin in your ears, the sweet smells of heavens gardens, and a painting by the hand of God. No I won't forget this evening. I did not want the ride to end, it felt like I was riding into a world that I had never seen before but always knew it existed some where deep in my heart. A place where God is and all my memories and loved ones and every good thing was available to me there. Somewhere I was loved, needed and wanted just for bein me without judgment or conviction. Felt like I was in the middle of heaven, healed, set free and loved. Just about when I was about to lay back and get totally comfortable we makes that last curve right into the center of town and the day dream was over.

Child you would have thought a parade had just hit town, people was just stopppin and lookin and lookin and stoppin to see us. Puddin pulls up to the Lilly of the Valley Kitchen and parks her car all proud and walks in the dinin hall to take as seat. Don't know about the valley in the name but the lilly was perfect cause it was all lilly white in the seatin area. Well honey the shit hit the fan when Mrs. White , you know the Majors wife, gits up from her table and comes over to ours and says "Na Lula you knows better than this, we gits together on Sunday the Lords day in the middle of town square and share our food and stories with yall. You know we do not share the same eatin place at no time; you know better than this. But I guess you have been hanging around some real bad trash lately, because we have never had any trouble out of you at all, before now." Then she looked at Pudding and says " I remember you even though you have seemed to improve your appearance somewhat and lost some weight. Do not matter thought a bitch is a bitch big or little, and a nigger wench that is a bought bitch ain't go clean up no matter how much of that rich smelling perfume she can put on. You can not wash dirt clean. Ms. Lula Mae the only reason yall still in here alive is because of you , other than that we would … "Then Pudding gits up from the table and kimbos her hips ready to fight when. Major White comes in and pulls his scared jealous wife over to her table and sits her down. Yall know, no self repectin white man would speak down at this wife to many times for a black woman so that poor man was caught, caught between a rock and a hard place. Caught between the woman he married to and the one he had passion for, for a moment I felt sorry for his low down ass. Puddin looks right in his eyes and says, in an almost beggin way "How have you been Major White? I shol is happy to be back in your town." Poor man he looked right in her eyes and you could see the tears swell up in his. Then he says, "Gal you din lost your mind and for sure you have lost your place or something, we can't allow you to sit up in here with decent hard working white folks and eat. Ain't yall got a colored place to eat at? I know yall do, because I let my prisoners get their meals from their. Ms. Luzy 's place is sitting over there just waiting for some customers of her … Na uhhh Ms. Lula Mae what is making the best damn biscut maker south of the Mason and Dixie line misbehave like this for ? Looks like you shoud have told Puddin here that this would not happen, not here in Friendly, not ever." I can't stand that old bastard actin like he got some kind of respect or something, he really ain't shit. He done licked the pink out of Puddin ass and done buried his face so far up her valley of hell, if she belch you can smell his hair cologne. For one thang he takes his prisoners over to Luzy's and feed them for free and another thang, I remember him down on his knees before Puddin. (Yall do remember what Ms. Lula Mae told yall she saw and keep quite about. I wish I had told somebody, anybody and I just might do that before I leave the white man's hell for colored folks heaven. Plus I bet he would be mad as a red head wood pecker if he knew Puddin told me he has a wart on his dick.). Puddin looks at the Major and his wife with the kind of hate that could make you sick to your stomach and then she says, " All I wants is to have me a good meal and some good liquor and go home." Major White says " You can get your good meal and good liquor on the other side of the track at Ms. Luzy's place. If you do not leave I will have to get the Sheriff to arrest you . You know better than this Ms. Lula, you know how we live here in Friendly, La. We all live together but we live together in our separate parts of town and on Sundays we let yall have privilege to our company and we treat yall like our children. We listen to your stories and tell yall some things about us. We understand yall is like children so we do not trouble your minds with all of our adult problems. We realize that yall's minds not quite developed yet to understand the white man's world. Na, becaue of my respect of the good Lord and the fact he put us in charge of yall I am giving you a chance to leave and don't come back here with no more foolishness. I know it might be hard for you to understand that is why we only discuss serious matters with out equals. You know if you was in Mississippi, Texas or Florida yall would be hanging from the ceiling while we eat. But here in Friendly we have compassion for our lesser people, that is the only reason you and Puddin ain't dead; but yall is pushing it. Hell we treats yall much better than we do them red heathens." Na ain't that a bitch we suppose to be happy cause deh don't treat us like they do the Indians. They just pissed at them cause they could not make them slaves. It would have been a bunch of bald headed white folk in this country for sure if deh had kept on tryin.

I am thinking of a million things I could be doing rather than bothering with these white folks about eating at they place. I could have fixed me and Puddin one of the finest meals anyone could eat. Could be sitting on my front porche smelling my perfume garden from heaven and listening to the frogs sing as the woods wake up for her night dwellers.

Could be donin a lot other things rather than trying to prove to white folks I deserve to eat in they place. Don't know why I let Puddin get me in this mess , when she is gone I still got to live here. I do not give a damn about being like them acceptin for their place in society and how they run every got damn thang, bastards. (Yall know because of them Ms. Lula go have to apologize to the lord for all this dirty talk.) "Ms. Lula, Ms. Lula do you hear what I am saying to you?" That is when I came out of my dream hearin the Major ask me did I hear what he was saying. "Yes sir Major White, I understands a whole lot better now. I do not know what got into me, don't know what made me think it would ever be okay for colored folk to make themselves confortable in the white man's world. I show do apologize to you sir and your wife and all the good white folk of Friendly, yall has been good to me, cause if it was not for yall Ms. Lula Mae would not have one dime in her pockets." "Na, Lula Mae you know we forgive you why don't you bring by 20 jars of them fig preserves, to the store in the morning, that will be your fine for breaking the rules. Oh and I need you to get there by sunrise, so yall gals had better be on your way." Na he can suck my soiled drawers for all I care; cause I don't give a damn about him messin over Puddin but he done messed over me na, takin my preserves.

CHAPTER 20

A fine Dinner in Jail

BOUT THEN HERE COMES the worst example of human being God ever created; Sheriff Watson, the white folk sheriff. Somebody had run and told him we was making trouble at Lilly's; you know this low down cracker basterd had a two by four in his hands. I think that som of a bitch was gonna hit us with that, for sure he was ready to put us both in jail. Lord please help us, because we is about to die. While Puddin starts to talk to the Sherrif I went to my other place, and started thinking about that beautiful sun set, started thinking whether or not God made it different for the white part of town or whether or not people just saw it different. A sunset is a sunset ain't it. Then Puddin pulls out some money and says this money just like your money, this money is made by the United States government and it don't say I just have to spend it at Ms. Luzy's kitchen. Then Sherrif Watsons neck turned as read as a blush apple. Oh god now that is the first time I ever really seen a red neck. He says, "Gal is you sassin Major White and disrespectin his wife? Then he moves closer to her with that two by fou. It was like a miracle all of a sudden Puddin changed her tone. "No sir Sheriff I may be some bit of a trash whore but I aint' crazy. I just lost my figuring for a moment,

I guess I thought I was still in Cuba or in some of them places outside of the United States, where everybody can eat together. I shol is sorry for upsettin you kind people, yall is been real good white folks, and yall treats yall colored folks like real good Christian folks should. I is so sorry for causin any trouble. I is gonna take myself and Ms. Lula Mae home and have us one of Ms. Lula Mae's fine meals. I shol am sorry for causin yall good Christian white folk problems, by comin in here and mis behaving." That right there let me know I was in hell when a woman this strong and proud had to bow down like a trained dog. Child I almost died because I could not believe that I just heard a woman so head strong about going in here to eat, just change at the thought of the white man's wrath. I had to hold back the tears in my eyes, but they started to fall, and I could see the smirks on them white folk face. They put us niggers in our place at the bottom of their feet. I felt like throwin up. I felt like fightin. I felt like dyin. The pit of my stomach hurt and I could hardly stand to here poor Puddin sound so pitiful anymore. Hell I needed a drink right then. I got scared as hell cause when you lets white folks know they right they really tear you another ass hole. Then all of a sudden Puddin said, "I just bet the good Lord sittin in here somewhere, lookin on at this and if he is, this is the reason I don't believe in him." Oh, Jesus, did she just say that, we was almost out of this shit. But no Puddin had to open her mouth, you could hear the people whisperin and they was lookin at us like they had seen the devil himself. I thank she scared them too cause blasphemy is somethin they teach hard about. No matter what they do deh don't believe in blasphemin deh God.

That mean ass Sherrif Watson looked at Puddin and says, "Gal is you tryin to be smart and blashpheme the Lord. Well, you shoulda thought about that before you come in here and bothered these good folks havin their meal. Git your purse. You too Ms. Lula Mae come on follow me to jail or one of these men will carry you; don't make me no never mind. I will hit a nigger wench in the head just like I do a hog. I done told these good folk just cause you train an animal don't mean they deserve to be treated human. Ifin I had my way you would still have sackles on your feet." I could see the look on Puddin's face and I could also see the how the Major was lookin at her too. His face was all red and sweaty, lookin and looks like he was tryin to talk to her with his eyes. Look like he was saying don't push the Sheriff. Sheriff Watson don't mind killin animals and he believes all colores is animals lessin deh is got his blood in em. We followed him jail holdin our heads down as we walked across town. What all them white folks did not know was none of them was go be eatin clean food tonight, cuase as I said our sisters was doin all the cookin. Hell, the sackles they done put on our minds is much worst than the ones they put on our feet anyway. Don't know how we go take them off. Wonder how much nigger filth dem good white folks go be eatin tonight ain'nothin worse than eatin a juicy piece of meat that use to be a dead rat. Na this is just between me and you; deh done ate a bunch of dead rats cause we catches em every now and then in our house. Most of the time we gives it to their cooks, hell that is the only way we feels like we is gettin back at em. A few of them be spared, just like a few of us be spared.

"Don't say it Ms. Lula don't say one word, I got my mind made up every last one of them go see what Puddin made of. When you is out numbered you smart to give in. I done licked more white ass than this, only difference was my face was buried between the cheeks. Puddin will not forget this night." Na we been sittin in jail for over 20 some odd minutes and then all of a sudden all kinds of food was brought over to the jail for us. Child we had roast chicken, steaks, them giant prawns with that special red sause, jambalya rice, garlic grits with fresh cheese and bacon in them(oohhh jesus), preserved water melon rinds, fresh baked biscuits, pecan pie and peachcobbler to die for. Ms. Cazzie Williams and her girls was runnin the kitchen tonight so deh brought the food over personal. Tell me that Jessie Mae and her girls was cookin for the Govenor of the state, tonight. Ms. Cazzie says "Major White sent all this over here for yall ladies. You could tell the colored gals was feelin real good about Puddin, by the look on their face, cause they know she the one pushed up the dinner thang. Maybe tht is why the damn food was so good, dem girls made it with love for us. Then that old stubborn Puddin looked at all that pretty food and tells Ms. Cazzie to take it all back and tell Major White he could stick it up his hairy ass. Then Ms. Cazzie says "Child I can not do that so you had just better take it and eat it and be glad you aint, got your self hurt over here messin with these good white folks. They is a lot better than some of the other white folks around here. Ifin you would have done this over in Summerview, La. they would have hanged you for deserte in the town square. Sheriff Watson is the sheriff over there too. You must have some good mojo bag, cause he do not mind hangin women, especially colored ones. So you ought to stop comin over here trying to cause trouble for all of us and just eat the got damn food. Cause I aint goin back and tell Major White none of that foolishments you is sayin. He is taking a chance sending this food. Ifin in his wife knew what he was doin he would not ever be able to explain it to her and he might could even loose his job. Most white men will grab them a bed wench some let their wife know and some don't. Major White don't want to rub it in Ms. Sallys face, so you just have to accept your place what ever that is. Seem like to me you might have been more than a little good time for the Major. But Ms. Puddin, your biggest down fall is you is a woman and you is colored and neither one of them adds up to freedom. Plus this is good clean food and a good meal can sooth your soul, child eat this food." Whole time Cazzie talkin she is winkin her eye at Puddin, she really put on show just in case somebody be tryin to listen at her. "Look Ms. Cazzie you take this back to that son of a bitch and tell him I says I knows what he really like and if he ever want to get it again he better come to Ms. Lula Mae's tonight." Ms. Cazzie tells her once again she was not takin that message back to the Major. Child I am almost finished eatin my food now oooooooweee and it was good. A good satisfiyin meal and I was alive to tell about it. Ain't but one woman that can cook almost as good as me and it is Ms. Cazzie that steak cut like butter it was so tender and good I wanted another one. I started to eat Puddin's, while she over there talkin to Cazzie cause she was shame faceted. By the time them two had finished talking and I was finished eating. The Sherrif came in and told us we could leave, he said "Ms. Lula I want you to go sit in that car and if you move I will have to arrest you again." Ms. Cazzie left and nobody but him and Puddin was left in that room. I was startin to get worried about the both of them, after about an hour or so. Puddin comes out look like she had lost her insides, she aint say nothin , she would not even look at me, you could feel her pain. Then all of a sudden she say, "I is good enough for them to lay up with me, roll in me, mess in me and they even pay good money to do it but I aint good enough to eat in that cheap little country hick shit shack that they thanks is a restaurant. I gots something to show these white folk before I leave this here town and I gots somethin to show myself too. To bad that bindin the Devil thang don't work for colored folks. Is you got some lye soap Ms. Lula I needs to wash some shit off me." We all had lye soap but we ain't bath in it or at least I never bath in it.

It is dark na and here we is headed back to my house in the pitch of night, but that full moon was just the touch we needed. I started to feel a little uneasy, cause I know that white folk can change they mind from prayin to lynchin fast as Jesus can say grace. All I want to do is get home. After I calmed down though, the ride seemed not to be so bad. Puddin was driving like the wind so I really could not here the woods like I wanted to but I could certainly smell the night. The air had just a tench of coolness in it, jasmine perfumin the woods and the moon was high and shinnin bright in the sky. I bet old Ma Jenea is cookin something up out in them woods. These is the kinds of nights you might see her walkin down the road durin full moon nights. That long gray hair that touched the ground always shined like spun corn silk at night and her yellow skin seemed to sparkle. She is a true healer but nobody still want to cross her to much, never know when you go need her. She one of them women you look at, speaks to but stay your distance. Cause ifin she looks at you and don't like you, you feels kinda sick. I mean it Ain't nobody know what she really was, she looked like a colored indian, but she talked like a creole, and she walked like one of dem African Queens.

As we get closer to my house I see that horse still tied by the tree. Now I have started to wonder who is it, so I asked Puddin to stop. Ms. Lula Mae "I can't stop I gots me some company comin and I needs to get cleaned up." I hope she don't think the Major go show up. Now I do not know who she got comin but I do know she did not tell me of it and I don't like it neither. That is my house and even if she is payin me she has to tell me when some one is comin to it. "Who you got comin at this time of the night Puddin? Plus I am concerned about that horse tied up over there. When we left it was there and it is still tied there. It is to close to my property and I want to know who the sam hell that is, pull this damn car over na." All of a sudden Puddin started rantin and ravenin all about how people likes to mis use her and how every body like it when they get a chance to treat her bad, din she pulls out her liquir bottle and starts to drink, swearing and cursing God and all the saints. I forgot about that horse because I am thinkin somethin is wrong with my friend. Anway she is still a little mad at me because I ate that food. Look I did not care how she felt that was a feast and I knew the cooks and I was hungry. Plus I knew we really was not in jail like talkin about it. I know they was making an example of us sos the Major could look like he was takin up for the white people and his wife. Shit I ain't gonna turn my back on Cazzie's cookin she is almost as good as me. Oh thank you Lord for gettin home safe. "Puddin I sure am sorry that our beautiful evening was ruined." She is go pay for cussin God out though. I might question God but I ain't done ever cussed him out.

CHAPTER 21

Something wrong with my House

As SOON AS I walked in my door I noticed my house felt different, but I looks around and everything seems to be alright. I just keeps having this feeling like something was wrong in my house. I ain't never felt this strange in my house before. I might have to go see Ma Jenea tomorrow myself apparently Ougalla must need to be woke up again. Aww no, no, no I did not mean that I meant, I need to go see the Preacher. Uh hell what I am lyin about if I go see him he gonna go see her. Every body gots somebody deh see, even in the Bible deh talks about the seers and watchers. Oh I knows about the book of Enoch and we knows about the Seventh Book of Moses too. We don't fool with it to much because the two headed doctors, the prophets and the spiritual workers mostly use it. Feel like I want to cry seems like my house is sick. Na don't know ifin any of yall ever had this, but it is a feeling you can not touch, its is like an itching under the skin that you can not scratch. I was to tired to heat up water for the bath so I just took me a little PTA (oh pta is a pussy, tit and ass whipe) and went on to sleep. I left Puddin up sittin in the living room lookin like she was ready to kill every white and every colored that liked whites too. Well I know she was not go be killin me cause I don't like em and I loves em cause I have too or once again let me say that is what deh Bible say I should do. Na I don't love em like I loves black folk I love dem with they kind of Godly love. You can take that like you wanna. I fell off to sleep hard, next thang I heard was a noise, squeak, squawk, squint, then I hears words "Ooh lawd Jesus, Jesus lawd have mercy. I am sorry, I am sorry baby. I aint go ever treat you like that again, never. My God, you a sweet chocolate bitch, put that sweet black ass in my face." I am thinkin I am dreamin a dream in hell cause heaven ain't got nothin to do with all this foolishness. Well not this kind of foolishness. When I finally got myself a wake , I realized I was not dreamin, but hell was having a hoe down in my house.

Then I saw them, Puddin straddled on top of the Major riden him like a wild bull. Then I hear Puddin say, "Na I want your low down ass to pull out of me mother fucker, pull out Mr. White." Why me, it always be me either fightingthe devil within or looking at his works on the outside. Lawd have mercy Puddin must have been on of his finiest works too. I hear the Major beggin for his life now, please, please, don't do it, don't make me pull out." I can't even get a little heat from this one, cause he sound so pitiful. Then that white man say, "You ain't got to call me Mr. White, call me whatever the fuck you want. Call me any got damn thang just don't make me move na, baby please please." "No got damn it you pull out of me na or I won't ever let you feel me again. Pull out." "No Puddin got damnit I ain't movin." Then I goes closer in the room and I sees her pullin a peral necklace from under his backside. I will never borrow that hoes' pearls again, never. He acted like he was about to run on my ceilin while she was pullin on them, it was all I could stand just watchin that shit. She looked like a witch ridin a broom pullin a string of demons out of that man's ass. I wonder what that felt like? I told yall she was the Devils prize whore. Then she stands up in the bed and I see Mr. White down on his knees, (It was worth all the spyin in the world to see a white man down on his knees before a colored woman, eatin her like she was sweet potatoe pie). Puddin say "You want to taste my sweet cherry blossom for the rest of you life, don't you Mr. Major?" "Yes, Puddin I want to taste all you got gal. You is one sweet bitch. " Don't call me no got damn gal, Mr. White." "After I finish tastin you baby is you go let me slide it back in from the back for a little while." "No Massa White , but you can suck me like I is a sweet drink, you old bastard." "Call me that again. "Call me an old bastard again Puddin." Oh Jesus, I felt some shame yall cuz I was starting to get a little titalated, cause all that talkin was gettin to me. Puddin is a real nasty bitch, yes she is. Then I watched him start to nibble at her woman self like a fish nibblin at a bait. Look like every time he got a good grip on it Puddin push his head back. That man started beggin her na, sweat drippin off him like a waterfall while she squirmin and moanin. Then she did it something I never even thought of before, that low down heifer turns around and puts her natural tail in that mans face. I just knew she was about to get her ass knocked off then, cause I don't know bout puttin your sweaty ass in a mans face. He did not hit her that nasty bastard look like he was trying to stick his nose in it too. See this is the reason why people be wanting to kill deh husband or wife when they catch em cheatin. I know I would not appreciate my husband bringing another womens ass home one his breath. See if he go home and Sally pull out her gun and shot him in the ass, he go be well deservant of it. Did I just hear him ask her to pee on him, well I ain't even going there, but he acted like he was tasten some of my sweet jelly preserves, that is when I heard the jar drop. She go pay me extra for using my fine preserves like this. And if that bitch piss in my bed, I am go grab her hair from behind and make her kiss her own ass. Oh my God, oh Jesus , Satan's harlot done hit the earth and she got white men ... well you know. I watched it all every bit of it until she turned around and sat on that man from the back and that is when he called it a day. That damn Puddin gets up and and looks at him and says "Na take your sorry ass home to your wife, you low down son of a bitch and be sure you rub a little Puddin all over her, kiss that bitch right in her mouth." But there was silence the kind of silence that you might hear at a catholic wake. Nothin, he said nothin, I heard nothin from him nothin . I thought he was about to kill us both that white man is gonna get up and kill us both, but that did not happen, he did not move. The death angel done came in the room. One dead white man two dead niggers.

CHAPTER 22

The Major of Friendly La is Dead

THE MAJOR OF FRIENDLY, Louisiana lay dead in my house in my room on my property. Now I am a dead woman, my house is burned down, anybody to close to me go die, and all because of another person's sins. The Lawd said come out from among them. Yes, I was tempted by money and now I am about to pay for it. I started screamin and hollering but nobody was go save me or hear me but God. Then Puddin says "Shut up got damit, let me think. I am not go die for this pecker wood, come on girl let me think." All of a sudden a voice said " Yall ladies need some help?" I passed out right there. When I came to, Puddin was still sittin there looking at the Major. Last I remember turnin around seeing Big John and that was it. I woke up in my bed, Puddin and Big John standin over me wondering if I was go make it I guess. Big John says "How you feelin Ms. Lula Mae?" I said "I am just fine John, I was just took off my feet when I saw you standin in this house and that dead white man in my bed ain't helpin." "Ms. Lula I been movin around here since early evenin I aint never left." "Looks like I done got my self a nigga problem." Don't nobody be comin around my place just hangin around. If he want to do that he need to find him a corner somewhere.

"Yall ladies left me to thinkin when I was here earlier, movin all around in the house, closin doors and windows, peepin out and lockin thangs up. Old Big John got to thinkin what is going on. I went around on the other side of the house and looked in and saw yall countin enough money to buy Jesus and all the Saints. Yall had more money than a two-headed doctor and bank robber." "So you been around here sneaking around in my business huh John. What right you have doing somethin like that nigger." "I was just curious Ms. Lula that is all, I really was tryin to stand guard for ya, never know who might be passin by to rob ya. Yall ladies look like yall need a man to do some heavy liftin." We don't need a damn thang nigga", said Puddin. Then all of a sudden she pulls that damn gun and points it right in Big John's face and says "We don't need no sneakin low down dirty dog to help us with a damn thang. Looks like we go be gettin rid of two men instead of one." Big John says "How you go get rid of that dead white man? If you kill me Ms. Puddin how you go get rid of me. But if you got to kill me, kill me like you did him." I hated John right then, he was just like the rest of them no counts. I looked right in Johns eyes and said, "I trust you Big John (I would have said anything to get what I wanted, he had his purpose right then). If I had to have someone hidin around here and watchin and sneakin and whatever eles you been doing I would rather it be you." "I am trying to figure how you meant that Ms. Lula, but there be one thing true about both of us, we both might be a little sneaky. You hired me here and gave me a good job. But you also needed some tendin to Ms. Lula, right. You know you wanted me, to do you, like Puddin just did the poor Major, ride you to death. Uh, don't fret girl I am a lot of man and I know ain't nobody perfect. I just want you to know you can trust me, just like you trust the good Lord. " Well one thang he did not know about me and that is I ain't never really trust the white man's God look at the trouble I am in now.

Na what we go do with the Major, God rest his soul. I can feel it in my bones yall there is going to be some kind of big confusion for us all if we try to explain bringing him to town. " Well, John you me and Puddin knows that we can not take the Major into to town. First of all everybody is goin to want to know why he was at my house or atleast pretend to wonder why. Child I have gone to another world now my head spinnin again. I see my life gone, then I see me in hell with Puddin and John burnin, cause that is what is goin to happen to us deh go burn us like deh burn witches. If only I had just keep on eye fucking men then John would not be here in all my business and Puddin would not have anythang to judge me by. People talk about looking and lusting but eye fucking ain't never got nobody in trouble, unless you a black man in the South looking at a white women. I can see my whole life just running through my head right now. Then I see what happens before we die, they go skin us and hang us and burn us alive like they did them Williams' cross the lane. Somebody had suppose to had touched a little white girl and for some reason they said it was Mr. Williams. Don't matter that he could hardly walk, could not see and was 72 years old. Dem white folk came from three Parishes and took that old man out and falyed him with a knife while he was alive . People could hear him screaming all over Louisiana, then after a while all you could hear was a faint moan of pain. Then you smelled human flesh being burned, all his children and grandchildren was there witnessing it. They made them watch while they hurt that poor old man, sure did oh and deh was singin hymns while deh did it sos Jesus could bless they deeds. They waited in ambush for anybody that came by his house that night and nights after that. It was something you will never forget. See them good Christians wanted to be sure that no one cut him down. His skinned and burned body just hung there until it rot. They was doing the bidding of their good Lord and savior or so they say. I says that because they had their Bibles in hand and was quoting scriptures while they did the Lords work. You can not do that kind of evilness unless the Lord gives you permission, right. Well that is exactly what is about to happen to me. One thang I am finding out is that sin is in the eyes of the beholder.

"Come on back Ms. Lula Mae come on back girl, you is loosing it don't go out on us now." My head was still fuzzy and I could hardly stand up, fear had taken me over. I hear Puddin saying "Alright Lula you can not do this now we got to think." All of a sudden I looks at Puddin like I have seen a ghost. I wanted to kill that bitch. Then I was thinking to myself; I could just go and turn her and John in. My Lord, the one of truth please give me the wisdom to figure out what to do. If the white folk God is looking and listening right now, I need you to turn your back on this like you have turned your back on us colored folk that has been suffering for so long.

Then all of a sudden Big John says "I got it". "Tells us, tell us how you are going to fix this. Tell us. Big Johns says "Ms Lula why don't you let me do men's business." Then he looks at me and says "Go get that good liquir you keep hid under your dresser in the bedroom." As I was coming back with the liquor I realized that Big John had looked in every part of my damn house. John took that liquor and poured it all over the Major, after he had cleaned him up. I was just standing in shock, still not believing what had just happened. You know that Puddin looked at me and says, "Come on and help us girl". I looked her right in the face and says, "Girl you is thinkin crazy, I ain't touching that dead man." I left and went outside on my side porche, not too many blacks had side porches, anyway next here comes Puddin. I wish she would have stayed in there with Big John. I just wanted to sit here in peace and remember what my house use to look like. Then I looked and sees Big John totin something in my rug over his shoulder. The rug that my great, great, great grandmother made me. First I loose my soul then I loose thangs that was made for me out of love. We done passed that rug around now for four generations, now. "Lawd have mercy" is all I can say. Then Puddin puts her arm around me and says "It is go be okay Ms. Lula." I looked at her with tears in my eyes and says, "I ain't go ever be okay with this, maybe this here is God talking to all of us. Maybe we need to repent of this and try to live a righteous life. I ain't did one thang but I am caught up in this just like I did. I done talked about how mean whites is and done wished a bunch of em dead but I ain't thougth I would have a man's blood on my hands."

"Ms. Lula you is the one got religion, I thank God just might talk to you. But, aint no God talkin to me ,see I is a scandalous woman, so all God ever do is peak down off his righteous Holy Throne to be sure I ain't even tryin to get to heaven. Plus, I ain't talkin Him either , cause I ain't got no reason to. He aint been talkin to me and most of the time his Saints is talkin about me and condemning to their personal hell. If this is how he teaches us lessons,we aint' never got to talk. And another thang I don't even believe in no hell sos can'nt nobody send me there. Don't believe in heaven but I done had a couple nuts that made me think I was there. Anyway Ms. Lula Mae, I ain't never met a church goer who did not take opportunity for your sinin. What I mean is you can buy your way out of sin. The peoples in da church that gives the most is the ones the Preacher and that Good Lord of your turn deh head on when deh is sinnin and messin over folks. I wish you would tell me I am lyin?" Well I ain't answer her about that cause I ain't go talk to no heathen whore about the Lords business. "Puddin were is John going? "He takin the Major for a little ride. You know Ms. Lula Mae I sure hate that the Major's old heart gave out on him. For sho this was one of the best fuckins I have ever done. I know it was good because my pussy was sweating and you ain't havin a good fuck unless your pussy sweats or atleast farts once or twice. You know about that don't you girl." What kind of heathen am I dealing with, is this woman sitting here telling me about her sweaty lady self and man is dead cause of it. Why is she telling me this? I don't want to know bout how she felt; I had seen enough. All I want is for the Major to be alive and me to get the hell out of Friendly without being skinned alive. I am sure now that Puddin is the Devils harlot and Big John is his pimp. I done got myself caught up in somethin and I don't know what to do. This here white man's God is done let me down again. Sad thang is when you believe in somethin and realize that it ain't for you, you wants to keep on believin, hopin to get Its' attention; wanting it to recognize how faithful you bein sos He kin bless ya. But to dis here God, your faithfulness and hope don't matter cause it don't seem like he care bout you at all. You know I wonder if that story about the Devil bein thrown out heaven is the truth. See I figures this ifin the Devil was given the Earth to rule din the real god of this Earth is a blood thirsty demon. Gots to be so, just gots to be so. Tell ya why cause everywhere in the Bible people was made to sacrifice animals, and some was bein called to sacrifice deh own children. Ifin God made us all why he needs so much blood to feel good. Well I don't believe that He do I belives the god of this world needs all that blood, to keep the people scared and to satisfy his hunger to be feared. That is what I belive see when a father loves his children he don't kill em. And us black folk is dispised by the god of this Earth cause he ain't lettin nothin good happen to us. We gots to keep our heads bowed down to people that hurt us and we is too scared to trust each other completely. So I recollect that old Satan his self is the god of this world and everybody tryin to do good thangs is his enemy. Plus ain't no such a thang is good no way. People just act a certain way sos deh look like deh better than other folks but Lawd if we could see what is in each other's hearts we would be throwin up all the time. We gots some people deh call retarded but you know what retarded is?

Anythang on this Earth that have one bit of sympathy and love in deh heart, na deh is retraded.

I stays up all night because I have no idea what the mornin might bring. My rooster had not even crowed yet. It must have been about 4:00 in the mornin and Earnest Walker come flyin up in my yard on his horse. He says " Ms Lula Mae the Majors truck was found wrecked on the bank of the Mississippi river and he is dead." My stomach turned, then I says, " Oh Lord what is Ms. Sally go do. Do yall know what happened? Mr. Earnest I have some mighty fine fat back and preserves in here would you like a cup of coffee and a little breakfast?" "No Ms. Lula, Ms. Sally go be carryin on somethin terrible when she gets this news, she don't know yet. I have to get to her so that she will say all the right things." It has started, I am already losing my blessed hand, nobody ever turns me down for a meal. I wonder if I can still cook, you know I wonder if my taste is still there. You got to have taste to be able to cook good, like you need rhythm to dance. Na I don't know what this old fool is talkin about, how he is going to see that a white woman says all the right thangs.

He just learned how to read this year and I thank she is the one that taught him. Course let him tell it, it was me that taught him, cause you know he could not say she taught him to read. But she can admit to telling what to thank. I can't see how he learned from me since we only spent a few early mornings looking a the bible and some of my newspapers. He really was not ever worth the time I did spend with him. Anyway that old fool pulls off without tellin me the details. I run in the room to wake Puddin; can you believe she woke up all cross and fretful, rollin her eyes at me. Huh, she better be lucky I am to scared to put her ass out. I tells her they have already found the Major's body and people moving around town. I even told her what Earnest said, how he had to get into town to see that Ms. Sally White says all the right thangs. A sure sign people already loosing their minds is a nigga tellin white folk what to do huh. Puddin turns an looks up at me all wrapped up in her silk night gown and says, " Miss Lula Mae, is we gonna have to put you sleep about this here issue? You so nervous you is bound to tell on us yourself. What you really care about some old man saying he going to town to help some white women speak, that aint that important girl. Why is you makin all this commotion about that? I needs my rest after last night I is pretty tired." I says "Puddin what is you so tired for you killed the Major with them evil hips and then you let poor Big John do all the hard work and me do all the crin and worring, ain't you got no scareds in you girl?" Puddin looks at me and says "Ms. Lula Mae is you asking me is I scared, me Puddin, Naomi Love? Why is I suppose to be scared, I learned not to be scared when I was a young girl."

" See Ms. Lula Mae you know ain't none of us was safe, not one colored girl or woman you know ever been safe. So every body jacked off on us. I was broke in like a grown woman early on in life it was brutal. You either go crazy or you go crazy, but for sho you ain't go ever be the same. We all knows women that get raped never be the same. Dis old man raped me when I was deliverin his goods to him. No why he raped me cause I wasn't but about 80lbs wet and looked like such an innocent little girl, most people said I looked like a little boy; but I wasn't as young as he thought. See I was savin myself for my Prince to come along and save me from hell. But anyway after he spoiled me and the white folk killed my uncle and took away the only protection I ever had. About a year or two after that mama and dem sent me to my Aunt Luzzy's cause she lived a good ways away and they wanted me to have a safe life. I was not at Luzzy's no less than three or four hours passed before she done sent word around about me. First man come around was this big old farty smellin man, big as John and stanking worst than a sunk nuts, call his self Willie Ross. I will never will forget his scent; he smelled like stale cigars and vomit. Huh, no what Ms. Lula that old man took me and play with me like I was a little puppy. All the time tellin me what a lucky girl I was, because he was go break me in. He was just breakin in a scab that had grown together hell I was still full of puss cause my insides had not healed proper from what that other bastard had done me. See he had a likin for little black girls and of course they was easy for him to get. Cause girls just aint worth to much whether deh black or white is deh Ms. Lula. I don't hurt from the outside; I hurt from the inside. I am go always hurt Ms. Lula and that is my hell. I bet I have thrown-up more than anybody you know Ms. Lula. If I could I would throw up the world I would, I hate this place. And I hates people, cause deh mostly evil pretending like deh is trying to be good. People is meant to be fucked over and I am just the one to do it."

Chapter 23

The Pain of Puddin

"See Ms. Lula after that sick feeling came all over my little body like I wanted to throw-up, but then comes the pain. The kind that makes you think death is the best thang that could ever happen to you. Felt like someone had took a dull knife and stuck it right through my bottom parts and just ripped them apart. I could feel the raw flesh of my insides burnin and tearin, then after a while I thank I passed out and when I came to he was still at it. Don't think I had even healed from what old man Burdock had done to me. Oh he was my first brutal rapist. Old Willie Ross, was like a raggin bull, forcin his self on me, blood all over me and him, but he keep pullin on me and pullin on me until he screamed and laid over. I was still cryin with blood all over me as he rolled over and stood up. You want to know what hate and pain looks like Ms. Lula, it looks like me. Know what my Auntee did when he roled over Ms. Lula? She came and got me washed me up , put milk in my all over me and poured some in me and brought me back to him again. I wanted to die right then Ms. Lula, but your good Lord did not let me die, he let me suffer. Just like he let all black folks suffer at the hands of his righteous chosen. If there is a hell somewhere my Auntee is bound to go and so is most of yall holy rollers."

"I was lookin at Willie Ross like the devil was in me as matter of fact Ms. Lula the devil did come into me; because right then I sold my soul to him, and I been a demon every since. I just laid there hopin he could see Satan in my eyes. Old Willie Ross must have seen him too, or either he saw that I wanted to eat his heart. See I wanted to kill him but I wanted to eat his heart before I did, so that bastard could feel my pain. That is how I knew the devil owned me right then. Ms. Lula I wanted to eat him alive. Maybe if I could taste the white man's heart I would understand why it was so cold. Old man Ross lost his erection, when he looked in my eyes. Course na he left and I never had to see him again. But others came back, over and over again. I have been topped by men and women. I learned to embrace fear a long time ago Ms. Lula, fear was my only company for a long time. So if you are still wonderin if I am scared Ms. Lula just stop. I am not afraid of the devil itself." "Child you mean the devil hisself don't you Puddin?" "No Lula I mean the devil itself. Since I been living I have seen yall so called devil in men, women, children, dogs, cats birds, so I just as soon believe that the devil is a it, cause it takes all forms. I believes the same about God, see Miss Lula to me the Devil is just God with a migrane headache. And deh both fucks over me."

"I know you do not understand all this foolish talk I am sayin Ms. Lula. So let's not talk about that old devil no more, cause the truth is he is the excuse people use for bein so low down. Let's talk about the fact that you need to stay out of town for a few days till all this thang dies down some. Ms. Lula since you up and all full of wonder, why don't you go in that kitchen and bake us some bisquits?" I just looked at at Puddin in amazement. Did this bitch just ask me to bake her some bisquits? How can she just take a thing and turn it soos, you looks so stupid for nothing. A man is dead and she is askin me to cook. Everythang I own is about to be burned up well not really, cause before all this blow up on me, two niggas I know goin down to the river. I ain't go hang, loose my house, or one more minute of sleep over a hoe and con man. If God is real or if he made up by the white man, I am go use him as my excuse for tellin the truth. White folk still thank you is contolled when you tell dem God made you tell the truth. I goes out on the front porch and feels the air; I feels the cold time comin in the wind. I looks over at my wood shed and

I looks out over my yard tryin to keep it in my mind. I is taking a long look cause ahhh , I get the feelin that I ain't go be here long. I feel like I am about to move away from Friendly. With all my money I can buy as many places as I likes. Ain't nobody go git my money. I will poison this whole got damn town. As a matter if fact, let me fix a few jars of special perserves. The good Lord did not bless me like this to let a hell whore, some saggy dick man, and some ignant muther fuckers take all my got damn money. You want to see hell come to dis earth let somebody try and take my got damn money.

Old Pete my rooster passed in front of my porch and turns and look right at me as if he had seen everythang , that sucker did not even give me a crow. Look like he was rollin his eyes at me. That was a show sign of trouble and big trouble it was. I was bracin myself for the worst and I was lookin at old Pete thinkin how good he gonna taste, if he keep on not crowing . In a few minutes he will be the main dish at the breakfast table. Then I start to think how long it is gonna take to cook him tender, it could take forever, because he is an old ass rooster and the older the rooster, the longer it take them to cook, because they are so tough. Maybe I ought to kill em right na; since he ain't got no manners. Naw, thank I will let him live he is a prize cock, that honorey bastard lucky. Something is wrong with me; I realize it too. I want to kill the rooster just because he did not crow for me. I want to start poisonin white folks just to start a panic and get the attention off the Major, sos I can get the hell out of town. Lord please help me. I is turning into a cold blooded murderer. I knows we all ain't got long to be free. I just stands there lookin out over my yard at the big old magnolia tree wishin I was it. I goes back in my house and opens all the windows and doors wishing, praying and hoping some good news comes through them. You know like an angel or something announcing that all this was a dream and a test. Hell I want everythang to back to the way it was before the Major came over here and climbed on top of Puddin. That whore kilt him with them evil hips and her lips. I looked right at her suckin the life out of that man. The devil did not make his whore fair. Oh Lord I want this to be a dream. But this is what you get when you mess with dem hoes.

Chapter 24

Big John Brings Back the News

As I is looking out the window I sees Big John comin over the walk, smilin and looking so fine. I must be crazy cause I is the only one out of these two that seems to be worried. "Good morning ,Ms. Lula Mae" he says. "Is you done made some of the best damn biscuits in these parts this morning?" I just looked at him and says , "No, hell no" and I turns around and walks straight back in my house. Well he ain't say another word to me. Big John just starts to work on the house while Puddin is getting dressed like she some lady or something, getting ready to go into town. I sees na what these two is, deh is the devil's children in my house. Puddin says " Ms. Lula do you want to go into town with me this morning. Seems like maybe you need someone to fix you some breakfast. Let's go over to Ms. Luzzy's place." I thought about going, then, I though about leavin my house all alone with Big John. After all he did just cover up Puddin's murdering hips and I know I don't trust any of them na. Course I am not gonna let them know it. I says no "I ain't going into no town this morning. Hell I might not ever go into town again." Then Big John says, "Well that's gonna seem mighty strange Ms. Lula Mae ifin, you never goes into town again. Sho you not goin cause you just don't want to leave me in your house alone?" I looks at Big John standin over there all easy in his self and I looks at Puddin getting dressed like she did not have a care in the world. Then I thought to myself if I want to know what is really going on in town, I had better go there to see for myself. "Ms. Lula, ifin it makes you feel any better, people is sayin the Major got drunk as usual, but this time he met his fate. So we ain't got one thing to worry about lady and I know yall done hide yalls treasure somewhere else by na, so what is the problem. Plus I ain't go take nothin from ya I cares about you Ms. Lula Mae." John must thank I am the woman who tied the goat.

Well this time the ride into town was not as pretty as my other rides have been. I had so much on my mind. But you really can not ignore the risen of the sun, see the sun demands you to look at it and pay attention to its' glory. While I looks at the sun rise, I thinks about how good God is to let us look on His great paintins in the sky all the time . Then I thanks me , Big John and Puddin ain't got no business enjoyin what God done painted in the sky cause we is hell bent for killin that man. Can't explain how I really feel right na. I don't know if you can understand me. Ain't nothin like bein scared, nothing. It just feel like you want to throw up, your skin be crawlin, your head get all stopped up, hell you just feel like you is holdin piss and can't go. I looks over there at Puddin and she all dressed up in her powder blue dress with white ruffles on it and a big full white hat broke down in the front with a powder blue rose on the band, white gloves and powder blue shoes, looking like a chocolate angel (That is why the womens really hated that heifer). You know she is a hoe but you have to give her credit for lookin good. No matter what she was wearing she was wearing it good huh. Course I was not lookin to bad my self, with my green dress fitted at the waist (Oh yall mother gots a small waist too.) with the little pleats in the tail of the dress and pokadots on it. Of course my hair was laying down on my back full of them heavy set waves. You know that look you get when you have platted your hair for a few days and tied it up. When you let is loose it just flows like waves on the gulf of mississippi. Oh, I am a fox na, nothin short bout me but my height, 5'3, waist like a wasp, and hips like a horse, paper bag brown and the finest cook in town. But all that did not make me feel any better, sittin here with this cheap tramp dressed like and decent woman. Look like we was never go hit town, then finally, we hits the bridge which seperates the town from the country. Here we is a murderin whore and a poor women who got caught up in trouble tryin to do her duty as a good Christian. Look what my big heart has done to me.

Well yall knows Puddin's braisen ass goes right to the Mayor's house and walks right up to the front porch and knocks on the door. Child I almost fell out. I could not believe what I was seein, better yet I really could not believe what I was doin. Well Ms. Bobby Jean Farque came to the door she be a little spit fire of a woman. She be known for not taking no shit off anybody, white, black, man or woman. White mens don't like her and black mens is scared of her especially when she decides she has a taste for one of em. They could not tell her no, lessin they git a charge. You knows the charge, the one they always used on colored men when deh catches one of dem with a white women. Oh yes Ms. Bobby Jean was a spit fire alright. She opens the door and looks like she been drinking all night, face all red and flush, hair looked to be nappier than any colored womens, especially around the edges, she must not had time to brush it. (Hummmm makes me want to wonder, a nappy headed white woman. Wonder if she got a little jigaboo blood in her. Could be she ain't never have no kids just went around adoptin em. No maam and no sir she ain't give birth to no babies. I ain't sayin she ain't never git pregnant though.) Her eyes was all blood shot, dress all wrinkled and she was bare footed. She looks up at Puddin and says "What in the hell do you want girl?" Then Puddin looks at her and says "I am just comin to pay my respect to Ms. Sally." Then child Ms. Bobby Jean says " HuH, I thought the only one you ever paid any respects to in this house was old dead Major White". Puddin looks right into her eyes and says "I never paid him respect or nothing else, if any payin was done he did it. And why is yall white folks actin like you did not know the arrangement. Why don't you just move aside and let me see Ms. Sally White please." Din Bobby says, "Sally your dead husbands nigger hoe is here." Then she turned and looked Ms. Puddin right in the face, as if to say "Watch it bitch." Then Ms. Bobby Jean moved, wait, wait a minute; I mean Bobby Jean moved. I don't call em Ms. lessin I am in front of them. She probably moved because that hang over she had was workin her nerves more than Puddin. We both walked in at the same time. Yall, once I got in the house I started to look around, you know to see if it is clean as mine. Cuz I had heard all about deh house from Cassie one of their maids. But it was different once you gits in on your own. You gits to see the dirt behind the front porch.

CHAPTER 25

Sittn in the White's House

WELL SHE AIN'T HAVE no dirt behind her front porch. Child that house was a sparkle in your eyes. She must have liked white a lot cuz just about everythang in it was white with either yellow, green or blue trim. White lace table clothes hand embroided, white lace curtins, white lace arm coverings on the couch. The table set was in white and silver, with little pink covered chairs around the table. My God, excuse me Jesus but she had snow white eyelet seat cusions (Don't worry my tale go be sittin on some cusions like these soon. May not be snow white but they go be eyelet cusions.) As far as I could see this woman keep it so clean around her, if a spot of dust showed up she would know right where it was. Southern women is known for keepin a clean house even the white ones. Ms. Sally White one of them white women who did not seem to like black men to much, except for her pet old Earnest. You ain't got one story about her and a black man. Course Major White jumped the fence all the time and everybody knows that too. Sos I figure maybe Ms Sally did not want anything black ever coming her way. Don't look like she wanted anything to dark around her; maybe that is why she had a white house. Anyway na I is wondering why is me and Puddin in this woman's house. Just when I finished figurin, Ms. Sally comes out from the back and looks at us both as if to say "What yall niggers doing in my got damn house." I swear I don't thank I ever saw her look like that at me. Before she could speak Puddin says, "Ms. Sally I sho is sorry about the Major us heard something bad had happed to him. I knows how much he loved you and I knows how much you loved him." I must say Sally did pretty good. I thank I would have had to slap such a brazin slut. Sally looked at Puddin and says "Did my husband confess his love for me while he was fucking you? Why is yall girls here na. If you not coming to bring me something you made or clean my house; I would prefer if you feet would not soil my dwelling. Only niggra girls I let in here is for that purpose and that purpose alone. Don't give a damn to much for your condolenses. Niggra's concern for me doesn't add up to nothing for me, or most other God fearing Southerners. And I know both of yall know that. So what hell do you want?"

By then Bobby Jean had brushed and combed through her nappy hair, washed her face and slipped on some shoes. That heifer takes a stance in the room like she was getting ready to whip some black ass. Puddin done sized up the room by na so she starts her cooning; but she used me. She says, "Ms. Sally, us girls came over to see if there is anything we can do for you. We understand we ain't worthty to come in your house or even be in your company. But whether we is or not, Major White was a whole lot better than most of these folk around here. That is how we felt about him in colored town. So Ms. Lula wanted to come over here and fix you one of her fine breakfast and bake you some of her fine cakes and thangs. We even bought you about 24 jars of fruit preserves and if you look real close you will see two jars of sweet watermelon rhine preserves. Not to mention two slabs of bacon and two slabs of salt sholder meat from them prize hogs."

Now that is when I wanted to kick her in her ass cause she done crossed the line. Here I am dressed as fine as any lady and I ain't got on no cookin and cleanin clothes and this wench din just offered me to clean and cook, like a house nigger. Plus, she done went and stole my preserves and bacon. What she don't know is that she is about to get her behind kicked. And I don't know which jars she took, she could have the wrong jars. Well right na you know what, I don't give a damn. Lord I am trying to stop cussin cause I know this mouth ain't suppose to go to heaven. I got a large charge against me cause this mouth been speakin like peoples of the world. I sure am go try to watch it, cause I needs all the holy credits I can get right about na. So I am go watch my damn mouth from now own. What got me was Sally and Bobby Jean kinda crooked their heads to the side, like they sizin me up. Din they looked at each other looked back at me and says, "There is the kitchen Ms. Lula Mae." Oh, I am Ms. Lula Mae now, they know got damn well I wasn't anybody that needed to cook or clean for them. But that is what I gits for hidin the Devil's lies. Then here comes the orders from Sally and Bobby Jean screamin em to me over each other, "Make three dozen biscuits, two apple pies, three coconut cakes, 2 grandma's pound cakes, one chocolate cake, two peach cobblers, and instead of bacon we want you to fry four yard chicks. We got a lot of people comin over. Oh and Ms. Cazzie and her girls go be here in a few minutes so you will have plenty of help, Ms. Lula Mae." I hate a biggity white woman, deh really pokin fun at me cause they know I don't want to do none of this. I guess Cazzie's girls go ring them chicken's necks, cause I sure as hell am not. I was two feet from kickin Puddin's ass through the door and ringin her got damn neck, right there on the spot. Oh, "Ms. Lula" says, Sally, "You thank you might have time to clean up the bathroom. Bobby Jean done throwed up her entire stomach this morning." Na I was go do my God fearin best for this woman since I was in the lions den. But these two done brought the Devil out in me. She makin me clean that bathroom for dirt, but she go be sorry she did that one.

"Will you please make us some of that ho cake bread too." Deh probably was gettin that in honor of Puddin. Din Puddin say, " Two bad Ms. Lula Mae did not have anymore of her fig preserves left." Ms. Sally say, "Oh we got some of her preserves we bought the last ones she bought to the store for sale. (What she really meant was she took every jar of preserves I had and keep them for herself). I bought them to the store and she took them straight home. I remember the towns people asking me why I cut my fig preserving short this year, lying heifer. She told people I left her short, but what Puddin did not know is that I had a cellar full of fig preserves. And as soon as I gets back home; I am go mark em up three, maybe four times the price and sell em to these white folks.

When I goes and opens this womens pantry it looks like my kitchen in there. She not only had my fig preserves, she had my pears, my peaches, my blackberry's, my strawberries, and my watermelon rinds too. Only thang different was the jars said Ms. Sallies Fine Fruit Perserves. She a Christian alright. She must have been lying to her out of town guest, telling them she made them , cuz everybody in this town knew I supplied the town with preserves mostly. Anyway, I looked around to see what she did not have; so I could find a way to get out of cookin for her. Well, that was a mistake she had so much I think the devil's jealousy tried to get into me. I thought to myself these white folks is sure crazy to talk down to me and ask me to cook for them, they better be glad that I serves a good and kind God. So I won't do em too bad. Better yet deh better be glad I know you suppose to reap just what you sow, or I would fix they ass up real good here today. I got three or four jars of water with mosquito eggs em, and that is what go be floatin in deh punch if deh push me to far. I will go home and get em. You know how sick you kin git if you drink water that mosquitoes done laid eggs in. Well no, yall probably don't.

You know I have read the Freedom Journal, so I know when white folks is being smart assed with me. I went on and started cookin she had everything right there at her finger tips, don't matter though cause I can have 10 times better than this. One thang I know for sure and that is if your heart is not in your cookin, you may as well put poison in their food and God knows my heart was in the pit of hell. So everytime they take a bite of this food, deh go be taking a bite of every minute of hate I have for them and their husbands and deh little kids too. That's right every dish I am making them is out of spite and that is worst than puttin filth in their food. As a matter of fact it is better, cause the poison of hate last longer. Eat well bitches. Anyway she has hot and cold water right into her house, they had started plumbing in white's ville first. You know she is just showing off with that big old café stove, it was three times the size of a regular kitchen stove. She ain't need no stove that big just for her and him. She had three ice boxes right in the kitchen with everythang you thought you wanted in them. I did not see where her smoke house was I am sure they had one ownin a store and restaurant and all. Her kitchen was as large two bed rooms with a dressing area. They got all this from the backs of lazy ass slaves, let them tell it. This is one of the finest sights I have ever seen. I was lovin all her cabinets, they was all glass, so I could see where everything was. I was almost scared to touch em. See I am kinda of heavy handed and I did not want to break nothin. I was really

205

just about to get going when a voice yells out from the sittin area, "Lula go to the car and fetch that fine elderberry wine you made last year." I was shocked Puddin din lost her mind in there with them white folks ordering me around like her slave or something. Then I thought about all that money and I says "Okay Ms. Puddin I is goin right na." Then I says under my breath "Bitch you just wait, you just wait," cause Puddin really getting under my skin na shit. I am a godly woman cookin in my good dress, for a bunch of nigga haters and a hoe. Din come here and found out this women been lying telling people she makin my preserves, and na I am having to play maid to these nigger whores. Yes, I just called dem two white women niggas too and deh is. All niggers ain't black as a matter of fact most of em is white. I is in hell so I guess it don't matter that Ms. Lula Mae is fired up na. You know I wonder how Puddin know my secret hiding place for my elderberry wine? Nobody knew that but me and the Lord. She been defilin my home. Umm just wait till I get home with this slut from Satan's harem; she been rumbling through my personals, aint know telling what else she aint din found. I am go make me some changes around my house. My house has been feelin strange, lately, for real, it has been feeling like it is being defiled. I realize now that I have given over to evil. Look at me I am serving evil and I can not say one word about it. I might have to make a trip to New Orleans soon. I needs me a low down conjuror.

As I was walking to that car I was wondering whether or not Mr Major's soul was in heaven or hell. I knowed based on what them white folks taught the Preachers to teach us in church, he was suppose to be in hell. I have always had my doubts about that one, seems like to me he should go to heaven. He did not kill anyone but himself. See if God made us and knows all about us he gots to be pretty got damn mean to put us in a place where we go burn forever and he knows what we go do already. But then again since white folk made heaven and created God in they image they can do pretty much do what the hell they want. Maybe the Major is in his heaven, he sure did die on his way there. I could never say these things like this in front of anybody else cause they would say I was not a Christian woman questioning hell and all. I pretty much believe hell right here especially ifin you black and ifin you white, you is in as much heaven as you can stand. All this dyin and lyin and hidin got me thinking now. What if a person did good all the time, and then just that one time they gits caught up in badness and die? Is a good and forgiven God go send them to hell for one badness? Or what about the thief on the cross they tell us about. All he did was steal and steal and at the last minute of his life he gots to go to heaven. I bet that theif was a white man, cuz ifin he was a black man, his black ass would have went to hell for sure. Maybe you can slip in and out of heaven if you just know the right words or is the right color.

Oh Lawd have mercy. See this is what makes me have to ask questions Lord. Some thangs just don't add up. The man you got over us as your spiritual example is getting more fury sandwiches than one of them New Orleans pimps. And not one thang has happened to him, he even got a few chaps. Everybody just go around pretendin like that is his God given right. I am kinda confused as to what is really right. Ain't coveting, fornication, adultery, lying, stealing and cheatin suppose to be wrong for everybody? Seems like to me you gots loop holes for preachers and politicians. But I am go stop questioning you cause I just ain't sure what side you onw. Well this walk to the car is just what I need to clear my head. We is in trouble if anyone finds out this white man was killed any where in Nigger town. Every thing go die including the grass, cause everywhere a black ass fall on it dem white folk go burn it. And they can do that if deh want but one of us go curse em before we die and a matter of fact a bunch of us go curse em before we dies. Us colored folks lives with one last cure on our tongue for the white man and you better know it. It is go be like what happened in Boottown when they thought a black man had sassed old man Billwoods' wife. They gathered up eight men and four women skinned em like catfish in the middle of town for all the heathen niggers to see while singing " Its go be over after while" and deh made the colores fry them chicken. See na these be the times I just don't give damn about this white man's God.

Well something strange happened in that town after that, the livestock, died, no crops would grow and the water went bad. Tell me every last one of them crackers lost they minds, running around tellin people they was seein skinned people in they rest. Could be true, since all the colored in that town made a trip to New Orleans to see the Queen Mother Viola Tamplet on a regular bases. She is nothing to play with, she know the poisons, the teas, the hoodoo, the prayers and she knows people. Tell me she helped them make a pac for revenge preva against that place and they cursed the ground. Course na it took a few years but all of them died in they sleep. Not just the ones that did it but all they family too. I don't know how to believe dis, cause seem like she could make the same thing happen for all us right now and end this. We go all be sellin our souls to the devil if them white folks even think that man was killed in my house. I don't understand why men like danger. The Major or no other man got a chance with a woman like Puddin. She can touch one hair on his body and make him have spasms down his spine. I know this to be true. You gots to be healthy to fool with a woman like that. Ifin there ever was a devil he knows Puddin and he knows to stay away from her too. Less he end up being her slave. That is why he sent her up here to us, cause he was to scared to keep her in hell.

Lawd , you know these white folks know how to live off they stolen treasure. I just noticed how fine this women's yard is. You know I feel like I am discovering a new world looking around this house. We all live right here in the same place and I done passed this place a thousand times and for some reason it all look new to me. A snow white picket fense, beautiful green grass, these is some of the largest zela's I have ever seen. These roses are twice the size of your hand in every color of the rainbow. These plums trees full of fruit she need to pick em and let me make some plum jelly. Satsuma trees branches breakin they so heavy with fruit, two big old fig trees and a yard full of gardenias just sos it could smell like heaven . I hate them so much, so much. Look like heaven is over here, but it look like heaven at my house too. It just ain't the same heaven. Don't give a damn what she got in her front yard though cause I have orchards full of the sweetest fruit in these here parts. Ain't never quite figured out how these people thank or how they God thank. I just know deh God don't think the same about me as he do them. I been figuring on this for a long time and something just aint right. I be thanking what in the hell is this God man thinking about, don't he know we have our doubts bout how fair he is not. I have my doubts bout all of it. I looks up and say Lawd show me the way as I was walking back to the house; seem like He heard me to cause a whirlwind came through. A breeze started blowing, trees was russlin, sound like wild animals was howling. Oh Jesus I thought the Lord was just about to show me some kind of big sign. I gets still, my heart is beatin, and my hands is sweatin. I am thinkin this white man God fixin to show hisself to me. I am go die, I am go die and he go send me to his white man hell. It was just a wind gust though. I was walking as slow as I could. When I gets to the screen porche I could sware I saw Puddin leaned down over Sally. Oh lord, is Puddin kissin on Sally, that wasn't no wind that was the Devil come riding on the back of the wind. Then I realized Puddin just being a good gal rubbing the neck of God's chosen. If you believed I really thought that then you believe everybody go be treated fair one day.

I must be loosin my mind. I found it though, when Ms. White, says "Lula will you hurry up and fry us some of that good chicken only you can make sugar." Lyin bitch she had the second best cook in Friendly, cookin for her, she just being hateful. I looked at her wit my kiss my ass eyes and was just about to tell her to go to hell then I remembered. I am a black woman in the Mayor's house. The last time a I heard a black woman stood up to a Major was over in Dentifa, La, she was put in a special made cell behind they house. He would beat and rape her everyday, after she had cooked and cleaned the house. She got pregnant too, tell me old Dufrye' made her drown every baby she had for him. He was pure evil cause he made her nurse every baby his wife had. They made her deh slave we all knew about her but nobody tried to help her. Here tell an old obay women from down Latfontu Bayou passed through to give Lucinda Bilbon her weekly herbs for her stomach aliment. When she seen that out door tolite where poor Ms. Gueschia was livin in. Some say she gave her the treatment to save your soul. Lady Gueshia crushed them herbs up and sprinkled them over the food for the Bilbon family none of them moved after dinner. She killed his entire family then she hung herself from they front porche rather than give them crackers the pleasure of killing her. Here tell even the white folk was scared to go to that house. They finally got up the courage to go and bury the family, but they left Lady Gueshia hangin here until she rotted and broke up in pieces. The buzzards came and took her body parts piece by piece until none was left. Huh, now that was something. Nobody ever settled in that place again. I came to my senses then. I got them some glasses and some wine and went into the kitchen, started baking biscuits and frying the damn chicken, hell atleast I did not have to pluck them. If they could stand to eat food that was cooked out of anger I could stand to cook the food. Yall know I am mad as a hell hound in heaven. Nothing worse than a arrogant hussie using me like I is some kind of damn slave and makin me kiss more white ass than usual. But I rather do what is needed rather than have more deaths on my hand, if I kin help it.

CHAPTER 26

Why is Bobby Jean Looking at me funny?

WHY ALL OF A sudden is Bobby Jean lookin at me funny, I don't like that look. And what in the hell is that deyis smokin it smell like skunk piss. I sware to God it smell like skunk piss. I ain't never smell no stanky cigar not like this. I wish they stop cause all of a sudden I is feeling light headed and scared too. Wait a minute I know that smell. I don't like it when white womens and black womens start enjoying each other too much. Cause that is always go be some trouble for the black woman. Plus it just ain't natural. Why is Bobby Jean lookin at me like that, what do that mean? I wanted to leave so bad, but I had to do my duty as a good Christian. Well after a couple hours passed instead of three women in the parlor drinkin wine, eatin chicken, biscuits and my fine ass preserves, the parlor filled up with people. Ms. Cazzie and her girls was such a help in getting things done and organizing the tables. Child these white folk was bringin the food. I told yall these southern white women can throw down. Pots of ettoffee, shrimp creol, stuffed bell peppers, rice dressing, candied yams, mustard greens and ham hocks, red gravey and jar fish, boudin, mountain oyster soup, I can't name it all.

I love how deh do their pecan pie. I told yall they can bake they ass off. It really was no need for all this food but I know everybody knew I was in the kitchen. See the word had spread through town I was cooking at Sally's house. I thank they just wanted to compete with me. It really did not matter what they bought they all wanted me to keep on cookin. Big Red Henry Boucheux bought in four boxes of slabs, (Oh for yall who don't know a damn thang slabs is big old sacalait, deh is fish.) they was all cleaned it was go be easy to fry them especially since he had fixed up a caldron full of lard and had it heatin already. But all he wanted me to do was season em for him. I did not have to cook them cause he can cook his ass off, most of them Cajun men can. They can cook and they can love. I tell yall more about the lovin later. Let me tell yall bout Henry Boucheux, he was about 6"5 broad shoulders, skin kinda dirty red, but he was one of them white men you might just look at twice and you might think about him in a certain kind of way. He had a way about him, he walked like he was all man. Big old tall bow legged white boy, with a third leg that seemed like it had a knot in it. "How you doing dare Ms. Lula Mae . I am bout to make your lips smack girl. Soon as you finish these fish I am go fry one hard for ya. I know you like em fried hard." I thank he was bein fresh, no I know he was bein fresh. What is wrong with me, my lips is gettin hard. He always made me feel kinda strange. That is one big fine white man, Jesus and he smelled like pine needles and fresh water. Any way, I noticed how when I spoke back to him I had a distinct southern drawl mixed with a little Cajun swing , it just came from no where. Even though I know we are suppose to be different and we are suppose to stay with our own, sometimes I think about what it would be like to be able to love who ever you wanted to. Just dreamin. It will be years and years up the road before we will be able to openly love who ever we want too. And to some people it will always be wrong for you to love who you want to.

Oh Henry Winkles Smith Johnson, the local attorney, insurance man, and all around demon; starts tappin the glasses to get everybody's attention. Then he says we need to stop a minute and say a prayer for Major White. Aww shit here comes the got damn prayer, the got damn prayer that makes it alright; the prayer where the good white God is gonna receive the Major's evil soul in heaven. Oh all that stuff I said earlier about him bein forgiven and goin to heaven that was only if he had done one bad thang. This son of a bitch here got a couple of books on the table. But we bout to hear the prayer that justifies every got damn thing Major White did as being obedient to his God. Mr. Henry Winkles Smith Johnson says, "Good Lord up above we all need to stop a minute and thank you that we are living. We know not the time or the hour we might leave here to travel on to that great white's only plantation in the sky. Where we will be served all day by good God fearing servants remade in your image. Hair straighten out, noses fixed, and skin much, much lighter and we humbly ask you leave them bucks in hell. We want to thank you for letting us be the first ones to walk on streets paved of gold and drink from the eternal fountain of love. And we want to thank you right now for giving our obedient and good servant their own section of heaven to live in. We thank you for giving us a chance to contribute to civilzing and preparing them to serve us in the hereafter. You is a mighty God and good one too, keeping us safe from those who may want to harm us. Oh Lord in the name of your loving son who came to free the slave's mind so he would always recognize his Master and serve him accordingly. We give you praise, glory and honor for allowing us to condition minds of these simple creatures so that our children will always have an inheritance of wealth by telling them what to do. All glory and honor is yours. For you are white as the driven snow, and your salvation is the red blood that flows through our bodies, and your eyes are blue as the heavens above. On mighty Father I want you to know we always keep you in our hearts. Thank you Lord for giving us the strength to tame the heathen and bring him to salvation. We bless you for giving us a warrior like Major White. A man who knew how to keep the order and take care of his wife. Take his soul in your bosom and ifin he is scared, give him a good mammy's tit to nurse away his fear. " Everybody had they head bowed and was prayin up a storm. Ifin it ever was a time when I was cursing it was right now, right this very minute. I was cursing them with their own book. If that son of a bitch thinks I am go be servin any body in heaven he got another thing coming. Huh, I dare yall to agrue and say a ignorant man can not pray, preach, teach, or start a religion. (Just listen at this prayer and you see what I am talking about). Johnson went on praying and tellin what he thank happened to the Major. I was damn near fallin asleep.

"My good citizens Major White died of a heartattack while he was driving home to be with his lovin wife. I can see the car as it went off the road into the miiiiiiighttttii Mississippi. I can almost feel that pain of his heart exploding and his neck breaking as he hit the water. That's kind of pain no good white man should have suffer that pain is only intended for nigg … " Then all of a sudden it was like they noticed a couple of niggers in the room me and Puddin, and the others in the kitchen preparin plates. Yall know them folk started to whisper the rest of their prayers like they was talking in secret. It was as if they did not believe we could hear them or understand what they were saying. We standing there big as day invisible in there world, only civilized by their standards, but not counted as human. Deh could have been talkin in tongues like Paul and dem and we would have understood that message. I guess they thought that our eyes buldgin out was us tryin to understand what dey were saying. Truth is we was waitin for lightenin to strike em. Lets say we was hopin lightenin struck em. When the prayers and lyin was over that room still had an air of quite over it like they needed to be careful just in case we could understand the language of civilized white folk. Can you believe they trying to keep secretes from maids, hoes, and gossips, the jokes in on them. I hate dem muther fuckers, wait I am go really have to watch my sinful mouth, God take it a way. I really do need your help. Here I am serving food, picking up behind em, trying to show some sorrow for this poor sinful bastard, that lost his life after a mid-night hump in a whores arms. These people is makin me have no regrets. I know one thang you shol is a patient God. I would have been sent me a bunch of warrin angels down here and killed these lyin sons a bitches. Especially if deh is saying I told dem to do all this evil shit deh is doing.

I am starting to feel a whole lot better, because seems like people are content with believing the Major's death was just an accident. One thang struck me funny as I was ease droppin on Mr. Winkles-Johnson and Sally Whites conversation. I heard him tell her, she needed to take care of everything real soon. I wonder what that meant? White folk always thinking about money maybe that is why they got all of it. Yes I am feeling pretty good now. All I have to do is find a way to get rid of Puddin and John. For one thang Puddin aint got all the money she think she have and Big John done over rated his dick. Ooow Child I can not wait to go home to my house. Jesus, Tree , Sky, Great Mother, Lawd, God, or Abondey my Great great great grand mother's God, please help me stay healthy long enough to spend all this money. Well I done had my full of today, and I am ready to go home. Strange thang them folks say I was a heathen before I knew their God and now that I know him, I am a liar and a murder. Maybe it is like this, if you don't know you are doing wrong you really ain't doin wrong. Like these dirty words I say. Who said they was dirty? How did they become dirty, fuck fuck, fuck fuck. I read somewhere that it meant fornication under consent of the king. And if it means that it ain't no dirty word it just got a dirty meanin. But yall who knows my favorite curse word is "white man". Why I say that is because when he shows up everythin that aint like him dies or wish deh was dead.

CHAPTER 27

Going Home With A Clear Head

WELL I LOOKED OVER at Puddin working the room like she pickin up tips for a hard nights service. I says, "Well, Ms. Puddin aint it time for us to be getting on home na?" Then all of sudden old Bo Riley a old red neck who loved black women as long as nobody saw him say, "Yea yall gals had better git goin, there might be some wolves in the woods tonight." Then he bust out and start laughing that bothered me, in my heart, I felt fear. See he was the kind of man whether he be white or black you just knowed you did not want him to have his hands on you. Old Gruffy, sweaty, stanky thang with them green toned teeth and bad breath, so bad, you thought his ass hole was his mouth. Plus I am just sho he got ass tics. He looked at us hard as we was getting ready to pack up and leave. But when Henry Boucheaux grabbed our stuff and took it to the car for us he took his eyes off of us, cuz he was no match for him. See big Boucheux was a man's man, he was fair and he was not known for hitting women. Old Bo Riley did not want to be made shame, cause everybody knowed deh had tension between em. Yall know Henry threw a bull once and everybody know he did not need much of a reason to kick Bo Riley's ass. Well me and Puddin head on back to the house and she sittin over there lookin like she just had the best time of her life, smilin and grinnin full of whiskey. I looks at her and and says' "Girl do you have any shame , do you feel anything anymore, what is yo problem? God is lookin at you and you sho is gonnna have to answer for all what you did. You is probably goin to hell and you probably go take me and Big John with you. Ifin anybody ever find this out we ain't go even have a church funeral, cuz our man of God probably won't even want to bury us in the church." Before I could get another word out Puddin stopped the car and looked at me and said, " Lula Mae don't you sit here and speak to me like you, your Preacher man or them holy whores are better than me cuz yall just like me. Yall just hidin it. You got harlots in yo pues, a pimp in yo pulpit, devils in your choir, holes in your pockets and all yall full of shit. Rotten holly god fearin shit. You heard everythang in there we off the hook. He died by an accident. Plus, I did not kill him, he should have been home with his wife; instead of buryin hid dick between my thighs. Aint my fault his heart gave out; plus that bastard did not even pay me first. But you know I gots mine don't you. Only difference between me and you is how we do thangs, not what we do. You hides behind the Bible and I dance before the Devil."

"What God dis is you say go judge me, huh. Is that the same God that gave them white folks the right to hang us, hoe us, sell our children, use our black babies on oak trees, for Christmas ornament to celebrate his birth, use our children as alligator bait. You aint forgot about the Farthenton Planation is you Miss Lula? The one where each Christmas it was death to be a little black babies cause old man Frisks would paint they little heads red, yellow, blue and green, dress em in white gowns and hang em like ornaments from oak trees. Not the same God that let our peoples be stole away from deh home destroyed our heritage, treat us like animals and force our men to be boys when deh is around. Me or you ain't nothing but gals and girls no matter how old we is. What is you talking about girl. Is you talkin about Jesus the one the white man beat us into worshiping. Deh brainwashed us into believin that we was nothing but heathens. Deh beat and killed us into worshipin their God. You know somethin is wrong with all this God stuff. How can a man kill a god, but they had the power to kill their's. And everybody knows deh killed him because he was a Jew man. Na white man down here hates a Jew just bad as he hate a nigger. He just tolerate of him cause that is who he gots to borrow money from. Oh yes, deh done did dem people so bad til deh all had to stick together and make deh own money. Na deh gots to go to him to borrow his money. See that Jew he go survive cause he got something they need , we go be destroyed Ms. Lula cause we something they want to forget. Deh either go kill us all or have us kill each other you watch. Ain't noboby colored go be left unless deh is a good hoe.

" You just as messed up as deh is Lula, scared to be yourself cause you know being holy is borin, as hell is hot. What you thank our ancestors worshiped before this man enslaved our minds, soul and body. Everytime you prays to this white man's God you is strokin his dick and everytime you fall on your knees before him, he is jacking off in your brain Ms. Lula Mae, everytime . What is dis God you talkin about Lula. What is He? Is He good? Is He bad? What is He? Can you tell me? You rich and to scared to spend your money. Who is this God? Who side is he on Ms. Lula? Seems like to me he betrayed us and enslaved us to cruel peoples. A God that teaches us to love dem when they is rapin us, beatin us and killin us. What fucking God is you talking about? What good has He done for you Lula, show me, show me how good he been to you, how good he been to any black folks. This the same God that is go judge me for being a whore. Is the same one that watched me be rapped and sodomized. He made me a whore Ms. Lula. He made me a whore and hoing made me rich. Don't you feel too good bout yourself Lula, cause you is made rich by a whore too. Everytime you think about this God and his God fearin people, think about how the mothers of those babies used for alligator bait felt. Think about whole strings of people being throwed off a ship in shark infested water, think about being skinned alive, hung, raped, burned alive, and then think how foolish you sound asking the God of these people to save you. I am glad you have hope and I am glad you accept their truth, but my truth aint there truth and they god is not my god. Opps let me change that, one of their gods is my god, his name is MONEY and money never fails. You find a man with enough money he don't need no God and he act like it too. For a ignant hoe I makes a lot of sense don't I Ms. Lula Mae. Na go on and Preach to the wind about your good Lord. Maybe a bird will pass by ya and piss on ya and bless ya."

CHAPTER 28

He's Not My God

"I KNOW YOU CONSIDERS me nothing but a cheap whore and maybe you and the white man's God is right. Being a whore helps me ease my pain for what been done to me. Everytime one of them white men favor my pleasing, plush pussy with they lips I enjoys it. I enjoys it three ways, it feels good, they kissin more than my ass, and they paying me for spittin my pussy juices all over they face and fuckin over them. Yes, Ms. Lula I fucks over them and trys to make it spit as hard as I can. The freest thang ever was is pussy, they just to got damn dumb to know it. They think I am good in bed, only if the truth were told. I am tryin to kill em everytime I hit the sheets. See some men buy pussy because they need to be in control, others is so damn ugly nobody in their right mind would have sex with them, sume is just lonely, din you got the ones with dem good wives to good to make that ugly face. But it don't matter to me; casue I will sell it to a broke dick dog if he got enough money. I serve a purpose Lula, what you do? Somebody gots to supply the world with pussy and I am just the girl. Who else go take care of all these sexually deprived peoples, if aint no good hoes around. See, I don't care as long as they pay my price and my price ain't cheap.

You wants me to feel bad if your Preacher don't bury me, why I bought your preacher for a thousand dollars. Didn't he make the ladies keep my name from ringin all over town so your house would not be shamed. Yes, indeed your preacher man did not give a damn about what I did, he took that money. By the way Ms. Lula Mae I got 400 of it back, your preacher likes to smell under arm pits. His nose ain't wide for nothin. See I do the thangs wives don't want to know about their husbands. Hell Ms. Lula Mae, I'll buck, fuck, suck, tickle nuts and hollow woah behind a fart ifin the money right. See a good hoe knows her job. Girl you gots to be willin to let a man sit the crack of his ass right on your nose and not flinch. You work a man ass hole right Ms. Lula he be comin back to you the rest of his life. I am a good hoe Ms. Lula, so anythin the wife, woman, or loverman to shy to do or thank deh is too saved to do; I gets paid to do. You thank your Preacher man just saw me once. Girl I made him thank he was special. First I listened to him, then I started to have treats for him; little thangs I know he like. I ain't never crossed what we did with the Bible, never did. I ain't go make fun of how nobody believe. Course I knows hoe's is all through the Bible and some of them was spared by the good Lord. Thank the Lord go spare me Ms. Lula? I started to fuck that wife of his but I just did not have the time. I could have too, she did not know it but I could have. How much you want to bet she aint had her flower picked in a while. All I had to do was get up on her and breath and she would have fainted. I know you thank I am low life shit Ms. Lula. But the truth is I am just a hard workin girl. I don't mark people for believing what deh want and I ain't go let nobody mark me for not believing, like deh believe.

"Ain't nobody go make me feel guilty for what I is doin or have done, nobody. Your God and his servants made me what I is today. See girl, I ain't never cried while sellin a little fury slice of pussy. But I cried a lot before I started sellin it. See when I was a young gul this man named Mr. Burdock raped me front and back. I was just a baby in most people's eye especially in my Uncle Marvin's eyes. See Ms. Lula I wasn't no more than 80 or 90 pounds a little boy shaped virgin, waitin on her Prince charmin. My mama sent me to take Old Bill Burdock his eggs. That morning he must had made up his mind he wanted him some little black girl for breakfast. No soon as I walked into his yard he knocked them eggs out of my hand and broke em. Then he says "Girl how you go replace my eggs, I done paid for them already, you gots some money?" Then he walks over to me and grabs me by my hair and threw me on the floor in his house. My hair was long then Ms. Lula Mae, it hung below my waist, but I always pulled it back in a poney tails. That is why it will never be long again. Betcha did not know this black girl could have so much hair huh Ms. Lula. He grabbed those pony tails and wrapped them around my neck pulling them so hard my scalp was bleeding and my neck was breaking. He took his concern out and forced it into me as hard as he could. You don't know about that kind of pain Ms. Lula. I was a virgin girl saving my self for the right man and this muther fucker comes along. Most folk said I looked like a little boy anyway. Lula he beat me and raped from behind over and over and over again. Then he turned me around and did my front part Ms. Lula . I stared him straight in his eyes, that is when he spit his baca in my eyes. Almost blinded me too. My eyes was hurting so bad and I could not see for a while. I was glad to be blind for a moment it made me feel like I was some where else. The baca burned my eyes so bad, I was not thinking about how he was hurtin my self down there. I did not know how to call on your God then but if your God is real, and he can see everything, then he should have had pity on this little girl here. He should have sent the angels to help me. Jesus should have came down from his throne in heaven and saved me. He should have had pity on me Ms. Lula.

Know why I crys when I tells this story Ms. Lula, cause it still hurts. But ain't no angels come, no Jesus came, no God called my name, no warrior to fight for me. Just me and this grown old man, hurtin me. Once he grunted and finished he threw me up against the wall and broke my arm and my ankle. He says, "Gal don't you look at me like you understand what just happened to you. Yall is really nothin but animals. I know you can't feel nothing, so don't act like you did. I just broke you in for your uncles and your step daddys. Hell you was kinda wide I bet your uncles din probably did this to you before. Plus I been looking at you since you turned 12. You just lucky I had somebody else in mind. If you tell anybody who did ya, we go kill all yall. Best you keep your mouth shut, ya here." Then he spit on me again and kicked me all they way out the door, like I was a dead animal. He just kicked me over and over until he got to the front yard. He said "If you is here by the time I go in and gets my gun, you is a dead nigger." I drug myself to the ditch and laid there until I could move. I was hurtin so bad I did not even have time to worry about what was in that ditch with me. See Ms. Lula he is the reason my Uncle Marvin Jones was killed, cause when I was crawlin back down the road full of blood and my Uncle Marvin found me. He grabbed me and held me and he cried and he cried and he cried, he said Button you will not see your Uncle again. You just need to know somebody did something. Just know that somebody did something. My Uncle Marvin went to that son of a bitches place and stomped him to death. He really did stomp him to death, he did not have no face or neck left for that matter not much of his body was left, he stomped him to death. Deh say wasn't nothing left of that sons of a bitch but his legs. My uncle lost his mind that day and he gave his life for me. He is my Jesus and he the only savior I ever knew and he is a colored man. He gave his life for me; he did not know I was go end up being a two bit whore. I am sorry he did it, I would rather have his love than his bravery. People say my uncle lost his senses because of what had been done to his sister when she was a little girl. Somethin like what happened to me happed to her ceptin she was about six years old I hear. I aint sure, but folk say that is why he took a spell and did that man like that. I bet he would have changed his mind if he knowed how I turned out. See Ms. Lula you can not judge me. Most people will do anything for some money. I aint hurting no body, I am supplying a service. Plus if you jugdge me by the standards of people who will do anything for money; then me and you and a whole lot of people go be pointin the finger at each other all the time. I am a hoe and I know it, but you don't know what you is Lula, you don't identify with nothing. I guess ain't nothing worst than too godly to see the hoe wrote all over your face.

I remember over hearing Uncle Marvin talking to mama and them. He was telling them that he could not leave like they wanted him to. He knew if he left them riders were gonna come kill all of us and half the coloreds for miles around. Uncle Marvin said " I knew I was go die soon as I saw Button's little broken body, but I rather be a dead man than have to live knowing that I did nothing about what was done to that child. I will see yall again. Don't worry about me, just get that child out of here, send her off, save her; I know she go be blamed for this. So Ms Lula if there is a heaven my uncle Marvin is in it. Anyway Ms. Lula the men caught my Uncle, shot him dead, skinned him and hung him in our front yard. They set a guard around where they hung him so we could not cut him down and bury him. We had to see him everyday just hangin there Ms. Lula. Where was God? Did I sin? Did my uncle sin? Was them men in power God's men, they was all Christians they was even singing old hymns as they skinned him. Some folk say they did him a favor cause they shot him first. I hear the man that made that shot lost his arm, cause they cut if off. Say them men was pissed off that he died so quick. So they God not my god, they ways not my ways, they thoughts not my thoughts and never could be. I got revenge for my Uncle Ms. Lula. For some reason ain't nobody bother me about what Burdock had done.

See Burdock had a son named Big Burdock, Jr. he was just like his daddy. About two years past and life was trying to get to normal; but I was ruined by then, no boys wanted to date me and most folk just shyed away from me, like I had done something wrong. Most of the time I was dodging men trying to do the same thang old man Burdock had done me. I slept with a blade every night. I was always cuttin myself too see how much more pain I could take. I was tryin to cut the shame and pain out of me plus, I was practicing throwing that knife. I was goin past marryin age na. You know how early most folk around here gits married. But for me Ms. Lula my marrying days was all over nobody wanted me, no maam nobody. Know how it feel to be hated and picked on for something you did not do. That is how I felt Ms. Lula, felt like I had done somethin wrong. All I did was go around thinkin about how I was go get back at all of them. I had a bunch of black folk I wanted to strike down too and I dreamed almost every night about getting back at them Burdocks. Well one day , I was out pickin snake berries, to make me a brew and ended up on the other side of Ms. Maylou's place. She was one of them obay women who actually lived in the middle of the woods in the prettiest and cleanest little house you ever wanted to see. We use to ride out to see her all the time. Every Wednesday, all the people from the church make a trip to see her. She such a sweet lady. Makes the best cookies you ever wanted to taste. I loved her rock candy, strings and strings of it was all over her house. She say what is you doing out here so far away from home Cher baba? I says " I am tryin to gets me enough juggers and snake berries to make me a brew". She says, "Child somebody done put a baby in you? I don't want to know nothin, take this and leave them berries you done picked already with me. I got a field full of juggers go cut me

223

about six don't stick yourself na. Who was it a Uncle, your step daddy, your daddy, one of the horney white men? Nevermind child don't tell me I can't choose sides." I just looked at her and started to cry. She can't chose sides and she is a woman? She gave me a whole bag of tea made from wormwood, beladona, and devils shoestring. You be careful how you mix it, it can kill you too. Don't put no more that two spoons to one pot that should be enough to start things to movin. If you goes beyond that you will never move again.

I picked me some black berries a whole basket full, got a bucket of eggs and headed straight to Burdocks's house. Whole time I am walking up there I am remembering what his daddy did to me. Before I got to the porch, Junior comes out with his gun cocked, ready to shoot. Well you wonder what in the hell was on his mind, cause he looked me up and down and then Junior smiles at me like he knew I would be payin him a visit for some pleasure. Then he says "I guess you realize what happened to you was not so bad after all. What you want niggar, you must want the same thing my daddy did to you a few years ago coming out here. He broke you in right, to bad he not here to see what I am about to do to you. Come here let me see what you got in that basket" . Now mind you Ms. Lula I had readied my self for some pain, I knew I was go have to feel something. I showed him the berries and the first thing he did to me was slap me down. He must have been hungry cause he grabbed the berries and put a whole hand full in his mouth. I guess deh was so good cause I had sprinkled sugar all over them. Next thing I knew he started to rub them all over my body, guess he never figured why I was letting him do this to me. Goes to show you how powerful a man thank his dick is. I had hate in me, the kind that makes a person sick, the kind that will make you do anything to get back at a person. Huh you should have seen him grabbin, lickin me and moanin like a dog.

Then all of a sudden he falls back and don't move no more. I had soaked them berries down in the tea, the sugar hide the bitterness. He started to shake a little and then his eyes looked like they was stuck wide open and he fell back. I kicked him to see if he could move. I know he could see me but he could not move. I am thinkin I am go skin his dick off. Then I stood over him Miss Lula and had the best shit of my life, child. He got a close look at the ass his daddy had raped. I could see the hate in his eyes when I stood up over him, but he could not move. Like

I could not move, when his daddy was rappin me. I wanted to cut off his dick and shove it in his mouth, but that was too good for him. So I just looked and looked at him then I peed in his eyes, he could not even squent. Don't look at me like that Ms. Lula I had to have somethin to clean all that shit off his face. There he was Mr. powerful man with a face full of my hate. I was as evil as he was and that is the reason I know I have a debt to pay one day, Ms. Lula. I poured water in his mouth too sos my shit could go down his throat. I am a monster. The whole time I was talking to him, telling him how his father destroyed all my feelings and my hope. I told him that because of him I would be the richest nigger whore there ever was. You think I am a hell hound don't you Ms. Lula, you think I am cheap, low and no good. Well I don't give a damn what you think. You have not walked down my road, so thank what you want. Anyway I patted his pockets but wasn't nothing in em then I felt this bulge around his waist it was a money belt, full of paper money. Then I searched all over his house tarin it up and there were bags full of gold and silver coins, paper money too. He could not move or talk he just laid there with hate in his eyes. I plucked out one of his eyes and bite it. It taste like a raw oyster. I just bit it to see, if it would help me see things like white folk saw things. But it did not help, all I could see was fear and hate. That's the only time I remember dancin and thankin their God. I thanked him that day, but that also was the day I died. I died Ms. Lula cause I became just like them Burdocks, no heart, no soul and no love. I did not sell my soul to the devil really, he just took it. Thank I don't stop and question whatever it is out there and ask them why me? Well I do, but I ain't got no answer back yet. And please do tell me it is a fuckin test; cause I ain't get a chance to study the book. Plus I ain't the only one in despire, every town I go to I sees colored folk living in despire and ifin deh ain't, deh tryin to forget deh every did. We could never do enough evil to payback the white man for how he done did us. So if you don't mind Ms. Lula take the God you was taught to serve to heaven with you. And when you get there and find yourself still going through the back door, remember it is a back door in heaven and that should make you feel just fine.

Anyway after deh found Burdock, Jr. thangs got real strange around our town. White folk did not come to ask us any questions. Nobody ended up hung for nothin. Not one word was said to us about Junior.

Some say the white folk was terrified because half of one of his eyes had been bit into. Others say it was the look of horror on his face. Then some say it was because he was alive but dead. Did not matter we all glad half our town was not dead. People started lookin at me funny though so my mama sent me to live with my Aunt Luzzy. That was a mistake. See my Aunt Luzzy was like most black folk in them days if you aint' their child, they might do anything to you. It was all about the money. You know my life was hell cause as soon as I got to Luzzy's the first thing she did was check me to see if I was broke in. She already had plans for me, I was old enough to work and young enough to sell. I left half the money I got from Junior in a box for my mama and Auntee Winnie. The other half I took , I needed every penny of if when I ran away from Aunt Luzzy's. I had to run anyway cause somebody had put rabid coon shit in in her oatmeal and she was dyin. I just knew people was go say I did it. Was not no cure for what she had either cause the two headed doctors did not even try to work on her. To scared she was go bite em. I was just a young woman ridin from town to town. I was always scared, always lookin over my shoulder but I kept movin, until I had just about spent most of that money I had. I had to settle down in towns where you had to be a scrared to make it. You can't even imagine in your worst nightmares Ms. Lula Mae some of the places I have been. I taught myself to read and write and I learned how to talk to people and bullshit them. The easiest thing to do is to bullshit people all you have to do is pretend they are smarter than you. I learned how the white man think, what he like, and I used what I knew to get what I wanted. I knows one thang about a white man he loves to be entertained in bed , on stage, in church and nothing is more entertaining to him than a woman dressed like a whore. You see Ms. Lula a white man's wallet is the extentionof his dick and if you make him feel important enough he will always share his extension with you. Most black men ain't have no extra money but it was that extra piece of dick that would get them a free fuck every now and then Ms. Lula. See Ms. Lula I will do it for free, every now and then.

CHAPTER 29

Give Me Back My Money

Ms. LULA SINCE YOU is feelin so got damn self-righteous give me back my got damn money. We pulls up to the house and my mind was thinking a lot of things. All about Puddin's story, the white man, his Christianity and his morals. I was almost in daze , but when we pulled up Big John was standin in the middle of my yard. What the hell ... any way uuuuuuuuummmmmmmm I sure do like him. I like him to much. I feel his hands on me when he looks at me. I feel him inside me when he touch me. I need to have him really really touch me . I can not help this I want to smell him and I want him over me covering me with his beautiful black ass. I want the pressure of his piece pennin me down. I know it is wrong what I am thinking but I want that man's sweaty cock right under my nose. I want that bad. I need that bad. I am not ashamed of what I am feeling right now. I need to feel him more than just in my day dreams. I am tired of sweatin at night rubbin my legs together like a cricket, my women is throbbin and hurtin like hell. Why should I care what a white God thinks about me. And I sure shouldn't have quite havin John cause Puddin showed up. I need a man, somebody who can lay it down and pick it up. Yall might not know what it is like to walk around moist all the time, well it ain't nice. Touchin yourself is good, but when there is not a candidate around to roll your jelly bone you got to take advantage of it. Then all of a sudden when I comes out of my daze I hear; "What took yall so got damn long Ms. Lula Mae", I says, "Who you talkin to nigga, you ain't got no right to speak to me like that. You just fixin my house you ain't plowin no permanent fields here yet." "I is sorry Ms. Lula I just been sick worried about ya considerin the company you was with." John did not even look at Puddin and she did not look at him. It is like they hated each. It is a strange kind of hate though, cause as soon as they are alone they go do it. We goes in and John starts to tell us we must be very careful very careful for the next couple of months. I says, "Why you worried John? Deh saying it was an accident." From what I hear Ms. White go get three times her life insurance on him.

What Puddin mean, give her back her money, huh, she ain't got no money that I have. What money I have is mine. Every dime I got from her I earned it. I put my reputation on the line. I was doing the work of the Lord, bringing a heathen to my blessed home. Her money, she better get something straight; that money is mine and I will do whatever it takes to keep it. She is in my garden of eden and she is the snake. I will buss a snake in his got damn head. I have the Lord on my side. She not giving me anything. I am meant to be blessed and she is meant to bless me. But if she tries to take my money I am go bless her with that 22 rifle. I'll pop that bitch behind the head like you do a hog.

Don't get me wrong, I do talk about how much money the preachers get, but I never say they should be denied their pay. It is hard teaching a bunch of sinners the path to righteousness and divine glory. Sometimes you have to go to hell to pull someone out. Sometimes you have to shake the hand of the devil to show him you not scared of him. And if Puddin mess with my money she'll think hound dogs from hell on her ass. A dirty bitch. I feel like a mint julep. This woman has made my nerves bad. I hope Big John is a smart man, cause if he is not then he done been through my house searchin. I gots holdin powder on all my stuff. If I was him I would not be touching that. Hate for him to get struck by lightenin while riding his horse on a clear day.

That reminds me of old Sam Delighte' a traveling salesman. He had everything you needed, tonics, fancy hats, shoes, tools you name it he had it. Well anyway he took up with Faralle' a well to do widow woman lived down Bayou Sameoldbullshiteverday' with her servants and that annoying little dog. We all said that dog was her husband. Everybody knew she had treasure on her place, cause for years the men was trying to get her to use the bank . She never trusted the banks. Well she took a liken to Sam and he soon stopped selling and settled in with her. They tell me, all they did was stay in bed. Well after he got her pregnant I hear he started acting up. Staying gone for days, spending her money all over town. The servants say he would bring men and women right in their bedroom when she was not home. They would be cooking in her kitchen and some even wore her clothes. Looks like that is a white folk thang. Cause most colored women got to much since for that, cause deh all know what is go happen if deh walk in and catch that. We know some of them hoes stole her jewelry cause we seen them wearing it. We all soon began to hate him. See Faralle' was just too damn quite and sad looking since the death of her husband, so you always wanted to help her. Hell everybody wanted to help her. So at first we was glad she had him even if he did use to have a wife. Anyway, one day she come home from New Orleans, that is where her doctor was; and there he was in bed with somebody's child. Faralle' took a spell and lost her baby right then and there. When she woke up she did not have the use of her legs. That poor woman was paralyzed with pain. Old Sam took that as an opportunity to really do her in then. Ruth Carson, was Faralle's friend so she went and told Sam all about where Faralle's treasure was. You know that old dog went straight to it and robbed her. What he did not notice was the little sprinkles of grain like powder on it. So he loaded up his wagon one of the most beautiful days god ever created, getting ready to leave her broke. Before he left he went to her bed and spite in her face and bid her farewell. Child, he got about three wagon lengths from the house and a bolt of lightenin came from the sky on a clear day and struck him on the top of his head. Then it struck the people who had stole her jewelry and clothes, and it struck the ones who had been in her house defiling it too. Now I am not much on folk stories but you can go to the po white folk and the rich white folk cemeteries, and they is all buried there. Farralle' buried a hundred dollars with each of them with a little note that said "All you had to do was ask". Strange thang after he died she got the use of her legs back and seemed to be doin okay. So if John don't want no lightenin looking for his ass he better not be snoppin around my house and puttin his hand where deh don't belong. The lack of money can do some strange thangs to people. And I don't like lack.

CHAPTER 30

What did them Two Nigras really want?

"Na, Sally what you thank them two little niggalets really wanted? Seem mighty strange they come all the way over here to see about you?" "No it don't Bobby Jean, they have been taught their place here in Friendly. They know how to serve us because we taught them. We ain't never had no trouble out our niggras to much because we always gave them enough freedom to be free in their world. We put enough lashes on them so they realized that their world and our world did not mix. But the most important thang we put in them was to always see us as the people God chose to deliver them from being heathens. Everybody admires deh deliver Bobby Jean don't you know that. We got us a set of well trained niggras, they well trained Bobby Jean. It did not take a lot of work either see we was not as cruel as some of them others. Instead of skinnins and hangins em my pappy would just cut half deh tounge out if deh talked back or did little thangs. Once you do that three or four times you gots a well run place. Plus, most the time our niggras wanted to stay with us , my daddy hated em so much, he did not rape em. He worked the hell out of them though and he let them keeps deh families, but he made it clear deh could never be equal.

I remember one time Bobby we had this one that called his self by a strange name or should I say his heathen name. It was Zinbalie or something like that. He was one of the most ungrateful mean nigras you ever wanted to see. My pappy took a liking to him and named him after his favorite mule Old Stumper. Which was a high honor for niggra. But he just refused to be called Old Stummper, he would not answer to that name. My pappy beat him three maybe four days but this one could take some ass whippings . So my pappy told all his stock they had them to stand in the fields mornin day and night until Old Stummper took his Christian name. Them niggras stood in that field for four days no water no, food, until their children started fallin out. Oh the smell from the fields was worst than passin a dead one on a tree. Pappy was getting ready to heard them to the river to bath, but a rain storm came and clean them up. We were sorry for that because it looks like that gave them more strength to stand. No matter what, them niggras stood we almost did not know what to do. Then my pappy bein the gentlemen he was told Old Stummper that he was go have to send him to the Delondaville Plantation. That was the one ran by Dr. Picknard.

You know he was one of our most honored men during that time, because he was the only man that had looked at a niggra's brain and heart. He was the first person that told us they had an ingrown tail too . You did realize they have a tail behind deh tail bone, Ms. Bobby Jean. That is the only reason we call them animals, it is a proven fact they got tails like monkeys. Well anyway he never did take that name and my pappy sold him. Dr. Picknard bought him for a good price too almost 1500.00. I guess explains why my pappy did not just kill him. Then another reason is we have strict Christian beliefs and a good Christian do not kill a thing because it is made a certain way. You might have to kill it if it gets out of control, but you don't kill it because of its' natural birth. That would be like me taking my gun just going out shooting my dog for being a dog. That is being a heathen Bobby Jean that is being like them, before we civilized them. You know we are still civilizing them? You see that Puddin how she come and made herself available to us. Ms. Lula is teaching her how she should act in order to live here, that is why they came . If you train one to be obedient and loyal they will train the others to be the same. We are gods to them, because we own their minds, we taught them what to think. One thing for sure our stock in them will last for generations and generations girl, cause we kills deliverers. Once you own the mind of anything, you own its' soul. If you think I am lying go to most of their homes, and you will see a picture of Jesus and you will see him as White, that lets you know how deh thank God should look. Lord forbid it to hell if they learn how to think. Even in their praise we are there, we use to let our people sing and shout deh way cause nothing sounds or looks better than a heathen praisin our Lord. My Pappy ran a smart plantation. He was just nice enough to gain their trust and just strict enough to put the fear of the Lord in them. It does not matter how free they think they are. Girl as long as they believe what we tell them, they will always be on the plantation. Bobby Jean, do you think there will ever come a day when niggras will be equal to whites?" "Sally I don't know, it could be such a day, after all we are teaching them everything we know." "No dear we are not teaching them everything we know, we are teaching what we want them to know. We ain't go ever teach em everything we know. You can't rule something that think it is equal to you. Tell you what you will never see a black face in our history book in America. And if you do they are in Africa or they are a slave, or some of those trouble makers. We always puts the trouble makers in the books, we want to keep every body thankin a certain way." "Well Sally I would not think I got all niggras fooled. That is a lot of people."

"Now the good Dr. Picknard said their brain is about the size of a small lemon that is why they speak broken language. That is also why they can't hardly read and shuffles their feet when they walk. They have to think how to make steps. Oh girl his studies showed them as one ignorant lot of people. But once you train them to do something they do it well. I use to always wonder why most of the field hands walked with that *chain gang stuffle* as we would call it. Until Dr. Pinchard explained it at one of his parties. I always thought it was because my pappy, would never let the field hands wear belts, so their pants was always falling down below their butts and they tryin to keep their pants up, while tryin to walk with dem chains around their ankles. You know on some plantations, the Masters loved to see their pants below their rock hard butts. You know which one I am talking about. But anyway that is the reason why I thought they did the *chain gang stuffle*.

Plus , we made our leg chains extra tight so it hurt when they would walk up straight and tall. They would have to bend over and suffle because their ankles and legs had to ajust to the grip of the ankle cuffs. But even after we took the cuffs off most of them continued to shuffle, see they are real slow. Most of them did not realize they were walking around free of the cuffs and not in pain or they had become numb to the pain. But anyway they just keep on shuffling thinking that every step they made out of turn would cause them pain. See what I am sayin Bobby once you get the mind the body go do what it say. See Bobby, Dr. Picknard say deh still shuffle like that because they really do have to think about how to make their steps; especially since they know the wrong step could be their last step. Look how Ms. Lula can cook, look how Cassie and them girls can clean, see how that Big John can build cabinets, cut up wood, plow your fields, and clip your grass, honey child he is well trained, well trained. Don't nothing sound any better than when they start singing the spiritual songs of praise we taught them. I just love to here them singing that one that ask the Master not to pass them by. See that song right there is teaching them to recognize they must go the Master for all their help. It teaches them to seek their Masters for help, favor and correction. Oh they sing it so well. It also teaches them to recognize their Master's as their Savior. That was the only song my pappy would let them sang on Sunday, in the fields or anywhere on his plantation, because that is the song that teaches them that their Master is their God. I see that frown on your face, because that is such a beloved spiritual and you probably thank we was using it the wrong way, but that is all you heard sung on our place.

I am sure the original meaning was something more divine and spiritual than what I am saying, but that is how my pappy used it. Girl you know how it is when you is tryin to train an animal. You use whatever tools you can to be sure you get the results you want. I am telling you we did not like them anymore than anyone else but we made them think we did and we always had double the crops of anyone else. Bobby Jean don't worry yourself about Puddin and Ms. Lula Mae, they really don't have enough brain power to do anything to complicated". "Sally, if that is what you feel about them, I will leave it alone, seems like you have it all figured out." "Yes, those two women that just left here, is doing what they are suppose to do, serve us. You know a Puddin can be quite useful, if you know what I mean. If I could buy her she would have all kinds of duties to perform on me." "Hahahahahha, you know Sally she is something to deal with, for the right price she will still perform them duties right now." "She don't even smell like one of them, she always have on rich perfume. My husband probably bought it for her. Powder puff pussy bitch. That girl don't know what a blessing she was to me though, cause I hated having White touch me." "Sally did you notice how they was not asking any questions; just being quite, going about doing what it takes to please us. Lula Mae Carson is the gossip for nine Parishes." "Asking any questions, I wish one of them gals would try to question me about anything. We both know the coloreds sneak around here and listen to every word we say and as much as their feable minds can understand they repeat. "

"Look most of them girls are doing most of us a favor; keeping them men busy while we chase the boys. Aint nothing is more exciting than having man who believes he is getting something so valuable it wil get him killed. All of us have played with a boy or two. Sometimes they be so scared you have to guide them all the way but when you mets one that is still close to being a savage he is different. He will grab you and enhale you like you is a fine perfume. His strong rough hands become gentle as a butterfly's fullter and once you teach him to taste the fairy milk between your thighs they are never the same again.

I remember this one called Big Bo from the Billings plantation next to ours, huh, he was something to see. His person was so large it saluted heaven every time he stood up. He had a tree trunk of a dick and I had made my mind up I was go climb it first chance I got. First I started off by giving him extra steaks and potatoes, he love steak and potatoes. Then I made sure he had fresh honey and biscuits every morning and a cake on Sunday. See we was as close to the Billings as God was to Jesus. Girl early one morning when everybody had gone to the basin to hunt, I got my chance. I had Ms. Mattie go fetch him and bring him to my bedroom. He might have been a savage but I wasn't. So it was not go be any fucking on the stable floor I saved that for a white man's treat. When he laid in my bed he just looked at me like he has seen heaven. He was big, but let me tell you he moved like he wanted to come back again and he did come back again and again. About nine years after I married the good Major he still was coming back. Then one day he showed up here with his bags and horse wanting me to leave with him. I could not have that so when

White came home I told him I saw that niggra peeping in my window, they did not kill em but he ain't seen nothing since.

I hear he got him a wife down round Plutache. People say he still big and fine and have a hell of a spread. You see how simple they are he really thought that I would actually disgrace myself and run off with him, huh. Deh say when people ask him about his condition; he tells them the Devil possessed him and made him peep at a blessed white woman and God struck him with blindness. You teach em what to think and they will think it. You teach them what to believe and they will believe it no matter how intelligent they think they are. It is called conditioning Billy Jean, conditioning. People been training monkeys for centuries Billy Jean. As long as we got pets we will never be lonely. Plus, there ain't no reason why I need to be denied compassion. Plus I got tired of Whites mercy fucks. Making love out of obligation never feels good for either person and Billy I know that better than anybody. I have cried more times than I can think of, when I am with White, knowing he go be with one of them before the night is over. Now mind you I don't envy them poor niggra girls at all. I am sure they hate every minute of it, but better them than me. Sometimes in marriage you do things because it looks right. Sometimes peoples find real love, the kind that make them never want to be out of each other's sight. Well that is not what I had for White and that is not what Major White had for me . The one advantage I have is that I am a white woman and that man of mine whats me off limits to the world so he trys to give me everythang while he is fucking over me. And if you get one that don't care enough to hit ya then you got it made. Most of them hit you cause you not her. So whatever I have to do to be happy that is what I will do. Why do you still have on that old dirty shirt Billy Jean?

" I aww don't know what to think about all that Sally. If it was a colored woman I would not give a damn about Major White or you. It's not like yall are the best of friends, so why would I come over to clean your got damn house and cook for you. Don't make sense for any colored woman to feel obligated enough to any of us to do us any favors. Puddin is probably still is your husband's whore and Lula Mae is the town gossip. When you ever known a gossip not to ask questions Sally, when? No it was something more behind that visit than meets the eye. But if you are okay with it I will just leave it alone, for now." "Well maybe they could not think of what to ask in this situation we have not finished refining them. Conditioning means giving them commands to follow not tryin to figure out if deh got question to ask us. Don't the Bible teach not to question God and ain't we their image of God? Then they no better than to question us, Billy Jean. One day they may advance to communicating with us on an intelligent level, assuming they have been properly trained in our institutions. Why have you let two niggelets worry you so girl? Look we have not taught them how to live in our world, we just taught them how to behave and how to exist in our world. They are not socially inclined people and they will never be equal to us as long as America's flag is red, white and blue. Hell, even if we give them a since of equality, we are still the ones that gave it to them, stop worrying about them two. I expect they will be coming back to see if there is anything else they can do for us. I hope some of them come over in the morning to clean this damn house for free. If not I will call Cassie and her girls and get it done for little or nothing. You feel like another drink of this fine elderbrerry wine of Ms. Lula Mae's before we retire for the night Ms Bobby Jean or would you like to go grind a while? We ain't grind since this morning. I need to release all this tension rather than talk about two little niggalets. Hell you is worrying like a nigger Billy Jean we ain't got to worry about nothing."

"Why Ms. Sally you don't seem to be morning the loss of the good Major." "Why would I do that Bobby Jean if it was not for that old obay woman and her herbs I would have just as many children for him as that niggra woman over in Fayeetville. Oh, yes I knew. I knew all about her it is kinda hard not to recognize your husbands face on a bunch of niggra bastards. I never faulted her she never had a choice, but I did fault him. How in the world could you allow for half animal, half human children to be born into this world with your face. It was hard not to see that red neck son of a bitch face all over each one of those children. He could not deny one of them. He the main one talkin about niggas is like dogs and cats they our pets. Well he was a pet funkin son of a bitch. Soon as my checks come I am going to send Ms. Reba Delonsha enough money to move away from here so I will not have to see any of them." Why you go send her money Sally? She shamed you." "She ain't shame me he shamed me. She did what she was told, like hitchen up to a mare and telling her which way to go. Hell yea, I am going to send her something, last thing

I want to run into is one of them boys with his face. I am going send her money for the services I did not have to do. You want to know the truth Bobby Jean, me and the Major would take on a visit once or maybe twice a year, but for sure he got some Christmas pussy. You would have to be a fool not to give it up for Christmas. Yall all know that no one in these parts ever got a better Christmas present than me. All them diamonds and not a damn place to where them, except in church on Sunday.

Everytime he would do it I got pregnant and everytime I got pregnant I drank the herbs. See he thought I was barren but the only thing I was not barrin was his children." " Well, how much you talking about giving this niggra?" "I am going to give her enough so she thinks I am a Saint. You see that piece of prime plantation the Farthering; well that belongs to our family or should I say the good Majors family. You know that was for White's old great great Grand Pappy's. Well she the owner now. Mr. Henry Winkles Smith Johnson got the papers ready for her and she gets, a 1000 dollars too. I'd say the good Major will be turning over and pissing straight up in the air in hell for eternity behind this one, fuck him. I hope he feels what I felt. The idea that a niggra owns his great great Grand Pappy's place will go down in history long after I am gone. It will be the greatest shame to his family name ever. See I ain't got no children to live that shame and that son of a bitch, was not my blood, so fuck him. People always figure that we is a bunch of heartless white woman. I know that is what most colored women say about us. They think we are heartless, they think we are so happy. They think we is to white to have real feelings."

"My point again about civilizing them. What woman could possibly believe that a man's wife would not have feelings, when her husband can't wait to leave her and go jump in bed over there in coon town. What woman likes going to fairs and seeing her husband's face on half the colored fucking population. You don't have a brain if you think his wife would not be hurt and ashamed. They call us heartless white women, but we are trying to exist too, we may not have on chains but we are just as enslaved. Shit what else can I do but be a wife and take some shit. I like not having to work, I like having my house cleaned. I like it all except the feeling of being owned. I can't say I know how niggras feel completely but in part I do. Bobby Jean I thank I am tired, lets go to sleep now girl. (Bobby Jean thinking in her mind, I will never have a baby, be just my luck that son of a bitch come here with nappy hair, dark skin, and a wide ass nose and fuck up everything for me. I am not suppose to know all this. I bet Sally would die if she knew what I really was. One fucking one millioneth drop of black blood got me hiding, but it is better than the alternative. I am not giving this up, forget being under privileged. I have not been proud of all of my choices, but I learned to embrace the benefits. Sometimes I am ashamed that I is passin, but I ain't crazy. Think of me what you want. I have witnessed what being colored means here and none of it is good. So the white world is the right world for me. I know what all yall is thinking but let me leave you all with this. Kiss my happy white ass.)

Opps, it was not my intention to release information about Bobby Jean in this book. But she was talking to herself and of course you can see what she is thinking. She is another story. Ms. Bobby Jean is our best kept secrete, she don't even thank no body knows. One thang I can say about my peoples is that they made it their business to know other peoples business. I was not go even mention Bobby Jean's skelton in the closet until she did. But yall did notice I kept mentioning that nappy hair. Bobby Jean's Great great grand ma was a quadrone, from the Carolinas'. That woman was whiter than any white women ever lived. Tall, blonde, with sky blue eyes and skin like milk. They tell me she would not even hold a black baby. She married one of the meanest Plantation owners in the area and she was just as low down as he was. Child she hated herself. They say she did not even want dark skinned colores on her place, they all had to be light skinned, that is how much she hated blacks. She had two children, they married white and their children married white, so you know what they looked like. Billy Jean brother was so damn fine he almost made you cry to look at him. He is about 6.3, 225lbs, big gray eyes, a strong physical build and I mean strong, he did not have a sign of a belly, none, nothing but muscle; and he smelled sweet as honey suckle rose. One day I passed as he was reparing the fense in front of his house and he was out there without a shirt on. He was all brown and toasty, little beads of sweat dripping off his body and his hair had curled up tight. Owwww Lord, I stopped and looked. I wanted to remember every bit of this fine picture, cause I was go use it later. Only one problem he had was that he was a good man. He dated one girl and he married her. He'd look at you, smile, tip his hat and go home to his wife and family.

Something about him made you want to offer him some pussy. You know like "Good morning Jacques, would you like a little pussy with your coffee?" Like I said I never bothered with the white men or Frenchmen passing for white on purpose; but he was an exception. If you saw him you would understand why. He was one, you wanted to catch you by the back of your neck and push you down on a hay stack. I could only imagine. Don't know how any black could be in him cause all of his children are lilly white. His wife, she is not just pretty she is one of the most beautiful women you ever wanted to lay your eyes own. Got a lot of ass and hips for a white woman. You will find that southern women in the deep south part of Louisiana gots ass. Life always presents a challenge, some you want to take up, some you want to pass by, he was one you wanted to take up. Of course if you mention this out of your mouth, you will probably end up under the river bank or maybe you just disappear all together, Billy Jean does have power. That is enough of this, lets get back to what our current issue is. Now this is a cup of hell piss.

CHAPTER 31

The Funeral of a Great White Man

BIG JOHN WAS CALLED to make the Majors coffin out of cypress and oak wood. He had two days to get it done. Don't know how in the hell is is going to pull that one off. Why them folks did not just buy him a coffin. The only way John is going to get this done is if he had already started on a coffin, poor man, he is in trouble. You know white folk bury their dead sooner than we do, so he had to hurry up and get it done. We all knows why too, it because they start turning black. Big John told us we must be very careful for the next few months, because you never know what might come up. He said it was something about how Ms. White was acting strange like, almost too relaxed like she was searching for something or waiting for something to happen. He said he was not sure about her because her and that Ms. Bobby Jean was looking at him like they was trying to put two and two together. I thank he was just reading into everything , because he was guilty. He knows he was the last hands on the Major. This whole situation could have been avoided if the Major would have been keeping his marriage vows. He really killed himself. But we would never be able to explain that to anybody. I keep seeing his face and I know it is because I have accepted blame for something that Satan's whore created. Damn, why did I let her back in my life? I always ask you to help me Lord and it seems like you lead me right into the middle of hell.

"Lula and Puddin seems to be getting a little to comfortable, about this Major thing. I tell them to be careful, they tell me I need to be calm. I got two days to make a coffin and the rest of my life to look over my back. Seems like I done got myself tied up with two scandalous women, one that thank she holy and the other one thank she slick. Ms. Lula Mae a good woman to take up with, but she ain't what I want to marry up with, she too free to be so holy. Some thangs a man wants his women to know how to do and some thangs he wish he did not know she did at all. Lula Mae always calling Pudding a ranced whore but she setting fields a fire like she got as much experience. She aint' got no cut on her. I ain't no fool I have been around and Lula Mae Carson, just soon cut my throat as to let me in her heart or own part of her wealth. She having a good time with me and I am having a good time with her. I likes make believe. If that girl thank she got me confused and in love, she can think again. I'd rather a paid for whore like Puddin anyway, I know she lying to me. These girls playing games, but old Big John got some tricks of his own. The thangs I have had to do to survive, they have not dreamed about yet. Ain't one place I ever went, somebody did not remind me I am black. Either some boy calling me boy or some man making me do what a boy ought to be doin. When you hold your head down all the time you gits to study dirt a lot. And when you study dirt a lot you knows it when you sees it." Puddin thank she done did some scandalous thangs to survive, huh, I gots stories too.

Makes me remember old man Ray Waller, he had a taste for watchin. Most times I am at his place he watchin. His wife always thought she was snickin and doing somethin and Waller be watchin while somebody pleasuring his wife for him. Sometimes you want to fight certain feelings, but it be feeling so good you forget for a moment and really starts to enjoy yourself. But that is when you scare some of them too, cause they really don't want you to enjoy it. But everytime I gots to plant this black cock in one of them hungry white guls, lord I loved it. I just loved it. Dem heifers lay open like big old cat for ya and that pussy bees good. Wonder what they would do if they knew I was really Sheriff Watson's son. He raped my mama when she was about 10 years old and she got pregnant with me, now that is the truth about Big Bad Ass John. I was go always be running anyway, cause most colored men who wanted to feel like a man moved around a lot. But now I got a reason to look over my shoulder, I got a white man's blood on my hands. Lula worth tryin to help though she is very valuable. Puddin can take care of her self, I ought to just leave here right na. Everything harder for me, every damn thang, being a man, tryin to get work, tryin to keep my mine right. Most places I go I gots to know how to act, sos not to scare these white folk. When you scare em they become worst. I don't get to have much comfort and there is not a place on the earth as comfortable as Lula Mae Carson's place. It is almost to much for a niggra woman or man to have. When ever I can find me some comfort, I take it, and Lula Mae Carson is as comfortable as it gets. Anyway the colored women adjust to all dis low down treatment better than us colored men. Somethin in us make us either fight or give up. Last year my brother got hisself put in jail, so he don't have to worry about makin it no more.

I never will forget the first time I lifted that heifers shirt up above them big juicy brown thighs, I knew I was in heaven or something like it. That Lula Mae a full woman, and she soft too. She smelled like fresh lemons and gardenias. She fine and her ass shaped like a perfect full moon. I'd have to be a got damn fool not to rock my self to heaven on that woman, she the kind you just want to lay in for a while. Big John aint' no fool, she good and she safe and I ain't goin nowhere right na. I ain't go tell what she taste like cause I am go have to kill ya.

Hell Sally White done paid me 500.00 to make this coffin, once I get it done, I am go kiss both these find ladies goodbye. Lula be talking to the Major in her sleep every night. She don't know I just sit up and watches her sleep. Some nights it is hard sleeping in a house with a women and another one is walking around half naked on the front porche. Some night it is hard as hell. Two nights ago that black bitch was standing on the front porche in the full moon light, with nothing on but a undershirt. She was bendin over picking up something. I damn near died, my knees was a fire. It was a fight trying not to run out on that porche and slide up behind her and shove dis dick up in her to the hub. I know what she could do, that girl there she go swallow me hold. She go buckle my got damn knees, she go make it worth every penny. I am go give her a little attention, been giving Lula a litte extra spice in her night cap, so she ain't go wake up. Look at that low down bitch, got damn my dick is hard. Come here girl. Big Johns loves make believe. Plus one thang I know for sure is all us coloreds like fish in one of them big old tanks. We gots room enough to swim, the water clear enough for us to see, but we blocked in. Truth is we can only go as far as they let us, it don't matter that you got sense enough to see and understand how everything is. Say what you want a man with a ten inch dick and a full sack of nuts finds it hard to bow down to any got damn thang, except for a good piece of pussy. I am sanking it to the rim with this woman and she aint' flinch. Let me take my time and be treated like a king. It feels good to be under the roof with two pleasing women, one for the money and one for the pleasure. It feels good being a man, no matter what color you is. Lawd this bitch got some good pussy, got damn, hell yeah I am go buy it. Plus mannn she taste like rain water from heaven's fountain, damn. I wish I could put her in a jar and drank her. See dis here is the kind of pussy you want to own. This bitch here is juicy."

"There is one privilege of being a man though and that is you a man. Even white men still see men worth more than women and rightfully so. We can make more babies, clear fields, build bridges, fight, hunt, you name it we just got more worth than women. Men who cook and clean always out do women. When it comes down to it we think different than these women, we naturally smarter than them. LeDale Cornbucker, he one of the worst men I ever came across. He was the kind that would hang ya, but make you fix his dinner before he did. I got caught up with him and his group while I was passing through Landfalls, Mississippi. One of them pissed off wives had burned down they hunting camp and they needed someone to build it back. Well, I had my tools and my skills, that is what got me out of hard time in the prison. See that old Sheriff, said somebody fittin my build had robbed the general store about two counties over and if I could not prove where I was I was about to go to jail. There I go to jail, everybody knew about this game, find a big black buck put him on the farm work him as long as you can and then out of no where set him free. (Don't move, just don't you move right na girl). That cause you ain't have no reason to have him there in the first place. Now most of em will let you go, but some of the low down son of a bitches keep you a life time. When the Sheriff told, Cornbucker I had carpenter tools, he bought my services from the Sheriff. You know that meant I was not go get a got damn penny. (Gotta keep my mind on something else or I aint' go make it a minute in this hot ass oven, damn dis some good pussy. Aww shit that's one but I ain't go stop. Dis bitch smokin cigarette, that is why I likes a hoe).

One day old Cornbucker got drunker than I done ever seen a man. He and Roy Weber was out behind the bayou at their corn still making brew. Roy Weber say "Cornbucker, what the hell we go do with all this new thinking our women been doing?" Cornbucker say "First mistake we ever made was letting them think they had the right to think. If we could have trained them like we did our coloreds life would be heaven. Instead we let em talk back and worst of all talk to each other. Web, we soften up when we start noticing them tears they be crying when we chastisin em. They don't know how hard it is for a man to keep up his punishment when deh start cryin. Ain't nothing worse than when deh be cryin in bed at night. Expecially when you can't go to buck town and get some of the sweetest tight pussy alive on earth. I ain't never care about what my women felt before, but lately it makes me feel like a piece of shit when she looks at me." " Dale you don't think them colored gals be wanting to be with us either do you. They hates us worst than our wives do." Roy says, "Hell man some of us really want our wives. I hope, all hope ain't gone. I love my wife but she is gettin sassy." " I tell you what has happened Buck, we let them get a taste of them colored men and they done runt our women. Making them thank they deserve to fornicate just cause we got the right. We started letting them tell us no and not giving a damn where we went and we let it happen, being greedy. It has back fired on us. I never thought I could feel shame or even bothered at all about what a women thought. But when my Sara Joe, looks at me with hate in her eyes, and can't stand for me to touch her at all; I feel small. You know I been smoking a pipe all my days. Now that women walks through the house literally cussing and slamming thangs, because she want me to start smoking outside behind the barn. Not in barn but behind the barn. Then she told me I had a foul odor and she ordered me this new cologne. I hate it. Can't go check my stands with it on. Hell everything in the woods go smell me comin so you know I am go have a shitty dick of a season if I got to keep wearing this high priced sunk piss. But if I ain't got it on she ain't letting me near her.

I don't want to loose my woman, but I ain't show I can keep on taking all this back talk. We should have left them black devils where they was at. (Shit Puddin, I see why they calls you Puddin, you is smooth, soft and sweet, don't move, don't move, it is gettin back up). Them colored women done bewitched us and the bucks done runt our women. Look Roy, all we have to do with our women is keep giving them thangs; thangs they can't get on their own. They minds like little children too, more toys you give em the less time you have to spend with them and the less trouble they cause you. I done decided I ain't taking no more back talk, and if these gifts ain't working I am go get me one of them special belts designed for hard headed wives. A man can only give so much." "Cornbucker, you don't know that a woman is like a piece of iron, the more you beat her the sharper she gets. One day she go turn around and cut you. You better keep using them gifts and thangs. I'd hate to see you without your ears boy. They only thinking about themselves anyway, we put up with a lot. Most of them don't know we knows when a woman want us or not, either they yell to loud or deh squeak like a mouse. Whether them colored gals like it or not they make us thank they do. Dem girls put a arch in deh backs."

" Ain't none of these bought wives we got foolin none of us man, they don't want to give us no satisfaction but lookin for every hard dick buck they can find. You ought to see how my wife and a few others come around the camp eyeing up big John. I ain't no fool, I knows they just ain't coming out here to see about the camp being built. Ain't that boy building us a nice camp though. I don't believe we got a carpenter around these parts can build like him. He too good to hang or whip, that boy go fix up my house and my barn before he leave here. You got anything you need done around your house Ray." Hell no Cornbucker, what ever I got needing to be done, I am go do it. I don't want him no where near my place. He probably a theif. Hell, his johnson hanging to the got damn ground. You right he is to good to hang or whip, so I am go keep him away. He the kind can make you rich a thousand times over, you want to keep him. Just between me and you he worth two or three wives; at least he go put out. The only reason I would hurt him is if I ain't have no other choice. Know what Roy I see what you mean. As soon as this camp is finished; I am go give him five dollars and send him on his way." That is the fist time I ever heard a white man admit how much more the black man is worth than a woman, any woman. Kinda felt sorry for them boys too, cause they had problems. Ain't a place I done been I have not had me two or three white women. Guess I looks like a big old oak tree to them, cause all they want to do is climb my trunk. I do kinda fancy them white women cause I likes how they hair feels on my thighs. (This got to be one of the best nights of my life. I feel full of power; this women right here is worth her weight in gold. Everybody on this Earth got a purpose and hers is to satisfy my aching dick. I am go have to stay away from her before I go broke. Only way I am go get something free from her is if she dead. Thank you Ms. Lula Mae for knowin this good hoe. There it is right there number two and this bitch could make a soft dick come.)

"Go take me a ride to Fille Platte and get me two coffins made from cypress and oak wood and make this money. If Lula and Puddin can keep it together until I am done with my work; I can make me some more money and disappear. (Damn that bitch Puddin is good, I bet she always good). Big John might be getting out of dodge pretty soon so I am go slip in this much as I can. When all this is over with I am go find me a good girl; one that is go do whatever I tell her and don't answer me back. Then I am go get married. It is hard to find them unsoiled at 15 year olds anymore, but it is one out there somewhere for me. I am go keep in touch with Puddin though, damn that bitch is good."

Child them white folks had some funeral for the Mayor. He had eighteen snow white horses pullin a gold trimed coach with his casket on it. The casket was too much, it had a glass front, looks like the Major was looking up at you. The black choir, the white choirs, all the boggie woogie bands and people from everywhere came to see this man buried. Us coloreds was not allowed inside the church except for to clean it up, and set up the caskets and flowers. Get it we still was in the church. But we had to stand on the outside and sing out there too. I did not really care where the hell I was I just did not want this man to get up. There was just as many white folk standing outside with us though; it was packed. I did not know he knew that many people. All his klan brothers' was there; I was expecting them to wear their sheets in honor of their fallen member, but they just wore the bands on their arms. His lodge brothers was their doing their hoodo ritual and several black preacher's showed up from other Parishes with their entire churches. It looked like the whose who of two headed doctors sitting around under the trees. I got enough

247

talasments to last me the rest of my life. Everybody had something and I got as much as I could. Child you never know when you go need some extra help. Some of these good Christians will throw a root on your ass in a minute. The Frenchman was there in all of their glory, looking white as ever. I saw a few that I was familiar with, in a friendly way and I smiled as I passed them and they smiled as they passed me. Lawd have mercy on us if any one ever found out that man was killed at my house; rode to death by a brazin whore, from hell. I would just have to leave my house with nothing but the clothes on my back. Let me make me some arrangements, right now I still got a bad feeling about all of this mess.

Ain't see Reba Delonsha, that was the creole girl that had eleven children for him. Oh lawd what is that poor girl go do now. She ain't go have any money, no pace to stay and she will never get a black man to take up with her; not with eleven head of children for the Major. She is a doomed woman, white people hated her and black people disowned her. One good thang will come out of this though, no more being raped by him. No more baring his children, maybe she should just leave. She probably did not come in honor of Ms. Sally White. That would be the civilized thing to do, but I think I might just would have showed up with every one of those children, looking just like that old red neck bastard. He could not deny them if he wanted too, they was pretty though, thanks to their mother. We all know the Major started her young, she was just twelve years old. Dirty old Bastard, son of a bitch. Reba was one of the prettiest little creol cuties you ever wanted to see. She looked like a little baby doll. The Major went to her daddy and gave him a 100 acers of land, six mules, a farm house already stocked and three hundred dollars for little Reba. All us women hated him, but all the men thought he was the smartest man alive. The only love that poor baby know is being raped by Major White. See, God you not go punish him for that right, cause you put them over us. I don't understand sometimes, that is why I am always asking these questions. My mind is limited lord and I need your knowledge and wisdom to show me the truth to these question I am asking. I am holding on to your truth and I need to understand why you lettin us suffer so much. Questions I would never ask men, I can always bring to you. Help me to understand.

We could see Ms. Sally thought the window sittin in the middle of the church cryin her eyes out, about this no good bastard. I sure in the hell did not understand where them tears were coming from. She must have had a onion in her handkerchief. He left her so rich she was sittin in church in the middle of the spring time wearin what they called a mink coat, with a diamond on her figure big as a got damn orange. Child her hair was all fixed up like one of them ladies we seen in books, look like she was about 15 or 20 years younger. Baby, that ironing board ass woman look like one of those slient movie stars. Well let me not call her an ironin board ass woman, I wish she was an ironin board ass woman. She lookin to got damn good. Cause I am takin me a nice long look, that woman ain't moanin. This is the first time I noticed that fine set of nursing tits she had or those well shaped legs she had. She has always been a strikingly beautiful woman, but there was something different about her. She was sitting there at his funeral looking better than she had ever looked in her life. Hell let me say this she was down right glowing.

I could hear the preacher just lyin his ass off in the pulpit. He said, Major White was a man of character, and Christian integrity, a good and faithful husband, awww shit I almost choked. He said, Major White knew the lord and called on him daily. I did hear him calling on Jesus while Puddin was whippin the evil hips on his ass. I don't know if he called on him daily but I know he called on him at the very end; so he was partially right, the good Major did call on the Lord. He said how good he was to all people and how he even treated the niggras like real human beings. If it was ever a time when I wanted to see a someone drown in their own spit it was now. All I wanted to do was kick his lying ass to shit. Then he becked over to the white choir and told them to sing *"Shall we gather in that Great Morning of Love"* and then he yelled to our choir and told them to sing *"Don't Pass me By Good Master cause I ain't go git t heaven if you don't open the door"*. I guess in the white man's world the Major was good man. Based on the teaching of their Bible he did exactly what they Bible taught in some ways. From what I done read it teachs it is okay to overshadow a little girl and impregnate her, people who lie and steal end up with all the wealth and blessing. It is okay for a man to have more than one wife and he can own several whores. Hell a women with virtue(that mean pride) can be replaced as a queen if she don't dance naked. We is black because we was cursed, to dismember bodies is okay, and slaves should pray for their masters so that they will treat them better, and to top it all off, if your God comes here and starts to preach equality and fairness for all people, kill him. And kill anybody else who preach the same message. I am not feeling to well, naw, something is uneasy. My house feels like it is catching a cold, my body feels like sin done took it over and all I do is dream about Major White. I got some serious cleansing to do. I might have to be asking some people to leave. Maybe this is a sign.

See there are a lot of things I have questions to you about Lawd. I it just don't make any sense to me the things that are happening to us. I have no doubt about your existence;I just need to know what we did to make you so mad at us. I know you see our pain. I know you hear us when we cry and you got to feel the fear we feel. Our men's backbones been broke so much he can't hardly stand up straight anymore. Our women been scared so much they no longer see their beauty. When you go come and help us. I thought you was black for a moment cause they hung your son from a tree. Just like they hang us from trees. What is it? Why we ain't got no real pictures of your son. I bet he is dark, he got to be dark, it is hot as hell over cross them seas. Seems like to me he would have been a dark skinned hard man. Anyway don't nobody know what God really looks like. So I can't see why he can not look like us. I keep questioning you because anybody else I ask this question to go answer it to suit how they think. And all the church people go say is "Don't question God".

One thing I have learned in this life is that there are a million excuses for losing but trying is not one of them. So I am trying to better understand, how such a wonderful and loving God can watch all this pain. Some of these books I been reading, telling me about how people been hurting each other since the beginning of time. I hope that could stop. I notice how black men automatically duck their heads when they are passing under Oak trees. I feel sorry for trees, something so beautiful and majestic in nature to become a representation of fear and trembling. Based on all of this bunch of holy bullshit; the Major is in the whites only section of heaven right now. I am in hell cause not only do I know we took a low life's life but I has been dancing with the devil the whole time. I thought he sent Puddin but he is Puddin. John trying to get settling rights at my house and now I got blood on my door. I am go start repenting right now. I got a trick for both of them though.

One thang I really liked about their funeral is that they did not do all that hollering and singinin until you shout shit. It was a lot of tall tales, wrapped up by two songs, a thank you for coming and a ride to the cemetery. Sally White sure did look like a fool with that big old mink coat on. I am glad she took it off. Child this woman has on a blood red dress at her husband's funeral, with a split in her skirt. Maybe she done lost her mind. Look at Pete Jeansonwe over their, I bet he got bags in his wagon to wrap up food. He comes to every funeral whether he knows the people or not. That dog takes away whole hams, pots of food and bags of preserves, and biscuits. He has no shame, just looks at you while he is gathering all the food he can; as if to say, "What the fuck you lookin at?" I would love to slap the shit out of him, I really would. He be looking at you with that one cock eye and them silver teeth then all of a sudden he might say "Yea, I am taking it and what you go do nigger? Stop looking at me for I gits me a got damn rope." "Yall know he peed on hisself until he was 21 years old and he sucked his mamas tit until he was twelve. We use to call him titty suckin pissy Pete, behind his back. This time he got his though, cause a old sunk got in the back of his wagon with all that food and sprayed all of it. I hear he was almost home when he realized it so that ole funk maggot did not have time to turn around and come back for more. Cause he would have, he ain't got no manners. His mammy must have been a cat. Truth is he could have loaded up two wagons and we still would not have missed any food. I thank I want to be burned up when I die. I ain't giving no bunch of hard hearted, self-righteous Saints the previlige of staring down on me in my death. I been looked down enough in this life and I ain't go leave here and have nobody coming looking down on me as I go over. I should tell em to bury me face down, so everybody can kiss my ass when I am gone, but the Church probably would not do that. I still might write that in my will. " Lula Mae Carson would like to be buried face down, so all yall good Christian folks and especially yall white folk can kiss her ass." That is one thang I liked about havin a big ass, when I walks out of a room I leaves a plain picture of what I want people to kiss.

CHAPTER 32

What she worried About

DAYS PASSING SLOW , gossip and idea's about what really happened to the Major no longer talked about. Sally White livin the life using Big John almost every other day to do extra work around the house. Honey she is adding on to it, tearing out rooms, buying new furniture, partyin and carring on something awful. She ain't act like no woman in moanin to me. Ifin I did not know for sure that Puddin had killed the Major; I would swear his wife had it done. It's like he died, she buried him and she never looked back. But you know I have had several of my white sisters say if they husbands die they would never marry again. When I say sisters I am talking mostly about the ones who you don't have to say Ms. and maam to and it ain't that many of dem. Everything that looks like it is good ain't. Sally ain't no real good Christian woman, I can tell na. Her, Bobby Jean, and Big John seem to be getting along mighty fine. He is spending a lot of time over there and he aint' been coming over here enough for me. But that is because of all them referrals he is gettin. You know Big John told me Sally White paid him two hundred dollars to build that casket, she must really like him. See I lets a niggar lie to me, he must have forgot he told me the real price. One thang for sure,

252

I ain't worried about them and John no more cause he told me he ain't never like no white women. John said he done had to think of all kinds of ways to keep his man up when he had to service them. He said that pale milky skin did not make him want to see the light. Told me deh makes him throw up. Na, I hope this man don't think I am a fool, most of them don't be thinking about color when deh is fuckin; deh be thinking about pussy and even I know that. But if he is a man of his word he might be telling the truth's so far I have not caught him in a lie. But he ain't to be trusted he helped cover up a killin. I knew once he went and started one of their jobs, he was go be too busy for any of us. They just like having a big buck around to do all their hard work. I kinda like having a big buck around too.

Big John is getting rich cause everything Sally get all the other ladies want. Ha women. I hear the men got together and begged Sally not to do one other thang on her house, because their wives is breaking them. Friendly looks like a new town. The Frenchmans is happy cause whatever John can not get to they are doing and they are doing a lot of work. I am just happy it is all over and we got off clean. Only if I can stop seeing Major White in my dreams. Puddin do not seem so happy these days. John he just teasin me every chance he get, don't seem like he go ever get finished working on my house and I don't care. But it was something different in Puddin, don't know if she was feelin sorry or if she was plottin something. She just was quite like and not interested in nothing. Did I tell yall she done put back on dem hips though. She was happy for a while and she gained her weight back. Well anyway people have deh ways. But I am go watch her, when the devil gets quite all hell bout to break loose.

Na I am not one to ever start nothing but one Saturday night I puts on the music (Didn't them white folk say the devil was over the choir in they heaven?), lets my hair down and takes me a drank and lights one of them special cigars Puddin had. They was different from the Cuban cigars they made you feel real good, real good. I liked the little cigars better than them big old ones; they just got a strong odor. All of a sudden Puddin and John got to dancing and pracin with each other. Na how long this shit been going on, thought they hated one another, huh. They sure did look good though, movin with each other's rhythm huh. Might I did not know any better I would say they were more than familiar with each other. But I know John had his standards and a woman like Puddin was not it; not for something long standing. Any man will take a quick fuck, but that is not who they want to be married to. See I don't do it for the money. I do it because I like it. Standards is standards. It is okay if he git a little of Punddin tale, she owe him that much.

We all feeling mighty fine, yall know what I am talking about, mighty fine, you know what I mean, grown folk stuff. You feeling like you deserve a little sin in your life and that sin you deserve just make you praise harder in church on Sunday. Well na, who is this coming up here unannounced? Oh my God it is Sho , didn't I say I was go call that girl by her real name. Well anyway Beluah come walking in my house big as day, like she owned it, lawd that woman was looking fine though, dressed up all fancy. Look a here na yall that heifer musta done put on bout 15lbs or so, which made her hips look round and full like a real woman, that gul build up like me. Here all us ladies prancing around dancing and one Big John, all us ladies and one Big John. Beluah was mostly interested in Puddin though so after a minute or two them two went into the back room. Nobody left up front but me and John and the Lawd and I am not sure that the Lawd was looking. I sure hope he is taking a nap; the same nap he be taking when we need help. Na, yall fixin to here a confession so pull out your Bible's, get the holy water, put on your judgment dresses, sharpen your firery darts and form your weapons. Yes, I did exactly what yall is thinking I did. John was standing over towards the window with his back turned to me. I took me another pull off my cigar, hit my wine and walked over to him and ran my hand up his leg and grabbed his concern. I had a hand full too. He turned around and laid a kiss on me like I ain't never been kissed before. I could feel it all in my spine. Then he took both of his hands and grabbed me by my hips and squeeze em. He was touching me gentle and sweet, then he fell on his knees, and yall then I felt something that made me know Jesus was real. It was his hot breath through my dress steamin my pleasure patch. Got damn this is just as hot as it was when deh actually puts deh tongue on ya. Lawd have mercy if this is suppose to be a sin, then sinning is a necessary part of life. Ain't nothing wrong with feeling this right, can't be, it just can't be. That man touched my women with this tounge, and that was it. I realized that I was just as much of a ranced woman as Puddin was. I realized that everything that I hated about her was everything that I hated about myself. This ain't got a damn thing to do with Big John. It is all about me and what I need right now, hell I might die tomorrow. But right now, at this moment I am going to enjoy every minute of this. I am go repent right now cause I will probably never do this one again. I am human and right about now I am just fucked to hell. That is right I said it " I am fucked to hell". You can judge me if you want but I won't be talking to you until tomorrow morning. Some women don't need a man and some women can't do without one. I know a thousand ways to touch my self and get pleasure. So don't thank I don't know what is pleasing to myself. I knows how to get pleased when I am being holy and I knows how to get pleased when I am bein unholy. If you can't put your own finger in your nappy piss patch, why is it okay for some body else to do it. My good friend Annie Wright, a good Christian woman once read this Indian book and it showed her the ways of touchin that did not require any imgination. She was accepted by both church women and women of the world. Annie demonstrated methods that did not require anykind of assistance. You just sit there and work your patch and all of sudden you falls back. Forget it I am not go tell yall about our sessions. Forget it. But any way she taught holy masturbation. Her way is righteous. Just sit there and squeeze until til ya spit. That way you ain't sinning in your mind, me I thanks of a lot of people when I am mind fuckin. Mind fuckin is good. Finger fuckin is good and tounge fuckin is good too but a good dick fuck is divine, Amen.

I never will forget the day we was having a talk, all of us women. The white ones too. It was about making it feel good. Do you know some of them women had never fainted before. Well when Annie finished they knew exactly what to do and I know they did it because it was a shortage on oil for a while around here. See me, I am one of those women you got to work the top, yeap cause my little woman sits straight up, so if you don't greet her first, she just sits there pissed off. Other women, all on the inside, every time you hit one of them it open their doors of heaven. Annie ain't shame she tells you in a minute she has ten men and they all knows what it takes to make her happy. Well I ain't got nothing against fingers but they don't take the place of warm body. I likes to smell a little man musk. I know one thang from this day forth everytime John licks his tonge out to me I am go drop to my knees. He was gentle and sweet and I willingly welcomed him in to water my garden. Call me what you want , think what you want, there is a bunch of ways to moan, in church, in sickness, in trouble or in bed. I likes the last one best. You ever been in a small boat on the water? That is how gentle John was stroking and rocking me; it might not last forever, but it will be good while it last. Shitttt ... then he started riding me like he was training a wild stallion. Got damn, got damn, got damn, dis man does have some good dick; Lord knows he do. He's take me for a run, and calm me down, take me for a run and calm me down. The last run he took me for, shut me down. I needed this and I am not ashamed, you see yall since I am finding out so much truth I am getting less and less ashamed of thing these days. I do believe that I am going to have to speak to God about this, but that is between me and God. I am trying to think of a way to tell John I need him to take his personal things to his house when he leaves. He comes over and stays and that is fine, but I want him to take his things with him. When men start leaving their personal things and work tools at your house they start trying to take over. Ain't a man alive go take ownership to my inheritance. My mother sold her soul to hell for it and I done took a lot of shit to keep it. Life don't always be bad or good, it just be life.

Puddin and Belauh in the back me and Big John in the front and God is in his heaven above taking a nap and the Devil is peepin at us. I feel off to sleep and woke up just as the light of the full moon was shinnin on his body. I saw the strength in his chest and the curves of the muscles in his arm. I could feel his body still steaming and best of all I could smell him. I rolled over and took the towel and dried up the sweat. Now I know this man was sleep, but his concern stood solid and tall like the stump of a strong oak. I always did climb trees as a litte girl. Only difference is I saddled this one like I was sitting on a young stud in heat. Easy and gental like, if you know about horses you know that you do not startle a stud in heat. Where in he hell did he learn to spank an ass like this. I likes how he spank ya, just enough for you to gitty up and stride a little. Something about a hard man with a gentle touch. Maybe I am just enjoying this too much. Maybe I am telling too much. But I got a lot of stories about life and life, is a lot of things. A lot of grown folk stuff. I likes that spanking thang. I bet old Lula Mae ain't shame tonight, plus I am go pray to God in the morning and beg his pardon. Yall don't have to quote me the danger of it. What if I die in the middle of sin? What if I don't? Neither question matters to me because tonight I am go thank God for these sweet moments of sinful pleasure. There has got to be something wrong with anything that teaches it is bad to feel this way. I am go quote my preacher na. "Every good thang comes from the lawd" and I ain't had nothing no better than this, in a long time. Plus, time is winding up, Jesus might be coming back soon. I hope when he does come back he does not take away grown folk pleasures. I also hopes he remembers who hung him on that tree and nailed him to that stake. That ought to make for some good white folk ass kickin.

CHAPTER 33

Ms. Lula Mae letting it all go.

You AIN'T NEVER HEARD me speak this way before, cuz I been trying to get to heaven well Ms. Lula Mae is letting it all go na. Dis what I see. I looks at Big John lying in my bed buck naked with little beads of sweat balled up on his body. Yes lawd, his strong muscular body, then I looks at his beautiful black ass and I mean his beautiful black ass sculptured like one of those greek gods. His feet was kinda ruff, his hands real ruff but he had a gentle touch, his hair curled tight and his eyes half open and here I go again. I took my tounge and tried to taste every flavor of his body, he was not even musky. I could really smell him. I was panting like a female dog in heat ha. My woman was feeling right womanlish and righteous. I lost my balance and fell on top of him. He sorta raised his head and looked at me and smiled; as I moved my welcoming hips and soft brown thighs all over this mountain of a man. I became alive again. I ain't braggin but child I got thighs and behind so if man like thighs and behind he can't help but like me, plus I am clean too, both spiritual and physical. John was saying thangs like " Ms. Lula keep on giving me the chocolate thighs girl deh so warm and soft, let me bite em, can I bite em. Then he says don't stop movin, don't get up , please don't stop". Yall know the talking makes it even better and when they go to talking in tongues that makes it even better. I am bad though cause I would stop and start again, yall girls know, playing. Plus, I use to ease drop on the elder ladies when they were in their sewing circle and they would be telling stories.

Yes, they said something about stopping and starting. They also said men can't stand it when you tighten up and hold it back. Now I know what was going on when they all took in a deep breath at the same time and released. Deh was squeezing deh funk pockets shut and openin dem up .Yes I was using everything I had heard and everything I had been taught throughout generations of womens I knew. I was slow rockin, fire grinding, grabbin and holdin, strikin the peg, swelling the belly, shittttt, Ms. Lula was working her garden. Yes, I was taking him to heaven and bringing him back to earth with the swaying of my hips and the cuddling of my woman. Big John was like a little baby crying for his ba ba. I gave him as much milk as I could. I was working on me a husband, long as he did not figure he was go own my part. That is why I need him to take all his personal things home. I am go let him bring them back but on my terms. If we get something together or he already got his that will be ours. He already know how good I cook now, he knows how good I taste. After he went off to sleep, I got up and aimed to go and get me a little mid-day libation. Seems like time had just passed us by. People lying around still drinking, smoking cigars, eating a little and falling back to sleep. When we woke up again the moon was shinning so bright and beautiful, it lite up my front yard like the early morning. I could see two shapes moving like cats in heat, hell they was even sounding like cats. It was Puddin and Beluah, out on the front porche. I watched em, touch each other, kiss and rub, child them was some squirrelin heifers. Looks like they was oiling each down and then all of a sudden they turned and put their heads on each other's woman. My eyes got hot and I know, I know my woman was throbbing like a drum beat, felt like I had to pee. I, I, I , thank I am , I thank I am, I am about to pass out. This has got to be heaven, I laid out and when I touched myself, it was like an oil slick. So, why waist a moment like this, why waste it. What is the worst could happen? One of the hottest thangs I done ever seen in my life was when Puddin and Beluah crossed up, I guess it was the way deh was grindin. So I went for heaven again, but when I opened my eyes Big John was standing up over me, touchin his self. He was watching all of us, I was not even mad at him, why deny him heaven. As soon as Puddin saw him she put her mouth on him , and before I could protest, Beulah put her mouth on me. Yall don't need to know nothin else. Noisey asses.

CHAPTER 34

The Morning After

NEXT MORNING WE ALL gets up and of course, I went into the kitchen to start breakfast. My house still had a strange feeling. Maybe it was because, I knew thangs would never be the same again. Thangs had already started changing, when I went into my kitchen John had started breakfast. Jesus this man can cook too. Them biscuits was pretty as mind (I know he got that from watching me, he stole my receipe. Na ain't that the devil, sitting around watching everything I am doing and getting all of my secrets. Huh gotta watch him what else could he be stealing. I want a man I don't need one), of course the jellies and jams was mine, beautiful fried bacon, fresh coffee and a fresh bouquet of gardenias on the table. I really don't like anybody cuttin my flowers. What the hell. How does a ruff and ready man know how to arrange flowers like that. Where in the hell did he learn to cook like that? He did not just start cooking like this over night; this takes know how. Let me stop complainin; glad I did not have to cook. But he to familiar, he even used my special vanilla in these hot cakes. You have to look to find my special vanilla. I am not sure I like that. I wish he was not one of them toe tapping men. You know the kind, dick so good every time you think of him you go to tapping your toes. I have had a few of them and Big John right there with em. Sweet as any man I ever been with. He stridin a little to long in my house though, some places and some thangs not for him to mess with. One reason I am still by myself is because I really don't like my thangs handled to much, unless I am telling you what to do and when to do it. He is going to far around here.

"Hey Lula", Big John says, not Ms. Lula but Lula. I have lost my respect already. "Yall come and sit down and taste what Big John can do for ya." I thought to myself I knows what Big John can do, Ms. Lula done already tasted Big John's wares. It is a happy morning, John is happy , Puddin and Beluah is happy God and Nature is happy, life seems good. Who is this coming up here this early in the morning? What is wrong with peole, can't I have some privacy. Plus how am I go explain, Puddin, John, and Beulah being her so early. It was Mr. Freddie Weller, he is in a panic, eyes all bucked, passing out flyers. He is screaming to high hell. "It's go be some got damn blood shed in Friendly. Hell done come to Friendly." I am like Lord have mercy Judgment Day done started. The Devil walking through Friendly and he started just where he should have. In town with them white folk. But that was not what he said was happening, he said , "Ms. Sally White was taken by force by Sherrif Jones. We thank he beat her and took her in the night." But dat was not it, it was a letter that Sally White had wrote. She left one to every citizen of Friendly, includin us black folks. It read like this "To all the fair and righteous citizens of Friendly. It is my pleasure to inform you all that I have been sucking Sheriff Jones dick for over six years now and am happy to say that he is the proud owner of half of Major Whites estate. You can burn that got damn house down as I do not give a flying fuck in hell as to what you fine folks may do with it, cause I am sure Puddin will never be able to own it. Every since the good Major had his first baby by that little girl; I have been having as many affairs as I can. Some of them was with a few of yall fine Christian women of Friendly's husbands. I am sick of every got damn thang that reminds me of Major White, so that is why I am getting as far away from here as I can. I know some good southern gentleman will look for a reason to burn down people's houses, hang innocent folk and blame all this on the Sheriff. Because that is what cowards do. But don't blame anybody eles blame me. From the very first time I had a black dick, I always knew I would have another one. And for the record Sheriff Jones dick is sweet as ripe sugar cane. Please put up your sheets no need to kill a bunch of innocent people. That is why I wrote this letter and printed copies of it at the news paper office. I do not want any of you for one minute to think that I was forced to leave this hell. To all of the fine Christian ladies of Friendly, if I hear one got damn word any of you have said about me I am gonna tell every got damn thang that any of you have told me about your worthless shit faced husbands. Din I am go tell your husbands how many of his friends you fine up standing ladies done fucked. Just remember we was all fuckin together and I know which one of yall is still kitty pattin. I know who the niggras are among us as well, and you know who you are too. I know you don't want all your fine white neighbors to fine out you have to claim one one thousandth black blood in your veins. It is a got damn shame that you do but God knows you don't look colored. By the way if yall force me too tell all I know, ain't none of yall will ever trust each other again. Yall have a good life, as I will be sucking Sheriff Jones dick as often as possible, in honor of Major White's generosity. P.S. To all yall caring colored women, thank you for seeing after my man. I likes the way you took care of him. May the Good Lord Bless You All. Ms. Sally White." They said he made her write at. Poor Mr. Weller, had tears in his eyes. He could cry all he wanted to do was hurt somebody anybody, he wanted to fix us all for what Sally had done. See, she shamed the hell of dem white folk. Child them sons of bitches was go destroy blacksville if deh had found out the black Sheriff had left with her and you better know that too. The flyer was offering a 10,000 reward for Jones. They wanted him alive he was a dead man. If they would ever catch him, the things they would have done to him, Satan would not have wanted to watch.

I guess I understand why they are acting so crazy; no body saw this one. Hell, I did not even have an inkerin about that situation right there. Them two sneaky low down evil devils. If some body had even mentioned the two of them, we all would have said, hell no. If I ever get my hands on Mr. limp dick Jones I am go chill the shit in his ass, what a two bit jip, muther fucker. I always had a feeling about him could not put my hand on it though. Sometimes he would be acting like he was trying to hard. Truth is the good Sheriff had him a business going. He never did one thing for himself, nothing. Somebody was always washing, cooking, cleaning and lovin him. He did not want for nothing. Now that is a dirty low down nigger bastard. He bet not ever give me the chance to fold his nuts back again. I mean he bet not give me a chance to fold his nuts back. I'm go pop em together with the palm of my hands. Old Bastard. People did expect Sally White was up to something but we thought she was rolling in the corn fields with one of the Major's friends. Sheriff Jones, however, was not in the running as a matter of fact no black man was in the running. We all suspected Henry, you know that big fine thang that brought all them big slabs to her house. Hell, he made since, but Sheriff Jones. A po ass nigger Sheriff. Ain't neither one of dem is shit. Who ever heard of a decent white woman runnin off with a nigger. Usually I want people to get away but I hope deh catch deh asses. Plus I thank Sheriff Jones was a little on the slow side.

So I asked Mr. Weller what we had to do with all this confusion. For he said "Nigger is you tryin to be smart with me I will fuck you up right na." I almost bust out and start laughin, he bout to take it out on me cause he thought he was to be easin up to Sally White. He said " I am here for that whore Puddin. Sally left her the house, the General Store, and the cafe. I coming to tell her if she take it we go kill her, you, and half of niggar town. I ain't coming back to say it again. Yall have a good got damn day." Then that son of a bitch spit on my porche. I hope is tongue rot out. What he did not know is that Puddin did not need none of that, she was already richer than all of them. He just a ignorant man, everybody know he wanted Sally White. This go kill him, he go be the laughing stock of the South.

He go be worst off than ole Geb Wilson. Geb took to diggin for treasure, somebody told him that them Massas use to bury one of their slaves with his money. Geb went around diggin up slave grave yards. Geb, went and got Louise Beatrice' one of them black, black almost pure African girls to take up with. Them yellow boys and white men loved that girl. Anyway Grason James always wanted Louise, so he told Geb, that most of the blacks that gave they life to watch they Master's money lived down in Florida. He told him that most men went down there hunting that treasure got enough never to come back. Grason, gave Geb over 400 dollars to help him on his way. Geb wrote home to Louise as ofte as he could. He must have stayed gone for over six years. When he got back Louise had three of the prettiest girls and a boy looked like he was a born logger. Grason told Geb he would give Louise back if he was go take her and the kids for his family. If not, he told Geb he owed him at least 200.00 dollars for taking care of his family. Next morning they say Geb slipped out of town and never came back again. People laughed at him for years, and they still tell the story of the man who left home looking for treasure while another man took his right out of his house. Geb was one stupid dumb ass. But he ain't go be alone na cause everybody know that Weller thought he was go git Sally White, here tell he had bought her a ring. I must be loosing my touch, I never saw that one coming. Them two deceitful people right there something else, I hope they can trust one another. I don't see how though, the way they been sneaking around. If I see Jones right now I might shoot him in the ass. He ain't shit. Typical nigger, used the colored womens hard work to make him look good for a white woman to run off with him. Typical common nigga. I kinda like Sally now, that was pretty damn good of her, pretty damn good indeed.

"Ms. Lula Mae seems like that fine ass Sheriff yall all been catering to done set yall aside for his swan. I know yall ladies must be feeling kinda used. See I never have that problem; you know feeling used. I learned fuckin was go be my profession a long time ago, so that is why I am so damn good at it. And once I was able to master suckin a man dick until his hemrrods popped out. I Knew right then and their that I was go be rich. My only competition was go be them white girls and most of them really hated having to do it. You don't think them white men giving me 300 and 400 hundred dollars for nothing, do you girl. I learned what men like and that is why I don't get used. You can't be no lady and please a man, he want to smell a little cat funk. I ain't never had one tell me he did not like the way I smell. Yall, holy women, gots one move and one sound, that is why your men end up letting me scratch their back. See men just want to sex fuck you and go bout their business, Ms. Lula." One day I am go tell Puddin, she ain't the only one know how to root and peg a man's concerns. She really got herself fooled by me. I just don't do it for the money; but if I decided to she'd be sharing quite a few of her customers. I might not tickle a mans' tail, but I sure can drain a nut. One thang about being a grown ass woman you can speak it like you know it. I might not tell everything I have done in my life, cause some thangs aint nobodys business but me and God. I remember when Vera Ratcliff decided she wanted to be re baptized in the church. See she was Catholic and we did not recognize no sprinklings. Well anyway she went to Reb and told him all about the affair she was having with Ruben Checker. He was our butcher and all around handy man. Whatever you needed done he could do. His wife Lillie Bell, she was an understanding women. Her husband was the most borrowed man in the Parish. It was a find Sunday morning in Friendly; we had just finished our town social, when all of a sudden Tom Ratcliff, Vera's husband came riding into town leaning side ways on his horse. Child that man jumped off his hores and caught Ruben by his neck, and it took four big men to break his grip. We all knew Vera was dead, but she was not when we got to her she was standing in front of a burned down house with nothing but the clothes on her back. Tom did not beat her or nothing but he left her with nothing. Only person got messed over in this situation was Vera; Ruben was still with his wife. His life went on as usual, here tell Tom remarried one of them Roboshow girls from LatNash. You ought to see the house that man built that woman. It is almost as big as one of them plantation homes. Poor Vera she opened up her a sewing shop, up around Thompson's Creek. I hear she is about to work herself to death. People say she is there seven days a week up until seven o'clock at night. Poor child if she had keep her mouth shut she would be livin in a mansion, with nothing but a little house work to do. She should have shot Rev. But now that I think about it, if she did not have enough common sense to know not to tell her husband something like that; she deserves to be slaving her life away. That is the reason why there are somethings I will never admit too, even if I had to swear it on the Bible. If God go strike me dead for telling a lie why I have my hand on the Bible then he go have to do it. There are somethings you just don't ever tell; expecially when it concerns personal sins. Who ever told the lie that people want to know the truth? Noboby wants to hear the straight truth. Think about it the first thing most people say when they hear how somebody really feels is that they are jealous, or being mean, or tryin to hold dem down. Only person you can be totally truthful with is the good Lord and you better watch what you say to him. Puddin ain't lying about them white men though, they have priced her out of the market for most colored men's wallets.

"Look at Lula Mae over there thinking on old Puddin'; I know she got more hoe in her than what I got in me. She just trying to get to heaven dressed like a lamb. Her God gots to be blind not to see who she is, but I do. She wants to challenge me right now about what I said about holy women. She can't though, because if she does she is go give me too much information about everything she has done. Ms. Lula doing good though she realizes that she is talking to a professional well paid whore, who likes it. I pays attention to everything and everybody. This makes me think about the time that Betty Wills, this little old country swamp whore, was trying to argue that all white men's cocks just pink. For yall that don't know it we gets together and talks about our customers. Anyway she had come down to the city for a visist and we was all sitting around getting drunk. I made a comment about purple cock white men. This little heifer looked at me and said "Them cocks must be old as you Ms. Puddin if they purple." "Yall know this little skully slut had messed up. She ain't know who she was talking to. First of all she looked dumb in a room full of old pros and second of all she was being down right disrespectful. I done been slapped in the face by more purple headed white men cocks than the South got cotton. Sure some is pink, some is brown, but I done seen my share of purple and age aint' have nothing to do with it. Goes to show I done seen more white cocks than her. Nothing makes me happier than seeing good god fearing folk like Lula Mae wanting to break lose on me but she can't, if she does she just gives me more information."

First thing my first madame taught me was, it ain't what you do anyway , it is how you do it. Most people will accept you if you show them one thing in the public and be somebody else in private. Even if they know who you really are or what you really do, as long as you act like you are not doing it and pretend to be clean they accept you. Yall know I am not lying. Sidney Paul love his men, he did. This man from the day he was born, coming up as a little boy did nothing but combe hair, make quilts and do exercise. Everybody knew this boy like men, but he married and had about six children, all of who belonged to the yard man. Cause he was not havin sex with his wife. As long as he was in church every Sunday, with his wife and family and did not talk about his love for men, people just said he was a curious man. Curious my ass he liked men and they all knew it. Hell his lover was the church panist. Who they also over looked especially when they was condemning people to hell. You know the harlots, like Jezebel, the lairs, the thieves, often times Revs would leave out the adulterers, fornicators and hypocrites. I wonder why? I always felt sorry for him, because he was forced to live a lie but everybody could see the truth. Take me for instance you can see that I am a whore, but I am a different kind whore. I am a high priced one, so I am different. It would kill Lula Mae if she thought, that I thought she was no better than me. We almost the same woman, except she is wearing a holy robe. I don't like robes. I likes fur, jewery, fine wine and good food and a good hard man piece with a fat ass wallet. Don't get all emotional and holy I am a professional whore made by the hands of good Christian men and women for their pleasure. Dogs in society need someone to chase. I am that bad luck black cat they talk about. I is always purring and persuading them doggish men, to be as doggish as they can. One thang about a dog he loves to sniff. I let em sniff right up into my hairy bank, next thang I know they is leaving a deposit or two."

"I know Lula Mae over there judging me and thinking she just as good a women as me, like she do about everything else; bragadacious bitch, but she ain't no Puddin. Hell, to bad she can't ask them three Frenchman (Real men from France) how they got to fighting over me. Child this all happened, while I was working with Madame Waset. These three French men wanted me to play their house maid. Each one of them wanted to take turns while I was bent over cleaning. You know the usual, screw the house made fantasy. Guess they did not think a big girl could have a grip like mind. We all have our little tricks, first thing I did was have them fold three dollar bills, so I could drop down and pick them up. They must not have ever seen that done before, because I could have swore a few knees had buckled. Once I snapped down on the first one he did not want to move, child. He just keep on going and singing some stupid shit. I hit that other one with my lips, you know my mouth is hot as a vulcano's ass. Then I oiled up my hands a little more and grabbed that other one. They was not ruff either. I was loving all this attention, plus they each had to pay me, so I gots triple the money, plus a huge ass tip. Did not take but about 5 or ten minutes either, before they all was laid out and I was taking me a little rest. Next thang I know here comes one of them done sit right down in my face, that is when I messed up his mind. I licked him from his crack of his ass to the tip of his shaft, I thank he was cryin. That sounds kinda of bad don't it, it is what I do. Don't read this part cause I have to be truthful. Child he turned around and kissed me like I was his most precious wife or something. Well when the other two got up they wanted to join in. Let me tell you he was not having it and that is when they started to act like animals. Them fools messed up a nice time, broke up the furniture and just kicked each others asses. All of them was good though; and they was nice looking. I did not mind taking on all three, they was worth it. It was alright with me that they got to tearing up in there, cause they must have had a years salary in them money belts. Madame Waset' had to call her boys in to kick em out. When the Sheriff showed up to take the report I knew I had made a huge hall. Everything in that room was mine and hers. That is why I always paid a upfront fee when I used the houses. Did not want any confusion about who gets the tips. Some houses let you use the room, but they take all the tips. I bet them men had a stroke when they realized all their money was gone. Madame smiled at me when I gave her the best damn tip she done ever got. She was soooo greatful and sweet. I see why she is such a well loved Madame. That women got a sweet pair of lips. Anyway I doubt if Ms. prissy ass Lula Mae go let a man sit his ass right down in her face and like it."

"It is time for me to change though. I want me a good a life somewhere. No more selling. I am just go do it for the pleasure. One thang about me I won't get bored. What some men won't do women will and what some women can't do men will suffice. I love variety cause it is the spice of life. It just makes living so interesting and tasty. Cocks is good and so is pussy, it is just according to what mood you are in. Good thang about being a women like me, I can have them both and it don't make me nothing, but a good whore. Now if I had got my hands on Mr. Sheriff, he would still be hangin around looking for me. But instead, Sally White done massaged his head and he done lost his mind. I bet she did it out of spite too. That boy did not have a chance. If they ever catch that boy, ain't go be nothing left to bury. This is when being a hoe pays off. All these good black women catering to him day and night and he done set them all aside. Took up with someone he can get killed for looking at. Serves em right, they should all be ashamed cause he and her made a plum fool out of them. One good thang about being a whore, shame does not exist in our world. Plus all of them good women would have talked about him like a dog if he had been seein me. They all would have been mad and trying to run me out of town. I would have been taking his money. Maybe that is why I never saw that cheap bastard. At first I thought he liked men. A lot of men who have a whole bunch of women like men. They just use the women to cover it up. Child I got stories and friends, from all walks of life. That is why no body can ever say Puddin went around judging people. Everybody know whores can not judge anyway, we just used by good people to express their bad behavior. If it was not for us whores how could you tell what a lady was. Ms. Lula Mae stop thinking on me over there girl. You know if you think it you may as well say it, it all has the same effect."

Bout two years din passed na the Preacher din had two more children by his new piano player. The new Major Mr. Johnson Budwall Smith liked being between Puddin and Beluah so much he bought the the land next to mind and built them all a house. Me and Big John not married yet, but he still bringing me his beaufitul black ass and I ain't got to cook no more. That man can throw down. I am still having dreams about the Major. Don't get why I can not get him out of my head. It is like he is huntin nobody but me. Big John has made a good bit of money, now wonder why he ain't left yet. We both wise enough to know we aint' go marry each other na . We keeps good company though. My soul has been restless, don't think I have had a good nights' rest in almost two years. Still talking to the good Lord, asking for understanding. Time I start making arrangements to move on with my life. I am still a young woman and it is a big world waitin to see me, just hate having to get on one of them ships. Most colored folks got a thang about ships, seem like they always bring us bad luck. Our ancestors were stuffed onto ships bring us over here ain't help none. And back some years ago the white folks big ship went down and killed a bunch of people. I would not have wanted to be colored on that ship, cause I know they all drowned. You know they was not go let them on a life boat.

Tonight is the spring dance, every body is getting ready. Now you want to see some fine dancing; just show up tonight. Them Cajun steppers go be there dancing up a storm. They must have started dancing together in the cradle. They move like one person with the music. Seein them swing around is a pretty site, but you aint seen nothing till they start dancing real slow. It's like magic or somethin. I am go let my hair down, get me a few shots, forget about my dreams and enjoy watching other people have a good time. Sure wish Big John had a mind to go somewhere for a few days, starting right now. Them Vincente' boys from the back basin go most certainly be here. Never forget the first time I met them. I was fishing up the levey, right at the mouth where the basin run out into one of them side ponds. I had about four lines going at once and this old boy named Bean, called hisself courting me was suppose to be helping me fish. Well anyway, a big fish hit one of my lines and I had to run to get it. This old man was standing on the bridge above. He said "Hey Cher bay bay, If you let em my boys will bring your pole to the bank." When I looked up and saw him and his boys; I damn near wet my pants. They looked like something that God had sent to earth just for me. Brown tanned skin, thick hair, big green and blue eyes and both of them boys was bow legged and the old man made me shame that I looked at him with lust; but I did. Cause he was a hell of a looker. I stopped for a minute to catch myself, that was the first time I could not make up my mind who I would have first. For sure I was going to have at least one of them. I am not perfect and yes I have to admit that when it was convenient for me I would enjoy all kinds of pleasures. Long after that I would go to that spot to fish, and almost every time I went there one of them showed up. They never minded asking colored women to dance and they did. Seemed like I was their favorite and everybody sorta accepted that. When they danced with you, you wanted it to be close to them, like you was melting into their bodies. Oh, and that myth that all of them are little put that out of your mind; or maybe I have just been blessed. I was probably being blessed, but I sure have been well blessed. Did I mention they are all married now? Well they are, but who cares they women been having our husbands for years. One good deed deserves another and fair exchange ain't robbery. Plus the good Lord ain't did them a thang, so he aint go do us nothing either, if we don't' get caught. Yall know something the white women never killed us when they found out we were with one of their men; mostly cause we was doing them a favor. Some of them would try and send us as far away as they could. Huh, but them white men kill your ass in a minute for having one of their women especially if you is a black man. A black woman pussy is a white man's luck and a white women's pussy show to kill a good buck. That is our little secrete saying, just between us black folk.

By the way, if yall don't think I know what you are thinking about me, you got another thought coming. I know yall calling me a hypocrite, judging my deeds, looking for a reason to tare me down. All because I am telling you the truth about life. Everything I am doing, I was suppose to do. If that is not so then God does not own my life and I have been wasting my time talking to him. I try to do things that help people know what is going on. I think if you live your life to where you don't do things to folk you would not want to have done to you; you are as good as a person can get. Nothing I have done up until now has ever really hurt anyone. My life is not so bad. I did not have as much money as I have now, before I met Puddin, but I had a whole lot more peace. My secrets was mine. My home was mine too. Now I share them both. I am not saying it is a bad thang, it is just different for me. I almost feel like I need them. Puddin and John just like beathing air, if they were not around I would die a slow lonely death. These two people have become a part of my heart even though I know they not right with God or man. Sometimes what we need and what we want may look like the same thing all dressed up at night; but when you undress it in the daytime you see the difference. According to how bad you need em you close your eyes to the faults. Truth is having them around is sending me to an early grave, but I would rather die than feel the loneliness of being alone. If the white man can justify everything he has done, I can justify everything I am doing right now. Yall don't know what it feels like to be coming up during this time. The only thing I have to look forward to is to die and hope that I gets me a good Master in heaven. I pray they lighten me up some and straighten out my hair, sos the other saints won't be so hard on me. If you black, white folk hate ya and black folk hate ya. If you think I am lying ask somebody real dark how they is treated. They will be the first to tell you that black peoples talk about them worst than white folk. My friend Mary use to tell me all the time how she just hated it when somebody would tell her she was pretty for a black girl. That is one reason she would never date them Frenchman men, because they was known for liking the real dark girls. Most of them light men liked them dark girls. It was not a compliment to her, because it actually meant that you ain't as ugly as most dark dark people. Plus most of dem lite colore boys thought deh was doin you a favor. Truth is deh hated deh color too and they just wanted to have some color in their children and we all knew it. Mary is a pretty women though and she fine as an afternoon shoe shine. There were always suiters just waiting to latch on to her, but they was all mostly them Frenchman and them yellow boys. It ain't good being black in the black race. I take it when we get to heaven we will all be washed as white as snow or atleast lighten up a little. See in this world for us right na we is still confused. People say we free but I know of atleast 20 workin plantations. Exceptin they don't call their free labor slaves, deh call them share croppers. Don't know if thangs go ever change for us but I can tell you that I ain't go leave no child behind to live this nightmare.

Never know what or who will come into you life and change everything about it. I know I was really battling for the Lord before that hussy Puddin set foot in my house. Puddin came to town one day and changed the life of us all. She made us free, she gave us spice, she made some of us pretty damn rich. She took our minds off the sin in our daily life. Then after she got us all caught up in her, she used her powers to blind us and made us think our wrongs was right. I still got something she aint got. I got repentence on my side; that is the only good thing I see about this heavenly adoption. I get to repent as often as I sin. Wait maybe I should not say repent, let me say I get to ask for forgiveness, cause I can ask for forgiveness as often as I sin without being held accountable for it. That is what my preacher say the Bible say. The only time I repent is when I am sure I am not go do that same thing again. I be careful how I ask for repentence. You got to be careful how you say certain things or they can get you in trouble. See Puddin don't think she needs to ask for forgiveness or repentance, that is why she go be in so much trouble. So, if the Lord is a true to the Bible, then everybody who have ever hurt, stolen, killed, judged, lied and coveted their neighbors belongs go be in a world of trouble one day. But not today, not today and maybe not for centuries to come. The day everybody is treated as true equals in this stolen land , will be the day of true judgment from a just God, who does not see color. Ms. Lula aint trying to be mean she is just keeping herself in the real world. I know if I had stolen something of value and built it up, I would not give it back and I would fight to keep it. That is why I know aint nothing here go ever be completely equal and it does not matter who has control. Plus you ever known a rich man to give you his money cause he felt guilty. Show me the way to him I got guilt trips of a lifetime to tell him about. This is one life I wish I could sleep through. Can't really determine what is right and what is wrong, cause what is right for me might be wrong for somebody else, it all according to who it is or what is is. So many thangs I can not figure out. Like when did I wake up and why did I wake up here? I can feel it in my bones that I should not be here, living in all this fear and hate. It is like I left heaven to come to hell. I am getting a little tired of talking now. Think I will just sit quite for a while. Satisfy my soul, lord, satisfy my soulllll, satisfy my soul lord, satisfy my soul. You can call me a hyporcrite, but I am a forgiven hyporcrite and aint a damn thang you can do about it. But before you say that look in the mirror, look in the mirror. That is what I had to do. What you got to say now. This story is about to end. By the way I danced my ass off with them Vincente' boys that is all yall need to know.

Yall know I has many many more stories to tell yall. Course this one ain't over just yet. Thangs is too good. My belief in God is so strong I got mustard seed faith. Seems like their God done truly adopted me in, cause we got off scott free, accept for them dreams. I keep seeing the Major lookin at me like I ought to be ashamed of myself. Well he ought to be ashamed of hisself. He the one died on top of a whore, not me. I got a man that I don't' have to feel guilty about having. Neither one of us is married. We aint got to hide what we is doin and we don't want too. Wish somebody in the church say something, so I can throw up Reverand Goodman's two new additions. Oh You know they have connected our towns, built a main street from one end to the other. Some white folk done bought property over in the flats and is building up the land. It won't be long now, and they go move blacksville further and further down the road. I am go hold on to my land, cause after a while we aint go have no where to stay. We too got damn money hungry, we just sell, sell, sell and it don't matter if the price is fair, we just sell. One thang my mama told me was not to sell our home. I would rather die the death of a red headed wood pecker, than to sell my home. They will never get this for little of nothing.

Puddin and Bealuah enjoying life and we all spreading fat. I been feeling kind of weak at the stomach. I thank I might be pregnant, I better take me a trip to New Orleans, shittttt, I ain't trying to raise no children now. Thank I will be going in the morning. I probably should have gone to Ms. St. Claire two months ago. I got gas movin all through my body, I can feel it creepin all over me. If I ain't pregnant I am fixed. But that can't be, cause the only one feeding me is John, and Puddin ain't got no reason to fret me. Plus all she ever do is boil pig feet and potatoes.

One thang my mama always told me was this, don't tell all your business. Have a secret place to run off too and never let your men friends know who all our friends is. When I told John I was goin to New Orleans he wanted to jump up and come with me. You know I was not go have that, just in case I needed to have a little work done I did not want him there. As luck would have it or as blessing go, Sister Willie Mae Coleman was the guest speaker at our women's day program. This is a Saint, she knows the way of the Lord and she knows the way of the wise women. A man ain't never crossed her door for help, she does no work for men, none. Hell the men don't know about her, she our best kept secrete. Know what else is a secret? She is my sister. Mr. Watson, was seeing another women at the same time he was seeing my mama. Oh, yes they had some shit with them back in them days. We found out about her when he was on his death bed. He told my mama to give her 200 dollars and 40 acres of land. Well, her mama came got the money, sold the land back to us, and we only saw them for Christmas. But we saw them every Christmas. See that back 40 directly behind our house; that is some prime rabbit hunting land. Child mens from all over the Parish come to hunt back there. So many rabbits back that you stepping on big balls of rabbit shit every two or three feet. Them men looks like they have a fever when they headed back there. You know if they don't stop to see what I got cooking they got a fever. Child it is 40 acres of rabbit gold, them hounds hit the ground rolling. All you hear is dogs and guns, dogs and guns. They been trying to get me to let them build some training pens. I aint go let no man build no training pens on my land. Next thang you know they go be trying to own it. Them white men can't wait to get their hands on my back 40.

Anyway, like I was saying it is good not to tell everything. Heart might mean to keep it, tounge might try not to say it, but need will betray them both at any given time. It is good to know people other people don't know you know. Know what else is good; having money is good. You know I had to invite sister Colmen over for dinner. The main reason is because she was not going to eat from any one else but me. I cooked her one of them Sunday go to meeting dinners fit for the Lord himself. She love Ettouffe, yall know I don't mess with Ettoufee to much that is what my cousin ate all the time. Yall know the one had them snails in her belly. She loved Ettoufee. But anyway I made a pot of that , potatoe salad, shrimp and grits, jambalyia, stuffed meletons, corn bread, shrimp creole, baked fish and two pots of string beans and potatoes. Yall know she love them old fashinon pound cakes with strawberry preserves on it, so I had to make three of them. One to eat here and two to take with her. I let her make the salk pork and okra. That is her treat to me. Some people say that this here God don't look after us and I am one of them. But I know for sure there is a God now. I know for sure. Sister told me the truth and she made me know my place.

CHAPTER 35

The Best Damn Funeral
Friendly, La. Ever seened.

TALK ABOUT A SAD day on the face of the earth, the news read. "None was found to be more beloved among the colores as Lula Mae Carson. A good Christian woman full of the glory of God. Heaven was missing their favorite angel. On, Saturday, morning Ms. Lula Mae Carson, was found dead after being run off the road about a mile from her house. Upon investigation, her house had been robbed, it is suspected that she must have walked up on the robbers and tried to get away in a car that belonged to Naomi Love. It seems as if she was ran off the road. A hard lick to the back of her head seemed to have been the reason for death. If there is anyone who knows of anything relating to this case contact Sheriff Watson. All comments will be keeip in the strictest confidence. If yall know of any relatives of Ms. Lula Mae, have them contact the Majors office before the Parish reclaims her assests." That is how the town paper wrote the story. You ever seen such a despicable group in your life. They better know that this God they playing with is real. I am a living witness of that. You just don't be talkin to your self you be talkin to God. And he be listenin I know.

Them old folks always said if you dance to the devils beat you go be his treat. Na yall know nothing but the devil in hell could stand around my coffin and carry on like that Puddin screamin my name out. Poor sweet sweet, woman of God, took me in and treated me like regular folk always tryin to save my hell bound soul. She don't know the spirit of the Lord is in the room with her and he got an angel of wrath with him. Oh Lord I could kill that rotten hoe. Then Puddin say's I will kill the son of a bitch black or white that took this good woman's life. Just then Sherrif Watson stood up in the middle of my funeral and say. "Na don't yall niggras get the wrong idea, ain't no bounty on on white man's head. Ms. Lula Mae was good a colored as there was , but she and none of the rest of yall, is worth a whiteman's life. Watch what you is saying here today gal." I wish I could get up and go right over to him and slap his face. What kind of mess is that to say at such a fine funeral. Give me a sword right now Lord, give it to me so I can stick it straight up his ass. I'd like to fix him some of my pass me not oh gentle savior and a litte of that Jesus keep me near the cross in it too. But I will never have the cycle of woman again. A girl can only drink so much tea. I hope he goes to hell. I want that old bastard to wake up in the middle of black folk heaven. Really, black folk heaven and I want him to have to live there in fear of his self. Every body in this life will come to the realization that there is a God. I still ain't figure what you be doin when we be calling on you. You don't hear us women call, you don't hear us colored folks call, you don't hear us poor people call, but then out of no where you will show up with a host of angels ready for war. I just don't get it. Lord did I just here Gabriel ask you to let him come to Earth and bring judgment on all of them. The Saints is throwing up all over heaven, this is just too much lying and deceit. The people who done ploted my end, crying like babies and calling my name. Ain't no nevermind though where I am going I won't see any of these devils anymore. Glad I got to be real before I had to pull up stakes and move on past the life I had been living. Some of the worst thangs that happen to you can bring about your change. Once we realize we not meant to be here always, we can accept our change and go on living towards our eternity.

Oh Pastor Goodman sure is putting down some serious preaching, that man done stood up in the Lords' chest. See that snow white and gold robe he is wearing he don't wear that except for Easter Sunday Morning.

But he is wearing it today for Ms. Lula Mae Carson's resurrection. Got on them white shoes too, and just look at Sister Goodman, child you know she had that dress special ordered. That is some fine hat, she got that from New Orleans, I know exactly what shop. Yall see that choir huh. Tell me something you ever seen a choir with gold robes trimed in sliver piping and all the choir books is new. Something just told me to make plans for my resurrection. So I started, I wanted to make sure everybody looked like what I wanted them to look like. Some of yall go say I am crazy, cause I don't mind releasing this life for another one. But yall gots to understand even I did not expect for life to stay the same to many things happened.

Child look at Reverand Goodman he done whirled around and touched heaven. Of course he is preaching over a good woman. (This was not cheap yall, I had to pay for all the trimming, plus the good Reverand cost 5,000, Mr. Undertaker, cost 6,0000) , they robbed me, but who cares it aint nothing but money. It is worth it for a find send off. The undertaker cost so much cause that man was on call for me. See yall I always had a fear of rotting before people found me so I had him start to pass by me in the morning and in the evening. I always wanted to be sure I was picked up soon after I past on , so I had that poor man on call. He was ordered to pass my house every morning right after the rooster crowed and every evening after he crowed. Six thousand dollars can get that done for you. I don't want my body stanking, always hated how that smelled. It's from passing oak trees in the south with ropes haning on them. That smell stays in your nose. I looked good in my casket. I changed my mind about being burned. (Why temp fate.). Child Reb, had an amen corner like you would not believe, some of them people I never saw in my life. But they was raising the roof for me and that made his sermon even stronger.

People was falling out all over the place. Not like it was at Sussie Bennet's funeral nobody liked her so the church went to sleep. I loved what undertaker Washington did with my coffin he nailed that sucker shut so not even the lord himself could get in. I could have been buried naked for all they know. See money is something else it can buy souls, it can buy love, it can buy respect and it can buy you the best damn funeral in the world. All you need to pull off a good funeral is two men that respect the dollar bill. I aint' need no lies told for me cause every body knew I was go have me a crown of gold and I do. No what else I found out, the world ain't paying attention to you. The world is too concerned with trying to exist. To say my cousin Eula was suppose to inherit everything I own if she wanted it. Nobody paid attention to her or asked her any questions. They ignored Eula Mae. I know I would have wanted to know who the hell was behind that black veiled hat. People still as hateful as they can be. They treated her like she was some kind of plague or something. See them white folk wanted to get my land and the colored folks wanted to finish taking every got damn thang that was not tied down or that the white folk aint' take. All that shit stopped when Eula showed up, with proof she was my cousin. Good thang Eula was superstitious and wanted to stay at the the bording house while she was getting things done. Plus she got to hear what all the people was sayin bout her dearly departed cousin, me. I don't know what Puddin and Big John would have done, not being able to get in my house. They was avoiding her like she had the small pox. I always believed in life after death, no matter what kind of death it was. It ain't nothing but change, just a process that is all. You leaves one senery and goes to another. We just spiritual time travelers.

After the funeral everybody met at Luzzies and my lawd what a feast it was. I counted 25 baked turkeys, with giblet gravey, fresh made cranberry sauce, mustard greens, collard greens, about 18 pots of those, string beans and potatoes, butter beans and okra, crowder peas and fat back, sweet corn mush, hot water corn bread and corn bread cakes, Fried chickens by the tables full, smother chicken and dumplings, 14 caldrons of seafood gumbo, jambalya , boiled crawfish, , boiled pigs feet and neck bones, 25 of the finest hams in the parish, (supplied by the white folk only cause they wanted to justify taking home so much food, plus they came from me anyway. You know they went and robbed my supply house as soon as they thought I was cold.). Every preserve we did in Louisiana was represented, watermelon rinds, muskydines, pears, peaches, strawberry, black berry and old lawd lets not talk about the cakes and pies. You know pecan pies is Southern tradition and them white girls can make the hell out of them. Grand ma pound cakes, jelly cakes, fig pies, chess pies, old fashion lemon pies, biscuits but they was not mine oh na not to mention them Cajuns had 16 caldrons frying sackalait, catfish, brim and cypress trout. Them Robashew boys bought in two alligators, and 12 turtles cooked every way they know how.

What a feast they had almost made me cry so many people came out even them damn quardruns. Well why not I was always nice to them plus they love my biscuits. They bought, two wagon load of pecan candy, crowder peas and rice, sweet corn bread, red beans and rice, boudin, lemon pound cakes, ripe to the rine watermelons, and 15 kegs of some of that homemade whiskey. Them people showe me some respect. Oh, lets not forget they bought 26 barrels of boiled crabs, corn and potatoes. I just never could trust them to much, they was just to white for me, just to white. But I ain't never treated them no way but kind. All this respect, good food and loving words is breaking this poor spirits heart. So many people claiming their love for Ms. Lula Mae Carson. I wish I could just sit here and continue enjoy this feast with them; it was a banquet just for me, wait it is all for me. If these people turn around and see me in here, that would clear the entire town of Friendly. Glad I got Solomon's mine out of my house before them good white folks came by. They snooped into everything, but they aint' even fine a piece of jewelry. I have always been a well prepared woman.

CHAPTER 36

Yall Niggras had Better Fine All that Money Yall Told Me About

PUDDIN, SHERRIF WATSON, BIG John all at my house. Big John say, "That was the hardest thing I ever had to do in my life. I really think I loved Ms. Lula Mae." Puddin say "I did love Ms. Lula Mae she was a good woman as far as good women go. But she was not a Saint either." "Puddin you is the devil" says Big John. Then Puddin say, We did what we had to do Lula was having to many bad dreams bout the Major. This whole thing was over and you the one keep telling me how she waking up in the middle of he night saying the Major was talking to her. You the one said she was saying he was one of Gods' Saints now. You are the one said she was go write a letter to the new Major about all that. For all the good that was go do her, me and Beulah is fucking him. You better be lucky she did not find out you was a two-headed doctor John or this would not have ever worked. She might have had sex with you but she would not have ever ate from you. My auntie always said they gits you in your stomach. That is why I don't eat from everybody. You filled her belly with snake eggs and gravey, not to mention you was saying the words. See that is why I don't like beans and rice. I know you was using elbow roots, and tad poles too. I use to see you at the creek niggar. I wonder is they still hatchin inside of her." "No women she been embombed. I feel like a monster, Puddin, she was good to me. I thank I was in love with her. But she was not so good she did not know I saw her taking the honey and parsley baths. That is when she wanted to keep me. I also noticed when she started to take them walnut baths to get rid of us too. She was not all together a Saint, but I still had some love for her." You did what you had to do John. You don't want to go to jail in the South tell him Sherrif. "Neither one of yall might not want to go to jail in the South gal."

"Look how smooth it all came together, we did not know she was go get robbed and we did know who ran her off the road. But we did know we need that body to get to the undertaker fast. Cause if anybody other than his greedy ass would have picked that body up with all them little critters crawling out of it , your ass was going to jail for murder John. They was go get you boy, cause somebody was go tell you was a two-headed doctor. (These is some evil people all I wanted to be able to do was scream out and say "The Lawd saw yall the lawd saw yall muther fucker and yall go pay for this one.") "I knew just when them eggs had hatched in her" says Puddin, "She thought she was pregnant. She did not know I knew she thought she was pregnant, but I noticed her trying to keep things down, hiding when she threw up, taking her temperature and when she said he wanted to go to New Orleans I knew she thought it. I knew it would not be long after that, it never is. You almost messed up when you gave her that wormwood, it was go kill them hatchlings. Good thang I stopped her from drinking the rest of it. Some two-headed doctor you is. So don't you come back here pretending like I is evil alone, we both in trouble. Hell, it is all your fault Sheriff Watson here right now, you knew she had wrote a letter and you did not think to move it." "Well, now Ms. Puddin you need me here, cause yall need protection from one another. Maybe Ms. Lula put that letter right where I could find it because she did not trust either one of yall. None of this matters to me, all I want is this King Solomon's treasure she is talking about. I sware Sheriff if I knew where that gal had hide this money I would be glad to split it with you. Nigger, you ain't splittin nothing with me, you go find this money so you won't go to prison. To bad Ms. Lula Mae not here now. Why you say that Sheriff. Well Ms. Puddin all she have to do is buy her a law man and I would get rid of both of yall for her. Don't look like she trusted yall at all." "No Sheriff it was Puddin she did not trust, she told me that all the time." "Just shut the fuck up John and lets find where that no good hefier hide all that money I gave her. John you say you been searchin this house before she died and you still can not find it. I am not sure I believe that". "I found it once then when I went back to look it was gone. Truth is she would give me anything I wanted so I never really looked for her money again. She ain't the only one with money though is she Puddin." "You need to stop talking out your head John. Don't feel guilty about Lula Mae she was a good woman but everybody know she was a got damn gossip and busy body. I bet a lot of people is sleepin easier now she gone. Sherrif Watson how long is you go be looking for them robbers?" "I don't know yall told me she had bags and bags of money, her letter say she had King Solomon's treasure, na yall is sayin you have to fine it. Some body might have to pay if it don't come up soon." "This one thang I know", says Puddin, she ain't never leave this town much and she loved this house. If I have to tear everyboard off of it we go fine that money. Na, here I is working between this cracker and this stupid nigger, old Puddin got a trick for them though. It' s go be the last trick I ever turn."

"I know Ms. Lula Mae was smart and stupid at the same time especially since she thought I was to much of a low life for Big John to fuck. I fucked him before she had meet him. I always remember the niggers I screw, cause they had to pay extra and he paid. You never forget a man that size coming in for some comfort. No what he paid for? He paid for me to spank him like he was a bad boy, yes he liked his ass spanked. He loved to eat cherries out you, I liked that. He use to change me like a baby and he loved for me to bury my face right in the crack of his ass, aww yeah, Big John was a big freak. See that bitter look he had when he was looking at me when he first met me; it was because I had his 200 gold coins. He bet me I cold not spit out change. I showed him I could and took his money. He did not have to worry about me telling it was business, just business. But I knew I was go be having him and I knew he wanted to have me. He did not like it the natural way either if you know what I mean, he liked a little ass with his meal. He the one told me Lula said she was not worried about him takin me serious cause I was just trash. I got a whole lot more of her dick than she did. One time I could still taster her pussy on him. I licked every bite of it off. It was my pleasure. The only thang I am glad for is that they had her casket closed, I did not want to have to look down in her face. See, me when my time come, nobody that looked down on me when I was livin, will have a chance to look down on me when I am dead. I want them to burn me sos, I can be conditioned for my new home in the white man's hell. Aww shit I don't believe in they hell. I just don't want know Johns, and Janes, and self righteous church folk looking down on me in death. I will get up if I have to and slap the shit out of em. I have done more work for the Lord than most of his Saints and disciples. Once I get out of this I am changing my life. I helped take a good woman's life. She had her selfish reasons but she opened her doors to me. She feed me and gave me comfort, yes after this one old Puddin quitin. Got me enough money to start life over anywhere I want to. Got me a real bank account in Paris, France too. Some thangs you keep to yourself. Gots me a good friend in Canada and I can disappear when ever I am ready and I am ready now. We hurt a good woman."

John and Puddin just knew they knew everything about Ms. Lula Mae, they did not think I had sense enough to take care of my self. What none of these people know is Ms. Lula had places they did not know about. See, my house was built to protect our people during slavery. My kin folk had just as much house under the ground as they did on top of the ground. There was no entrance from the main house to the tunnels and you had to know exactly what oak marked entrance. Once you in it, it was like a general store. Everything I had in my house was in the tunnels. Each tunnel lead to freedom. I could be in them and hear everything going on in my house. My peoples was freedom fighters. That is why I am so blessed. We had our secret place that went from town to town underground. Puddin don't realize I knew where all of her hidden money was every dime, plus how in the hell you go hide something on my property. Hell she hide it about two yards from our tunnels and I just drug it right up. Just wait until she go to get that. There were so many times I stayed under there and listened to her and John I can not count them. I told yall they was go be doing it every chance they got. Another thang Puddin ain't hide all her money there either.

"Look I am go give yall till tomorrow morning to come up with Ms. Lula's treasure then somebody go be hung by the evening. You can bet on that, good day I gots Sherriffin work to do, yall go and find that money.

If not you go see how bad it is to lie to the law. Boy go fetch me a drink and take this parlor furniture and load on my truck. Son of a Bitch, this mother.., done took my parlor furniture, he deserves death. Can you believe this. I can not wait until it is his turn.

CHAPTER 37

Judgment Comes
Sooner Than you Think?

"PUDDIN IFIN YOU KNOWS where that money at you better tell it."" Look John my pussy got pockets but they ain't big enough to tote around all that money. Now you done looked every where but up my ass, go get a candle." "The Sheriff aint' playin na Puddin he is go kill us dead. I don't know any white man want to be made no fool of by no colores. You better tell it." " John do you think I would lie to you , we is all we got. I am in your corner baby. We is both been searchin and searchin this house and it is solid as a rock no money in site. Wonder if Lula buried that money somewhere." I made John go dig up the graves in the backfield, the gardens, the bait beds, damn near everywhere a shovel could dig we dug and no money. Then I thought I got enough money for myself; I am just go take mine and get the hell on. They probably will hang Big John but that is what he deserved. Well got damn, I goes to the uprooted oak tree down the bayou and my heart failed, my chest is gone. I am go kill me a nigger cause nobody but John could have got that, he was always snooping around. I am go kill him dead. One thang for sure I can search in peace, I put enough belladonna in his drink to knock him out for two days. I aint go kill him, cause I don't want to cheat the Sheriff out of his hanging. You know what; I am go do to him what he did to Ms. Lula. Soon as I said that, the Lawd showed me a nest of them fearful brown spiders. I grabbed them and took em back to the house. While he was sleep, I shoved those eggs down his ears. You should have seen all those little babies crawling down his ears. Now in about a month or two if he is still living he go have some real bad headaches. Ha, we will see na nigger. We will see. It was hot so I laid myself down in Lula Mae's bed the same one I was having Big John in every chance I got. Took me a long satisfying rest, dream about how good I am about to live and how I am gonna spend all my money. I am go leave all this po ass trash, go somewhere, and live like a woman ought too.

"Yall, get up in there; I say get up in there." You know a good spirit can get startled too. It was Sherriff Watson low down ass at 5:30 in the morning yelling from his truck. " I ain't got all day where is that money. Big John was the first to run in to meet him. I could see them two talking but I did not know what they was saying. Look at him being the perfect boy, running to meet Master. Only thang Puddin did not know was that, that Master was his daddy. Sometimes being unseen is a good thang, cause what I saw next was like a moving picture show. Sheriff Watson tells Puddin "Gal your time is up" and then all of a sudden Big John grabs Puddin and holds her down. Sheriff Watson , slaps her over and over and over and then he says, "Na you go stretch out for me like you did for all them paying men you cheap bitch. I am go teach you about lying to the law and stealing from dead people." John was holding her down then he turned her over first and the Sherriff just pushed himself in her, they both had her from the back. Can yall tell me why that low down bastard had to stick his pistol in that girl? She screamed and screamed but no one could hear her, then she was quite, no sound, no smart words, and no loud laughing, nothing. Puddin was gone, gone the way she meant for me to be gone. I wanted someone to pay for what they had done to me but I truly did not want to see how these men was using her. The Sheriff must have had a lot bottled up in him cause he was riding her like he had not had any in a while. He probably had not either; he was one of them men you did not even want to take money from. Plus, he had took Puddin before, he knew how good she was, so he was trying to get all he could this last time. Don't know how he could feel anything with her laying limp like that. Then all a sudden John said "My turn na boss," that man put his face right down in all that mess and grunted like a hog. That is the nastiest son of a bitch I done ever seen in life or death. God I am about to blaspheme now. Jesus Lord have mercy; clean my soul from his filthy presence. I cannot believe that was the same man I had made love to so many times. I wish I could throw up. Oh, lawd have mercy on poor Puddin's soul, cause no matter what had been done to me, she does not deserve this. I just could not take seeing a women being done like that by these men. Once John finished he beat her face and beat her face, as if he was trying to stop her from looking at him. The Sheriff had to yell to him to stop. "John, stop na boy, take her body to river and throw her in it." John gits in her car and takes her body over to the river bank and throws her in it he could have just as easily carried her on his back to do that. He just wanted to drive her car. As I was lookin over the hill by my oak trees I saw her floatin down the river like a piece of trash. To make it all worst look like she got caught up on a beaver damn, you know they was go eat her. I know it was wishful thinkin but I could swear look like she was holding on to that damn and looking back at the Sheriff and Big John. Ain't it strange Puddin was damned in this life and she ended up being caught on a damn in her death? Maybe, maybe she not dead, but that all it was wishful thanking, nobody human could survive that kind of beating. Sheriff Watson left John to clean up the mess. Ain't nothing ever did in this world is hide the eyes of the almighty is always looking on. Somebody go pay for this evil right here. Who is this riding like the wind coming up the bank, well hell it is Mayor Johnson and Sheriff Watson. Major Johnson was yelling at John "What is you doing with Ms. Puddin car boy, where she at." Before he could say one word, Sheriff Watson shot and killed John dead. John eyes bucked wide open like he had seen the devil himself then he fell into that muddy Mississippi River, like so many of our ancestors. There he goes floating down the river like an old broken log, just like he sent Puddin down that river. I will never doubt the judgments and good favor of the Lord again. How you die is much more important than how you lived, to me. I'd rather have a crown of glory than end up in a den of beavers or alligator bait.

The Major just stood there crying in disbelief. Old Sherriff Watson went to get back in his truck; in all the excitement, he lost his bearings. That man plum forgot he was in Louisiana. One of them black stump tail cotton mouth moccasins had fell out of the tree right in his truck. When that sucker got in his truck and that moccasin hit him, it was all she roll. He was gone, that snake must have been sent by Puddin, maybe her getting caught on a damn, was like her pointing her finger and cursing them. I told you we always have one last curse. Cause looks like that old stomp tail was waiting for the Sheriff. I bet he was one of them evil jet black ones too. You could hear him holler and scraping to get out, but he did not stand a chance with that old moccasin. Huh, Puddin got her revenge on them both and the Lawd took his vengeance for me on all of them.

Friendly, was not the same, they had lost the best woman ever born and raised there. Ain't go be another Lula Mae Carson, to bake, preserve and give them the truth about situations. These people go be lost around here, while I am living in heaven. This woman is a new creature now, gone to enjoy what heaven is really like. Beulah Mae, left Friendly soon after everything was over and moved to France. Yall know she could because she never had to spend any of the money she earned while she was working. Best thang her mama ever did was turn her over to Ms. Rose Delauche. Nobody in Friendly ever found Ms. Lula Maes' treasure. Most people think it was a lie anyway. Now they did believe that Puddin might have had a little money, but trying to find where a whore done hide her money is like, trying to find where the white man hid his consciousness. Shit you go be looking for a lifetime. They aint never found Puddins' money either. Tell me Beulah and her new friend Eula Mae Ms. Lula's first cousin opened up a school for wayward girls and boys. They housed two thousand children, some of their parents worked for the school so they stayed there too and they were building houses for their employees. Ms. Eula Mae was a good woman but she could never shut up, or at least that is what people said about her. She made the girls and women dress the same and she made the men and boys dress the same. Everything had to be in perfect order. That might have been the only real fault she really had, she liked things perfect. Ms. Eula Mae Johnson was an heir to several sugar cane plantations in the islands. Aww honey child she was old money, old dirty money. Most people could tolerate Beulah, but they say that Ms. Johnson did not do anything but brag on how good her life was and how she was taught manners and so on and so on. Them was two of the most private women you ever saw in your life. Both of them traveled a lot, all over the world. But you best believe they never left at the same time. One of them was always watching over their school and their money. They lived quite lives telling and writing stories all about a place call Friendly, Louisiana, all their trips and what they thought God was thinking. Strange thang, Eula, found all of Ms. Lula Mae's journals, child she is still reading them till today. The thangs she found out about people in that little town made her laugh and laugh. She keeps reading them over and over, I think that was her way of keeping Lula Mae alive. After all she is one hell of a women to have had the pleasure of knowing.

Here tell me when men went to drill for oil on Ms. Lula Maes' and place they found tunnels full of fine jellies, preserved figs and stacks of books from the towns people houses. Nobody wanted to claim Ms. Lula Mae Carson's place, people believed it to be hunted by her spirit. No seriously, as greedy and low down as people is, nobody wanted to move into Ms. Lula Mae Carson's house. They knew only one spirit belonged to that house and that house belonged to one spirit. Ms. Lula Mae sister, Sister Willie Mae Coleman, would go and stay there but she is a strong woman of God. If it were not for her aint no telling what might have happened. People say they have passed there and seen the lights on at night and looks like a women who favored Ms. Lula Mae is standing on the porche. But it ain't nobody but Lula's sister and her friend from out of town. The house never looked like it was unkept. It was still alive. The white folk bought some of the land from Ms. Lula Mae's cousin, but honey child they did not touch that house. The house was left there in the middle of 100 acreas of prime land with nobody living on it. Friendly not only lost Ms. Lula Mae, but the coloreds lost their preacher and the undertaker. Not long after Ms. Lula's funeral both of them just took off and left. What preacher you ever heard of just take off and leave his flock. Hell got a place for him and he know it. That is just down right disrespectful, wonder what he was scared of. I knew the Undertaker was gone cause he aint have no reason to stay. Plus he aint have me to look after no more.

Eula Mae Johnson was one of the most prolific storytellers of her era. People came from miles around to hear her tell stories, in both French and English. The students in her school, excelled in poetry, play writing, storytelling and math. Yeap math, she was never very good in math, so she made sure everybody else was. One of Eula's favorite stories was about a Sheriff that was bought out by the ghost of a dead woman, but he never got a chance to spend the money. Amazing story.

Not too much have changed in the south, people still people. You can't change a system ain't never meant to count you in. It might take centuries before blacks is considered almost equal and you had better believe they go be almost equal. Long as the long arm of religion is alive in their heads black folks go always respect they Masters, because that is what they religion teaches em. Tell me it don't and I am go call you a got damn lie, I sure am. Some thangs don't change though, New Orleans still known for their fine bordellos, good food and wild nightlife. A new woman has come to town, named Sweet Mama Rose, she has some of the finest girls on this side of heaven, hear tell. Nobody knows where she came from, but she got one of the sweetest voices you ever heard next to Puddins'. She is one of those women who don't like men much, they say her woman hangs on to her like a baby suckling at they mama's tit. Too bad Puddin did not make it, she could have teamed up with her and they could own Louisiana. Instead, she is probably done floated to the Gulf and out to the sea by now. They never found her body though; you know she was bad, even Jezebel had her hands and feet left. Women like that either live or they die. I doubt if any angels was on call to grab Puddin out of the water after the Sheriff and Big John finished with her. Don't know where Puddin is, in heaven or hell but I do know that where ever she is people better watch out. I am just glad she not in Paris with us.

I am glad my spirit is free to roam now, nothing is worse than being boxed all up in a coffin. And livin in the South being black is just like bein boxed up in a coffin. Hell, so yall know we been boxed up all our life. It is good when your spirit is free. The South has some beautiful places, the land is welcoming and the air is always full of sweet smells. But the smell of burning flesh, lynchings and rape still is the common denominator for blacks. Lula Mae and Beulah found their way to heaven and a new life. Everybody else got exactly what deh deserved. The blossoms in France smell as sweet as those in the South, but they do not last as long. One thang I know for sure and that is if you repent enough to them white folk God, he will do something for you. He will send you a sign or a sister, or maybe he will let you over hear what your enemy is planning for you. Either way he will look out for you if you talk to him enough.

Just because you think you are better than a Hussy, does not mean you cannot show one some Christian Charity to one. It just might pay off. Well na it is time for me to take a rest and float to the other side of heaven. I love Venice. That is one of the pleasures in Heaven, you can rest whereever and whenever you want to. Bonsoir. Ms. Lula Mae shol likes to travel. Oh lawdy, lawdy, lawdy trouble don't' last always, oh lawdy lawdy lawdy , trouble don't last always.

Oh before I go "Don't be defined by some one else's opinion of you, it is just an opinion" Where is my olive oil. You know I should have named this story "The Repentance of Lula Mae Carson".

Now yall know Ms. Lula Mae just love to tell these stories; ups, I smell my biscuits in the oven. I don't believe in letting my food burn. Owww wee child, I wish yall could taste this.